THE PROVING
GROUND

VALLEY OF THE PEACEMAKER
BOOK TWO

THE PROVING GROUND

W. E. DAVIS

CROSSWAY BOOKS • WHEATON, ILLINOIS
A DIVISION OF GOOD NEWS PUBLISHERS

The Proving Ground

Copyright © 1996 by W. E. Davis

Published by Crossway Books
            a division of Good News Publishers
            1300 Crescent Street
            Wheaton, Illinois 60187

Cover design: Cindy Kiple

Cover illustration: Steve Chorney

First printing, 1996

Printed in the United States of America

Library of Congress Cataloging-in-Publication Data
Davis, Wally, 1951-
   The Proving Ground / W. E. Davis.
      p.   cm. — (Valley of the peacemaker ; bk.2)
   ISBN 0-89107-884-3
   I.Title. II. Series: Davis, Wally, 1951-   Valley of the
peacemaker ; bk. 2.
PS3554.A93785P76 1996
813'.54—dc20   95-47119

04	03	02	01	00	99	98	97	96
15	14	13	12	11	10	9	8	7	6	5	4	3	2	1

DEDICATION

To my daughter,
Jessica

CHAPTER

ONE

THREE TIRED MEN on three tired horses moved slowly up the dirt road, their only consolation being the gathering clouds that provided some shade from the noon sun and the nip in the air, a portent of foul weather soon to arrive.

The eldest of the three, a man with long, bushy sideburns, a scraggly beard, and a receding hairline hidden under his ragged hat, rode in front, tall and erect in the saddle despite his fatigue. To his right rode a man several years his junior and several notches uglier with a weak chin and a protruding upper lip but whose eyes belied the intelligence the rest of his face hid. The third man, riding thirty yards or so in front of them, looked about with excited shifting eyes. He wore a small, sandy-blond mustache and would be considered by most women to be attractive, certainly the best-looking of the three.

"How far is it?" he asked the others.

The bearded man answered without looking back. "You asked that an hour ago. I said we were close, and we still are. An hour closer, in fact."

"My horse is plumb wore out."

"They all are," he was told. "We'll get new ones in town."

"With what? We're broke."

"Not for long. Now shut up."

He fell silent. They continued riding, their eyes fixed on the road ahead and the building clouds above. After rounding a lazy bend in the road, the steep canyon walls fell away and parted, and they found themselves in a treeless, winding valley. A small creek paralleled the road. To their left was a narrow trail that wound up and over the hill with a chain across the mouth of it where it met their road. From the chain hung a small sign.

"Here we go, what's this?" the youngest man noticed. He rode closer to read. "'Private property,' it says. 'William Bodine.'" He thought a second, then the corner of his mouth curled up.

"I'll be back," he told the others. "If I'm not back in a few minutes, follow me on up."

Jim and the bearded man just looked at each other and shrugged as the youngest member of their party led his horse down into the gully and around the post to which the chain was attached, then up the road. They couldn't see a house or anything else, nor could they hear anything, but there was no doubt what was in these hills. The same thing in all the hills for miles around: a gold mine!

They'd waited about ten minutes when they heard a distant, muffled shot, so low that they weren't sure what it was at first.

"You hear that?" Jim asked.

"Think so. Must be he wasn't too friendly, didn't want to part with it easy."

Sure enough, they soon saw a cloud of dust as a horse and rider rode hard down the trail. But he was not running scared. He shouted, stood up in his stirrups, and raised a large cloth sack with both hands as he skidded to a stop at the bottom. The bag appeared very heavy.

"Borrowed a little something to tide us over," he announced.

Jim rode over next to him and looked inside the bag his partner held open. He whistled low.

"We got ourselves a little gold. Now we best be moving on. No sense tempting fate. Anyone see you?"

"He was alone in the house. Didn't see no one else."

Jim opened his empty saddlebags and dumped in the gold. It had been left in its gleaned state, raw nuggets and chunks such as would be scraped from an amalgamation table before being melted and poured into brick molds. He figured they had several pounds, plus a few hundred coins of various denominations, money the miner had apparently already traded the mint for.

"Best we split up," Jim said. "Don't want to take no chances. When we get to Bodie I'll keep going and arrange some new horses. You two ditch these nags and spend the night, then take the next stage out tomorrow. We'll meet where we were going in the first place. It's far enough away to give us some breathing room and not so convenient to follow us to."

"Just like that, our prayers are answered," the eldest of the three said, gazing again at the saddlebags that held the gold. "What'd I tell you?"

"Just in time," the youngest man noted as a dark cloud passed overhead and snowflakes began floating lightly down over the men and their horses.

The season's first snow had been falling for several hours, having begun around noon. The flakes were large and many, but this was not a blizzard. There was no wind to drive them, so they drifted casually onto the town and its people, whitening rooftops, streets, hat brims, and shoulders. It would not stick. Indian summer would come, the snow would melt in a few days, then return a month later with a vengeance.

This was Bodie, California by name. Gold by trade. It had been called Deadwood, South Dakota; Telluride, Colorado; Angel's Camp, California; Elkhorn, Montana; Aurora, Nevada, and a hundred other names in a hundred other locations, but the gold would eventually die out, and the towns would soon follow suit. The people would pack their belongings in their wagons, leave behind whatever didn't fit, and head for more fertile ground where the cry of "mother lode!" had been raised, leaving their homes and stores for the die-hards to disassemble and burn in their stoves.

So many people moved so often throughout the West, they could easily be considered gypsies—gold gypsies. They weren't all miners, not by a long shot. True, the lure of gold was at the bottom of it all and was mentioned on many of the pages of their diaries and journals, especially those pages upon which they bid good-bye to their homes as they prepared a move to another camp. But not just the miners and speculators were numbered among the gypsies. Butchers and saloonkeepers, doctors and ministers, ladies of questionable virtue, gamblers and gunmen, all of them saw the elephant.

And so Bodie was the most recent of the gold camps to become a boomtown, and the people had been streaming in steadily for several months since word had been broadcast of the strike at the Empire Mine. Hardy people, they were unmoved by stories of Bodie's winters with its blinding snow, twelve-foot drifts, death by freezing or any number of endless illnesses. Or of the gunfights in the saloons and streets. Those things were all just a part of life, and in spite of all the negatives, life in Bodie was said to be good.

The snow had little effect on the citizens this morning. They moved about as they did every morning, going to or coming from their work at the mines and mills or running errands. Few strolled without a purpose. Even the unemployed—the gamblers, rowdies, layabouts, fallen angels, Chinese, and scattered Paiutes—ventured out only when there was a need.

The jailhouse door opened onto King Street, just a block from the growing Chinese district. Deputy Matthew Page emerged, closing and locking the door behind him, and stepped out into the street. He pulled the sheepskin collar of his worn leather coat around his neck, adjusted his flat-brimmed hat, and trudged down King to Main Street, his gloveless hands jammed into his coat pockets.

A duly-appointed Mono County Deputy Sheriff, Matt Page was assigned to Bodie, serving as its only jailer and law enforcement officer.

Matt nodded a greeting to a rosy-cheeked soiled dove, hurrying from the apothecary with a precious bottle of laudanum for her ailments. Blonde, curly hair, slight frame, well-built but not immodest in dress, she smiled in return but did not slacken her pace or give a second look. Matt let her pass without any further interest.

He was headed for the Quicksilver, a small cafe run by Sarah, his wife of several months, for a hearty, hot breakfast but then decided to delay it awhile and complete an unscheduled round of saloon inspections. It was his way of keeping ahead of the problems and of fighting off the boredom of routine.

The gumsoled boots he favored were quiet on the boardwalk, and he slowed at the door of the Bessie to peer inside. None of the saloons were using their swinging batwings due to the cold weather, so the Bessie's full doors were closed. Matt put his face next to the irregular glass and saw most of the patrons huddled around a pot-bellied stove in the center of the room. A few men sat alone at the fringes, choosing to warm their hands around the neck of a bottle rather than by the fire.

He could see nothing more as his breath had fogged the window, but there didn't appear to be any reason to try. Matt moved on, his cheeks stinging and his nose threatening to run, and continued down the street and back up the other side until all the saloons had been checked.

Only the Nugget, the last on his schedule of stops, proved interesting. It was lively, the air filled with chatter and outbursts of cursing and laughter and tobacco smoke. Matt went inside, as much to warm himself as to investigate it for lawlessness.

The Nugget was one of the newer saloons. The bar itself was of imported cherry wood, hauled in on the back of a wagon by the owner who brought nothing else of value with him. Paying cash for a new building, he installed the bar and opened for business even before the tables and chairs he'd ordered had arrived.

Behind the bar were many photographs and some crude paintings, all of women in various stages of undress and luridly posed. And one picture of a fine racehorse. The walls were wallpapered in vertical stripes, and strategic kerosene lamps lined the entire room. Their odor and smoke was unmistakable, but no one cared. Every bar was the same in that regard.

With two stoves and three faro tables, the Nugget catered to the miners, giving anyone who ordered a drink a free pickled or deviled egg and salty jerked beef. Of course, after eating it, they'd be thirsty and buy another round, and after a few more they'd be stupid enough to stagger to the faro table and let their pockets be picked. This, plus the general inebriation of all the patrons, led to more than a few eruptions, even between good friends.

Violence was not a stranger to the Nugget.

Matt entered unnoticed as he surveyed the crowd, many of the patrons being miners who had worked all night and just gotten off duty, their tin lunch buckets on the floor beside their booted, filthy feet. At this time of day the only other patrons were the unemployed . . . either by choice or because there were no openings at present in the mines or mills.

These two groups—the miners and the unemployed—had factioned, each claiming one of the stoves around which they huddled. A few neutrals stood at the bar, claiming allegiance only to their glasses. They were noisy and boisterous but, for the most part, kept to themselves. There was no reason to fight; they all suffered from the same cold weather and the same thirst.

A few men wore their guns openly, stuck into their belts or sticking out of their pockets. Rarely did a Bodieite wear his pistol in a holster; it sent a message that he was looking for trouble, and it usually found him. But no man worth his salt would walk through Bodie unheeled. What with all the people streaming in, it just wasn't safe any longer.

As Matt stood surveying the crowd, the door opened behind him. A miner brushed past, jostling the deputy without apology. Matt held his peace and watched the man, whose bushy mustache was gray with snowflakes, head for the nearest stove. He set his lunch bucket on a table and shoved two men out of the way, putting his hands out toward the stove and warming them.

Unfortunately, he had chosen the stove claimed by the rowdies and layabouts, and his rude treatment of two of them was met with an immediate protest and demand for apology.

"Hey, watch yourself, mole!" a dirty man in a bowler spat.

"I'm cold. My coat is thin," came the miner's reply, his teeth chattering to underscore the point.

"We're cold, too," protested a bearded man. "That don't give us the right to go knocking folks over."

The miner ignored them, rubbing his hands together to defrost them.

"We're talking to you," the bearded man said, his tone harsh.

Trouble was brewing, and Matt slowly undid his coat to give him more freedom of movement. He didn't want to tip his hand yet, to show the badge of his office pinned to his blue, woolen shirt, preferring to handle the problem in a more subtle fashion if at all possible.

The miner bristled. "All you do is sit around the stove all day, sleep in chairs or on the tables by night, swilling what free drink you can finagle and trying to keep warm. Stand clear and give an honest, working man a chance."

Bowler stood abruptly, knocking his chair over, his fists clenching and unclenching. In June they would have already taken to fighting, but with the weather as it was, their blood was too thick, and it would take them a while to warm up to the task.

"I don't reckon you'd care to take that back, would you?" His tone was threatening and unmistakable, the ultimatum had been issued. And yet, it was a fair request, and by implication, the problem would be solved if the miner complied.

The rest of the patrons, more miners than not, had been watching in silence from their seats around the other stove or had turned their backs to the bar to watch. Faro had even been put on hold. But before the offending miner could rise to the challenge that had been flung in his direction, a man wearing miner's boots and a banker's suit stood and addressed the other party in a booming voice.

"Excuse me, good sirs. We of the profession were as you once upon a time . . . destitute and in need of work. We have become fortunate to be employed, as you no doubt shall be also in due time. When that day comes you will hunker around this stove. Let us remain in peace." He moved his arm out toward the miner. "Come, Frank. You can have my seat."

"Thank you, Mr. Wellman." Frank began moving toward him.

"Just a durn tootin' minute!" protested the man in the bowler, rising and addressing Thomas Wellman, a foreman at the Empire mine. "He still owes me an apology!"

"Well, now, good sir, that is a matter of opinion, I'm sure. As I see it, Mr. Cooper's offense was to seek some heat for his cold body just come in from the snow. Why he would owe an apology to you for that is quite beyond me."

"He bumped me."

"This is a crowded place, sir. Men are bumping each other with frequency and no one demands an apology."

"I aim to get one just the same," said Bowler.

"And I will see to it," said the bearded man, rising.

"I see that you are serious," Wellman said. "But can you count? How many of your party are there, and how many of ours here?"

"We have equalizers," the bearded man said through clenched teeth.

This was shaping up very quickly and proved to bypass fisticuffs directly into a shooting match if Matt didn't do something soon. He'd hoped they could be civilized, but the rift between the factions had apparently grown. It was then Wellman spied the deputy.

"Good sir," Wellman told the bearded man, "if it is your intent to let firearms do your talking, may I suggest you think twice. Behind you stands the law, with a hogleg to back it up the likes of which you haven't seen. I wouldn't be surprised if that gun suddenly appeared in his hand while we are even watching, as though it could leap out of the holster strapped to his leg and into his hand of its own accord."

All eyes turned toward Matt, who was surprised but remained stoic, drawing a breath and holding it while standing erect. He met the eyes of all in the room while parting his coat to reveal both badge and gun, playing along with Wellman's bit of theater. That he had come in without being seen or heard added to the mystique Wellman had spread. Matt nodded at Frank Cooper, the pushy miner, who scurried to Wellman's side.

"Taking sides, Deputy?" Bowler asked.

"The side of the law, that's all," Matt told him. "There will be peace in Bodie. I'm so against violence I don't mind using it when I have to prove my point. Mr. Cooper, you give this gentleman his apology so we can all go about our business, and I don't have haul any of you gents to my cold, dreary jail."

The man in the bowler was beyond the acceptibility of an apology, however, and in a swift motion reached into his coat pocket. But Matt was ready, and before the man could withdraw whatever he had dipped for, Matt had covered the ground between them, grabbed the arm, then swept the man's feet out from under him.

As Bowler sprawled on the sawdust-covered planks, a small pistol slid out from his leather-lined coat pocket and clattered to the floor beside him. Matt plucked the weapon from the sawdust and pocketed it. The man glared at Matt from the floor, growled something under his breath, then picked himself up without Matt's assistance.

"I gave you fair warning," Matt said. "No man jerks a pistol at me and stays by the fire. Come on." He led the man toward the door, then stopped and turned. "It's over, men. Mr. Cooper?"

Frank Cooper turned to the man he had offended, now a prisoner of the deputy. "My apologies, sir. It was not intentional, and

I did not want the thing to come to this. Upon your return please allow me to buy you a drink."

But it had come to this, and the man in the bowler would not be appeased by an apology too late to be of any value. He'd return, all right, and accept that drink, then kill the man. At least, that's what his eyes said. He turned and let Matt take him to jail.

Matt locked the cell and gave him a blanket.

"What's your name?"

"Patrick O'Shea."

"New in town?"

"Two days."

"Have you eaten this morning?"

The man was subdued but only as a volcano is subdued before erupting. "No."

"I'll get some breakfast for you. The penalty for your offense is a night in jail, but since it's so early you can spend the day. I'll let you go after supper, unless you want to demand your day in court, in which case you'll have wait until tomorrow to see Judge Wadell, who's in Bridgeport today. I doubt the snow will delay him."

"I plead guilty," he said quietly, "although it wasn't you I was drawing on. It was that other fella."

"Same difference," Matt said. He buttoned up his coat to go out again. "I was headed for my breakfast. I'll come back with yours."

"Thank you."

Matt locked the man's pistol in a desk then stepped out once again into the cold, securing the door behind him as before. It wasn't as cold in his jail as he let on. His stove was fully stoked and served a smaller area than the saloon, so his charge was plenty comfortable.

But he figured Patrick O'Shea hadn't learned his lesson. "I'll have trouble with you yet," he muttered quietly as he turned and walked up the street. He'd have to keep an eye on him.

James Nixon's small, wooden chair creaked in protest as he leaned it back on the two rear legs, his own lanky legs now propped on top of the desk, crossed at the ankle. His shoes dropped small specks of muddy snow onto the open ledger, into which he had just recorded that day's inventory of explosives.

Working the powder magazine for the Queen Anne—head monkey, as his position was affectionately christened—Nixon kept track of the powder, fuses, sticks of dynamite, and other explosive substances stored in the room with him. He received the new shipments, checked out supplies to the powder monkeys working the Queen Anne, and stood guard over the rest of the stuff. It wouldn't do to have powder disappearing.

The magazine was a small, board hut on the side of the hill, midway between the town proper and the entrance to the Queen Anne shaft, relatively isolated from any other structures, except a miner's shack that had been put up recently between the magazine and the edge of town.

Inside the magazine, besides Nixon and his chair and the desk that supported his feet, was a row of shelves along the back wall opposite the only door that held boxes and cans of powder and fuses and caps, all clearly marked. The desk occupied the corner left of the door, the remaining corner was bare, a testament to the small stove that used to be there but had been removed when Nixon blew it up the year before.

Some powder had gotten wet, and he had attempted drying it in the stove. Fortunately, it was a small amount, and he had stepped out of the shack when it went off. He'd also had a comfortable chair, but it was destroyed by pieces of the stove. The foreman of the Queen Anne thought losing that chair—and the realization of what would have happened to him had he been in it—was punishment enough, so they retained him. Knowledgeable powder men were hard to find. But they didn't replace the stove.

Nixon sank deeper into the coat he wore, turning the collar up around his neck. He cursed the weather, cursed the town, and cursed the gold for being in such an inhospitable place as this. Then he opened his tin lunch bucket seeing what there was to eat.

With the incessant pounding of the mill not too far off, small noises escaped Nixon's notice. He couldn't hear, or just didn't pay any mind to, the scratching along the back wall. Then there was a rapping, and this made its way into his consciousness.

"Eh?" he said, looking up and turning his head around, trying to pinpoint the sound. It rapped again.

"What is it?" he asked louder, letting his feet down to the wood floor.

"I say in there," a muffled voice outside called in hoarsely. "You best get out while the gettin's good. You got about ten seconds."

"What's that?" Nixon said. "Come again?" He stood slowly and stepped toward the back wall, but the voice did not come again. Nixon scratched his head and was about to shrug it off and go back to his lunch when he heard a hissing. Not as a rattlesnake hisses or a steam vent hisses, but a quiet, crackling hiss that every powder man knows only too well.

Someone had lit a fuse.

With the seconds ticking away in his mind and confusion faltering his actions, Nixon peeked through a space between two boxes. There it was, burning brightly and out of his reach.

. . . Three . . . Four . . . Five . . .

Abruptly, Nixon realized there was nothing he could do but run. Who had done this and why mattered not a whit at the moment. He turned and bolted toward the door, his cold hands fumbling with the latch, and pulled it open, taking a running stride out into the snow.

. . . Eight . . . Nine . . .

The Quicksilver was quiet; though crowded with men, they were uncharacteristically stifled. What talk there was barely exceeded a whisper, the predominant sound the *chink* of forks and knives against china plates. Whether it was weather that subdued them, the good food, or respect for the cook, no one could tell.

Rosa Bailey bustled from table to table serving the patrons hot biscuits and ham and keeping their mugs full of her dark, rich coffee. Her somewhat expanded girth did not slow her down as she flew from the kitchen to the customers and back again, her full, bright-blue cotton dress billowing behind her.

In the kitchen, Sarah Page was busy rolling more dough for biscuits, slapping ham into the hot cast-iron skillet and jumping back as it spit and spattered, and cracking eggs into a bowl, then whipping them with a fork. She wiped the back of her hand across her forehead and sighed, then with a satisfied smile returned to her tasks.

Rosa came with a wry grin and dumped a load of dirty dishes on the board next to the wash basin.

"I'll get them clean in a minute, Sarah," she said as she put a pot of water on the stove. "You've got a customer out there."

Sarah brightened. "Matt?"

"Of course. I poured him coffee already. The man's mighty chilly. Looks like his face has been slapped both ways, it's so red."

"It better be the cold." Sarah pushed at her hair. "How do I look?"

"My word, child. You live with the man. Didn't you see him this morning?"

"Yes, Rosa, of course. But not for long. And that was several hours ago."

"Sarah, you must love him something awful."

"It's awful indeed. I love him so much it hurts."

"I had a man like that once, believe it or not. Just because I used to . . . well, you know. Just because of that doesn't mean I wasn't capable of love. He wrote me great letters, full of wonderful things. He asked me to come marry him, live in Kansas. I just didn't know what to do."

"What happened?"

"He stopped writing. To this day I don't know what's become of him. Got tired of me saying no, I suppose. Found a woman nearby him who wouldn't keep putting him off." She stared off as if in a trance as she wiped her hands absentmindedly on her apron, then suddenly snapped out of it. "You go on. Matt's a waitin'. I'll get his plate. There's only a couple folks left, and I just filled their mugs. Your morning rush is about over."

"Thanks, Rosa. You're a dear." Sarah reached behind herself and untied her apron, hanging it from a knob on the flour bin.

"I ain't nothing of the kind, Sarah Page. And don't you forget it." They shared a laugh as Sarah rushed out of the kitchen and joined her husband.

Matt stared vacantly out the window at the lazy snowfall, sipping his black coffee and planning his day. A soft touch on his shoulder brought him out of it.

"Good mornin'," he said, looking up. Sarah leaned down to kiss him, but stopped short when she realized a couple of men at the next table were watching, so she fussed with Matt's silverware.

"What are you so deep in thought about, Matt?"

"Oh, nuthin' really. How's your day so far? Here, excuse my manners." He stood and pulled a seat out for her, then, when she was settled in, he resumed his. His hat and coat were already draped on the chair on the other side.

"It's cold, that's for sure," she said, wrapping her arms around herself and faking a shiver. "Makes working over a hot stove a blessing in disguise."

Rosa came to the table with the plates, setting one before each of them.

"Rosa!" protested Sarah. "You needn't bring me anything."

"Nonsense. You need to keep up your strength. You sit here with the deputy. Enjoy yourself. I can take care of things for a few minutes." She patted her employer on the shoulder and wandered over to a couple of miners just finishing their sausage and corn.

"She seems to be doin' better," Matt commented, cutting a piece of ham with the edge of his fork and sticking it in his mouth. "Emotionally, I mean. You know."

"Losing her daughter Nellie was a blow to her, of that there can be no doubt," Sarah said. "It was really tough at first. She didn't have any skills to speak of. I think she even snuck back to Bonanza Street a couple nights, just so she could feel useful."

"Yeah, I saw her. I didn't say nothin', and she tried to keep herself hid from me. You know, I hear talk around town."

"Talk? What kind of talk?"

"You know. Amongst the women. I suppose you've noticed not too many women come in here and very few of the married men."

Sarah nodded. "It's so wrong, Matt, to treat someone that way. Since Rosa got the hang of things, she hasn't been back. She told me she isn't going back, either. She's done with that life."

Rosa passed by and they both busied themselves eating, Matt commenting how good it was for Rosa's benefit. She just smiled and continued into the kitchen.

"It's not just Rosa they're avoidin'," Matt said after she was gone. "It's your restaurant, too."

Sarah gazed out the window, watching as the ground was blanketed. "In a few weeks we might not be able to see out because of the snow. You realize that don't you?"

"Yeah, I reckon." He watched his wife as she watched the snow, then said, "So what are you going to do about it?"

"Do? About what?"

"The dropoff in customers."

"Nothing, Matt. Not a thing. It's just the weather, that's all. Besides, if people want to stop eating here, that's their choice. I'm not going to let Rosa go, if that's what you're asking. I need the help, and she needs God. She needs to know people care, that God cares. If I turn her out now, she'll be lost for sure."

"I'm glad you feel that way, Sarah. I just don't know how bad things are going to get. The women just don't like associating with prostitutes, even reformed ones. They—"

The rest of his sentence was cut off by an explosion east of them. The windows shook, the dishes rattled—a few of them breaking—and everyone dove for cover. When it stopped, Matt ventured a look outside. A column of smoke billowed up from the side of Bodie Bluff. Someone shouted, "Volcano!" One of the miners thinking of leaving the restaurant peeked outside from under his table.

"The powder magazine at the Queen Anne!" he corrected. Matt jumped up and rushed out, followed by the two miners who had forgotten to pay. Sarah didn't notice. She threw a shawl around her shoulders and, as Rosa rushed out of the kitchen, told her she'd be back.

"Boil lots of water, Rosa. No telling what we're up against here." Rosa nodded and hurried back into the kitchen, and Sarah ran out of the Quicksilver and up the street, joining scores of others who were doing the same. Matt was already out of sight.

CHAPTER

TWO

WHEN THE EXPLOSION FIRST ERRUPTED, Rosa dove immediately for the floor and was cowering under a table even before the deafening sound had subsided. Glass from a broken window scattered across the floor toward her. As it came to rest and all seemed over, she chanced a peek out the window, seeing a column of smoke rising from the base of bodie Bluff. She shouted, "Volcano!" but was quickly overruled by the miners whom she could hear hollering in the dining room. She knew, from her many conversations with miners, that up on the hill was the Queen Anne powder magazine and that it held two tons of blasting powder in it at any given time.

The Quicksilver quickly emptied, and, despite Sarah's instructions, Rosa was drawn outside by the awful sight of the smoke rising above the town and spreading out because of the wind. She knew many of the men who worked on that hill. Every building in town had been shaken by the blast, and glass and debris were everywhere. The concussion had blown out windows all over the camp, had knocked goods and china from shelves and had taken the legs out from under several men. Horses ran loose through the streets and panic swept through the people, especially those who had husbands and brothers working in the mines and mills. But cooler heads prevailed, and the town quickly began mobilizing as people streamed up the hill to help, some with bandages or blankets, a few with wagons to haul off the injured.

Rosa ran up the hill, wondering how it had happened and who was involved. She had many friends among the miners and hoped it wasn't someone she knew. She nearly smiled when she realized that probably wasn't possible, since she knew just about everyone.

The old Queen Anne hoisting works nearby had been reduced to rubble, as was the boarding house next to it, but the mill, being far enough away by design, was untouched. The powder magazine itself was a black, smoking hole in the ground surrounded by a mountain of debris. Two injured men writhed on the ground not far away.

As she arrived at the scene, some of the injured were already being treated. A few medical supplies had arrived, having already been gathered by some of the merchants, and Sarah was busy treating some of the superficial wounds, mostly folks cut by flying glass and debris. Rosa caught a glimpse of Matt as he raced toward the boarding house, and she heard someone shout that a woman and child were buried.

She wandered over and watched as Matt got as close as he dared and called into the remains of the boarding house.

"Hello! Are you all right?"

They listened, and soon a weak female voice responded. "Yes . . . we're alive." A cheer went up.

"Okay, we're coming in for you," Matt shouted. "We need to know where you are."

"I'm down here, under this pile of rubble!"

"Yes, we know that. But whereabouts? We want to clear the way."

"I'm by the piano!"

An exasperated Deputy Page looked around. "Anybody know where the piano was in this house?"

A man on the other side of the wreckage said, "Next to the settee, I think."

Matt muttered something to himself and then shouted down to the woman. "Okay, I think I can follow your voice. Where is your baby?"

"He's next to me, he's all right. The piano tipped over but was stopped by the settee."

"I told you it was by the settee," said the man on the other side.

"We're under the piano," the woman continued. "It protected us."

Matt directed the rescue effort, having the available men form a line. Board after board was carefully lifted off the pile and passed down the line, then thrown out of the way. It took about a half hour until they could see the woman. The baby started crying, spurring the men on to resume their labor, and in fifteen more minutes, the space over the woman was big enough for a person to crawl through.

Matt scanned the crowd.

"Who'll go down?" he asked.

"It's not safe," someone declared. Others murmured agreement.

"Yes," Matt said, "that's why we have go down there. There's a woman and her baby trapped."

But no one came forward. Without another thought, Matt stripped off his coat, his outer shirt—the one to which his badge was pinned, a badge that could get caught on things in a narrow space—and unbuckled his gun belt. These he hung over the end of a piece of lumber sticking vertically out of the edge of the debris, putting his hat on top of it all. He hurried to the edge of the wreckage and shinnied head first down into the hole and disappeared.

When someone cried out that the deputy was going in, Sarah jerked her head up from her tasks and looked up the hill, trying to determine exactly where it was Matt was going. Then she saw the remains of the boarding house, and she knew. She hurriedly finished wrapping a wound, then ran to where the crowd watched in silence.

Under the rubble, Matt crawled to the woman, told her something encouraging, then checked out the piano. It was being held in place by about two inches of wood resting on the settee. The slightest disturbance would break it free to fall on the woman and baby.

Matt grabbed the baby. "Be still, Mother. I'm gonna take your baby out, then come back for you. Where do you hurt?"

"My arm. I think it's broken."

"Okay, you sit tight. I'll be back." Matt crawled out carefully, holding the eerily quiet baby to his chest with one arm, careful not to lose his grip nor allow himself to relax and crush the baby under him. As soon as he could see a face, he shouted up, and a man moved cautiously to the entrance hole. Matt handed the baby up to waiting arms. It was passed along the line and finally thrust into the arms of the closest female. Rosa looked down at her dirty, bruised bundle, deep in her own thoughts; then the baby cried and shook her out of it. She began at once to clean him and treat his little cuts and bruises, talking to him gently and cooing to settle him down.

Matt went back down and sandwiched himself between the woman and the piano. Finding a broken board, he wedged it in place between the piano and another piece of lumber. *Doesn't look too strong,* he thought. *Hope it holds long enough for me to get out.*

"Okay, your turn," he said to the woman. Then he yelled to the men outside, "Go ahead, we're ready!"

The men began once again removing boards and debris, making a clear path for the woman. Rosa held the baby and watched, biting her lip. Under the debris, Matt looked up and realized the piano was face down toward him. He could reach the keys with one hand and plunked a couple of them lightly. It worked. Carefully, he played taps. Outside, the men heard the piano, wondering what it meant, and stopped working to listen. Then they recognized the tune and laughed.

"That's Matt," one of them said. "He's letting us know he's fine." They feverishly returned to their task.

When the way was cleared, two men clambered down and took hold of the woman. They pulled her up and out of the wreckage, while she screamed from the pain in her broken arm. Just as she was freed several boards moved, and Matt saw the piano shifting. He began to pull himself out from under it, but the board he had wedged in gave way and the piano slipped off the settee. Matt scrambled, throwing caution to the wind, and just before the piano landed he jerked his foot out of the way and scampered up the waterfall of wood, taking blows from the moving lumber as the piano crashed behind him in a cacophony of sound, the debris of the boarding house collapsing on top of it. Sarah screamed, but Matt emerged on top, bruised and bleeding, but unbroken. Two men grabbed him and dragged him to safety as the structure fell with a roar, shooting dust and debris in all directions.

Rosa gave the baby to its mother, placing him in her good arm with a pat on the cheek for both. Sarah came over with bandages and sticks, and splinted the broken arm so the woman could be safely moved, then mother and baby were put in back of a wagon and driven down to the doctor's place. Sarah crunched through the snow to Matt and the men, who were all congratulating each other, while others began the grim task of searching for more victims. Rosa watched them in silence as they reunited in an embrace, but it was not a long reunion. There was much to do.

Sarah played the nurse some more that morning, treating the minor wounds and freeing the doctor to take care of the major ones. Rosa shuttled back and forth from the Quicksilver, bringing bandages and food. They both finally collapsed from exhaustion in the restaurant, coughing and wheezing. They rested awhile, drank some coffee, then Sarah bundled up and went out again, searching for Matt. Unable to find him, she returned to the restaurant.

She entered the deserted restaurant and sat down in the first chair she came to. Rosa was trying to clean the place up but was too tired and not accomplishing much. With all the excitement, no one was coming to dinner, so she had leaned the "closed" sign in the window and drawn the blinds.

Matt sat with the other rescuers and the men in charge of the Queen Anne. They were silent, both from their exhaustion and the knowledge that many more people could have died that morning.

"What's the count?" Matt asked quietly of Thomas Wellman.

"Three severely injured, a few superficial, plus the woman and baby."

"That's rough. This is not a good day in Bodie. Who are the badly injured?"

"Pete Lamboy and Oliver Melton, both of them miners. They were unlucky enough to be walking past when she blew. James Nixon was somewhat fortunate. He had been in the building just seconds before the explosion. Don't know why he isn't in tiny pieces. He's unconscious, over at the doc's. Doc Curtis says it's too early to know how he'll fare. He'll let us know if Nixon wakes up so we can talk to him about what happened."

"And the other injured folk?"

"Most of them hit by flying debris. Some of them were in town, near windows. Cut to pieces, a couple of them. We're real lucky there aren't more dead."

"A good gunfight usually kills more than this," commented Fred Smith, supervisor of the Empire Mine and Mill. He wasn't making light, just stating a fact everyone knew.

Matt stood up. "I best be gettin' back to my duties. See you men later." He turned to leave. "Oh, Mr. Wellman. Thanks for your help in the Nugget this morning."

"My pleasure, Deputy."

Matt straightened his hat and trudged down the hill into the center of town. Crossing Green at Main, Matt stepped around the ever-present Paiute, Cornbread Tom, occupying his usual morning position in the center of town, apparently unaffected by the calamity up the hill. He was seated on the boardwalk, legs curled, his feet in the street. Whether a hot day in the middle of summer or a day such as this one, there was a good chance Tom would be in place here.

Occasionally he'd vanish for parts unknown and a day would pass without Cornbread, but he'd return the next with a live badger, which he'd sell to a member of Bodie's sporting crowd for the purpose of fights with local dogs, a mining camp gambling tradition much frowned upon by the women. The fiercer the badger, the more money Cornbread would make for bringing it in.

Cornbread Tom, self-named for his favorite food and the man whose wife introduced him to it, had a wikiup somewhere outside town where his squaw Tom Annie remained, waiting for Cornbread's return after his daily morning forays into town for handouts. Cornbread wasn't incapable of working, he just chose not to.

Of indeterminate age, Cornbread had accepted the arrival of the white man into the area with mixed emotions. Yes, it would mean a change in Cornbread's way of life to some degree. It would mean oppression. It would mean the taking of Paiute land by the white face. But to Cornbread it would also mean a source for work when he wanted, handouts when he didn't. What did the land mean to Cornbread? He could neither possess it nor subdue it. Who could possess something so vast? And subduing it was a joke. The best any man, white or Indian, could ever hope to do was manage to exist for another day. Ultimately, the land would remain, unchanged, when there was nothing left of a man but bleached bones in the sand.

Matt respected the Indian, knowing him not to be the lazy freeloader others—and, at times, Cornbread himself—made him out to be. He was self-controlled and mysterious, much like the Chinese whom the Paiutes hated, as much for their irritating speech and strange customs as for their industriousness. And it was mutual. No one disliked the Paiute more than the Chinese, and both sides were comfortable with their racism. That's just the way it was.

It was because of this Matt noted, with some apprehension, a lone Chinaman in heavy clothing scampering down Main Street on the far side, on some secret and necessary mission that drew him from the friendly confines of Chinatown into the hostile environs of the white man. For while the Paiutes were disliked and largely disregarded, the Chinese were feared by the whites, as people fear anything they don't understand.

Matt knew Cornbread Tom would see the Chinaman, though Cornbread would not likely betray it immediately. His reaction would depend upon what the Chinaman did, which direction he traveled, and whether or not he noticed Cornbread. Matt knew, by some sixth sense he had about the situation, he should stay until the Chinaman had passed.

At the least, Matt would be delayed by a minute. At the most, he'd have to break up a fight. After all, it had happened before with Cornbread and another Chinaman. Cornbread had been the loser that day.

The deputy continued on up the street but paused casually at the dry goods store and stepped back into the alcove at the door, watching. Cornbread remained seated, his fur blanket drawn around him, head tipped slightly forward to keep the falling snow out of his face, something the narrow brim of his woven basket of a hat couldn't accomplish.

The Chinaman continued without slowing, giving no sign he was aware of the Paiute. Matt breathed a sigh of relief as the Chinaman was abreast of Cornbread across the hundred-foot span of Main Street. In a few steps, the Paiute would be out of the Chinaman's line of sight. The deputy began stepping out to resume his return to the Quicksilver when Cornbread suddenly rose, letting his blanket fall, revealing a snowball in his right hand. As quickly as an energetic boy, the Paiute cocked his arm and reared back, then threw the snowball across the street with rifle-shot accuracy, plunking the Chinaman square on the back of the head. This had been no ordinary snowball; Cornbread Tom had formed it around a rock, and the Chinaman was knocked clean off his feet. He jumped up with a shout, turning circles to spy out his attacker, his fists flailing in the air, and his high-pitched voice jabbering in his native tongue.

Then he detected Cornbread Tom, standing on the corner across the street laughing uncontrollably. The Chinaman wasted no time charging across the intersection in a direct line for the Indian, the size of the Paiute no deterrent, his anger suppressing his sense. He launched himself headlong into the man, and before Matt could reach them, they were wrestling in the snow.

A small crowd, alerted by the strange cries emitting from the combatants, not unlike the squeals and growls one could expect from the badger and the dog, gathered to watch the two heathens—as they viewed them—grapple, and the sight was enjoyed by all, with a few bets made on the fringe by a couple of members of the raucous crowd. They cheered on their favorite, groaning in sympathy as a successful blow was landed or cheering the one delivering it, but the situation went from comic to serious when the flash of a knife blade was seen, most likely in the hand of the Paiute, although no one could be sure. A woman screamed.

Matt stepped in, but the flashing knife would not permit him to join the fracas. Having no alternative, he drew his Colt's Peacemaker and capped off a round into the air. The two combatants took the hint and rolled off each other.

Neither appeared to be injured and the knife lay in the much-disturbed snow between them, unclaimed. They stood up, glaring at each other and preparing to move on, when the Chinaman noticed something in Cornbread Tom's hand that caused him to emit a howl.

His queue. His precious long, black pigtail.

He reached behind himself to confirm it, grabbing the stub of his hair, and anger welled up, spilling out of his mouth in a verbal barrage that made several women cover their ears and hasten away, despite their inability to understand the words. Only the gun still resting in the deputy's hand kept the fight from resuming.

Reluctantly, Cornbread Tom handed over his prize to the deputy upon demand, and Matt gave it back to the victim. He snatched it from the lawman and walked away, pointing his finger at the Paiute and dishing out innumerable threats. Cornbread just shrugged.

Matt gave the instigator back his blade, knowing its utility and ceremonial significance to the Paiute, and told him to get scarce for awhile.

"They'll be looking for you, Cornbread."

Cornbread nodded. "Take Annie Tom to Bishop. Yellow man there no angry." He smiled sheepishly, knowing full well the Chinaman's anger was his doing. He picked up his furs and plunked his basket back on his head as Matt broke up the spectators.

"Show's over, folks. Move along now."

"It's a free country," one of the sporting crowd declared, but not so loud that Matt could tell who had said it.

"Fine," the deputy said with a shrug. "Stand out here and freeze. I don't give a hoot." He spun on his heel and trudged up the sidewalk, stuffing his hands deep into his coat pockets and scrunching his shoulders, raising his collar farther up his neck.

CHAPTER

THREE

MATT HEADED STRAIGHT for the Quicksilver and, in a few frozen minutes, was there. He stumbled in, dirty and wet, shut the door behind him and shucked his coat, dropping it where he stood, then hurried over to the stove without saying anything.

Sarah walked over to him, putting one hand on his back, the other on his arm. She leaned into him, her head resting on his shoulder.

"It's a mite chilly out there," Matt said, rubbing his hands briskly.

"I was worried about you," Sally said. "What possessed you to crawl into the rubble? You could have been killed."

Matt glanced at her over his shoulder. "There was a woman down there. And a baby. Someone had to get them out."

"Why you? You're the only husband I've got."

"I'm the deputy sheriff," he said, as though that explained everything.

"Yes, I know," she said, turning her head and staring out the window. "But how does that qualify you for rescues like that?"

"No one else was going," Matt said, his brow knit. "There wasn't time to stand around discussin' it."

Another look, but he held her gaze this time.

"I don't understand, Sarah. It ain't like you to complain about things like that. What's up?"

She shook her head and said nothing.

Matt could only shrug. Sometimes he'd seen other women get moody like this, and there was nothing that could be done about it. His own mother, he remembered, got this way on her wedding anniversary every year after getting word that Pa'd been killed at Vicksburg. Now it was Matt's turn to become melancholy about his mother. How he wished she'd known that Jacob Page was indeed still alive, albeit with one less arm, and living in California.

Suddenly he thought of something and bolted upright in the chair.

"What is it, Matt?" Sarah asked, concerned.

"Whoa. I forgot about my prisoner."

"Prisoner?"

"Yeah. Took him in this mornin'. Little problem at the Nugget. I need to take him some lunch. Can you rustle somethin' up?"

Sarah sighed. "Sure, Matt." She turned slowly and retreated to the kitchen while Matt stayed by the pot-bellied stove, rubbing his hands and sipping coffee.

She emerged a short time later carrying a tray covered with a checkered napkin. "Here you are. Beef and bread and some coffee. And a slice of apple pie. It's all I have considering the restaurant was closed today, and I didn't do any cooking."

"Don't sell yourself short, Sarah. Shoot, this is a feast. Word gets out we feed our prisoners like this and I'll be spendin' all my time arrestin' people. Thanks, honey. I'll send Nathan Carswell over to replace that window or patch it temporary if he's out of glass. Wish I could stay and help, but I've got duties." He took the tray from her.

"I understand, Matt. Rosa and I can take care of it. I'll see you tonight, okay?"

"Okay, Sarah." She began to turn away. "Hey, wait a second." She stopped and lifted her face to him.

"I'm sorry," she said with a smile. He leaned down and kissed her. She gave in to it and kissed him back until Matt almost lost a grip on the tray. "I'm just worried, that's all," Sarah said when they broke.

"About what?"

"You . . . us."

"What's to be worried about? Nothing's any different today than it's ever been."

"Yes it is, Matt. Bodie's growing, getting harder for one man to handle. We're busier and I'm . . . there's a lot different. And when you went down there today, I had the feeling you weren't coming back."

Matt gazed at her a moment, then broke into that bittersweet grin of his she found so irresistible.

"I'll always come back," he said. "Lord willing, of course."

Doc Curtis leaned over the patient, watching the man struggling to breathe as he stretched out on his stomach, his back so chewed up by the blast that he was unable to lie any other way. His breathing was shallow and his back barely moved. He seemed to have remained unconscious since the explosion.

There was little Doc Curtis could do for him. The wounds were numerous and severe, and many continued to ooze despite the doctor's best efforts to pack them. Nixon had lost a lot of blood, had some damage to internal organs caused by the percussion as well as the shrapnel, and now it was only a matter of time.

Nixon groaned, something he had done several times, even in his unconscious state. But this time, a word escaped his lips. At least, it sounded like a word. Curtis put his ear to Nixon's face and urged him to say it again.

"If you can hear me, James, what did you say?"

Though his eyes remained closed, his lips parted. "Make . . . me . . ." He drew in a difficult breath. "Make . . . well . . . man . . . p . . ." But the last word was nothing more than the *puh* sound. Nixon would never finish his thought. His breathing had stopped, and almost immediately his skin began turning yellow and waxen as the blood stopped circulating.

Curtis was sad. He had always liked Nixon. But he was not surprised. Those wounds were fatal. Curtis had known that the moment Nixon had been brought in.

He pulled a sheet up over him and stood silent for a moment, wondering what to do about the man's message. *Make Wellman p.* Make Wellman what? Obviously a reference to the foreman of the Empire Mine, but what did Nixon want? Make Wellman *puh.*

He ran it through his mind, and suddenly a shiver ran up his spine, shaking his shoulders. Make Wellman . . . *pay*.

Could it be that Wellman had something to do with the explosion? Had the old feud between the Empire and the Queen Anne flared up again?

Doc Curtis sat down hard in a chair by his examination table and stared at the sheet-covered corpse. Somebody had to be told about this.

Balancing the tray with one hand, Matt stopped at the door of his jail and fished out the key, but as he reached up to stick it into the lock, he realized he needn't have bothered. The door was ajar, and as he pushed it open slowly with his foot, he saw the damage to the edge of the door and the door jamb. It had been pried. He set the tray down on the stoop and silently eased his Peacemaker from his holster, then shoved the door fully open.

There was no one in the office. He stepped in quietly, heading toward the door that led to the cells. It was unlocked, though he'd made sure he locked it when he left. Peering through the barred window in the door he could see the cell door standing open and the keys lying on the floor. He didn't need to go in to know that his prisoner was gone. He turned toward the desk immediately as he remembered that's where the keys had been, locked in the drawer with the desk key in his pocket.

Sure enough, the desk had also been pried.

Matt went out and picked up the tray, setting it on the desk. He looked around the room, his hands on his hips, and thought. Then, coming to a conclusion, he abruptly stormed from the jail, leaving it wide open, and charged into the snow, his boots crunching on powder several inches deep and still falling. He stomped down the boardwalk, then crossed Main Street as he neared the Nugget, dodging behind a two-horse wagon struggling up the street with a load of wood from Cottonwood Canyon.

He took the two steps with one stride and kicked open the door. He had the immediate attention of everyone in the place, but there were only two men he was looking for . . . a man wearing a bowler and his bearded friend. Breathing fog with the door still open behind him, the deputy did a slow turn of his head as he scanned the room, but the men he sought were not there.

"I'm lookin' for Patrick O'Shea and his friend!" Matt announced.

"Ain't O'Shea in your jail?" an unshaven drifter asked with a tobacco juice-spattered smirk.

Matt hooked the leg of his chair with his toe and jerked it out from under the upstart, sending him sprawling into the sawdust and the chair flying.

"I ain't in the mood," Deputy Page growled. "Any more of you want to be funny?"

There were no takers.

"All right. Like I said, I'm lookin' for O'Shea and his friend. During the tragedy at the powder magazine someone let O'Shea out, and I've got an idea who." He addressed the miners around their stove. "Any of you men see when he left the room?"

They all shook their heads.

"We all left, Deputy," one man ventured slowly. "The place cleared out. In fact, your jail may have been the only building in town with someone in it."

"Not fer long," said someone out of Matt's line of sight, getting a few muffled snickers, but by the time Matt swung his head around, no one's mouth was open.

Matt relaxed, knowing he wasn't getting anywhere here. He straightened his coat, adjusted his hat, turned on his heel, and strode out of the Nugget.

As he walked back to the jail, where he intended to sit down, eat his prisoner's lunch, and think about what to do next, someone across the street shouted for him.

It was Thomas Wellman, and he was running across the snow-covered street, hailing the deputy. Matt stopped and waited for him in front of the butcher shop.

"Deputy," he said, trying to catch his breath. "Excuse me a second, I ran all the way."

"What is it, Mr. Wellman?"

He caught his breath. "You've got to come look, up at the powder magazine."

"More victims?"

"No, no, thank the good Lord, not that. We think we know what happened."

"Was James dryin' some powder in the stove again?"

"That's what we thought at first. But we found something that looks, well, puzzling. Maybe even sinister."

Matt stepped off the sidewalk in the direction of the powder magazine. Wellman moved with him, trying his best on stubby, tired legs to keep up with the lanky lawman.

"Are you sayin' it was intentionally discharged?" Matt asked.

"Well, I'm not saying it. But I think if you look at what we found, you might draw that conclusion."

"Mr. Wellman, I hope you're wrong," Matt said, his face grim. "Because if you're not, it would be murder."

"Yes sir, Deputy. It would indeed."

They maintained silence the rest of the way, Matt preferring to see for himself rather than waste time listening to Wellman describe what he was about to look at anyway. Near the ruins, where men milled around, Matt spied a familiar figure, that of a one-armed miner to whom he bore a striking resemblance.

"Afternoon, Pa," Deputy Page said to his father, Jacob, a miner himself and the man who superintended Bodie's newest mine, the Bodie Unified.

"Afternoon, Matt." His voice was not its usual jubilant self.

"I take it you've seen what I was brought here for?"

"'Fraid so, son. Look here."

Jacob Page led Matt to the side of the magazine—or at least where it had been—that was farthest from town, the uphill side. He knelt down and with his remaining arm—the one the Rebs at Vicksburg had let him keep—pulled aside a tattered board. "When it was found I made everyone skedaddle so's you could eyeball it for yerself."

Matt dropped to both knees in the snow beside him and squinted into the shadow. The snowfall had slackened, making his task a might easier than it would have been otherwise. He examined and gazed, then bent closer and looked some more, then finally sat up and stared at his father.

"What am I lookin' at?"

"Oh, my word, Matt. It's as plain as a tick on a baby's behind. Right there!" He stuck his index finger in and touched the stub of a cigar, firmly stuck between two boards.

"So?" Matt said.

"So Nixon don't smoke cigars. That's fresh. It was crammed in there by someone passin' by. Not even old Noah would do a blame fool thing like that. There ain't a kid in town would toss a cigar in a powder magazine."

"Ain't many kids in town smoke cigars," Matt pointed out. "What does that prove? That someone was careless?"

"No, that someone stuck it in there on purpose."

"Why?"

"To blow it up, of course."

"My question is, why would someone want to blow it up? And who would it be?"

"Well, we don't rightly know that yet," Thomas Wellman said. "Maybe an enemy of the Queen Anne or an enemy of James Nixon, I don't know. That's why we brought you up here, to show you this so you could investigate it and find out who blew the powder magazine and killed these people."

"Are you sure this cigar did the deed?" Matt asked. "Now don't get riled, Pa. I'm not questionin' you that it did. I'm just askin' how you came to that conclusion. I'm tryin' to get educated."

"Well, it's like this," Jacob Page said, his voice strained like it had been when Matt was ten and got caught chasing the chickens and scaring them so they wouldn't lay for a couple of days. "Where this cigar is, there ain't no way for it to have gotten there without bein' stuffed through a crack in the wall from the outside."

"How do we know that's where it was? I mean, the building blew up. Maybe it was somewhere else."

"It blew out the other way," Jacob Page declared. "Stand up, see for yourself."

Matt obeyed and could indeed see a pattern to the debris. From where he stood, it was like the explosion went away from him toward town. All of it pointed back to his position.

"Okay, it blew from here out. How do we know ol' Nixon didn't do it, on purpose or on accident?"

"Like we said, he don't smoke cigars. He chews. He learnt it don't mix for a powder monkey to smoke, so he took up the chaw. Good practice, if I say so myself."

"Maybe someone else was in there, and they did it."

"We questioned ever'body and nobody admits to it."

"Naturally," Matt said.

"No, we believe 'em," Jacob said.

"Okay," Matt said. "Let's go on the idea it was intentional. There would have to be a motive. Who's got a hate for the Queen Anne now?" He looked from his pa to Wellman.

Wellman shrugged. "Don't look at me. They're miners just like we are. All them scalawags like you met in the Nugget this morning, they got a hatred for all of us. Maybe it was one of them."

"Maybe," said Matt. "What about Nixon? He have any enemies?"

"He's Irish ain't he?" Jacob Page said. "Sure, he's got enemies. But they don't blow each other to smithereens. They go to fisticuffs or jerk their six-shooters, and that's only when they get likkered up. It ain't like them yellow-bellied braggarts to skulk around and set off a powder magazine."

Matt walked slowly around the ruins of the building, inspecting the ground carefully, almost like reading trail sign, something he'd gotten pretty good at since coming to California.

"Where was Nixon found?" he asked.

"Right about where you stand," Jacob Page said. "His legs was kinda uphill from the rest of him."

"Was he on his stomach or his back?"

"Stomach. His front was mostly okay. It was his back that was pretty chewed up."

"So he had his back to the blast. Was he blown to bits or mostly intact?"

"Oh, pretty much in one piece, I s'pose. More or less."

"Then he wasn't in the shack when it blew?"

"Nope."

"Why not?"

"He was runnin' away, most likely. If he was inside, you wouldn't a found much of him. Mebbe a piece of him here and there."

"Then he was outside the shack and moving away from it."

"Yeah," Jacob Page agreed. "I s'pose so."

"He knew it was going to blow," Wellman considered the idea thoughtfully. "Nixon knew the magazine was going to blow."

"Okay. But how'd he know?" Jacob Page wondered.

"Only two ways," Matt concluded. "He set it off and couldn't get out in time, or someone gave him a warning."

Thomas Wellman and Jacob Page stared at each other. The conclusion was obvious since Nixon didn't smoke and had no reason to blow up his own powder magazine on purpose. Someone had told him to get out, but he didn't get far enough away. Either he thought about it too long, or it went off sooner than someone expected. Their first conclusion was right, the explosion had been set by someone else and it was indeed murder.

"Well," Matt said with a pronounced sigh, "let's hope Nixon has something to tell us."

Jacob Page and Wellman gave each other a glance, then Wellman said, "We'll never know. Doc told us a while ago he's gone."

Without comment, but with the information visibly weighing on him, Matt returned to the cigar and gently picked it up. It was long and plump and soft when he squeezed it between his thumb and index finger. He held it under his nose and drew in a large sniff, then rolled it around in his fingers.

"Did you fellas see this?" he asked.

"What?" Jacob Page asked, moving closer. Matt held out the cigar and turned it slowly so his pa could see the circular burn around it, like the markings on a barber pole.

"What do you make of it?" Matt asked.

"Looks to me like a fuse was wrapped around it," Wellman said, stepping over to take a look. "Wrapped the fuse around and stuck it in through the crack so it hung into a box of powder, then crammed the cigar in the crack to keep it in place. When the cigar burned down far enough it lit the fuse and in a few seconds, *kerblooey*!"

"So Nixon fer sure had some time to git," Jacob Page speculated. "Why didn't he?"

Wellman shrugged. "He wasn't the brightest of individuals, God rest his soul."

"Where'd someone get the fuse?" Matt asked.

"Look around," Wellman told him. "There's pieces of fuse all over the place, an unfortunate by-product of the trade. It'd be simple enough to come by."

Matt stuck the cigar gently into his shirt pocket and, turning on his heel, took off toward town at a trot, leaving Wellman and his father to muse over the remains of the building.

Matt traveled straight to the tobacco shop and went in, the door ringing the little bell hanging above it as he entered. The pungent yet pleasant odor of cut tobacco leaves for cigarettes, cigars, and pipes greeted him first, before the shop owner, whose back was to the door while he straightened his shelves, had the chance. He turned at the sound.

"Good after—oh, Deputy Page. Nice to see you. Don't tell me you're taking up the chaw? No, the pipe. You look like a pipe man."

"No thanks, Mr. Gordon, although it is mighty tempting on a day such as this. A pipe, I mean. Must be nice to wrap your cold hands around a hot pipe bowl while warming your insides at the same time."

"That it is. But if that isn't why you're here, to what do I owe the pleasure of your company?"

"This." He fished the cigar out of his pocket and handed it to the curious tobacconist, who accepted it with a puzzled look.

"Cigar," he said. "What of it?"

"What can you tell me about it?"

He rolled it between his fingers, smelled of it, and measured its circumference.

"Not very expensive but passable. Good filler, cheap wrapper, burns hot. They wear well in your pocket, take some abuse and still smoke good. End was bit off, not cut. Strange burn mark around it, no idea what caused that. This is the cigar of a man of little means, who doesn't give them away and would smoke them if they were as hard as a log. I'm surprised it's as long as it is."

"Why?"

"Because men that smoke these don't toss them away, they put them out on the bottom of their shoe and save them to finish later."

"Do you sell them?"

"Are you joking? It's what I sell the most of, next to plugs of chaw. Very few around here except for the lawyers and mine owners can afford anything else."

"How long ago did you sell that one, if it came from here?"

"That's a pretty tall order, Deputy. I do believe it came from here, though, because it's so fresh. Maybe yesterday, maybe even today."

"Can you tell me who might have bought it?"

"What's this all about, Deputy?"

"That cigar set the powder magazine off."

Gordon looked at the cigar, as if seeing it in a new light. He set it down on the oak counter as though it were something sinister that would contaminate him, then looked up at the deputy, his face as serious as a snakebite.

"That was intentional? Is that what you're saying?"

"That's the possibility I'm lookin' into."

"Whooee," he breathed. "This is serious. Let me think."

He put his hand to his forehead to consider the question of *who*, but was interrupted by the doorbell tinkling the entrance of another customer. A woman of ill repute sashayed up to the counter and ordered a bag of cigarette tobacco and papers. She plunked some coins down on the counter and accepted the bag he offered without comment, eyeing Matt up and down the whole time she stood there. She paid for her items and received a small sack from Mr. Gordon, and as she prepared to leaved, she gave Matt a yellow-toothed smile.

"My, you're a young one to be totin' a star. I'm up at Number 3 Bonanza. Look me up sometime."

She turned and walked out, popping her hips a little for show.

"Brazen little hussy," Gordon said. "But some of 'em are like that. Personally, I'd sooner hit the top of my foot with the business edge of a shovel. Don't know what these men see in 'em."

"You married, Mr. Gordon?"

"Yep. Ten years come June."

"Loneliness, Mr. Gordon. They're lonely. I'm not so young I don't understand that. Surely you know it, too."

"Oh, I do. It's just that you'd have to be awful lonely to hanker for the likes of her."

"Many of them are. Not that I condone it, you understand. Not for a minute. But I do understand it. Now, you were saying . . . ?"

"Ah, yes, the cigar. I believe I've had three men buy those in the past two days. I know two, but the other was a stranger. Yesterday, Mr. Fred Smith of the Empire came in, bought a whole box. He can afford the good ones, but he's cheap, and he smokes them nonstop. Plus he likes to give them away, make everybody think he's a high roller. This morning two men made a purchase. Bob Kitterman bought one . . . maybe two, I don't recall. The stranger bought two."

Kitterman. Matt knew him, sort of. Worked the drill under his father, lived in Uncle Billy's boardinghouse owned by the Empire Company. Seemed like a nice sort. That left the stranger.

"This stranger," Matt said. "Can you tell me what he looked like?"

"Like every other man who comes to town. Dirty, in need of a shave. Maybe a beard. I wasn't paying that much attention. Long sideburns, but his hairline was receding a mite, I think. He had a hat on, so it's only a guess. I'm afraid that's all I can assist you with."

"That's been helpful, Mr. Gordon." Matt picked up the cigar and slid it back into his pocket. "Thanks."

"You're welcome." As Matt began moving toward the door, Mr. Gordon hailed him. "How about just a try?" he asked, holding up a new cigar. "On the house."

Matt smiled. "I'd rather hit the top of my foot with the business edge of a shovel, Mr. Gordon. But thanks just the same."

CHAPTER

FOUR

THE SNOW HAD FINALLY STOPPED FALLING, leaving a good six inches covering the town. The sky was still dark and overcast, but it figured to break up by nightfall. By tomorrow evening the snow would probably all be gone, except that which rested in shadow all day. Bodie's streets would then be all mud, but to most citizens that would be just another minor inconvenience, more a topic of complaint at supper and in the saloons than a genuine hindrance.

As Deputy Page moved steadily down the boardwalk, he tipped his hat to a couple of the town's fairer citizens, who smiled shyly in return, then whispered giddily to each other after they were past him. He was oblivious to it, though, and when he was abreast of the Empire Boarding House, owned by the mining company for its employees to reside in and travelers to use as a hotel, he stepped out into the street to cross to it. Stopping to let a buckboard pass, then hurrying to avoid one coming the other way, he recalled as he crossed Main Street the days not too long ago when one could lay down in the middle of the street any time, day or night, and not be disturbed.

He entered the hotel, nodding to a pair of hardy men taking up space on the porch in the two rockers in spite of the cold. Some of the boarders sat in the parlor, one of them reading a week-old paper from Aurora, Nevada, two others playing a rousing game of checkers, both of them smoking familiar-looking cigars.

"Where's Billy?" Matt asked one of them.

He jumped two of his opponent's men. "In the kitchen," he said without looking up. "Thanks, Mr. Kitterman."

He waved a response, and Matt turned, relieved that Kitterman was no longer a suspect. He went into the kitchen where Uncle Billy O'Hara, a former slave and riverboat captain's assistant, tended a bubbling pot on the stove.

"Smells good," Matt said.

"Matthew!" Billy said, happy to see his friend. "What are you doin' here this close to supper? Don't tell me Sarah done throwed you out." He laughed, knowing it wasn't true.

"No, 'fraid not, Billy. I just came by to talk to you, get your ideas on something."

"Sounds serious. This have anything to do with the powder magazine?"

"Yeah, 'fraid so. What did you hear about it?"

The large man stirred the pot and tasted a spoonful of his stew, a heavy beef broth into which he had poured cut potatoes, carrots, onions, okra, and his own special spices, which he would reveal to no one. Some said it was sugar, some said it was a pinch of gold dust, others plain old Bodie dirt, and another contingent opted for strange oriental spices purchased in Chinatown. Sarah told Matt it was a combination of salt, pepper, and curry powder from India. Not enough to make it hot, just enough to make it interesting. Everyone said it was good.

"Ah heard it was an accident. James Nixon carelessly dryin' powder, wet from snow seepin' through cracks in the wall, by puttin' it in the stove."

"That's what he did last time, only not so much that it killed him. Do you really think he'd do it again, only more so?"

"No, Ah s'pose not," Billy admitted. He stirred the stew one more time pronouncing it done, and rang the bell. In moments, men started filing into the kitchen to get themselves a bowl of stew and a hunk of bread with fresh-churned butter and stove-boiled coffee.

"Come out here, Matthew," Billy said, drying his hand on a towel. "They can tend to themselves."

Matt followed Billy out to the parlor, now empty, and they sat in two old, upholstered chairs in the corner by the lamp table.

"So, what's the problem?" Billy asked. "Ah take it it weren't no accident. That's why you're involved."

"You're right, Uncle Billy. It was murder."

Nothing surprised Billy anymore, not after all these years of hard living in a fledgling mining camp. He just nodded.

"Someone stuck this in between the cracks. It burned slow enough to let him hightail out of there, but not too slow because Mr. Gordon, the tobacconist, says these kind tend to burn hot."

"You want to know who smokes these," Billy concluded.

"If you can find out, I'd appreciate it."

"Kitterman does."

"Yeah, I know about him. But the two he bought, he and another man were smoking out on the porch just now."

"Ah don't know any others offhand, but Ah'll keep my eyes open."

"Thanks. I've got another problem, too, Billy."

"What's that?"

"I had a prisoner. He tried to draw on me this morning when I got between him and a miner, Frank Cooper, who was havin' a little argument over manners . . . rather, Frank's lack of them."

"What do you mean, you 'had' a pris'ner?"

"When I went back to the jail after the explosion, he was gone. Someone had snuck in and pried him out. He would've been out by now anyway, with three good meals in him, but I guess he just didn't cotton to the idea of being locked up."

"Many men don't, even when they got nowheres else to go," Billy said. He thought for a second. "You say you arrested him before the explosion, and after the explosion, he was gone?"

"Yep."

"Did you consider he might have a partner, someone who set the explosion to make sure no one in town would be a witness to the escape?"

Matt stared at Billy, his friend and mentor. "No, can't say as I did. I was thinking it was an enemy of Nixon's or the Queen Anne's."

"Might not be a bad idea to try and look at it that way," Billy suggested.

"But why commit a murder just to spring a man from jail a couple hours early?"

"Was it a murder? Or a plan gone bad?"

Matt thought. "No, it looked like Nixon had warning. He was running out when it went off."

"Whoever set that cigar there told him to flee," Billy said. "But it went off before Nixon could get far enough away. Ah'd look in the direction of the man you lost from your jail."

"But he has an alibi. Me."

"He must have a friend."

Matt snapped his fingers. "That he does. A man in the Nugget took up his cause before I arrested him."

"They'll be together," Billy predicted. "And with this weather, they might still be in town. But they'll be hard to find, make themselves scarce."

"Chinatown," Matt concluded.

"Likely," agreed Billy. "But you be careful. A man who wants out of jail a few hours early might have something to hide."

"Like what?"

"Like his true self. Your man might be wanted somewhere for somethin' serious and was afraid you'd find out."

Matt took off his hat and wiped his hair back, breathing out a sigh. "Thanks, Billy. Sometimes—no, most of the time—I think you'd be better in this job than me."

"Ah have experience in the world you lack," Billy said, "because of mah age. But you got skills in other areas Ah could only aspire to. Give it time, son. You'll be figurin' these things out on your own. Jus' takes time. Now hadn't you ought to git home, see what Sarah's fixin' for supper?"

Matt smiled and stood. "Thanks, Billy."

Billy remained in his chair. "You be careful tonight."

"I will."

Matt strode out of the boardinghouse as Billy watched, like a proud father watches his son.

Sarah set the plate on the table in front of her husband, steam rising from the meat and potatoes.

"Sarah, I don't know how you do it," Matt marveled, drawing in a whiff.

"Me neither, today," Sarah admitted. "It was quite an interesting one, don't you think?"

"If you only knew," Matt said.

"What's that mean?"

"After I eat, I got some work to do."

"Oh, Matt. Do you have to go out?"

"I'm afraid so, honey."

She set her own plate down, wiped her hands on her apron, and took her seat across the small table from her husband. Before she could protest anymore, Matt bowed his head and began praying, and Sarah was forced to follow suit.

"Father, we ask Your blessing on this fine meal," Matt prayed, "and we pray for Your strength tonight. Be with the families of the man who lost his life today, and may he be resting peacefully in the bosom of Abraham. Amen."

"Amen," repeated Sarah. "Now what's all this about you having to go out? What's so important you can't enjoy an evening at home with your wife, sitting by the fire?"

"Don't make it any harder than it already is, Sarah. Golly, sweetheart, your daddy is the sheriff. Surely you know he sometimes had to go out at night." Matt cut a hunk of potato and stuck it in his mouth, washing it down with a gulp of fresh buttermilk, a rarity in Bodie but possible today because of the cold.

"Ma never liked it none."

"Did she complain?"

"No," Sarah admitted quietly. "But I'm not Ma."

"No, and it don't bother me none that you complain. Shoot, I'm complainin' on the inside. But I still got to go out."

"Why?"

"That explosion today, it was done on purpose."

"It was? Why would someone do something like that?"

"Don't know for sure, but I think it was a diversion so they could get someone out of jail."

"That man you arrested this morning?"

"The same."

"So, what are you planning tonight? Should I wait up?"

"I've got to find them, and I don't know how long that will take. It's best you don't. Besides, you've got to get up early for breakfast at the Quicksilver."

"What's wrong with tomorrow, when it's daylight?"

"They might be gone by then. The weather's breakin', and first chance they get, they'll be headin' out of town. It's got to be tonight."

Sarah knew there was no point arguing with him. Her father had been devoted to duty like Matt—it's one of the things that made Matt a good lawman and made Sheriff Taylor hire him in the first place. All she could do was sit home knitting by the fire and reading the Bible and praying God would bring him home safe. After that, it was all in God's hands. Sarah sighed, wondering how people who didn't believe in Jesus could possibly make it in this world with all its trials and heartache. People like Rosa Bailey.

"Well, you be careful," Sarah said needlessly. But she didn't know what else to say. "Have a good time" just didn't sound right at a time like this.

Matt finished his meal and wiped his mouth with his sleeve, ignoring the napkin by his plate, then pushed his chair back and put on his hat. He stepped over to his bride and leaned over for a kiss, lingered a second or two longer than he might if he'd only been going out to pick up a sack of flour, then pulled on his leather coat and buttoned it up.

They exchanged looks but no words, and Matt turned and strode out into the cold moonlight.

The cold had driven everyone indoors, and Chinatown's streets were deserted. Matt strolled past the butcher, where naked ducks hung in the window, and the Joss house, the Chinese place of worship, where mysterious red characters had been painted on the door.

Bonanza Street on the edge of Chinatown had foot traffic, men hurrying to or from the cribs, and Matt wondered if he'd have to check every one of them. He'd be mighty unpopular around town if he did.

He decided to try the opium dens first. If men were hiding out, they'd want a place that would give them a refuge all night, not just for an hour or two. He remembered the trouble he'd had at Mr. Song's den before and the large Chinaman he'd punched. That man wouldn't likely be rolling out the red carpet.

Keeping his badge in place this time, he went to the den and decided on the direct approach. The door was shut, so he grabbed the cold brass knob and turned. As the door opened, he was hit by a rolling cloud of smoke that nearly bowled him over. He staggered but maintained his grasp on the door and fought his way inside, coughing.

He gazed through the yellow haze, searching the faces for the owner of the den, Mr. Song. Then he saw him as the man pattered out in his black slippers and yellow silk robe from the back room to greet the new arrival. Matt figured he must have a cord attached to the door that rings a bell in the back room somewhere. Mr. Song's face was all smiles as he approached, until he was able to see through the smoke and recognize the deputy.

"No trouble here," the man said in his broken English. "You go now."

"I don't want any trouble, either," Matt told him. "This is official business. I don't want to shut you down right now, I just want to find someone who may be hiding out here."

"No one hide. Regular customer. Go, please."

"Not so fast, Mr. Song. The men I'm looking for might be regular customers of yours. But he and his partner killed some folks today. You heard the explosion today, didn't you?"

"No hear."

"Sure, Mr. Song. Okay, I guess I'll just have to do it my way."

Matt opened his coat slowly while holding his gaze on Mr. Song and cleared leather, pointing the pistol toward the ceiling. He cocked it.

"Okay, no shoot," Mr. Song said. He pulled on a rope hanging from the ceiling, and in a moment, the large Chinaman came out to do his master's bidding.

"Deputy look for man," Mr. Song said. "You help."

The big man squinted his eyes and regarded the deputy suspiciously, then looked at Mr. Song and nodded once.

"Okay, he help. Tell him what men look like."

Matt gave him the description of the two men from the Nugget. The Chinaman thought about it, then nodded and motioned for Matt to follow him. He disappeared into the back room. Matt trailed along, trying not to lose sight of him in the smoke.

No sooner had he passed through the door than he was struck on the head from behind. He folded, collapsing onto the dirty floor, his hat knocked from his head. But he wasn't whacked unconscious and groaned as he tried recovering. Someone jerked the pistol out of his holster while two others grabbed his arms and yanked him upright, then dragged him to the back of the place and threw him out into the snow, his hat flung on top of him. The door closed with a bang, and Matt was alone, just him and his headache.

He lay there for a bit, trying to comprehend what had happened so suddenly. He rolled over, pushed himself up to a sitting position, then found his hat and stuck it on his head and, with much effort, stood all the way up.

Okay, what went on in there? he wondered silently. Was that a payback, a warning, or just unfriendly Chinese? One of these days he'd find out, but right now he needed his wound checked. He could feel the warm blood running down the back of his neck. Besides, he no longer had his pistol.

He stumbled to the boardwalk and clung to a porch rail, trying to get to his feet. He heard the light steps of someone approaching but ignored them.

"Are you okay?" a female voice asked.

Matt looked at her, but couldn't quite focus.

"Oh, you're hurt. You need someone to look after that for you. Here, my place is just around the corner. Say, aren't you the deputy? I saw you today in the tobacconist."

Matt squinted and peered at her. Sure enough, it was the soiled dove he had acknowledged earlier.

"I'm okay," he said.

"Nonsense. You won't get three blocks like that. Come on, I'll fix you up. Don't worry, ain't nothin' gonna happen. I know you got a pretty young wife. But she's sleepin' at home, and you need help here and now. It'll be our little secret."

She took his arm with both her hands and guided him off the porch, leading him to her crib on Bonanza.

It was a small place, just a bed and a chair and a table, but it was home. She set Matt down in the chair and helped him off with his coat, then wet a rag in the bowl on the table and dabbed at his wound.

"Nice bump and a cut. They musta hit you with a gun butt or something."

"I don't know," was all he could say.

"Well, you'll be okay. Here, take a little of this. It'll kill the pain." She held it out to him.

"What is it?"

"Laudanum, of course."

"No thanks." He pushed it back.

"You need it."

"Don't need medicines."

"Look, Deputy, it'll get you back on your feet sooner than not takin' it. That way you can get back to your work and take care of the men that did this to ya."

Matt didn't have to think. He grabbed the bottle and took a tiny swig, about a capful, then handed it back to her.

"Thank you, Miss . . . ?"

"Just call me Betsy, Deputy."

"Betsy. Thank you."

"Don't mention it. You may be the law, but you ain't never done any of us bad. You're a man just like any other man, and your wounds have to be taken care of. That's me, Betsy, the little Bonanza Street nurse." She laughed, then said, "Only I don't compare to that Sarah of yours."

Matt turned his head and looked at her askance.

"Surprised? Don't be. We know what you and Sarah done for Rosa Bailey after the awful death of her daughter Nellie. Not too many of the good folk of Bodie—or any town, for that matter— would do that for one the likes of us. We may be prostitutes, Deputy Page, but we got hearts."

"But today, in the tobacconist's—?"

"Just havin' a little fun. If I acted like I knew you, Mr. Gordon might've got suspicious. You know?"

Matt was silent as the woman dressed his wound and wrapped a clean cloth around his head.

"There. Now see if your hat still fits. Good. Nobody'll notice. Now you get on out of here, I got customers."

Matt stood and gazed at the woman's face. Pretty, but not too, her body covered with decent clothing, but the coat hanging over the back of the chair was tattered, and her gloves had no fingers. He stored the information away and pulled on his coat.

"I don't know how to thank you, Betsy."

"You already did." She watched in silence as he buttoned his coat.

Matt smiled. "Good-bye, Betsy. See you around, I guess."

"Best not," she said. "Unless it's happenstance. Here, let me check outside first. Wouldn't want folks gettin' the wrong idea."

She opened the door just wide enough for her head and peeked out.

"Okay, streets are clear." She held the door open wide.

Matt hesitated, then touched the brim of his hat and stepped out into the street.

He didn't see the man standing in the shadows down the street, watching him.

CHAPTER

FIVE

MATT STRODE OUT OF CHINATOWN, defeated for the moment. He could see he'd get very little cooperation from the Chinese, and he wasn't positive his quarry had taken refuge there anyway. He stopped by the jailhouse for his spare revolver, and while he formulated a plan, he took a moonlight stroll of the saloons. Maybe someone there knew something and wouldn't mind telling him.

He chose the Nugget first, both because it was where the trouble started and because it was the closest. He shut the door behind him as he went into the warm room and headed straight for the bar, ignoring the customers except to keep an eye out for the men he sought.

It was much more crowded than it had been that morning, and the additional bodies helped warm it. A full contingent surrounded the faro table, and there wasn't but one or two open spaces at the bar. Matt saw the owner in his usual spot behind the bar, selling a beer he'd brewed himself to a thirsty miner.

"Water," Matt said as he leaned his elbows on the polished wood.

"Water?" repeated Nate Holcomb. "What on earth do you want—oh, it's you Deputy. Sure, one water coming up."

"You got any coffee?" Matt gingerly felt the back of his head where a large knot had formed just above the hat line. He could feel it through the cloth Betsy had wrapped around it.

"Yeah, got some on the boil now. You want that instead?"

"Both."

"Coming up." Nate filled the glass and the mug and brought them to the deputy. "Any problem here?" he asked suspiciously.

"Don't know," Matt said. "Why, you havin' one?"

"No, no, it's real peaceful."

"The miners and the layabouts keepin' peace?"

"Yeah, Deputy. It was just them two this morning caused a problem. The man with the beard left right after you hauled O'Shea off. Neither of them been back."

"You hear what happened?" Matt took a sip of the hot, bitter brew and asked for sugar.

"About the powder magazine, you mean?" Nate asked, handing Matt the sugar bowl.

Matt nodded.

"Yeah. Someone set it off on purpose. Heard some of the miners talking about it. Opinions differ as to who and why, though. Some say O'Shea's friend. Others say it was the husband of a woman the powder man was seeing. Then there's the old rivalry between the Queen Anne and the Empire I heard about. Of course, that was before my time."

Matt drank in silence.

"What do you say, Deputy? You seem awful quiet tonight, not your usual friendly self."

"I'm nursin' a headache. Got cold-cocked in Chinatown lookin' for them two."

"They get you?"

"No, I don't think so. It was a payback from ol' Mr. Song. Something that happened a while back."

"Seems to be a lot of paybacks going on here," the bartender mused.

Matt nodded. "Thanks for the coffee, Nate. If you get wind of them two, would you let me know? I'll be around town."

"Sure thing."

Matt touched the brim of his hat and left the saloon, not paying any attention to the men he wound his way through, and went back out into the cold.

As he had that morning, he went to every saloon in turn, going in each one and surveying the crowd. As might be expected, he happened upon several fights along the way, but most were broken up without any problem and the combatants returned to their routine. Matt was in no mood for gunplay, and he was short-tempered, a man of few words. In the Bessie, an errant punch had clipped the deputy's face as he stepped between two men breaking up a row, and a hoist engine operator from the Queen Anne suddenly found himself in the sawdust, looking up . . . from one eye. Matt figured that was punishment enough and left the place but not before he checked for the wanted men.

With no place left to search and Chinatown just too hostile and uncooperative, Matt strolled down to the stable to see about his horse. It had been several days since he'd ridden Blister, and the Morgan was probably lonely. Matt figured he'd talk to him some, tell him his problems, and feed him a hatful of oats before calling it a night.

He entered the big doors, closing them behind him. The stable was cold and he shivered, wishing he was already home in the nice warm bed, cuddled next to Sarah. Blister blew as he smelled his master and pawed the ground.

"Hey, old boy," Matt said, unlatching the gate to the stall. "How are you, huh? They treatin' you okay in here?"

Matt stroked the horse's velvet nose, and the animal nuzzled him. Taking a brush from a nearby hook, he lovingly stroked Blister's neck.

"I miss the good ol' days, don't you? When we could ride the range tracking folks, run free, sleep out under the stars, cook some grub over a campfire. Things are different now, ain't they?" As if understanding, Blister dipped his head a couple times. "That's right. But it's good, Blister. I love Sarah. I like my work, except when I get knocked on the head like this. You know, that opium den is a real sore spot with me. I tolerate the ladies, you know, because if I went on a rampage with them, the men would string me up in a heartbeat. Now, we'll have to work on that problem another way. But I got to do somethin' about ol' Mr. Song. He's killing people in there with that stuff they smoke. Them people look mighty sick. They need God, but they're takin' the poppy instead. It don't make no sense, does it, boy?"

Matt glanced about the dim interior of the livery. His eyes lit on his tack and the long rope hanging from his saddle. With that, an idea formed. He'd been assaulted tonight, so someone should pay.

But he was just one man, and what could one man do? Not much maybe. But one man and a horse . . . now that was a different story.

"Blister, how'd you like a run? Your feet are gonna get cold, but they'll be movin', so it shouldn't be much of a problem for you."

Grabbing his gear, Matt saddled the Morgan, which began to get excited. Day or night, hot or cold, Blister didn't care. He just wanted out, wanted to run.

Matt led the horse out into Main Street and closed the big doors behind him, then rode slowly up Main Street. Bodie was by no means dead at night, what with the twenty-four hour shifts at the mines and mills. The great steam engines that drove the stamps ran continuously since they were so hard to get started, which meant the mills and therefore the mines ran continuously too. Men still came and went at all hours.

A man on horseback was another matter, especially in this weather, and Matt got a few stares from the curious but paid them no mind. He turned on King Street, rode past his jail, and went directly to Song's.

Matt pulled his right leg over the saddle and slid down from Blister's back, took the rope from the saddle and walked silently on his gumsoled boots to the door. There he tied one end of the rope to the door knob and uncoiled it, tying the other end to the pommel of his saddle. He hoisted himself back and drew his pistol, firing it several times into the ground. The sudden series of small explosions was a shocker in this still, dark night, but Matt didn't wait around for a reaction. He whistled and dug his heels into Blister's flank, and the horse leapt ahead, galloping up the street and flinging snow in all directions, steam blowing out his nose like a freight train.

The rope fed out and finally went taut. Matt kept riding, and Mr. Song's door exploded off its hinges with the splintering and ripping of wood. Matt reined Blister up and turned the horse in time to see the den empty of frightened, confused, and drunken people. Then he saw the silhouette of a large Chinaman, his queue flailing out behind him. The man ran out into the street, turning in a circle to see who had done this, then spied the man on horseback fifty feet up the street. He shouted, and Matt dug in his heels again.

Blister ran, and they passed the dislodged door, now lying silent in the snow but still attached to the rope. As they neared the

Chinaman, Matt veered away and ran past him, causing the man
to turn while shaking an angry fist. That was his undoing. He did
not notice the rope, did not see it go taut, did not see the door being
dragged by the rope behind the horse, and did not know what hit
him as it mowed him down.

Matt heard the crunch and wheeled Blister around. He released
the rope and rode back to the fallen Chinaman, who lay face down
in the snow. Matt jumped down and rolled him over. He still
breathed but had been knocked senseless. Matt felt around the
man's massive waist then opened his coat and retrieved his stolen
Colt's six-shooter, sticking it in his belt.

"Fair's fair," he said, and backed off as a group of Chinamen
wandered up cautiously. "Go ahead, take him." Matt directed.
"And tell him if I ever see him again in this town, he'll regret it."

The men nodded and dragged their unconscious comrade back
into the den. Mr. Song charged out of his den protesting as Matt
mounted his horse, shouting at the deputy in Chinese. Matt reached
into his pocket and drew out a coin, which he flipped to Mr. Song.

"You fix your door," Matt said. "Next time, when I come
callin', you be more hospitable. Understand?"

Song bit the coin, looking up at the deputy first in anger, then
in wonder, and then looked back at his injured bodyguard. He
understood. He turned slowly and retreated into his establishment.

Matt coiled his rope and loped his horse back to the livery, and
after removing the saddle and giving him a quick hay rubdown,
headed toward the big double doors to go home.

The evening had not been a total loss.

But as Matt was on his way out, a voice called to him from the
shadows inside the livery. Matt swung toward the sound while slapping leather, his Peacemaker solid in his hand and ready for action.

"Whoa!" the voice called. "I'm not heeled!" The man stepped
into the light that shone in from the street, both his hands shoulder high and fingers up.

"That was a durn fool stunt, Noah. What do you want?" Matt
asked, irritated at the town character for surprising him.

"Sorry. I didn't mean startling you there, Deputy. I got some
information for you."

"About what?" Matt relaxed the muzzle of his gun, then
dropped it into its holster. Noah Porter was full of information,

most of it firsthand to hear him tell it, like who said what to whom at Appomattox, and how he pointed out the first nugget at Sutter's Mill to John Fremont. But Matt usually listened to him anyway. Sometimes he could glean a little bit of color from Noah's mountain-sized piece of quartz.

"Them men you're looking for."

"What about them?"

"I know 'em. They're wanted back in Iowa or Kansas or someplace, and in Nevada. I seen 'em on a wanted poster in Virginia City last year."

"Was one of 'em Jesse James, Noah?"

"No, course not." He waved the deputy off. Matt grinned a little, but due to the dark, Noah couldn't see it.

"What are they wanted for?" Matt asked.

"Well, in Nevada they robbed a man of his gold as he was on the trail to town from his digs. They fled right off, and a posse looked for 'em, but they were never found. Rumor had it they were good at changing their appearance. For all we knew, they were still in town." He chuckled. "They might even have been in the posse."

"So, how is it you recognize them now?"

He waited a second to answer. "Truth is, Deputy, I used to run with them, afore I knew they was no good. Now, as I recall, there was three of 'em in Nevada . . . or was it four? Maybe both at different times. Anyway, I'm sure it's them. I wasn't in on that gold heist, don't think that for a minute, Deputy. Do you think I'd come to you if I was? No siree, I was in jail on a drunk charge. You can write the sheriff there, he'll back me up."

That was the first plausible thing Noah had said. Maybe there was some truth to his claim after all.

"Okay," Matt said. "Assumin' that's all true . . . and I'm not, mind you . . . what's your reason for telling me?"

"They owed me a cut from some honest work we did. We were employed for a time, guarding a stage carrying a payroll. Gave 'em honest money to live on between robberies, I see now. There's a reward for them now, thousand dollars each. I couldn't catch 'em alone, and neither should you."

Matt wasn't surprised that outlaws and gunslingers would be hired to protect payroll shipments. Many sheriffs across the West, in fact, were really outlaws, hired because they were good with a pistol. What this man had to say made sense.

"Okay, Noah, tell you what. You repeat this tale to someone else and if he goes for it, we'll put our heads together. The big problem I still have is, where are they? It's one thing to surround 'em and take 'em down. You gotta know where they're at to do it."

"Well, I don't know where they're at, but I know where they're gonna be at sunup."

"And where might that be?"

"I happened to be followin' 'em when they stopped in at the stage office durin' all the festivities at the Queen Anne and bought two tickets out. Let's go see your friend, since I can see by your face you ain't inclined to believe me." When Matt gave him a surprised look, Noah said, "Don't think I don't know what people say about me. Well, maybe I do stretch things every now and then. But what I'm telling you tonight is gospel. When your friend—Uncle Billy, I'm a guessin'—when he hears my story and sees I'm tellin' the truth, I'll tell you where you can find them." The man smiled. "Business is business."

Matt had to grin. "Fair enough, Noah. Let's git. It ain't gettin' any earlier."

Sarah Page set the plate down before her husband, her left hand clutching tightly over her breast at a shawl to fight off the morning chill that seemed to creep in through the wood house. The sun had not yet risen, but already Deputy Page's plan was in motion.

"I'm sorry for making you get up so early," Matt said, then downed a large gulp of her coffee.

"It's my duty," Sarah said. "And I'm happy to do it. You haven't been to sleep all night, have you?"

"I caught a nap. There was a lot to do and little time to do it."

"So, are you going to tell me who patched your head?"

Matt took a bite of fried ham. "Just some stranger who was passin' by and took pity on me, laying in the road like that. They wrapped me and sent me on my way."

Sarah was more worried than suspicious. "How long can you continue this job alone? Bodie's getting too big for one man."

"Speak to your pa," Matt said. "He's the sheriff of Mono County. He makes the decisions."

"Is it my place to speak to him?"

"No," Matt conceded. "I'll do it when I see him, later today if my plan is well-founded."

"I don't want to hear about it. I'll just worry," Sarah said. "You know, what you told me about how you retaliated at Mr. Song's . . . it wasn't a very Christian thing to do."

"It wasn't retaliation," Matt corrected. "It was justice."

"To pull the door off the building, then run the man over?"

"He was guilty of assault . . . on me, I might add."

"He didn't assault you."

"He led me to it."

"Even so, why not let the courts take care of justice?"

"Sometimes, Sarah, the courts can't administer justice. The laws of this state allow the evil of addiction. Is it wrong to wrest the pipe from the hands of its victims, those people who are slaves to it? Is it wrong to make running an opium den difficult?"

"I suppose not, when you put it that way. But where will it end? Will you kill Mr. Song?"

"Of course not. I had the opportunity. And if I were to have tried to take the big Chinaman into custody, I would have had to kill him and perhaps a few others before it was through. Or be killed myself. Don't get a lot of cooperation in Chinatown."

Sarah was silent, then asked, "When will you return?"

"If my plan works, if the men I'm lookin' for do what I think they're gonna do, I'll be back in a couple days. Maybe three. Until then, Uncle Billy's going to assume my position. He's got plenty of friends to call on if he needs it. I was hoping you and Rosa could help him out with meals for his boarders, if you don't mind."

"You know I don't."

"Billy'll appreciate it, that's for sure. And when I get back, we'll . . . we'll do something special."

"Like what?"

"I don't know. Give me a chance to think about it, okay? Look, I gotta go." He stood up and took his bride in his arms, pulling her into him and holding tight, smelling her hair and kissing her forehead. She tilted her face up so he could kiss it, and he didn't disappoint.

After Matt had let go, stuck his hat on his head, and breezed out the door carrying a small carpet satchel, Sarah was still swooning.

CHAPTER

SIX

THE FIRST STAGE OF THE DAY scheduled to leave town pulled up in front of the Bismarck Hotel. A man in a long, black coat and large-brimmed hat worn low over his face boarded first after tossing his bag up to the teamster on the roof. He settled in, resting his chin on his chest—having apparently gotten up earlier than he liked—and soon was joined by several other passengers, none of whom arrived together. A tall man with a shaggy beard, a clean-shaven gent, his suit dirty but otherwise in good condition, and a man in miner's clothing and boots with no hat each took their turn. None of them had any luggage.

The door was closed behind them, the horses *yee-hawed* into life, and the stage pulled out into the middle of the street as the first rays of sunlight crested Bodie Bluff.

The bumpy trip to Bridgeport would take them several hours, with only one scheduled stop to water the horses about halfway. The passengers were jostled, but none complained, this being the nature of stagecoaches. The man in the long black coat slept undisturbed by the rough ride.

"Morning," the miner said to the clean-shaven gent, who grunted a response. The tall man with the shaggy beard ignored them and looked out the window at the majesty of the snow-capped Sierra Nevadas as Bodie receded in the distance.

The miles passed in silence as none of the men volunteered to be the first to open conversation. The man in the long black coat slept without snoring, the others kept to themselves or stared out the window. It would prove to be a long trip if this kept up.

"Chaw?" The miner finally offered his plug to anyone who would take it. He held it out, but no one accepted. "Smoke then? I got a ceegar or two I'd be glad to share."

"I'll take one," the man in the black coat said, apparently not sleeping after all. He glanced up at the bearded man, who was riding backward and still gazing out the window. The bearded man met his eyes out of the corner of his own for the briefest instant, then gave a subtle nod.

The miner extended the cigar. The man in the black coat reached out for it with his left hand, but instead of taking it, he swiftly grabbed the miner's left wrist. In the same motion, he drew a large, black pistol from inside his coat and pointed it at both the miner and the clean-shaven man as he tipped his head back, revealing his face.

"Good mornin', Mr. O'Shea," Deputy Matt Page greeted. "Or whatever your name truly is, since I doubt that one to be factual."

Patrick O'Shea, masquerading as the miner, tried pulling away from Matt, who immediately fired a round past his ear and out the window, then let go of his wrist and in the same motion recocked his gun while drawing a second hogleg from under his coat and pointing it at the other man—who had been bearded the day before—beating the other outlaw who had begun to go for his pocket. The bearded man snatched his false whiskers from his face, and the two captives recoiled at the sight of the gun the man held, the third revolver eradicating all hope of escape from their thoughts. They had never seen Red McDougal before—a miner Matt had arrested for fighting several times but who had recently reformed—but the outlaws were well-acquainted with the Remington pistol Red now trained on them, and they needed no other introduction. At the sound of Matt's shot, the stage driver reined the horses to a smooth stop and lithely jumped down from the driver's seat.

"You got 'em there, son—er, Deputy?"

"Yessir, Mr. Page," Matt shouted back. "They're apprehended." He spoke to his prisoners. "Stick them arms out the windows."

They obliged, under the obvious threat of violence, and Jacob

Page manacled the men's wrists together, not an easy task with only one arm, but he had plenty of time. Matt leaned over and relieved both men of their weapons as a rider on horseback drew up alongside the stage.

"Nice horse, Deputy," said the real stage driver. He jumped off Blister's back and tied the animal to the rear of the stage, then hopped back up into the driver's seat. Jacob Page remounted the coach and took the seat alongside him.

"Think you might let me drive some more?" he asked the teamster. "It was right fun."

"I don't know, Jacob. You ain't never let me run the hoist engine at the Unified."

"That can be arranged."

"Somebody get to startin' this thing," Matt shouted out the window. "We got a lot of road to put behind us before the next snowfall, you know."

With a creak of the wood coach on the leather straps suspending it and the snort of the high-spirited horses, the stage once again moved down the muddy track, destined for the county seat. Matt plucked the cigar O'Shea still held from the outlaw's hand.

"You know, maybe I'll take it after all," he said. He moved its length slowly under his nose while taking a whiff. "If I'm not mistaken, this smells just like the one I already got . . . from the Queen Anne powder magazine."

O'Shea and his balding, formerly bearded partner from the Nugget incident gazed at each other with eyes wide, and both of them slunk down in their seats.

Matt grinned at Red McDougal. "Thanks, Red."

"My pleasure," he said, not taking his hard-set eyes off the outlaws. "James Nixon was a friend of mine."

The stage rumbled over the narrow track, now muddy from the melting snow but rocky still, and the passengers were jostled to their teeth. The prisoners were quiet at first, apparently given to their fate for the moment but not consenting as to their identities. The balding man, a good ten years older than O'Shea, gave his name as Jesse James, which Matt knew to be false, but he branded him James for conversational purposes. The two men sulked, ignoring each other's gaze but taking in the view out their side of the coach: the rolling hills covered with snow, melting in the early morning sun, no clouds remaining in the azure sky now that the storm had passed.

After a time, O'Shea cleared his throat getting Matt's attention. The deputy swung his head slowly toward the outlaw, his face expressionless.

"What did you mean when you said you got another cigar just like that one?" He nodded toward the pocket where Matt had slipped the store-bought cheroot.

"That's a silly question, don't you think?"

O'Shea knit his eyebrows, then raised one of them. "You're obviously presuming something I'm unaware of. You say you have another cigar like mine, but what of it?"

"Because they're the same," Matt explained. "That's the significance of it. The one I have was used to ignite the Queen Anne powder magazine, and while the whole town was attendin' the tragedy, you were sprung from jail by your friend."

O'Shea's face went ashen. "That's not true."

"What? That you were sprung from jail? I suppose you're not really here next to me, handcuffed to your friend . . . you're sittin' back in the cell wonderin' where the deputy is with your breakfast."

"No, of course I'm—"

"Or that you were sprung illegally? Since I didn't let you out, there can be no other way about it."

"No, Deputy, that's not what I'm saying. I'm telling you I had nothing to do with the explosion."

"Ooh," Matt said theatrically. "That was just a coincidence of major proportions, I take it."

"I have no idea," O'Shea said. "I had nothing to do with it."

"Two of those cigars were bought at the tobacconists the day before. One was used to light the powder magazine, the other you just offered to me."

O'Shea looked across at the other prisoner, who ignored him, then back at Matt. "I smoked the other last night."

"You have the butt?"

"Well . . . of course not. Nobody carries around cigar butts, except them old Injun fellers who hang out around town bumming whatever they can get off good white people. You can't expect me to have the butt."

"No, I suppose not, but that ain't my problem either."

O'Shea didn't answer Matt, but looked across at his friend. "Tell him, would you?"

"I beg your pardon?" James regarded O'Shea with that *I've never laid eyes on you* look. "Why do you address me? We never met before boarding this stage this morning."

"I . . . uh, no reason, good sir. I ask your forgiveness."

James resumed his scrutiny of the countryside while O'Shea looked down at his free hand, resting in his lap. Matt grinned knowingly, then adjusted his position in the seat for more comfort—although the effort was largely futile—and brought his hat back down over his eyes. His Peacemaker remained at the ready in his hand to his side, out of O'Shea's reach, his second gun having been put away to give him a free hand.

At the usual rest stop location, Willie reined in his team and brought the coach to a stop. Matt alighted quickly, followed by McDougal, and went around to the opposite side. McDougal remained on post at the open door.

"Here's the way it is, gents," Matt told his prisoners. "One at a time you can come down. I'll go with you to the tree yonder and bring you back. Then the next man goes. Try running and I'll shoot your legs out from under you. If you think I can't do it, you're welcome to try me. We've got water if you want it, some bread and jerked beef. Anything else will have to wait until we get to Bridgeport. Who's first?"

"He can go," James said, nodding toward O'Shea. "I'm fine."

"Okay." Jacob Page had climbed down by this time and taken a position on the far side of the stage, just in case someone had a wild hair sticking in him. The teamster was already tending his horses.

Matt had Red unlock the cuff on O'Shea's wrist, then relock it around the window post of the stage. O'Shea slid toward the far side of the coach and stepped off lightly. By then Matt had come around and joined his pa. He motioned with his pistol for O'Shea to move out. O'Shea did so in silence, keeping both hands elevated without being told.

When he finished at the tree the hands went back up and he walked to the stage as ordered, then took his spot and Matt replaced the handcuffs as before. The rest of the men took their turn as Willie finished tending the horses, and soon everyone but

Matt was back aboard the stage. He had stopped just as he began to climb in, catching a glimpse of a rider coming his way from Bridgeport. Even from a half-mile off he recognized the easy lope of the rider's horse and the way he sat erect in his saddle. Matt walked ahead of the coach to greet him.

The man on horseback stopped his sorrel with a word, some twenty yards shy of Matt. He scrutinized the lawman for a second, then raised a hand in greeting. Matt returned it.

"Charlie Jack," the deputy called. "How are you doing?"

"I do well," the Paiute called back.

He rode on up to Matt and threw his right leg over the pommel of his saddle and slid off the horse with no hands, landing quietly in his white man's boots on the moist earth of the trail. He wore the garb of the white man and a flat-brimmed bowler, formerly black but now gray from years of trail dust and the sun. His only weapon was a knife, sheathed in leather and hanging from an old belt.

They grasped each other's hand in friendship.

"Why Deputy ride stagecoach?" The Paiute asked. "Horse lame?"

"No, he's tied up in back. I've got two prisoners in there." He jerked a thumb over his shoulder at the stage. "Takin' 'em to Bridgeport. They're wanted in Nevada."

"Nevada strange place. We no want bad men here."

Matt chuckled. "They want 'em so they can put 'em in prison," Matt explained.

"Better whip or drag behind horse. Then put to work. In prison they just sit, eat. We pay, they no work. Bad idea."

"Probably," Matt admitted. "I'd never thought of it like that. Maybe I'll suggest it to someone."

"Is that father?" Charlie Jack peered into the sun to the man sitting next to the teamster.

"Sure is," Matt said.

Charlie Jack grunted and walked to the stage. When he passed the horses he stopped under Jacob Page and looked up.

"What are you up to, you old savage?" Jacob said good-naturedly.

"I ride to Bodie, say good-bye for winter."

"Don't like the snow, eh?"

"Charlie Jack and all Paiute no like snow. Too cold. White man crazy to like snow, stay in Bodie when snow so high must look up to see top." He shook his head, unable to fathom the depths of the white man's mind.

Matt clapped the Indian on the shoulder. "We've got to get going, Charlie. It was good to see you. Where are you headed?"

"Go south for winter, like duck." He smiled. "Duck and Paiute think good. White man, not so good."

Matt laughed and returned to the wagon while Charlie Jack remounted his horse. The Indian waved.

"Tell Sarah I'm okay, would you, Charlie? She's in the restaurant. You know where that is."

Charlie Jack nodded, then held his hand up to Matt's father and spoke quietly to his horse.

"Good-bye, Charlie," Jacob Page called after him. Willie whistled and gave the reins a shake, and the team blew and pawed and sprang to life, straining at their harnesses as they set the stage into motion.

Sarah and Rosa busied themselves repairing the damage from the day before and getting ready for opening again. By seven o'clock men were already on their way, and as Rosa finished the details and set the tables, Sarah rushed into the kitchen to begin cooking. She had already put the biscuits in the oven, and the coffee was ready, so the first customer wasn't disappointed with a delay. She had fresh butter and a jug of maple syrup, hot biscuits and coffee, and strawberry jam. For many, that would be enough.

It was an easy matter to throw some ham into the skillet, crack a few eggs, and whip up a tub of flapjack batter. Soon the orders began coming in and Sarah's morning flew by, keeping her so busy she hardly had time to think of Matt or long for his return.

She wanted to tell him but not when he had something pressing on his mind—she wanted all his attention. She knew she'd have to wait until he returned. Sighing, she surveyed her kitchen with her hands on her hips while she thought about what to do next, then cracked some eggs into a bowl and whipped them with a spoon.

Later she and Rosa sat down with coffee mugs full of herb tea and thought about the upcoming lunch hour.

"You seem awful distracted this morning," Rosa ventured cautiously. "I don't mean to pry, but is something bothering you? Tell me it ain't none of my business and I won't ask. I mean, I'm concerned, Sarah. You were there for me—still are, in fact. I just want to return the favor."

It's okay, Rosa. I . . . I just wish I could spend more time with Matt, that's all."

"He's got an important job. Takes a lot of his time. You know that. He had the job when you married him."

"I know. But I remember my daddy. He was never this busy."

"Your pa's sheriff in Bridgeport. It ain't like Bodie, not being a gold town. It doesn't have the Chinese, the unemployed, the ladies of ill repute . . . well, it has those. Just not as many as here. And Bridgeport's winters aren't anything like they are here. People there can move about all year long. Here, people get cabin bound. Nothing to do but raise Cain. What I'm saying is, Bridgeport doesn't have near as many problems as Bodie. Bodie's growing and gonna continue to grow as long as the gold holds out."

Sarah was silent.

"I know," Rosa continued, "that probably ain't much comfort to you, but it's true. You got a good man who loves you. I can tell by the way he watches you when he comes in. He won't take his eyes off you. Give him some room to be a good lawman, Sarah. You have a whole lifetime ahead of you. He won't always be deputy here, and he won't always be so busy."

"What you're telling me, Rosa, is to be patient?"

Rosa smiled. "That's it in a word."

"Okay, you win," Sarah conceded. "I'll try. But it'll be hard. Especially with him gone now."

"You got the restaurant, child," Rosa reminded her. "And me here, to keep you comp—oh my, who's that coming in?" She had glanced out the window at a man climbing off his horse in front of the restaurant.

"An Indian," Rosa said, sucking air through her teeth. She began retreating to the kitchen.

Sarah turned and looked at the man.

"That's just Charlie Jack," she said. "Don't you remember him? He was at the wedding."

Rosa took a closer look as the Paiute mounted the boardwalk and headed for the Quicksilver, relaxing as the recognition hit.

"Oh, so it is." She laughed self-consciously. "Sorry. I had a bad experience once with an Indian."

Sarah wondered what that could have been but didn't have time to inquire because in came Charlie Jack. He was removing his hat and coat as he caught her eye and smiled at her.

"Miss Sarah."

"Charlie Jack, what a nice surprise. Do you have time to sit, have something to eat?"

"Charlie Jack must go," he said. "Just stop say good-bye, see Miss Sarah in spring."

"Going south, are you?"

"Yes. Deer go south. Charlie Jack go south. Matt say hello."

"Matt?"

He nodded. "See on trail. Take bad men to Bridgeport. They sad."

"Oh. Well, thank you Charlie." So Matt's plan had worked, and he was safe. Sarah was relieved.

CHAPTER

SEVEN

DEPUTY PAGE SLAMMED THE CELL DOOR shut on the prisoners as Mono County Sheriff John Taylor—also Matt's father-in-law—looked on from the leather chair behind his desk, his feet comfortably occupying the paper-strewn top.

"You confirm their identities?" he asked his deputy.

"They ain't talkin', but my pa went over to the telegraph office to send a wire to Virginia City. We should know pretty soon."

"Good." He turned to the man who'd helped bring them in, Red McDougal. "As soon as we know for sure, we'll arrange for your reward."

"Ain't mine," Red said. "Belongs to ol' Noah Porter back in Bodie. All I need is fare home."

"Fine with me," the sheriff said. "Stage back leaves in the morning. I'll see you get a room on the county."

"That's fine with me. Can I go on over to the hotel now, or should I wait?"

"Naw, you go on over. Matt, maybe you can go with him. Then round up your pa and bring him down to my place, have supper with us. He's going back on the stage too, ain't he?"

"Yessir. He took leave of work and will have plenty waitin' for him when he gets back."

"You're gonna stay for a couple days, of course," the sheriff pronounced. "The judge is gonna need to hear your evidence about the powder magazine so he can bind them over for trial in a couple weeks. For that matter, you'll have to come back for the proceedings."

"It's too bad Bodie doesn't have a full-time judge. It'd save having to bring all my prisoners here."

"Wouldn't matter. All felonies get tried in the county seat, which is Bridgeport. Mighty inconvenient in the winter, but until Bodie grows, it'll remain a municipal court district."

Taylor looked up at their guest. "You go on, Mr. McDougal. The deputy'll be along in a minute."

"Thank you, Sheriff." He bowed out and shut the door behind him.

"Listen, Matt," Taylor said, taking his boots off the desk and leaning forward in his chair, his arms resting on the desk and his hands clasped. "I don't know if I trust this Noah feller none. There's something smelly 'bout a man willing to turn in his friends for money."

"Even if they're wanted by the law?"

"If they really are wanted. They say they never laid eyes on Noah. Don't have any idea who you're talkin' about."

"Don't matter to me none. We still got 'em for the powder magazine."

"They say they didn't blow the powder magazine. I heard them complaining."

"Yeah," Matt admitted. "So? Not many guilty men come right out and admit it."

"Do you have a witness?"

"I've got the cigar they used, and one just like it O'Shea had on him when I arrested him. Plus the motive: creating a diversion so the older one could free O'Shea from my jail. That Nixon didn't get out in time may not be their fault entirely, since they warned him to run. It's even questionable they knew how much damage the blast would do. There's something about dynamiting a train in their past. Least that's what Noah told me he thinks he remembers."

"You think them warning Nixon to get out will exonerate them for his death?"

"I hope not. By all rights it shouldn't. But it's possible they didn't intend to kill anyone—leastwise, we can't prove they intended to—and as I read in the law book you gave me, that makes it second degree murder."

"You their lawyer?" Taylor leaned back and pulled the makings for his pipe out of the drawer, stuffing a wad of cut leaves into the bowls and lighting it, blue, pungent smoke drifting throughout the room.

"Hardly. That's just the truth, that's all. Ain't that my job, to search for the truth?"

"Yep, that it is. But it might be you're going to have to do better than you've done to prove that's the truth. You got to prove they put that cigar there. What's more, O'Shea has an alibi . . . you. He was in your jail. Now how could he have had anything to do with it?"

"Well, I suppose he couldn't. But the one who calls himself Jesse James—"

"It wasn't him who had the cigar in his pocket but the other. A small distinction, maybe, but some lawyers can take nuthin' and make it look like the biggest alibi in the world. You see, son, you got some evidence but not enough to convict them. Fortunately, we don't have to let them go just yet, considering they might be wanted men. That'll give you some time to make your charges stick. I think Judge Wadell will go kindly on you and hold them over based on the circumstances. But without more proof, you won't get a conviction. Not in this town."

Taylor relit his pipe that had gone out while Matt frowned over this turn of events. It had all seemed so obvious before. He was relieved that these were wanted men anyway—at least he hoped they were—so it wasn't a total loss.

Taylor saw the dilemma on Matt's face. "Don't let it worry you, son. You did a good job, putting this together. Had quite a little adventure with it too, I hear. You're doing good work."

"Thank you," Matt said, somewhat relieved. "You know, sir, it's getting a little difficult to police Bodie alone. It's getting real rowdy with all the people coming in. Most of them don't have work, and they sit around all day just thinking up trouble."

"Yeah?"

"Well, I was wondering . . . what are the chances of getting some help? Maybe a deputy."

"You're a deputy."

"An assistant deputy."

"We call them police officers."

"Okay, what are the chances of gettin' a police officer to help me?"

"Slim and none," Taylor said. "Mostly the latter. Costs money to pay a police officer. Where's it gonna come from?"

Matt shrugged. "I don't know. I don't know much about county financin'."

"Neither does the county council, but that's another tale. Tell you what I'll do: I'll check into it. Maybe I can rustle up someone to work part-time for you. Or you can call on him when you really need him, just so long as it ain't all the time. The key to sheriffin', Matt, is to be tough. Let the people know you mean business. Now, the way you handled that Chinaman, that's the right way. Didn't take no help. Don't need to waste time with courts."

"Sarah didn't like it."

"What's my little girl got to do with this?'

"She's my wife, sir—"

"Dad blame!" He slammed his fist on the table. "I know she's your wife. I gave her to you, remember?"

"Yessir, but she said it wasn't Christian."

"Did you agree with her?"

"Well, no . . ."

"Thank the Good Lord for that!" He settled down and leaned back in his chair. "Just because we're Christians don't mean we walk around lettin' people beat up on us. We're lawmen, and we have a job to do. As long as we don't break the law outright— man's or God's—then we do what we have to do to maintain peace and uphold justice. My word, Matt . . . you've killed a man or two. Don't she know that? Did she tell you that wasn't Christian?"

"No sir. She knew I had to do it."

"Well, you had to take care of that Chinaman, too. If you didn't, you'd a had to kill him sooner or later. I'll bet you a month's wages you don't have any problems from them people for a while. If you hadn't done what you did, they wouldn't give you a moment's peace. Them and anyone else who heard about it. You done the right thing . . ." He smiled wryly. "And you done it real good, too. I wish I'd thought of that."

"Thank you, Sheriff."

Taylor stood and stretched. "Mr. McDougal's waiting for you at the hotel, best get on over there. Here, give the clerk this paper." He quickly wrote out a note on county stationary and folded it once before giving it to Matt. "I'll see you and your pa in a little bit for supper."

"Thank you, sir," Matt stuffed the note in his shirt pocket and hustled out of the office.

They sat around the dinner table, staring at the feast steaming before them in bowls: whipped potatoes with thick, brown gravy; fresh green beans; hot bread with cranberry preserves; and a juicy roast; with baked apples for desert cooling in the kitchen but announcing their presence with a drifting, sweet odor.

"Ma, you outdone yourself again," Sheriff Taylor announced.

"Yes, ma'am," Matt agreed.

"Gonna make it hard to go back to Billy's cookin'," Jacob Page declared.

"Don't you talk that way, Mr. Page," Irene Taylor scolded. "Billy's as fine a cook as there is in these parts. He just doesn't have time to do it up like this. Most of the time I don't either, especially since it's just John and me now. Most of the time we eat simple."

The sheriff patted his stomach. "Couldn't tell it to look at me," he said proudly.

"You look fine," Matt told him.

"Don't we sound humble," Jacob Page observed. "Justa telling each other how wonderful we are."

"Now, Jacob," the sheriff said, "Matt can compliment me all he wants. Course, it ain't gonna get him a raise."

"Ain't a raise he wants," Jacob said.

"Pa!" Matt warned.

"That's okay, Matt. I know what you want," the sheriff said. "And I know that you know you ain't gonna get it by tellin' me I look nice. Now let's all stop this nonsense and eat."

He reached for the bowl of potatoes, but his wife cleared her throat. Taylor gazed at her cockeyed, then remembered.

"Oh, yeah. Shall we all bow to give thanks?" They did so, and Taylor prayed. "Thank You, Lord, for the table spread before us, for the bounty with which You have so greatly blessed us. Let's eat. Amen."

They chorused the *amen*, and everyone dug in.

A half hour later they were devouring the baked apples when Taylor made a suggestion.

"Matt, since we got a few days, what say me and you take that trip we been thinking about."

"What trip is that?"

"Walker River, what else? Do a little fishing."

"Ain't it kinda cold?"

"Not where I go it ain't. It's end of season, but they'll be there, and they're hungry, too. What do you say?"

"Sure. Okay."

"Jacob? You want to go too?" Taylor asked.

"Thanks, John. I'd like to, but I took two days off as it is to help Matt with them criminals. I need to get back to Bodie."

"Fair enough, then. Maybe next time. Matt, we'll head out before dawn. Pack for overnight so we don't have to hurry."

"I'll get you some food for the trip," Mrs. Taylor said.

"Excellent. Thank you, honey. What say we retire to the parlor for a smoke?"

They all got up and eased out to the parlor, but Matt hung back and began to help Mrs. Taylor with the dishes.

"You don't need to do that, son," she said.

"That's okay. I always helped ma."

"Well, you're a grown man now, Matt. You belong in there with the sheriff and your pa."

"I don't smoke."

"No, but you can sit there with them like you do, join the conversation. You need to get used to it. That may be your pa and father-in-law out there, but you're one of them, not a boy. You've earned the right to think of yourself as an equal. Now git, before I switch you."

She smiled and winked, and Matt, with a sheepish grin, handed her the dishes he held and left the room.

Before sunup Matt was in the livery saddling Blister and packing his meager provisions into the saddlebags—enough for that day and the next—and strapping his bedroll and duster behind the cantle of Blister's saddle. Sheriff Taylor came in shortly, still holding a mug of coffee and several slender poles in his other hand.

"You ready?" he asked his deputy.

"Yep. What about the prisoners?"

"I asked Harvey Boone to take them some food. He's done that for me before. He shouldn't have any problem with them."

Matt nodded. Harvey was a good man, and, like Sarah in Bodie, Harvey's wife Mary also ran a restaurant, the Argonaut. Matt hadn't had a chance to see him yet this trip, but he planned to do that before he left town.

They mounted and rode out into the predawn streets, vacant of anyone else here in a town that had no twenty-four-hour concerns. Only the saloons were open early and stayed open late, but even those places were dark from two to six A.M.

The air had a bone-cutting chill to it but nothing like Bodie would be this morning. Oh, it snowed in Bridgeport all right and stayed all winter, but it wasn't immobilizing as in the higher elevations.

They rode all morning, a friendly sunrise greeting them as they passed through Devil's Gate. Just beyond the pass, the smell of sulfur and a plume of steam from the far side of a low hill heralded their approach to a hot spring, not an altogether rare occurrence in Mono County. They rode to the edge of the spring and dismounted, picketing their steeds to a post set in the ground nearby for just that purpose by some previous visitor.

"Stay away from that one," Taylor warned, pointing to a bubbling pool several feet away. "Peel your skin right off. I once found a man in there. From the chest down he was nothing but a skeleton."

"How long had he been there?"

"Best we can figure, a day and a half."

Matt pulled off his boots and unbuckled his gun belt, dropping it onto the ground where he piled the rest of his clothes, except his long underwear and hat. His union suit he shucked just before he stepped gingerly into the main spring, then slid down up to his neck, sighing audibly. Sheriff Taylor followed, and soon the two of them were relaxing in the hot spring, the cold temperature of the air around them irrelevant.

But they couldn't stay there all day and soon had to climb out, don their duds, and remount their horses. They still had another hour to go before they reached Taylor's favorite fishing hole, a wide bend in the river that was always still and deep, and had plenty of tree branches hanging over the far bank for the fish to hide under. There they could drown some worms and haul up two-pound trout to their hearts' content.

The man in the bowler hat, known to Matt Page as Patrick O'Shea, paced in the tiny cell, the frustration apparent on his young face.

"Bob, would you relax?" his partner suggested, following his own advice by stretching out on the cot. "You're making me nervous."

"Your plan didn't fly, Cole," Bob said in disgust. "'Change our appearance and catch the stage,' you said. 'These rubes will never figger it out.'" He growled his displeasure. "And calling yourself Jesse James. What was that for?"

"You listen to me, Bob Younger. I ain't never steered you wrong before. Saying I was Jesse James is so far-fetched they'd never consider who we are. Besides, this is only a temporary set-back. Look here, we're in Bridgeport, almost halfway to our destination. We got the ride we paid for, didn't we?"

"Yeah, we got that all right. But that wet behind-the-ears deputy was holdin' the business end of a pistol on us the whole way. That ain't my idea of comfort."

Cole Younger laughed at his brother. "I figure that deputy's about three, four years older'n you, Bob. If he's wet behind the ears, that pretty much makes you soaked." He howled, while across the cell Bob's face reddened, more in anger than in embarrassment. But he didn't dare say anything against the eldest of the three Younger brothers. Next to Jesse James himself, Cole Younger was the finest criminal mind in the West, and Bob, for all his sputter and spit, held his brother in high regard.

"And who's this Noah character who supposedly fingered us?"

Cole smiled. "Don't you remember? He that's simpleton who held our horses when we robbed them miners. Did it for two bits."

"Oh, yeah. Next time, let's tie them to a tree or something. Or kill the man who holds them before we leave."

"Stop worryin', Bob. We'll be long gone before they confirm who we are."

"How do you figure that?"

Cole coughed, cleared his throat, and nodded for Bob to grab some cot and stop pacing. Bob did so in silence.

"When our breakfast comes, we'll break on out of here," Cole said matter-of-factly. "The sheriff and his deputy are gone. You heard that Harvey Boone tell us so when he brought our supper last night. That means all we have to do is take care of him, find us a couple horses and some guns, and we'll be on our way."

"Shoot, we might as well rob the bank while we're here."

"I'm against that," Cole said. "It's just the two of us, and we don't even know how much they got here. This town don't look like much."

"Now Bodie, a gold town, that would've been a good haul."

"And it would have, if your hot head hadn't got you arrested. I told you before, while we're out here letting things cool off back home, we gotta lay low, blend in with the crowd. It don't pay to go making no waves."

Bob nodded contritely. "Sorry, Cole. I really am. That green deputy and his red-haired miner friend just got to me, that's all."

"You gotta learn to let that stuff go, Bob. It'll get you killed. The last thing we need is some country sheriff thumbing through the wanted posters and recognizing our faces. I'm mighty displeased I had to shave as it is." He rubbed his chin. "That took a while to grow."

"That scraggly beard made you look like an old man," Bob said, a smile twitching at the corners of his mouth. "What with that nearly bald head of yours and all."

Cole threw his hat at his brother. "Don't let Jesse hear you say so. He's prouder of his beard than I was of mine."

"He's got a baby face," Bob pointed out. "He needed a beard."

"Land sakes, Bob, shut up."

"What? He ain't in here with us. Last I heard he was in Utah."

"You'll get into the habit," Cole cautioned, "and one day it'll just slip out, and that'll be the end of Bob Younger."

"Aw." Bob waved his brother off and tossed his hat back to him.

"Get some sleep," Cole said. "We got a full day ahead of us tomorrow. Heaven knows what we're gonna have to do to get us some horses and guns." He snorted. "What are they thinking, leaving that store clerk in charge of two of the most notorious criminals the West has ever seen: the Younger brothers."

"Two of the Younger brothers," Bob corrected. "Jim's waiting for us in Markleeville, in case you forgot. Besides, they don't know we're the Youngers."

Cole put his hat over his face. "Oh, yeah, that's right. Too bad. I bet they'd feel right proud to know they caught us. Right proud."

"Let's tell 'em when we leave," Bob suggested, stretching out on his cot.

"Best not," Cole said. "We don't want every robbery in California laid to our account just due to us being here. We got enough trouble of our own without soliciting more."

"You're right as usual," Bob conceded. "You know," he added thoughtfully, "it sure was lucky, that explosion on the hill so you could break me out. What was that, a powder magazine?" Cole grunted softly as Bob went on. "It ain't right, though, them blaming us for it. Why, I was in jail, for Pete's sake!"

Cole didn't respond. He had fallen asleep.

"Boy, Cole," Bob muttered, more to himself than to his sleeping brother. "I don't know how you do it. One minute you're talkin' to me, the next you're sawin' logs."

He settled in himself and folded his hands across his stomach. Soon both brothers were fast asleep.

The tray was heaped with steaming breakfast food. Mary Boone had covered it with a cloth for the trip to the jail.

"You be careful, Harvey," she told her husband. "Don't let them try anything."

"Don't worry, hon. I'll be fine," Harvey assured her as he picked up the tray. Her old revolver was stuck in his belt. "I did it last night with no problem."

"That doesn't mean today won't be different."

"Dear, do you think Sheriff Taylor would've left me with this task if he thought I'd have a problem with these two?"

"No, I suppose not."

He leaned over and gave her a peck on the cheek. "I'll go on over to the store after I drop this off. I'll bring it all back at lunchtime."

She nodded. "See you then."

Harvey balanced the tray with one hand as he opened the door, then stepped out into the clear, cold morning air and headed up the boardwalk to the sheriff's office, which was on the same side of the street as the Argonaut. He'd married Mary not too long before Matt married Sarah. He and Mary had known each other casually for years, but they'd never really paid too much attention to each other, Harvey because he was married and Mary because she was so busy. But then Harvey's wife took sick and died, and after a year he realized he was eating nearly every meal at the Argonaut, and the attention he was getting there exceeded the service the other patrons received.

It wasn't long before he woke up, and in due time, he and Mary were hitched. Since Harvey was busy all day in his general store, Mary asked if she could keep the Argonaut open. Harvey said it was fine, only she'd have to close it up or sell it when she had children, and she readily agreed. So far, that hadn't happened. Harvey wasn't concerned, but Mary wondered about it. She wasn't getting any younger. She was nearly twenty-five, almost an old woman.

Harvey keyed his way into the sheriff's office and pushed the door shut behind him with his foot. Walking to the back where the cells were, hidden from view from the office by a wall, he set the tray on the floor so opening the cell would be easier. The prisoners appeared asleep, not stirring except for their chests rising and falling rhythmically.

Harvey unlocked the cell door and swung it open, then pushed the tray in with his foot. It scraped on the floor, the silverware *chinked* together, and the coffee mugs rattled on their saucers.

Harvey turned to leave, but before he'd taken a full step, something had flung itself around his neck and was constricting his throat while he was manhandled back into the midst of the cell. Both wrists were seized, and he was unable to grab for the gun in his waistband, though it would have been pointless since another hand had already yanked it out and was poking the business end of it not too gently into his ribs.

Harvey tried talking, but the arm encircling his neck was too tight. Then his wrists were freed, and he was shoved onto one of the beds, his head striking the wall a glancing blow. Frightened, Harvey kept his hands in plain view and twisted on the bed for a look at the prisoners, to gauge their intent.

He needn't have worried, though there was no way he could have known that ahead of time. They virtually ignored him, locking the cell door behind them as they hurried out. As the younger one disappeared, Harvey heard him stop and saw him stick his head back in.

"We're gonna let you live," he explained, his face drawn and serious, "because we ain't cold-blooded killers. But you let out a warning and I'll shoot you, sure as I'm standin' here. We'll be out of town in a few minutes. You give it an hour before you holler, or you'll live to regret it." Bob thought about that and laughed, then corrected himself. "No, on second thought, you'll not live to regret it." He laughed again, maniacally, and was gone.

Harvey thought about what the man had said and decided he wouldn't risk it not being a bluff. He laid himself out on the bed and stared up at the ceiling. A few moments later the smell of Mary's cooking found him, and he glanced over at the tray on the floor. If he ate slow, that might be just enough time for them two to make it out of town . . .

CHAPTER

EIGHT

THE OUTLAWS HUSTLED UP THE STREET, trying not to look too suspicious while keeping watchful eyes on the other folks moving about.

"What's your plan, Cole?" Bob asked.

"Pretty obvious, Bob. Get a couple horses and some guns."

"Where?"

"Wherever we find them."

"I suggest we get the guns first."

"Well, ain't you the smart one!" Cole spat. "Of course we get the guns first. If we get the horses first, someone's liable to start shootin', and we won't be able to shoot back."

"That's what I figured, Cole. You don't have to be so blame critical."

"Shut up and keep your eyes peeled."

Bob didn't answer, knowing his brother's temper, and did what he was told. They kept to the west side of Main Street as they headed north to the edge of town, their only gun being the one they took from Harvey, which Cole wasn't sure would even shoot. Of course, unless they encountered someone recklessly stupid, they wouldn't have to find out. He stuck it in his waistband but kept his hand near it.

In a few blocks, they were rewarded. A cowboy, fresh into town from one of the nearby ranches that surrounded Bridgeport, stepped out from an alley where he'd paused to refresh himself. He wore a weather-beaten beige duster and a fairly new, black Stetson, his face sporting a bushy mustache, his cheek bulging from a wad of chew. Cole caught his eye. The man tipped his head in greeting, but before he realized what was happening, Cole had jerked the pistol and was pressing the end of it against the man's nose.

"Your gun, mister," the outlaw told him quietly through clenched teeth. "Get it, Bob."

Instinctively the man raised his hands while Bob lifted the cowboy's hogleg from its leather scabbard hanging from a thin belt strapped around his waist and over his pants.

"Take the whole thing, Bob," Cole demanded.

The cowboy caught on quick and reached down slowly with one hand to unbuckle the rig.

"It's tricky, let me do it."

"Slow and easy," Cole cautioned.

"Only way I know how." He undid the buckle and let Bob take the gun belt from him. He kept his eyes on Cole's, knowing that was the best way of reading his intention. It worked with cows, and it worked with men. Better with men, most of the time. Cows often didn't know what they were going to do until they'd done it.

"Get them hands higher," Cole ordered.

"If'n I reach any higher, I'll be grabbin' feathers off ducks flyin' south," the cowboy complained. "Look, I ain't gonna put up no defense. I may look like I can't tell a skunk from a house cat, but I know when someone's got the drop on me, and I'll tell you, I ain't anxious to be lookin' up at the sky and seein' nuthin'."

"You're a right-smart cowpoke," Cole said.

"Now give me your hat and coat," Bob ordered.

"Ain't you never satisfied?" Cole asked, scowling.

"No," Bob told him plainly. Again, he made the demand.

"My hat?" the cowboy protested. "I just bought it last year. It's almost brand-new."

"Dead or alive," Bob threatened.

"It's yours," the cowboy said. "How about givin' me yours since you only got one head. I'd sooner walk around town nekked than without a hat."

"That's fair," Bob said. "It's just a trade then." He exchanged

hats, plopping the cowboy's on his own head and slipping on the
coat.

"You got a horse?" Cole asked.

"Please, mister, not my hoss," the cowboy begged. "We been
together a long time, me and him. We're like . . . well, he's part of
me."

"I got some hot lead gonna be part of you if you don't give us
your horse," Cole threatened. "And tell me where we can get
another one."

"Well, if'n you gotta take him, Ol' Gimpy's around the corner,"
he told the outlaw, his voice breaking. "Maybe, when you're done
with him, you'll send him back. He can find it. Just cut him loose,
okay? As fer another hoss, I can't help you there. I just rode in
myself. You could always try the livery down the road." He jerked
his head toward the north end of town.

Cole eased the hammer back down, which eased a sigh from
the cowboy, so Cole quickly snapped it back again as if reiterating
his threat.

"No goin' for help," Cole said. "You squeal, we'll come back
and shoot you deader than your last meal. Make no mistake about
that."

"I believe you, mister," the cowboy said. "Don't you worry
none. I'll just wait right here with my mouth shut until you two
gents are nuthin' but a memory."

Again Cole released the hammer, then stepped around the
man, and he and Bob ducked down the alley. The cowboy stood
still as he'd promised, then, when the outlaws were out of earshot,
a wry smile broke out on his weathered, rawhide face.

"Always hated that hoss," he muttered. "If I said he had a brain
the size of a pea, I'd be payin' him a compliment. And that saddle's so wore out, it stopped creakin' five years ago. Good thing
my hoss was tired and I left him in the remuda restin' up. Let 'em
steal that nag I was usin' in the meantime." He sighed as he turned
to walk away. "Gonna miss that hat, though." He strode lazily up
the boardwalk on bowed legs, his hands in his pockets, whistling
a tune.

Cole and Bob found the horse as promised, still saddled and
with a rifle in a scabbard tied to it. Without even a cursory glance

as to the soundness of the animal, Cole instructed Bob to mount. With his little brother in the saddle, Cole jumped up behind him on the animal's rump and off they rode.

The livery was where the cowboy had said it was, and Cole lost no time sliding off the back of the ragged horse and darting inside. Not a minute later Bob heard a hollow thump and a groan inside the livery. Cole returned about two minutes after that astride a piebald mare, carrying a tangle of leather with a strange holster on the end of it. This he flipped to Bob.

"What this mess?"

"Shoulder rig," Cole told him. "It's all he had." With a jerk of his head, Cole dug heel into the mare's flanks and turned her northward, heading out of town at a gallop, leaving Bob to follow as best he could on Gimpy, whose name, he was discovering, was appropriate to the animal's strange gait. As best Bob could tell, the animal was lame, or at least had been so at one time, as her gallop, though plenty fast, was irregular. It wasn't so bad he couldn't stay astride, but she took a lot of coaxing, and he flapped his elbows as he rode to maintain his balance.

Thus armed and astride, Cole and Bob Younger kicked their horses and rode as hard as the horses could run, anxious for Bridgeport to be nothing more than a memory.

Sheriff Taylor and his young deputy stopped for lunch under a big tree within sight of their goal, letting the horses wander in the dry grass of the meadow and eat as they pleased. Taylor decided to make camp there, since it was an easy walk down to the river, and Matt built a fire for boiling coffee while Taylor unwrapped some cold fried chicken and biscuits his better half had made for them that morning.

"Here, let me take care of that coffee," Taylor offered.

"It's no problem. I can do it," Matt said.

"Yeah, I know. I've had your trail coffee."

"What's the matter with it?"

"Too weak. Tastes like dirty water. I'll make us some muleshoe coffee."

"What's that?"

"You'll find out. Go find me a muleshoe."

"Where?"

"Anywhere. This is an old prospector trail. There's mule shoes all over the place out here."

Matt was puzzled but knew better than to question the sheriff. He walked down the trail, looking in the dirt and in the sagebrush that lined both sides of the narrow track, dug around with the toe of his boot and with a nice, straight stick he had found. When he looked up, he was several hundred yards from their camp.

Then he found it. A small shoe, maybe three-quarters the size of a horseshoe. He picked it up out of the dirt and brushed it off, then took it back to Taylor. When he got there, the sheriff regarded him.

"What took ya?"

"Mule didn't want to give it up," Matt said.

Sheriff Taylor looked at Matt blankly, then howled at this unexpected response. He took the shoe from his son-in-law and dropped it into the coffee pot.

"What are you doin'?" Matt asked, surprised.

He looked in the pot. The shoe had sunk.

"When she floats, it's ready," Taylor explained. He put in more coffee grounds. "Ain't strong enough till she floats."

"If it's all the same, I'll have mine now," Matt said. "That thing wasn't clean."

"What do you mean it ain't clean? Didn't you clean it?"

"Nope. Didn't have anything to clean it with."

Taylor shrugged. "Oh well. It oughtta be clean by now."

Matt picked up a chicken leg. "Think I'll pass on coffee."

"Here." Taylor held out a tin mug full of hot brew he'd been hiding behind him. "I poured it already. That's just water for cleanup." He grinned.

Matt took the cup, feeling a little foolish for believing the mule shoe coffee yarn, but grateful that Taylor felt comfortable enough with him to do it. They enjoyed lunch while Taylor explained how to fish the Walker River to greatest advantage.

Lunch finally over, they took their fishing gear and hiked down to the river. Blister and Eli, both loyal, contented horses, didn't need picketing. They knew their masters and knew they had it good. There was no reason to run off. They grazed nearby, happy to be free of their saddles, while the two lawmen sat on the grassy bank of the river, their worms sinking into in the pool, dancing on the end of their hooks and teasing the trout. Taylor broke out his pipe and puffed contentedly on it while Matt leaned back and enjoyed the solitude: the singing of the water and the birds, the breeze whispering through the aspens and cottonwoods.

It wasn't long before Matt's pole began dipping as a trout nibbled the bait.

"Wait a second," Taylor instructed. He watched the pole. "Easy, easy . . . Now!"

Matt jerked the pole up hard and snagged the fish, and the tip bent wildly as the trout tried swimming away, fighting the line and the hook in his lip.

"Okay, good job, Matt," Taylor encouraged. "Keep the line taut, tire him out. Don't let him go under the roots over there. Crank that reel in a bit. Little more. Okay, I see him. That's a nice one. Back yourself up the bank some, pull him closer to shore so I can grab him. That's right."

Taylor reached out to haul in the fish but suddenly groaned and flopped over, a split-second before Matt heard a distant noise. For a moment Matt was frozen, not understanding what had happened, then he realized the sheriff had just been shot.

He dropped his pole and rushed to his father-in-law, who had fallen partially into the river. Matt dragged the man up the bank and spread him out on his stomach to inspect the wound. It was in his back, just off center and not quite midway up, and bleeding. This was serious. Taylor's eyes had rolled back, and his breathing was labored, but once out of the water, he slowly regained consciousness. Matt pressed his hand on the back to slow the bleeding until it could clot.

"What . . . happened, Matt?" Taylor asked, coughing. Brown fluid sprayed from his mouth, and Matt hoped it was tobacco and spit rather than blood.

"Sniper," Matt said. "From over there."

"Go . . . go get him," Taylor ordered weakly.

"You're hurt bad," Matt told him.

"Do your . . . job, Deputy." He coughed again.

Matt got up reluctantly, then drew his revolver and ran through the brush from the river's edge, not in the direction he thought the shots came from, but skirting around and approaching from the assailant's flank.

He stopped and listened. Noise, that of someone running

through the brush. He moved ahead, keeping down as much as possible while trying not to step on brush or rocks, but wasn't very successful at it. Then a horse whinnied, and he heard someone mount up. Matt rose carefully and saw the assailant's backside as he kicked his horse into motion. He capped off a couple of shots, but they were futile, and he had known it ahead of time. The man was a good two hundred yards away. Even if he was astride Blister now, it would take too long to catch up to the man and bring him back. By then, Sheriff Taylor would be dead. The man rode hard, not looking back, and Matt couldn't get a good look at him.

Running back to the area where they'd left Blister and Eli, Matt whistled for the Morgan. They met near the edge of the meadow, and Matt was relieved the horses hadn't been tampered with or run off. Fighting the urge to mount up and give chase, he threw open the saddlebag and dug out his monocular, then ran to the a nearby rock outcropping and clambered up to the top. From there, he could see the road north and a cloud of dust. He pulled open the monocular and put it to his eye, focusing on the retreating assailant. The man wore a dusty coat and a black hat with a curled brim. His elbows stuck out oddly when he rode, not tight against his body. He was soon joined by a second man who rode out from a stand of cottonwoods. The gunman slowed. The men talked. They then picked up the ride again, and both of them hightailed out of Matt's sight.

Matt slowly pushed the monocular together and jumped lightly down from his rocky perch, replaced the spyglass in his saddle bag, then stepped into the stirrup and onto Blister's back. He rode to where Eli stood watching them, his ears pricked, knowing something was wrong but not understanding. Taking hold of the horse's reins he led Eli to the river and his master.

Matt passed the location where the gunman had shot from and jumped down from his horse, kneeling in the dirt for a better look. There was a unique disturbance in the dirt where his legs had been as he hid, and the remains of a handrolled cheroot, still smoking, lay on the rock where he had placed it in preparation to shoot but then had left it in his haste to flee. Matt checked the footprints, noting the style of boot, and collected the cheroot end. He scouted the area and saw the expended cartridge, the brass glistening in the sun. Picking it up, he saw it was a .44 Winchester, which corresponded to the sound the gunman's weapon had made when fired.

Matt looked around for tracks left by the gunman's horse. These he found without difficulty, and upon inspecting them closely, noted the extreme wear on the outside of the shoe of the left front foot. The horse had a little gait problem, probably from birth. It was no handicap to the animal, it was all he had ever known. Judging by the way Matt had seen him run, he had learned to overcome whatever disability he might have. But it was not a high-dollar horse. Whoever owned him didn't have much money.

Matt led Blister and Eli the rest of the way to Taylor's side and knelt by the sheriff.

"Did you . . . get him, boy?" Taylor gasped.

"He had too big a head start, sir."

"Go after him."

"I can't."

"What do you mean, you can't? He . . . shot me!" He punctuated his outrage with a spell of coughing.

"I've got to take care of you, sir. I can go after him another day. There's got to be a reason he shot you. He'll be back, to find out if he finished his business. I've got to stay and make sure he didn't. Let me take a look at that bullet hole."

Taylor didn't protest. He knew the young deputy was right, and he also knew his situation was grave. Experience and pain told him the bullet was in a bad place and had to come out before he could be moved. And since they weren't near town, and there were precious few farms and ranches in the area, it was all up to Matt Page. Taylor's best hope was in him. The lawman could otherwise only pray for a passing carriage with a doctor in it, a highly unlikely coincidence.

Matt used his knife and opened Taylor's shirt. The wound was neat, the blood clotting nicely. It seemed to have entered at an angle. Matt figured the sheriff must've been shot as he was bending over for the fish. That meant the bullet had traveled upward, so he tried feeling around to see where it ended up. If there was spinal damage, Page knew Taylor was in a world of hurt. He might even be paralyzed for the rest of his life.

"Can you wiggle your toes?" he asked Taylor.

"Not with my boots on," the sheriff said with some difficulty. Matt's probing had left the man gasping for breath.

Matt pulled off one of the boots, exposing a dirty sock with

numerous repairs in the toe and heel. As he watched, the sheriff's
toes curled slightly then relaxed. It was all Taylor could do.

"That's good. Can you feel this?" Matt asked, running a finger
up the bottom of Taylor's foot.

"Dadgummit, Matt, I . . . sure can." Good, he still had feeling.
That was a relief, but Matt still had to get that bullet out. They
didn't want it moving into the spine or a vital organ when they
packed Taylor off to town. The trip would kill him.

Matt removed his hat and wiped his forehead, then put the hat
back on, shading his eyes from the sun.

"Okay, Sheriff. I got to build a fire for water and to sterilize this
knife. You don't happen to have any whiskey, do you?"

"Of course I . . . got whiskey," Taylor grunted. "What do you
think I am, some heathen?"

"You sit tight. I'll get that lead out in a few minutes."

"Like I'm going somewhere," Taylor muttered.

Matt covered the wound and trotted to Eli, taking the saddle
off the animal's back. They were staying a while, so there was no
sense giving the horses saddle problems. He fished around in the
sheriff's saddlebag and found the bottle, then took it to him for a
sip. Matt whistled for Blister and removed his tack as well, then
gathered some sticks and built a fire, using flint from his own gear.
In a while, the knife was red-hot and ready. Matt pulled it from
the coals to cool and prepared Taylor's back by soaking a rag with
whiskey and setting it on the wound, letting the alcohol dribble
into the channel in his flesh. Taylor squirmed and cursed the pain
but didn't complain to his doctor.

Matt bowed his head before lifting the knife and prayed. "Dear
God, this is Matt. Matt Page—"

"He knows who you are, boy," Taylor grumbled. "Give . . . give
me that bottle and get on with it."

"Oh . . . yeah, of course. Dear God, I pray that You will guide
my hand and watch over Sheriff Taylor. Amen." He gave the sheriff a sip of anesthetic.

Matt emptied his lungs, then filled them again, but held his
breath as he put the blade to his father-in-law's back.

He used the knife as a probe, feeling along the channel until the
point of it touched the lump of misshapened lead. Now came the
big problem: getting it out. He'd watched doctors do this with

modern medical tools, long two-sided things he didn't know the name of, or scissor-like thin pliers they called . . . force-its, or something like that. But he had none of those implements. Just that fixed-blade knife.

His eye lit on the fishing poles still lying on the bank of the river. They were thin, especially at the end, and a metal ring was stuck on the end to hold the line. He raced down to the river and brought them back, his fish having escaped. With the knife, he cut one pole a foot from the end, severing the line as well, leaving him a thin shaft with something he could push past the bullet to pull it out with.

They were both fortunate the bullet was stuck in muscle. Had it gone any deeper, Sheriff John Taylor would be a memory, and Matt would be packing him home draped over the saddle. As if was, Taylor had a chance if the deputy was able to get the bullet out.

Matt gave the sheriff another swig, then soaked Taylor's neckerchief with whiskey and stuck it in his patient's mouth for him to bite on. He began to probe with the fishing pole tip, thinking how he was still using it for fishing, just of a different sort. The channel was large enough, and it went in easily—from Matt's perspective. Taylor squirmed and bit hard on his neckerchief but didn't cry out.

The deputy had marked on the shaft the depth of the bullet, and as that mark reached the sheriff's skin the probe stopped. Matt had found it. He slowly rotated the rod tip until he was sure the small metal ring was clear of the bullet, then pushed it deeper a half-inch or so and rotated it back a half turn. If his calculations were correct, the line guide would be just past and behind the bullet. He pulled gently, his touch on the stick light, and in a fraction of an inch, the pole stopped. He took a deep breath.

"Okay, Sheriff, here we go. Hold on."

Taylor squinted his eyes shut, clamped down on the neckerchief and nodded once. Matt pulled easily, feeling the resistance as the bullet was forced through the channel of succulent flesh. Because of its pulpy, wet nature, the channel was actually not as big as the bullet that caused it, meaning every movement of the bullet caused pain. Matt didn't let up, however, and his diligence was rewarded. The bullet popped out, followed by the pole tip, and Taylor's body relaxed, his breathing deep and regular. Matt reached up and took the neckerchief from his mouth. The sheriff didn't stir.

Matt cauterized the wound by removing the lead bullet from one of his unspent cartridges and dumping the powder down the fleshy channel, now enlarged from the probing of his knife and the fishing pole. It flared when he lit it, and Taylor howled, then passed out from the pain. The smell of burnt flesh and gunpowder nearly made Matt ill, but he held his breath and doused the area one more time with alcohol, then put a clean bandage over it—one sleeve of his union suit—holding it in place with a torn-off leg of his undergarment. Then he crawled off to recover.

Sitting with his back to a tree, knees up, Matt rested his head on his arms. His shirt was soaked, and he shook from the release of tension now that the task was finished. But his success was still in question, for though Taylor breathed, he was still unconscious from the pain.

Preparing for a long night, Matt built a fire near the elder lawman and covered him with both bedrolls, his own as well as the sheriff's. It wasn't dark yet, but Matt knew the sheriff would need all the warmth he could get. There were no caves in this area, no shelter to speak of, so he could do little but trust God for clear skies and still air.

When Taylor came out of it he'd be hungry, so Matt took the remaining fishing pole and went down to the river bank. He baited a hook and tossed the worm into the water, then settled in. It was one thing to actively hunt for food, quite another to sit and wait for a fish to get around to biting a worm Matt couldn't see.

But he didn't wait long. A tug on the pole made him sit up and tip his hat off his face, and another tug told him to set the hook. He jerked the pole tip up sharply and the fish was snagged. Matt brought it in quickly. He grabbed the slimy trout and pulled the hook out of its mouth, then threaded a line through its gills and tossed it back into the river, anchoring the other end to a root sticking out of the ground. Under other circumstances, he'd be having great fun. Today it was a necessity, which took the fun out of just about any task.

He rebaited the hook and tried again and within a couple of hours had four decent fish, plenty for supper. He returned to Taylor's side with his catch, stoked the fire, and checked his patient. Taylor was breathing regularly. Matt sat near the fire and cleaned the fish.

"Thank you," said a muffled voice nearby.

Matt raised his head toward the sheriff. "You awake?"

"No, I'm a talkin' in my sleep," the sheriff said. He hadn't moved but turned his head for a look at his deputy.

"How you feelin'?" Matt asked.

"Like I been shot in the back and operated on by a meat-handed deputy with no tools. You get it out?"

"Yessir, I did."

"How?"

"Went fishin'," Matt said. He didn't tell the man he'd ruined one of his poles, and Taylor didn't ask further. Some sixth sense he had developed over the years told him he probably didn't want to know, leastwise not just yet.

Taylor ate little, and Matt's own appetite was suppressed by the gore he'd seen. He ended up wasting two fish, tossing them into the bushes for the critters.

They settled in by the fire, and, while Taylor slept, Matt stared up at the stars, thinking of Sarah and how much he wished he was at home with her, to hold her and smell her lilac water. For a moment, he wished he was a farmer and could shuffle into the house at the end of a hard day . . . at the end of every hard day . . . and eat a fine dinner and sit by the fire, reading the Good Book while Sarah embroidered, a dog spread out by the hearth, children doing their schoolwork at the table, an apple pie baking in the oven.

He fell asleep with those thoughts but dreamed of gunmen and bullets.

CHAPTER

NINE

DEPUTY MATTHEW PAGE had saddled the horses, spread the coals of the previous night's fire, and packed everything else behind Blister's and Eli's saddles. All that was left was helping Taylor onto Eli's back so they could ride home.

But the sheriff was still prone on the ground, sound asleep. Matt hated waking him, preferring he get as much sleep as possible, but they had to get moving. Bridgeport was a day's ride away as slow as they were going to have to go, and the sheriff needed a warm bed and medicine to fight infection. All Matt's efforts would be in vain if he didn't get the the man to a doctor.

Leaving him here and riding back for help was out of the question. The sniper might return or be lurking from a hidden vantage point even now, waiting for an opportunity. If Matt rode off alone, the sheriff would be a sitting duck, unable to defend himself.

They could wait and hope for a passing wagon, but they were well off the main road, and the chances of that were less than slim. So Matt made the decision to move him. Now all he had to do was convince the sheriff it was necessary. And trying to convince the sheriff of anything was like trying to teach a mule to knit.

Matt waited, sipping on the last drops of the coffee he'd made before snuffing the fire. He still had some in the pot if Taylor wanted any . . . it was a small matter to dump it out and tie the pot on one of the leather thongs hanging from the saddle's front jockey. The cup would rattle around nicely inside the pot, unless he stuffed it with rice grass to keep the noise down.

Taylor stirred and groaned. Matt moved over next to him and sat on his haunches, waiting. The sheriff moved again, his face set in a grimace, and finally opened his eyes. When he managed to focus, he saw the concerned face of his son-in-law staring at him pensively, sucking on the edge of a tin cup.

"You got some for me, or'd you hog it all?" Taylor grumbled, his voice cracking from a parched throat. Matt reached back, grabbed the pot, and filled the cup about halfway. The coffee wasn't overly hot, but it was drinkable. He handed it to the sheriff, who turned on his side with a wince and drank it all in one gulp.

"That's mighty good," he said. "Did the shoe float?"

"Bounced out when I dropped it in," Matt replied.

The sheriff looked over at the horses. "We goin' home, is that it?"

"It's time, don't you think? You need a doctor so he can correct what I did and give you some orals. You ain't well, not by a long shot."

"Don't say them words, boy."

"What words?"

"Long shot. Makes my back tingle."

He was becoming his old self again, Matt noted wryly. A good sign. His wits were sharp.

"Think you can get up onto old Eli?"

"I can ride him for a spell once I'm up there. It's gonna be gettin' there that's the hard part."

Matt looked around and saw what he needed not too far away: a sloping rock dropping off on the other side, total height about three feet.

"We'll stick Eli next to that," Matt said, pointing with a nod of his head. "I'll help you hike up to the top, then you can step on Eli like he was a rocking chair."

"I'll give it a go."

"First, I need to check that hole in your back, see what's happening. Lay down on your stomach."

The sheriff obeyed without argument, both men understanding their slightly altered roles in light of the circumstances. He handed Matt the empty cup and eased himself down, letting out the breath he held once he was settled. Matt untied the makeshift bandages and inspected the wound. It was red and ugly around the edges, the first sign of infection. A day, that's all they had. Any lingering out here could mean trouble. Blood poisoning. Loss of mobility. A bad infection moving into his spine. Disability. Loss of the use of his legs. Any number of things. They could waste no time.

"Looks pretty good," Matt said.

"Let's get on home, then," Taylor said. "It hurts some, but I'll make it."

Matt replaced the bandages, tearing off a piece from the remaining arm of his underwear, wishing he had something clean to put on the sheriff's injury, but it would have to do for now.

Matt helped Taylor stand, the sheriff wavering on weak legs he hadn't used for nearly a full day. He threw an arm around Matt's shoulders, and the deputy stood under him, letting the sheriff lean on him for support. When he'd gotten his legs somewhat, they walked to the rock, Taylor doing his best to stay upright. The strain on his back was evident in his face, but he said nothing. There was no point; it had to be done.

They inched up the rock and Matt whistled. Blister, recognizing his master's whistle, came over instead, his head down. Taylor realized the dilemma and summoned enough wherewithal to whistle for Eli, who pricked his ears and looked over, and seeing his master, followed Blister to the rock.

As if sensing what they were to do, Eli came alongside the boulder and stood rock-solid as Taylor threw a leg up and slid into the saddle, grabbing the pommel to keep from sliding off the other side. He winced and let out a yelp as he came to rest. In a moment it passed, and he breathed a tremendously relieved sigh.

"Okay, Matt. Ready as I'll ever be. Hope she holds out."

"Me too." Matt jumped down, then stuck a foot in Blister's left stirrup and pulled himself onto the Morgan.

"You take it easy," he told the animal, and thus they began their long journey home.

Before they'd gone five feet, Matt offered a prayer under his breath, both for a trouble-free journey and for Taylor's healing.

They rode slowly, so slowly that both animals strained at their bits. They weren't used to walking like this on the open road. Blister especially was anxious to put some ground behind him in a hurry, but both horses yielded completely to their riders and restrained themselves.

Matt was frustrated, too. This pace was too slow, for Taylor as well as for himself. Every hour he went without treatment increased the chances of serious complications . . . if he didn't die outright.

If Taylor knew too, he didn't let on. He sat straight in the saddle, which Matt figured was the most comfortable position considering the location of his wound, but as the day wore on, his posture slouched in spite of the pain. He was too spent to maintain it. And at their last stop for water and jerky, Matt could tell Taylor had developed a fever. His face was flushed, his eyes half-closed, beads of sweat on his forehead that the cool air could not have caused. They'd not make it back today. He couldn't travel much farther without some rest and serious nutrition.

Matt scanned the countryside trying to get a fix on exactly where they were. Ahead of them, maybe ten miles, was Devil's Gate. After that it was just a couple of hours, maybe four at this speed, into town. Perhaps, once through the pass, Matt could hide Taylor off the trail and ride ahead for a buckboard to bring him back in.

But that would have to be tomorrow. The sun was still fairly high in the partly cloudy sky but would fall fast. They needed to stop soon and make camp while Matt still had time to find a good spot and catch something for them to eat.

All day Matt had kept an eye out on the country around them. Anyone following would have had no trouble keeping up. A man on foot could pace them. Someone keeping off the trail would have had trouble not being seen in several places where the vegetation was sparse and the land flat, but they could hang back and wait until their prey had made it to the trees again, then close the gap.

Matt tried thinking of who might have wanted to shoot the sheriff. He even asked Taylor once, but the venerable sheriff just shook his head. There were too many men he'd jailed over the years, but none that stood out as vengeful.

A spout of steam rose a mile or so ahead, off to the right. Matt watched it and remembered. The hot spring. That would be good for the sheriff, he figured. Clean out the wound, invigorate him, maybe even help break the fever. Shoot, maybe they could even camp near it, let it keep them warm. It was far enough from the road.

"Let's get to the hot spring, Sheriff," Matt said. "Can you make it there?"

Taylor nodded and stiffened his back to show the young deputy his resolve, but where the spirit was willing, the flesh was weak, and he soon had slumped again. Matt came up next to him, ready in case his father-in-law and employer began sliding off Eli's back.

As soon as they made the hot spring, Matt jumped off Blister and led Eli to it. He eased Taylor out of the saddle, feeling for himself the fever that raged through the man. Taylor didn't protest as Matt undressed him, removing everything, including his bandages and underwear, everything but his hat. Matt suppressed a snicker at the sight. Taylor understood what Page was doing and stepped himself into the spring with a little help from his companion.

"Mind that wound, now," Matt cautioned. Taylor nodded, and Matt could see the relief spread across his face as the hot water and steam began its work. There was a grimace as the first contact was made with the wound, but in a few minutes, it passed as he became used to it.

Matt tended the horses, keeping a wary eye on Taylor and the road below them some hundred yards off. This was good. The springs were above the road up a small rise and afforded a good view of the countryside. Behind them, the rise turned sharply upward into a high hill. The bad part was, any campfire they made would be visible for miles, but it was a risk they'd have to take.

With both animals picketed next to some succulent rabbit-brush, their tack removed and coats rubbed down with dry grass, Matt cut some sticks and made a small lean-to at the upwind edge of the hot spring with the roll of canvas they'd brought just in case they had encountered rain or snow. As he hoped, the slightest breeze filled the lean-to with steam. Matt remembered the times he had a cold and his mother would fill a pan with hot water and have him sit with his face above it and a towel draped over his head, trapping the steam. This lean-to would not only trap the sul-fur-rich steam, it would also provide some heat for the sheriff all night as well. Matt could sleep off to the side, up the hill a ways, affording himself a better view.

He checked his patient. Taylor was breathing regular.

"I've got to get a rabbit or grouse or something," Matt told him. "You want to get out?"

Taylor said his first words in half a day. "I ought to. I'll shrivel up until I'm just a big wrinkle if I don't."

"Feeling better?"

"Yeah. Fever's still there, but it ain't so bad. Here, help me."

Matt took the hand Taylor offered and pulled while the sheriff climbed out. Matt took Taylor's bedroll and wrapped it around him. Soon Taylor was dried off and back in his clothes. The wound looked about the same, Matt noticed when he wrapped it, but at least it didn't look any worse.

He remembered the time he'd been shot during the aborted capture of the prison escapees and what Charlie Jack had done for him. A poultice and some sage tea, that's what had helped him through. Course, his wound wasn't near as serious as Taylor's. But still, maybe that would help. He tried remembering what all Charlie Jack had used.

"I'll be back," Matt said, setting up Taylor's bedroll on soft ground and dropping his saddle blanket at the head of it for a pillow. He figured he had about an hour of good daylight left. That ought to be enough to catch one lousy, little animal for supper and grab a handful of leaves for tea.

Taylor grunted his response as Matt took his rifle and a small leather bag to carry what he'd gather and trudged away. He walked a half-mile away from the road, then cut up the rise, over the small hill, and spied a small copse of cottonwoods and aspen. There he hoped to find the meat and the leaves he needed. He proned himself on the grassy ground, his rifle at the ready, and waited. The leaves he could get anytime. He didn't have much daylight left for shooting game.

He didn't wait long. A rustling in the grove that wasn't the wind caught his attention. A jack was venturing out, making tracks to his hole for the evening. He stopped and sniffed the air, and Matt was glad the breeze hadn't changed direction. He was still downwind. He brought the Winchester up and closed his left eye, sighting in on the rabbit and began squeezing the trigger.

The rabbit looked from side to side, then tensed as it prepared to run, but suddenly it fell to its side at the same time a shot shattered the air to Matt's right, maybe a hundred yards off. Matt was startled but stayed on the ground. There was someone else out here, and they too were getting ready for evening supper. But who was it? Was it the men he'd seen riding away after shooting Taylor? Maybe a prospector or a trail bum. Matt remained motionless, waiting for the shooter to emerge and claim his prize, keeping the Winchester at the ready in case it turned out to be someone disinclined to friendliness.

Matt watched a man emerge from the rocks and skulk up to the rabbit. Matt waited, watching the man look around, then gather the jack and turn to go back to his camp beyond the rocks or wherever it was. Matt didn't know of any trails back that way, so the man must have been keeping off of them. That could mean he was a desperado, but he didn't have the look of the man Matt had watched ride away through the spyglass. Could be the unseen partner. There wasn't enough light for Matt to tell.

Matt waited, debating whether to follow the man or let him be for now. He still needed some food for himself and the sheriff, and some leaves for tea and a poultice. After that, maybe he'd look the man up. Then again, maybe he'd just leave him to himself. Taylor was unprotected right now. Anyway, the man hadn't been too careful about shooting. Maybe he didn't know there was anyone else in these parts. If he had been trailing them, would he have fired his gun like that?

No, Matt concluded, the man didn't know they were there. Still, he judged the best course of action, since he knew nothing about this stranger, would be going straight back to camp. He had a mission and that was getting Taylor to a doctor before something serious happened to him. Then he could worry about tracking down the assailant, something he was downright anxious to start.

The rabbit shooter disappeared over a rise, and Matt got up, making his way quickly to the grove. He found the bush he'd hoped to find and took several handfuls of leaves, stuffing them into the bag he carried over his shoulder. Another jackrabbit startled him, fleeing out of the bush and over his feet, but Matt kept his rifle down. He didn't want chancing a rifle shot here, not within earshot of the other man. He sighed and hiked back to camp, hoping Taylor wasn't too hungry.

"You get something?" Taylor asked, not rising to greet his deputy. "I heard a shot."

"Wasn't me," Matt explained. He dropped his gear on the ground. "There's someone else out here tonight. He bagged my rabbit before I could get off a shot."

"Maybe he'll share it," Taylor speculated.

"Can't take a chance," Matt said. "Might be the man who shot you."

"Did he see you?"

"Don't think so. I was layin' low for a spell before the rabbit showed up. He was behind a rock, and I didn't see him until he fired." He poured water from his canteen into the coffee pot.

"Think he's a bad sort?"

"Couldn't tell. Let's just hope he doesn't find us."

"What'cha up to there, Matt?" Taylor asked, watching his deputy crushing the green leaves in his fist.

"I'm makin' you some tea. It's a Paiute remedy Charlie Jack taught me."

"He was probably trying to poison you, and it didn't take," Taylor said.

Matt smiled. Taylor was making wisecracks, so he must be getting better. The deputy crushed more leaves and dropped them into the pot, then built a small fire and set the pot over it. Soon the water was boiling, and Matt grabbed the handle, using his neckerchief as protection for his hand, and poured the liquid into a cup. It was nearly dark now, the only light being what the fire gave off. The night would be cold, he knew, and he was grateful for the warm steam from the hot springs next to them. They could tolerate the sulfur smell for one night. He handed the cup to Taylor. The sheriff took it without comment and drank it down, then handed the cup back to his deputy. He coughed and closed his eyes.

"Well?" Matt prompted.

"Well what?"

"How was it?"

"What do you mean, how was it? It's medicinal. It's supposed to be horrible. You ever taste medicine that was good?"

"No, can't say that I have," Matt admitted.

"We got any flour?" Taylor asked.

"A little, I suppose."

"Can you make some biscuits? That'll fill us up, hold us over until tomorrow. It's not far to Bridgeport, I'll make it . . . I think."

Matt checked his saddlebags and found enough flour mix for a pan of biscuits. He set about making them and soon had them frying in the small, cast-iron skillet. They ate them dry, washing them down with more tea. It wasn't as bad as Matt remembered, and he wondered if maybe he'd done something wrong.

They settled down finally to sleep, and Matt lay under a canopy of stars. The clouds had dissipated, and he was grateful. The last thing they'd needed was rain—or worse, snow. If it held, they'd get up at first light and be back in Bridgeport in time for a late breakfast.

It took Matt some time to fall sleep, however. The idea that someone might be watching them kept nagging at him, and seeing that man on the far side of the hill earlier was a puzzle and a worry to him. What was he doing here? Any other night Matt would've hailed him, and they would've shared a campfire and some talk. But not tonight. Matt prayed, keeping his eyes open, asking God to keep watch over them through the night and to bring the sheriff around in the morning, giving him strength to make the trip home.

Matt fell asleep with the prayer still on his lips.

Rosa Bailey hustled down the boardwalk, a basket hanging from her left arm, her right hand clutching at the collar of her greatcoat and keeping the neck closed against the chill. In the past she never hurried, not because of her size but because she never had any place to go that was particularly important. In fact, she could wait around, whether in her crib or in the dance halls, and wait for the men to come to her.

But now that she had put that life behind her and worked a respectable job waiting tables and taking her turn in the kitchen, her life had some purpose.

She had always thought that would be drudgery: slaving over a hot stove for hours, mixing, plucking, beating, measuring, rolling . . . those were things other women did, women who didn't have a real purpose in life, just some addiction to the way things had always been. Bear the children, do the washing and cleaning.

Rosa scolded herself. If only she had considered those tasks worthy of her before, perhaps Nellie would still be alive and Rosa would be the teacher rather than the student. She also had to laugh at herself, for she found she actually enjoyed doing those things. She felt pride in her accomplishments when her cornbread or biscuits came out of the oven and more so when she heard the appreciative moans of the men as they tasted her work.

This morning she was headed to the general store for supplies: flour, sugar, corn meal. And to the butcher for fresh meat. She'd stop at the produce stand for his daily offerings as well. This week Sarah was going to let her plan the menus.

Rosa wanted to tackle an apple pie, too, so Sarah told her which apples were best. They had plenty of cinnamon but were short of the other necessary ingredients. And vegetables and meat. Those things they had to buy every day, which Sarah usually did in the afternoon after the lunch rush while Rosa did the dishes and pots and pans and set the tables in preparation for the supper hour.

Larger restaurants would be open all day, and a few of the chop stands—counter eateries inside hotel lobbies and saloons that sold fried chops and steaks and other easily prepared foods—were open almost twenty-four hours. There wasn't a time of day that a hungry man, be he miner or gambler, couldn't find something hot to eat, so long as he had the money to pay for it.

Rosa entered the general store, her opening of the door tinkling the little bell above and announcing her arrival. There were a few people inside, but none of them paid her any mind, not even looking up to see who had come in. A scruffy, bearded man was pawing through the Levi's heavy cotton duck pants with the rivets at the ends of the pockets, looking for his size. Rosa recognized him but couldn't place the name. In the canned goods, a man was reading labels, although by the look of him, Rosa suspected he was more or less guessing at what they said.

A woman was browsing through the bolts of colorful cloth along the wall, her back to Rosa. Rosa didn't recognize the woman right off, though she knew, at least by sight, most of the women in town, considering there were so few of them in relation to the number of men.

Rosa consulted her list and went to the counter at the rear of the store where the owner stood, waiting for customers to ask for assistance. He wore his hair parted in the middle and slicked down with hair oil, his face clean shaven except for a large, bushy mustache that he trimmed on the bottom even with his lip. He wore a black vest over a starched white shirt, and a gold watch chain hung between the pockets.

"May I be of some assistance to you, good madam?" he asked with a smile as Rosa approached him, the look on her face telling him she was about to request something.

She consulted her list. "Yes, please. A sack of flour, two bags of sugar, and a bag of salt."

He chuckled. "You baking for the entire town today?"

Rosa smiled back. "Hope so. This is for Sarah at the Quicksilver. Could you deliver it this afternoon?"

"Certainly. I'll have a boy come round with it after he gets out of school. Shall I tally that to her account?"

"Please."

Rosa hadn't noticed, but as she said "Quicksilver" the woman admiring the bolts of calico jerked her head up and eyed Rosa with distaste. As Rosa waited for the order to be tallied the woman sauntered over in her direction. Rosa noticed her and recognized her face as belonging to one of the women in Sarah's sewing circle from church. Rosa smiled shyly, almost apologetically. The acknowledgment wasn't returned as the woman looked past her and at the shopkeeper.

"Excuse me, John," she said.

"Yes, Mrs. Bascomb?"

"I don't mean to pry," she began slowly, which Rosa knew meant as sure as the sun rises in the morning that she was about to do her level best to do just that. "I'm a friend of Sarah's, and I don't recall her ever leaving the job of making purchases for her restaurant to someone from Bonanza Street. Are you sure this woman isn't going to take these things somewhere else and leave Mrs. Page with the bill?"

John Kline, the shopkeeper, was momentarily taken aback but quickly recovered. "The merchandise is being delivered," he told her. "There's no way that could happen."

She tittered. "Oh, my, yes, of course. That is true. I'm so sorry." Her apology was directed toward Kline as she continued to ignore Rosa. "I was just looking out for my friend's interests."

Rosa's face flushed, and she could feel the heat of it. A year ago she'd have poked the woman in the mouth. It wasn't a mistake; it was a calculated insult. The woman knew she worked for Sarah; she'd known it for several months, as soon as the sewing circle got wind of it. There'd been no mistaking how they felt about it. This wasn't the first time she been insulted by one of them, although usually it wasn't this blatant.

The former prostitute held back, though, biting her lip to keep from spouting off and giving credence to their complaints. She quivered as she suppressed the urge to lash out, both verbally and physically, but her eyes flashed her anger in no uncertain terms.

Kline was uncomfortable. Not at all pleased with the cattiness of the woman, she and her friends were nonetheless good customers, and he didn't want the loss of their business by chastising her for sticking her nose in where it didn't belong. He knew who Rosa Bailey was and understood how the women of Bodie felt about the soiled doves, especially those who tried shouldering their way into the social circles. That Rosa was a *former* soiled dove was irrelevant to them, and to Kline as well, although he would never turn away a paying customer. Indian, prostitute, Chinaman . . . the color of their money was all that mattered. And Mrs. Bascomb's personal beliefs were none of his business.

"So, Miss Bailey . . ." he said slowly, forcing a hesitant grin. "Will that be all?"

It was more a plea than anything else. *Just leave, if you don't mind,* he was saying.

Rosa finally took her eyes off Mrs. Bascomb, determined to act more the lady than did her detractor.

"Yes, Mr. Kline, that's all." She turned and hurried out the door, the tinkling of the bell echoing in the silent store as everyone, including the miner and the man at the cans, watched her go.

The miner brought a pair of jeans to the counter, setting them down so Kline could wrap them in brown paper and string. While he waited, he locked eyes with Mrs. Bascomb.

"You'd do well to keep better track of where yer nose gits stuck," Jacob Page said quietly so only she could hear. "One a these days yer gonna poke it into a hornet's nest."

He turned away before she could respond and paid Kline for his pants, then grabbed his package with his solitary arm and strode out of the store. Mrs. Bascomb watched him and *harrumphed*, then tossed her head back and spoke to Kline.

"Of all the impudent men."

"W-was there anything I could get for you?" Kline asked. "A few yards of that pretty blue—"

"Just looking," she cut him off haughtily. "Good day."

He acknowledged her, although it didn't matter as she was already halfway to the door.

The man at the cans came to the counter with his purchase.

"What was that all about?" he asked.

"You must be new in town," Kline guessed.

"Been here a week."

Kline nodded. "Just a representative of the good women of Bodie making them they feel is beneath know where they stand. Everyday stuff here."

The man nodded. "Women," he said, and he and Kline put the incident from their minds.

Rosa walked even more hurriedly than normal, her anger welling up inside and causing her to rush, burning it off. It was that or find someone to sock. And she was beyond that kind of behavior, she told herself. She wouldn't let some old biddy, some pious, better-than-thou, uppity . . . *witch* cause her to stumble.

She took a couple turns around town, avoiding King Street, which led to her old haunts, lest she be tempted by the familiarity to return. She couldn't go back to the Quicksilver yet; she hadn't finished the errands. Besides, Sarah would ask what had happened and would take up her cause for her, but Rosa fought her own battles.

And right now, her biggest battle was with herself.

For thirty minutes she stormed the town's boardwalks, mindless of others and the stares she got. When she had settled sufficiently she took a deep breath and checked her list. Produce. She needed apples and a few other things. She took account of herself, located the produce stand, and headed for it.

But just before she got there she was waylaid by an old friend, one of the gals she formerly oversaw at the dance hall.

"Rosa, is that you?"

Rosa stopped, recognizing the voice. She couldn't be rude. Besides, she'd always liked Betsy.

"Betsy?" As Rosa turned she put a broad smile on her face. "Why, look at you! Don't you look grand?"

"My, Rosa, I'm so surprised to see you. Some of the girls said you'd gone to Nevada."

"No, Betsy, darling, I'm still here. Never left town, not even after . . ."

"Oh, my, Rosa," Betsy said, softening. "I'm sorry. I didn't mean to remind you of that."

"That's okay, Betsy. I hardly ever stop thinking about her."

"I also heard you went to work for the sheriff's wife," Betsy said. "Is that true?"

"Yep. In her restaurant, the Quicksilver."

"I never figured you for domestic things," Betsy said, shaking her head.

"She's good to me," Rosa told her. "You should come by sometime."

"Oh, come on, Rosa. You know better than that. I wouldn't be welcome."

"Not true. Them folk—the Pages—they're real nice folk, not judging others all the time like some."

"Like most, you mean," Betsy said with a sneer. "But you're right about them. I saw the deputy the other night."

"Do tell. Where?"

"Bonanza Street. Where else?"

Around the corner, out of their sight but not out of earshot, stood Mrs. Bascomb, listening. She'd seen Rosa coming and ducked into the alley, afraid of what the wild, evil woman would do to her. At Betsy's revelation, Mrs. Bascomb threw her hand up and clamped it over her mouth, her eyes wide. Just wait until the others heard this. She picked her skirt up and rushed down the alley, taking the long way home.

"What was he doing there?" Rosa asked, unaware of Flora.

"He got hurt at Mr. Song's and kinda passed out almost. I bandaged his head and sent him on his way. He's a good man and sure in love with that little bride of his."

Rosa smiled. "Ain't he, though? Listen, I'd love to stay and chat, but I've got work to do. I'm baking a pie for the social Saturday next. I need to practice."

"A pie? For the social?" Betsy laughed uproariously and slapped her thigh. "Listen to you, Rosa Bailey. You've gone society on me. If that don't beat all!"

Rosa beamed. "It ain't such a bad life, Betsy. Beats what you do all to he—to heck, that is."

"Even cleaned up your mouth. The change is purt near complete, Rosa."

"I gotta go, Betsy," Rosa said, giving her a hug. "You don't be a stranger. You're welcome anytime, understand?"

"Sure, Rosa. Sure. You too."

They parted with a final wave, and Rosa made her way once again to the produce stand, determined to bake the best apple pie Bodie had ever seen.

CHAPTER

TEN

THE KITCHEN OF THE QUICKSILVER was hot near the stove but much cooler by the walls where the Bodie weather seeped in through the cracks, despite the best efforts of Sarah and Matt to plug them. But right at the moment that's where Sarah preferred standing, letting the wall cool her back as she leaned against it.

The door opened and shut, but before she could sigh and brush a lock of hair from her forehead and push herself away to go help Rosa with the provisions, Jacob Page stuck his head in the kitchen doorway.

"There y'are," he said with a bearded grin.

"Oh hello, Jacob," Sarah said, mildly surprised. At his request, she had long since stopped calling him Mr. Page. Said it made him feel too old. "I thought you might be Rosa."

He ran a hand over his whiskers. "Naw, she got two arms. I only got one, in case you ain't noticed."

Sarah laughed and invited him in.

"She'll be along soon, I reckon," Jacob told her, spying a plate of cookies cooling on the counter and snatching one. "Saw her about town."

"Can I get you something to go with that?" Sarah asked, giving her father-in-law a scolding look. "Coffee? Milk?"

"Milk? You tryin' to poison me? As fer coffee, that's right temptin', but I kin wait till supper, I s'pose."

Sarah was a bit puzzled. If it wasn't something to eat he wanted, why had he come? He was usually busy during the day.

As if reading her mind, Jacob said, "I jes' stopped by to see how yer doin', Matt bein' away an' all."

"I'm fine," she assured him, a slight tint of suspicion in her voice. "Why? Did you expect there to be a problem?"

"Well, no, not really. I'm jes concerned 'bout ya, that's all."

He wasn't fessing up completely.

"Look, Jacob . . . if there's something I should know, please tell me. I'm a grown woman, I can handle it."

"Kin ya?" He squinted one eye at her. "You kin handle a lot a things, that's fer shore. But a gang a women bent on yer ruination—I'd sooner kiss a mad mama grizzly after swattin' her cub than try to unravel that knot."

"Oh, the good women of Bodie, is that it? What have you heard, Jacob?"

"Well . . . I was in the general store when Miss Bailey come in with yer list, and Mrs. Bascomb was there, an—"

"Flora Bascomb." Sarah knew what that meant. Flora led the delegation to rid Bodie of anything and anyone she deemed unacceptable. "So, what'd she do?"

"Well, she kinder stuck her nose in where it don't belong . . . She hinted to Mr. Kline that maybe he oughter double-check with you on the order. I think she was trying to say that maybe Miss Bailey was over-orderin' and was tryin' to steal from ya."

Sarah stomped her foot. "Oh, that woman!" she said roughly through clenched teeth. "I've half a mind to—what'd Rosa do?"

"She jes' smiled and went about her business. Mr. Kline didn't argue with Mrs. Bascomb none, but Miss Bailey's jaw was plenty tight. I think if it were jes' the two of 'em, Miss Bailey woulda decked her one."

"I might've myself if I'd been there."

"Aw, no, you wouldn't," Jacob disagreed. "You ain't like that."

Sarah smiled. "You're probably right, Jacob. And I'm glad Rosa didn't do it, as much as Flora deserves it. It wouldn't do Rosa any good to retaliate. She's under enough pressure as it is."

"You too, Sarah . . . or ain't you noticed."

"Me? What can they do to me?" She was playing coy but knew full well what Jacob was talking about.

"Not come to yer restaurant, that's what," Jacob declared. "And they can tell their husbands and the husbands of their friends. Pretty soon, yer only customers'll be single men, and even some of them will git pressure from Mrs. Bascomb."

"How can that happen?"

"Clyde Bascomb's a stockholder in the Empire."

"Oh." Sarah understood that kind of silent pressure. Flora would put the screws to her husband, who would pass it down the line, getting her off his back. "Well, Jacob, there's plenty of single men in town who don't work for the Empire. I guess we'll just have to rely on them for business."

Jacob shook his head. "I wish there was somethin' I could do to help, Sarah."

"Aw, don't worry about it, Jacob. God's in charge. He can deal with treacherous people like Mrs. Bascomb, especially since she claims to be a Christian."

"Ain't my notion of what a Christian should be," Jacob said.

"Don't get me wrong," Sarah added quickly. "I'm not saying she isn't a Christian. I'm just saying that she claims to be one, and if that's true, the Bible says God will deal with her. It's entirely possible to be a Christian and still act improperly, just as people who aren't saved can do good things. But God doesn't let those who are really His children stray indefinitely."

"Most of the fallen angels, way I hear it," Jacob said slowly, "are more Christian in their actions than the so-called good women of Bodie. Aside from their jobs, I'm talkin'."

"What do you mean?"

"Most of 'em got hearts as big as all outdoors. You have an outbreak of influenza, or a fire makes people homeless, guess who'll be doin' most of the carin' fer the sick and displaced? That's right, the ladies of Bonanza Street. Happens in every gold camp. I guess they understand what it means to be down and out. Makes them care more than regular folk fer those in need. Seems to me Mrs. Bascomb and her like could take a few lessons from the wh—from the ladies of questionable virtue."

"Rosa's that way," Sarah reflected. "Could be you're right."

She sighed and the conversation lagged, then Jacob, picking up another cookie, asked, "So, what're you gonna do?"

"What can I do? I'm not sending Rosa packing, if that's what you mean. And I can't make Mrs. Bascomb stop being like she is. Only God can do that."

"Well, I ain't much of a prayin' man, but I'll do what I can. And I stand behind you all the way. You know that."

"Thank you, Jacob. You're a dear." She touched his arm and stood on her tiptoes to kiss him on the cheek. The grizzled miner blushed visibly. "I do wish Matt would hurry back," Sarah sighed. "Him being here might keep them from getting brave and trying to run Rosa off."

"I wish that was true," Jacob said, popping the cookie into his mouth and brushing the crumbs from his whiskers. "But them kind are like mules. They don't care who's watchin'; if they wanna kick, they gonna kick."

Sarah said good night to Rosa, and they both walked out so Sarah could lock the door behind them.

"Uh, Rosa," Sarah said as the other woman turned for home. She stopped and looked as Sarah. "Yes?"

"Would you, uh, care to join me at church tomorrow?"

Rosa smiled and shook her head. "Honey, you got enough troubles without having me show up at your church services."

"Please, Rosa, don't think of me. It's for you that I ask, not myself. I don't care what those other women think."

"No, I can see that you don't. But I do, Sarah. It wasn't so bad when I was in my element, livin' life the way I chose. They stayed away from me, and I stayed away from them. But me tryin' to fit in their world, well, it just ain't workin' out so good."

"You're not—"

"No, honey, I ain't goin' back to it. Don't worry. But I may have to move on, as soon as I save up enough. I'm kinda stuck between a rock and a hard place right now. I can't leave 'cause if I do and I get to a new town with nothin', well, it'd be too easy to have a relapse, if you know what I mean. And if I stay here in Bodie, I'm destined to be shunned and looked down upon by the very women who think so little of my past life. It's like they don't really want us to change, they just want us to go away."

Rosa let her head drop a little. Sarah could tell she was on the verge of tears and moved to her, putting her arms around the woman.

"Don't be doin' that, Sarah," Rosa complained. "What'll people say?"

"Hang them," Sarah said. "Come on, you're coming with me." She took Rosa by the arm and led her down the boardwalk toward the home she shared with Matt.

"What for?" Rosa inquired, while letting herself be led.

"Just to visit," Sarah said. But she had more in mind. Like teaching the woman some things a good wife ought to know, like sewing and knitting and maybe reading to her a little from the Holy Writ. You never knew, there were plenty of men in town who were anxious for a wife, regardless of her background. Once married, there wasn't anything the good women of Bodie could say.

"Look, I still ain't goin' to church with you," Rosa warned.

Sarah laughed. "That's your choice, Rosa. That's your choice." There was one thing Sarah knew for a fact: Christ couldn't be forced on anyone. It had to be their decision.

Sarah lit the stove and put the teapot on the fire while Rosa took two china cups and saucers from the cupboard.

"Been a while since I drank tea outta something like these," the woman said.

"Oh, those old things," Sarah decried. "Hand-me-downs."

"Still, they're pretty."

Sarah scrutinized Rosa out of the corner of her eye as the woman examined a cup admiringly, rubbing her hand gently over the fine, colorful, handpainted decorations. Sarah found it both amusing and touching that such a seemingly worldly woman could enjoy fine, delicate things such as these, then chastised herself for the thought. There was no reason why Rosa should be any different than any other woman, despite her hard life and wayward past. She still had inside her what God had created, what he placed inside all women.

"What do you do when you're home?" Sarah asked suddenly.

"Beg pardon?" Rosa set down the cup.

Sarah blushed. "I'm sorry. That was an impulsive and nosy thing to ask. Please forgive me."

"No, it's okay," Rosa assured. "I'm curious about other folk as

well, I just never had the courage to ask. Nor the opportunity." She
thought about it. "I don't do much, I guess. Sit around and try to
keep warm mostly. Stoke the fire, mend a few things, work on my
face." She laughed heartily, the first big laugh Sarah'd ever heard
from her.

"Do you read?"

"I know how. I just don't have no books."

"No? Would you like some?"

Rosa shrugged. "I suppose it couldn't hurt none."

"Good. I have a few I'd be happy to lend. We'll look through
them in a bit. Oh, the tea's done." With a potholder, Sarah lifted
the teapot off the top of the stove and poured the steaming water
over the leaves at the bottom of the cups. They sugared and
creamed their tea to their individual tastes and took them into the
parlor, sitting next to each other on the sofa.

Rosa took a sip, then glanced at her young friend wistfully.

"Why're you being so good to me?" she asked.

"I'm not. What I mean is, I'm not being particularly good or
anything. I don't know. What do you mean?"

"You know what I mean. All the other women don't want me
around. Is it because of Nellie you're doing this?"

"I feel bad about Nellie, that's for sure," Sarah admitted. "So
does Matt. Especially Matt. He feels responsible. But it's not out
of guilt or pity that I befriended you, Rosa, or even Christian duty.
I happen to like you, I needed help in the restaurant, and you
needed a job. It's as simple as that. Don't go trying to read too deep
into things. There often isn't anything there."

"You're not like all the others," Rosa told her. "They wouldn't
touch me with a ten-foot pole. If that's Christian love, well, no
thanks. You can have it."

"Don't judge God by people, Rosa. Really, it's just Him and
you and no one else, especially at the end. And He loves you."

Rosa's face was stern. "*Pah*. God loves me. Then why'd he take
my Nellie?"

"I can't answer that, Rosa. Sometimes things happen that we
don't understand. But everything that happens to the Christian is
for their good and is by God's design. Remember, Rosa, God had
a Son, His only Son. And He sent Him here to die a horrible death
on the cross. And Christ was perfect, free from sin."

"Then why'd He do it?"

"So He could save us and take us to heaven one day. He died in our place, took the punishment we deserve. The truth is, people all the time complain about God being unfair. Why did he let the powder magazine blow up? Why did He let Alvin Sporger—a good Christian man with a family, by the way—slip on the ice and fall two hundred feet down the shaft last month? I don't know, Rosa. But I know that we all deserve to die because of our sin, and by God's mercy He saves some of us."

Rosa was silent, and Sarah began thinking about the good Christian women in town. Just how real were their claims? Were they really saved, or did they just play at religion because it suited their idea of what a good American citizen was supposed to be? Didn't the Bible say that true Christianity produces good fruit in a person's life? There certainly wasn't any fruit on some of those dead trees.

"That may be true, Sarah, what you said," Rosa admitted, "but I just don't know."

"Well, you think about it. And please, don't reject God just because the people here are full of sin. You're a sinner too, you know."

Rosa nodded. "Maybe it's too late for me anyway."

Sarah shook her head slowly. "Not as long as you're breathing." Sarah decided to leave it there, not to press Rosa too hard right now. She wasn't ready for harvest, not yet. What was that Reverend Edwards always said? You can't pick green fruit.

Sarah's eyes lit on her knitting basket. "Say, Rosa, do you know how to knit?"

"Huh? Knit? Of course not. When would I have ever learned how to knit?"

"I don't know. When you were a little girl, I guess."

"I didn't learn nuthin'. My ma was always gone. I practically raised myself."

"In that case, you did a pretty good job. You turned out pretty good for someone who raised themselves."

Rosa blushed. "Not really."

"Well, I think so. Anyway, would you like to learn?"

She shrugged. "I don't know. I don't see a real need for it."

Sarah smiled. "Give you something to do besides pat your face

in the evenings. But it's up to you. I'd be happy to show you anytime you're ready."

She got the two of them more tea, then Rosa decided it was
time to go and left quickly. Sarah thought the woman was somehow uncomfortable, more so than she was when she came over, so
Sarah knew the seeds had been planted. She wasn't quite as vehe-
ment in her contrariness to the gospel, but Sarah figured she still
had a long way to go.

If only Flora Bascomb and her group weren't doing so much
damage right now.

Sarah put on her best outfit, her Sunday meeting outfit, and
walked with a light step to the Miner's Union Hall where services
were held, her head up, but not so far she could be accused of being
snooty. She made it to the Union Hall early and without confrontation, picking a seat near the back. As folks filed in and scattered throughout the hall, the piano tinkled hymns, hymns Sarah
had known since she was little, and she found herself humming
along. Then Honorable Reverend Horace T. Edwards took the
podium, offered the opening prayer, and the service began.

They sang a few songs, and Sarah noticed by some discreet
peeking that the most vocal members of the opposition to her
"consorting" with Rosa were singing the loudest, with pious looks
on their pinched faces. Even Molly Carter, who for a time had been
Sarah's closest friend in Bodie, was beginning to have that appearance. Her husband, Joseph, a hoist operator at the Empire, caught
Sarah's eye and smiled, but he quickly dissolved it and looked
away when Molly caught him. She herself glanced at Sarah, not
with a look of disdain as Sarah would have expected, but more of
apology. It was brief, however, and she didn't look again.

They settled into their pews, and Reverend Edwards read the
announcements.

"A pie and costume social is planned for Saturday next," he
said, "at 7:30 in the evening, here in this hall. All are invited, and,
ladies, bring your best pies because there will be a judging. To
make it interesting and fair, all those entering will be asked to wear
a costume and mask so their identity will not persuade the judges.
Men are invited to dress up as well in the costume of their choice,
and there will be prizes for the best, male and female. Afterward,

there will be constrained dancing for those inclined, nothing faster than a waltz. Punch will be provided by the Men's Fellowship Committee."

The ushers were then summoned and assembled at the front with the baskets, and after a prayer of blessing, the baskets were passed among the faithful and collected at the back of the room. The pianist, on loan from the Hardrock Cafe and Saloon, played another hymn, then vacated his stool, donned his hat, and retreated quickly to his regular job before any of this religious folderol could rub off on him. Reverend Edwards again stood at the podium, opened his great Bible, and commenced with the sermon.

Sarah tried listening, but the familiar story of Adam and Eve sinning in the Garden of Eden (with the part about their naked-ness left out due to the mixed nature of the congregation) did not hold her attention, and she found her mind wandering. Mostly she thought of Matt and wished he was back from his trip. She didn't understand why he had to keep leaving. He was deputy sheriff in Bodie, yet spent as much time in Bridgeport or parts in between. It was bad enough that Bodie was becoming more than one man could safely handle, especially someone like Matt who refused bru-talizing the ne'er-do-wells like so many of his counterparts in other towns she had heard about. Except for the Chinaman.

That it was the best way to keep people in line she also didn't understand; she just knew it wasn't right to treat people that way. If they did something wrong, they deserved punishment. That, she had no problem with. Like everyone else in town, she had little sympathy for evildoers. But sometimes the punishment seemed far worse than the crime and perhaps even premature on occasion.

But those were stories she'd heard from people who'd come to Bodie from other places, and she didn't know how true they were. What she did know was that Bodie had divided itself into two loose factions: those who approved of Matt's methods and those who thought he was too soft. And it seemed to her that both sides were made up of all the wrong people. Many men from the church thought him too easy on criminals, along with many of the rougher element themselves. They respected a tough lawman.

Some of the more distinguished citizens, those who considered themselves enlightened and forward-thinkers, thought Matt was a touch too harsh, preferring that the law best be used to correct flaws in people's character rather than to simply punish.

The more she thought about it, though, the more she realized that those people were in the minority, and Matt would just wave them off when they presented their ideas to him. Once he offered a man his badge if he thought he could do a better job than Matt had done, but the man quickly declined, and Matt told him to keep his opinions to himself until he was ready to put them into practice.

Suddenly, Sarah became aware everyone had bowed their heads, and she snapped back to reality and followed suit as the preacher prayed the benediction, then rose with the rest of the congregation and filed out into Main Street. The sun shone bright, and all traces of snow had fled, but the air still had an edge to it, and she drew her shawl around her tightly. She stood outside, waiting, as the men and women filed out of the Union Hall until she caught the eye of Molly Carter. Sarah smiled and waved.

Obviously uncomfortable, the woman pretended she hadn't seen Sarah, but her husband pointed her out, making the ruse impossible to maintain. She smiled weakly and nodded, and Sarah seized upon it as an opportunity. She made her way quickly to Molly's side.

"It's been a long time since you've come over for high tea," Sarah noted. "I'd love to have you again, if Joseph doesn't mind."

"Not at all," Joseph Carter said before his wife could signal him to decline.

"Why, of course, Sarah, I'd l-love to," Molly said. She glanced at her husband, but Sarah's gaze prevented her from giving him a scolding look.

"Good!" Sarah said. "After lunch, then. Say, three o'clock? We can talk over old times."

"Certainly. That would be fine," Molly consented, her heart not in it, but unable to weasel out of the engagement.

"Thank you for letting her go," Sarah told Molly's husband. "With her due so soon, it's a wonder you'd let her out of your sight."

"It's another couple weeks," Joseph said. "Besides, she's in no danger with you. I hear you're quite the doctor when the need presents itself. Why, the way you—"

"Oh, how you do go on," Molly chastised her husband. "It's embarrassing how you build people up in front of everybody."

"Sorry, Mrs. Page," he apologized. "Didn't mean to do that."

"That's okay, Joseph," Sarah said.

"Shall I bring some cookies?" Molly asked, making it a point to be proper now that she had no alternative.

"That would be nice," Sarah said. "Some of your fabulous sugar cookies would be good. You still make them, don't you? I know how furiously you must be making things for the baby."

"She still has time, and they're even better than before," her husband said with a grin.

Molly regarded him. "So, they weren't very good before, is that what you are saying?"

He laughed. "Not at all, my pet, not at all. Listen, Mrs. Page, we better be going before I put my foot in it too deeply."

"Good-bye, then," Sarah said. "See you this afternoon, Molly."

Molly nodded curtly and turned her very pregnant body around. Joseph smiled again at Sarah and followed dutifully after his wife.

Sarah watched them, noticing out of the corner of her eye some of the other women staring at her. Ignoring them, she turned on her heel and strode toward home.

She was bothered, there was no question about that. Oh, not by the women who watched her as she walked away. Most of them were the tongue-wagging variety, hard women who led hard lives, made all the worse by their constantly furrowed foreheads and their penchant for gossip. But Molly . . . she and Sarah had become good friends, even though they'd only known each other about six months. But in the last few weeks, Molly'd become closer to the other women and drifted away from Sarah.

Sarah knew why: Rosa Bailey. The women didn't approve of Sarah allowing Rosa to mingle with their husbands at the restaurant. Because of Rosa's past, they believed she would be a bad influence on their men. It was common in gold camps for the ladies of the evening to be ostracized. The soiled doves expected it and didn't go out of their way to bother the "good" women of town. But Rosa had done what few of them ever did: turned her back on that way of life.

Only they weren't of a mind to let her forget that. Forgiveness, something they all claimed to believe in when it came to their own sins and which they fully expected every time they did something wrong and got caught, was something they did not extend to women of questionable virtue.

They sat in church with lemonade faces, piously singing the hymns and listening to the sermon, nodding their heads now and then when some particularly profound point was made, but the rest of the week disregarding two of the basic lessons of Holy Scripture: love and forgiveness.

Sarah shook her head. She was sounding just like them. They weren't all bad. They didn't do anything outright. For the most part, they were kind, helpful people. They'd bake bread for the needy, bring food to the infirm, get together for quiltings. But on that one issue, they were adamant. Prostitutes were not to be abided!

Sarah threw open the door to their little house and tossed her shawl onto the back of a chair. She dropped onto the small divan they'd bought secondhand and wished Matt was home to complain to about it. Maybe he'd know what to do. Sarah smiled slightly. If nothing else, he'd hold her and stroke her hair.

She sighed. He was hardly ever home, it seemed. A frown appeared as the smile faded, and she sulked. But it was short-lived. She had to get ready if Molly was coming over. Sarah hoped she could reach her, make her understand that Rosa was trying to reform, but it wouldn't take if the "good" women wouldn't accept her into the fold.

They'd drive her back to Bonanza Street, then cluck their tongues and say, "I told you so."

Sarah bowed her head and prayed for God's guidance.

Water bubbled to a boil in the tea kettle on her small stove while Sarah fussed in the parlor, fluffing pillows and flicking a feather duster over the furniture in a final touch-up before her guest arrived. Her emotions were more than mixed as she toiled, they were jumbled and churning within her.

She was glad Molly was coming over, apprehensive about the forthcoming confrontation she expected yet hoped could be avoided, and angry there was anything to Molly's visit besides two friends getting together to enjoy each other's company.

Sarah knew she was in the right and knew that hiring Rosa had been not only proper but what God had wanted her to do. Rosa was grieving over the death of her daughter, a death brought about, in the final analysis, by the life into which Rosa had led her. Rosa wanted out, and Sarah had the means to give her a helping hand and make it possible for Rosa to provide for herself other than by selling her body to the men of Bodie.

But Sarah also knew where Molly stood . . . on the side of Flora Bascomb and the other women who followed her lead. What Sarah didn't know was whether or not Molly was a willing accomplice.

She hoped that was not the case.

Jacob Page had been right, Sarah thought as she straightened the doilies she'd crocheted and draped over the arms of the second-hand divan and upholstered chair, not the only items of furniture Matt had picked up used in Bridgeport from Harvey Boone. Mrs. Bascomb was a poor excuse for a Christian . . . if she was a true Christian at all.

Sarah was horrified at herself for the thought and immediately asked God to forgive her for judging the woman. But the idea continued to nag her and a Scripture verse came to mind . . . *By their fruit ye shall know them.*

Mrs. Bascomb was bearing rotten fruit, and she was spoiling the whole barrel.

"Lord," Sarah prayed in a whispering voice, "please change her heart. And use me to accomplish it, if it be Your will."

Light steps sounded on the porch, then a *tap tap* at the door. Sarah looked toward the ceiling in a final, silent plea for strength, then smoothed her dress, took a breath, put on a smile, and opened the door.

Molly stood there, heavily bundled against the cold, her head down, and her arms full with a basket. Sarah greeted her with sincere warmth and urged her inside.

"Here, let me take this," Sarah offered, latching the door and relieving Molly of her burden. "It was so good of you to come over."

"Thank you for asking me," Molly said, while avoiding having to look Sarah directly in the eye.

It seemed to Sarah the sentiment was forced, but she accepted it graciously nonetheless. She peeked under the checkered cloth that covered the top of the basket.

"Um, they look and smell delicious." Molly had obviously just made them, which meant she'd spent the hours since church slaving in the kitchen . . . and probably grousing at her husband for talking her into this liaison. She'd also changed from her Sunday best into a more reasonable outfit, a loose-fitting sack dress that didn't hide her pregnancy, even under her heavy wool coat.

Sarah set the basket on a nearby small table and took Molly's coat and hat and muffler and hung them up.

"Please, sit down, Molly."

"Thank you." Molly glanced around the room and selected the upholstered chair, settling into it, yet remaining uncomfortable.

"Tea?" Sarah inquired.

"Yes, if it's not too bothersome," Molly said. Her words were proper, but her voice was strained.

"Be right back, then." The tea pot began to whistle. "Just in time," she said with a lilt, trying to liberate some of the tension between them.

She returned in a few moments carrying Molly's basket of cookies and a tray with her delicate tea cups, bowls of sugar and cream, and a covered dish full of genuine Chinese tea leaves, purchased locally on King Street. They discussed the weather and Molly's pregnancy while they made their brews and placed a couple cookies each onto their saucers. For all the undercurrent running through room, the two women both tried to give no visible sign of it.

"You must be excited," Sarah said, admiring for an instant Molly's bulging stomach."

"Yes, I am." She smiled and looked away from Sarah, resting her hand on her belly.

"What are you hoping for?"

"A boy. Joseph and I both want a boy."

"Did you pick out a name?"

"Joseph the Third. Joseph's father was a Joseph also. It's kind of a family tradition.

"Good Bible name," Sarah said approvingly.

They fell silent for a moment, then Sarah sighed audibly. She couldn't hold it any longer.

"Molly, we've been good friends ever since you came to Bodie last year."

"Yes, we have," Molly agreed. She wouldn't look at Sarah but stared into the brown liquid in her cup.

"I'd like to stay that way. It's not good for friendships to cease, especially for no good reason." She paused to let Molly respond if she wanted, but Molly said nothing.

"What's going on, Molly? Tell me, please!"

Molly's eyes began watering.

"Sarah, I don't have any choice—"

"Any choice? Any choice about what?"

"You know, the ladies in the church, even the other ladies in town who don't attend church, but especially the ladies in church . . . they don't approve of you having that . . . virtueless woman working in your restaurant."

"Well," Sarah began, "I'm glad someone finally had enough courage to put it to me direct. But what does that have to do with our friendship? And for that matter, what's wrong with Rosa working for me at the Quicksilver? Yes, she used to be a woman of ill repute, but she's put that behind her."

"She still is a woman of ill repute, don't you see, Sarah? She always will be. She can't deny her past."

"What does this have to do with anything?" Sarah blurted, raising her voice slightly. "What are you *ladies* trying to accomplish? Tell me, Molly."

Molly was on the verge of tears. "They want you to let her go, Sarah. They can't associate with her. You know how it is."

"Which means they can't associate with me," Sarah concluded. "Well, I understand why they wouldn't want to socialize with the Bonanza Street crowd. But Rosa left there, Molly."

"They—we don't see it that way," Molly said.

"No, I can see you don't. As along as she works for me, the Quicksilver is forbidden, is that it? And I'm someone to be avoided."

Molly nodded hesitantly, tears flowing freely now. Sarah couldn't cry, not just yet. She was too busy seething.

"This is not a very Christian thing to do," Sarah pointed out.

"But the Bible says we are not to have anything to with whoremongers, Sarah, and that's what Rosa is."

"Was, Molly, was. That's the point. She turned from that. We're supposed to practice forgiveness. Jesus was the friend of sinners."

"Well, of course *He* was . . . He's the Son of God."

"He's our example. What about the woman at the well, Molly? And Mary Magdalene. And Rahab, who hid the spies. Listen, Molly . . . Rosa is no longer a prostitute. Can't you understand that?"

"But Flor—we think there's too much of that still a part of her. It hasn't been very long and—"

"Flora. Flora Bascomb, is that who's behind this? Well, let me say this, Molly. Sounds to me like the problem is Flora, and the others are worried that too many of their husbands know Rosa and the other girls a little too well. Isn't that it?"

Molly raised her tear-streaked face to look at Sarah, her mouth agape. Clearly, she had not considered this possibility.

"No." She shook her head. "No, of course not. In fact . . ."

"What?" Sarah urged after Molly faded out. Molly looked away. "I can't say it."

Sarah leaned forward. "Molly, despite what's going on, I still consider us friends. What Flora and the others are doing is just plain wrong. Yes, Rosa used to be a harlot. But she's not any longer, and to keep away, she needed someone's help. I was there and the Lord told me in that still, small voice, that feeling you get in the pit of your stomach . . . He told me in my heart, Molly, to extend a hand to her, so I did."

"I wonder if you'd feel the same if you knew where Matt was the other night." Molly said it in a rush, and her face betrayed her own surprise at it. She looked as if she was trying to take the words back and swallow them, but it was too late.

"Excuse me?" Sarah said, puzzled. "What does Matt have to do with this?"

"Oh, Sarah, I'm sorry. I didn't want to be the one to tell you. I really didn't."

"Tell me what, Molly? You've no choice now."

Molly took a deep breath. "He was seen coming out of one of the girls' cribs the other night."

Sarah was stalwart. "He's the law in Bodie," she pointed out. "His work takes him to a lot of places he'd never go otherwise. I'm sure he had a perfectly good reason . . . if that's the truth. Who saw this?"

"Sarah, Rosa was seen talking to the other—to the woman

after that—and the woman was heard to say she had entertained Deputy Page."

Sarah was stunned. Her breath left her, and she felt light-headed. If she had tried to stand, she would have swooned.

Molly set the tea cup down and stood. Her hands were shaking.

"Sarah, I'm sorry. I really am. I don't mean to leave you with that, or be rude, but I have to go. Please . . ." She could say no more and ran out of the house, leaving her cookie basket behind.

The room swirled around Sarah, and the blood pounded in her ears. This couldn't be true. Matt had no reason to go to one of the doves. No reason at all. Flora was behind this lie. It had to be her. No one else would be that vicious.

Sarah collected herself and prayed loudly for God's help. She wished Matt was home. He'd take care of this problem. He'd go right to the Bascombs' place and settle it once and for all.

Rosa! She'd be able to denounce the lie. Not that anyone else would believe her. But Sarah would, because she knew Matt was innocent—

A cramp suddenly rippled across Sarah's abdomen. She curled up in the chair, holding her arms across her midsection and moaning softly, and continued to do so for five or ten minutes, until the pain subsided and finally disappeared, leaving her sweating and exhausted, and with a severe headache. Slowly she pushed herself out of the chair and made her way to the bedroom, clutching at the wall to keep herself upright, then flopped onto the bed.

That's when it finally let loose, and she cried until she was over-taken by sleep.

CHAPTER

ELEVEN

THE TWO LAWMEN were both awake before sunrise. Taylor pushed himself to a sitting position while he watched Matt set the pot on the coals for coffee, then saddle their horses. Few words were passed between them, Matt's mind occupied with thoughts of getting the sheriff back to town while avoiding their assailants, and of the man on the other side of the hill. Was he to be feared?

To Matt, it didn't matter. There was no time to find out.

"You feelin' okay?" Matt asked the sheriff as he helped him stand.

"What diff'rence does it make?" Taylor asked, his voice weak and his words slurred. "We got to get going no matter how I feel." He saw the look on the deputy's face and added, "But thanks for askin'. I feel bad, like I got a hot poker stickin' outta my back. To be honest, son, you might have to tie me in the saddle before long or ride up there behind me."

Matt considered that as he again used a rock to give Taylor some ease in getting up onto Eli. The old horse sensed something was amiss and stood still, not even giving ground when the injured man plopped hard into the saddle. Matt handed Taylor the reins, and he took them but didn't let go of the pommel. He slumped forward, and the young deputy realized that the proud lawman was in dire straits. He didn't look like he'd make it ten minutes, much less the several-hour trip that lay before them.

At least they weren't being actively pursued. Let the outlaws trail them if they wanted. Once Matt had Taylor safely back, they'd wish they'd kept riding.

Matt mounted Blister and nudged his flank with his heel. The Morgan shook his head and stepped forward, knowing he had another restrained day ahead of him. Eli moved alongside Matt's horse, and Matt kept the animals close so he could reach out to steady the sheriff if the need arose.

They had gotten out of sight of the steam rising from the hot spring when the creaks and rattles of a buckboard arose behind them. Matt turned in his saddle, slipping his Colt's revolver out of its holster with as little motion as possible while he continued riding. The wagon, with one man aboard, was gaining on them. There was no way to outrun it, and Matt still didn't know if he needed to try. After all, the sniper and his partner were two men on horseback, not a single man in a two-in-hand buckboard.

No, it was the man from the night before—whoever he was. Matt could tell by the stocky shoulders and thick neck. Friend or foe or something in between, Matt had no choice but to stand prepared. He kept the gun beside his leg, inconspicuous, but cocked it to save time later.

The wagon approached, and the man hailed them from fifty yards out with a wave.

"Who is it?" Taylor asked, his eyes unable to focus.

Matt said nothing, waiting for the man to get within range, concentrating on the wagon driver's hands.

"Morning!" the man shouted. He slowed down as he came abreast of the two horsemen. "A mite chilly to—Deputy Page? Is that you?"

Matt was startled and for the first time looked at the man's face, surprised to see an old friend.

"DeCamp? Fred DeCamp?"

"In the flesh," DeCamp answered. "That Sheriff Taylor with you?"

"Yeah," Matt said. "Fred, he's been shot. You ain't by any chance headed to Bridgeport, are you?"

"You bet," DeCamp said as he jumped down from the wagon. Matt discreetly slipped the gun back into its holster and swung himself down from Blister's back. He joined DeCamp by the sheriff and helped the quickly weakening man down from Eli, which wasn't hard as he virtually fell off the horse. They loaded him into the wagon, made him as comfortable as possible, and Matt tied Eli to the back of the buckboard.

"He was doin' pretty good but took a turn during the night," Matt said as they readied to leave.

"How'd this happen?" DeCamp asked as he climbed up into the seat. The leaf springs creaked under his weight.

Matt stuck a foot in the stirrup and pulled himself up. "We were fishing down at the Walker River. Someone snuck up on us and shot him, then hightailed it outta there. I saw two men."

"Was this two days ago?"

"Yeah. How'd you know?"

"Think I saw them two. They were riding hard, didn't so much as look at me as they passed. I was just out of Coleville at the time. They were in a hurry, that's for sure." He gave the reins a shake and his team moved out, jerking the wagon a little as they started, then settling into a peppy gait. Taylor rolled around in the back but didn't complain.

"Did you get a look at them?" Matt asked.

"Not much. One man was riding kind of funny, though. His elbows all sticking out like he wasn't comfortable."

"That was the shooter."

"The other man, he had a hard look to him. His face was in shadow under a big floppy hat brim, so I couldn't see it. But he was wearing a black coat and tucked his pants into his boots. That's all I noticed. Sorry."

Matt thanked him. "That's a lot, my friend." Then Matt silently thanked God for sending DeCamp by.

As they pressed toward Bridgeport, Matt asked after DeCamp's family, his wife and daughter. "And how's little Samuel?"

"Growing like a weed. Annie treats him like he was her own. It shames me, the way she does. I'll tell you, Matt, it's enough to cure any man of the wanderlust. She's more woman than I deserve."

"Most women are," Matt said. "Don't know why they put up with us."

Thankfully, the trip home was without incident, just the occasional complaint from the suffering Taylor, for which neither Fred DeCamp nor Matt Page begrudged him. They came through a pass and below them the town spread out at the end of a long, wide valley. Matt signaled to DeCamp that he was going on ahead, and Fred gave him a wave. Matt dug his heels into Blister's flanks, and the horse shook his head, twisting it from side to side and flipping his mane while he snorted. Then the great muscles tensed and rippled beneath Matt as the Morgan sprang forward.

They raced down the road at a gallop, the likes of which Matt hadn't experienced since his first day with this mount—and on the same road. At this speed, the horse was smooth, not jarring his rider, and Matt lowered his head near the animal's neck.

Exhilarated, Matt lost himself in the feeling of the ride, forgetting for a moment the troubles that beset him. He longed to keep riding, to ride until neither he nor the animal could go any farther, then make camp by a stream and enjoy roasted sage grouse or rabbit and sleep under the stars.

But it wasn't to be. The life of leisure he had once enjoyed was over. He had a wife, a job, and a great task ahead of him that could not be neglected. He wasn't sorry for his choices; he loved Sarah deeply and wanted to be with her even more than he wanted to ride Blister to the ends of the earth. But he had to admit, he would miss the way his life used to be.

He passed the first buildings before he began slowing, then headed directly for the doctor's office. Pulling a leg over before Blister had come to a full stop, he jumped down and the momentum carried him at a run onto the porch and into the office while he shouted for Doc Madsen. Blister stood untethered outside, dipping into the nearby water trough.

In a moment, Madsen appeared outside, followed by Matt, and looked up the road as he shaded his eyes. Soon the wagon bolted into view and in a minute or so entered town. Matt whistled for Blister and mounted, while Madsen retreated into the office and then emerged with his black bag in his hand. He began trudging up the street toward Taylor's residence.

Matt waved for DeCamp to follow and rode to Taylor's house a couple blocks away. Mrs. Taylor had come out in her apron when she heard Matt shouting for her, drying her hands on a towel.

"What is it, Matt? Is everything okay? Where's John?"

"Coming up in the wagon," Matt said, sliding off Blister's back and tying him this time to the fence. "He was shot. I think he'll be okay. The bullet's out. But he needs medicine. Doc Madsen's on his way."

But before he had even finished, she'd dropped the towel and was running to meet her husband. DeCamp reined his horse to a stop in front of the house, then jumped down and joined Matt and the doc at the rear of the wagon. The three of them carefully lifted the feverish Taylor out of the buckboard and carried him into his house, a worried Mrs. Taylor walking alongside holding her husband's limp hand and speaking to him, sprinkling in prayers with her encouragement.

When he was safely in bed, Matt retreated outside with Fred DeCamp.

"Nice of you to help," Matt said, shaking the man's hand. "You coming along probably saved his life."

"Aw, I don't know about that. I'm just glad I could lend a hand. Well, I've got to get moving. I've got some supplies to pick up."

"Maybe I'll see you later around town," Matt said. "How about the Argonaut for lunch in an hour or so?"

"Works for me," DeCamp said. With a grin, he touched the brim of his faded and worn felt hat and climbed onto the buckboard.

Matt watched him drive away, remembering his first meeting with the man and his family in the secluded cabin during a rainstorm, when all of their lives had just about been lost at the hands of two desperadoes. He shook his head. It seemed so long ago, so far away.

Matt leaned on the fence rail, and Blister nudged him playfully with his velvet nose. Matt absentmindedly rubbed it, thinking of Sarah, pining for her. He wished, even prayed, that he wouldn't have to go after the men who shot the sheriff but knew he had no choice. He was the law now, even though he was officially assigned to Bodie; Bridgeport's lawman was out of commission.

The trail was too cold for rounding up a posse, and Matt knew he'd have to go it alone. Once he found them perhaps he'd be able to rustle up some help, so long as there was a place nearby to rustle it up from. But until then, it was just him. Him and Blister.

And God.

Maybe the odds weren't so bad after all.

The screen door creaked and slammed. Doc Madsen appeared on the porch, rolling his sleeves down. Matt waited for him at the gate.

"How is he, Doc?"

"Better than to be expected," the doctor said with a raised eyebrow. "What'd you take that bullet out with?"

Matt grinned sheepishly. "The tip of a fishin' pole." He shrugged. "It was all I had."

Doc thought about it. "Good idea, Matt. It worked okay. But you should have boiled it first. He's got a severe infection. Now, don't go looking like that. He could have gotten that anyway. I'm just saying, next time sterilize your equipment by boiling or sticking it in the fire. He owes you his life, there's no doubt about that."

"I heated the knife," Matt said weakly in his own defense. "I never thought about the fishing pole."

"Next time you'll do better."

"Doc, I hope there ain't a next time."

Madsen smiled and clapped Matt on the shoulder. "Amen to that." He opened the gate. "See you later, Deputy. I left instructions with Mrs. Taylor, and I'll check in on him tomorrow. She wants to see you inside." He turned and walked back toward his office.

Matt hurried inside and found Mrs. Taylor in the parlor, waiting.

"He's asleep," she said. "Doctor Madsen cleaned the wound and gave him something to fight the infection. I have to keep an eye on him for the next few hours, but I wanted to say thank you."

Matt put his arm around his mother-in-law's shoulder. "Aw, that's okay, Ma."

"How's Sarah?" she asked.

"She's fine," Matt said. "You sound worried."

"I am. It's a hard life in Bodie, to be sure. But running that restaurant as well . . . I just worry about her health, that's all."

"Her health? Is there something wrong with it?"

Mrs. Taylor looked at him, puzzled, then moved her eyes quickly from side to side as she searched for what to say. But Matt could tell she was keeping something from him.

"What is it?" he asked, the bottom beginning to fall from his stomach. "Is there something wrong she hasn't told me? She's seemed a little under the weather lately. What's the matter?"

"Oh my," Mrs. Taylor said quietly. "She hasn't told you, and now I've gone and let the cat out of the bag. I've spoiled the surprise."

"What's going on?" Matt asked again, becoming agitated in his ignorance.

Mrs. Taylor sighed. "I guess I've no choice now but go through with it, otherwise you'll worry needlessly." She took a breath. "Please forgive me, Sarah," she whispered, and, reaching into her apron pocket, pulled out a letter, handing it to Matt. He recognized Sarah's handwriting even before he read the envelope. It was addressed to Sheriff and Mrs. John Taylor.

Matt pulled out the letter and unfolded it, then read with a wondering, fearful expression. But before he had finished, it transformed into a mile-wide grin, and he gazed up at his mother-in-law.

"She going to have a baby!"

"Yes, dear. She's going to have a baby."

Matt threw his arms around her and danced her around the room, making Mrs. Taylor giggle in spite of her concern for her husband. Matt whooped and Mrs. Taylor shushed him. The deputy reddened and immediately stopped dancing. He gave Mrs. Taylor a hug, but he quickly broke off as his attitude soured.

"What's the matter?" she asked, putting her hand on his arm.

"I want to take her in my arms and tell her how thrilled I am and how much I love her, but I can't go home now."

"Why not?"

"I've got to go find the men who shot the sheriff."

"Oh." She couldn't argue, couldn't tell him he didn't have to go. She'd lived with a lawman too long not to know they had a job to do, a job no one would do for them. And even if their duty didn't require it, she knew Matt, just like her husband—were he in this position—would complete the task anyway.

"Well," she said, brightening up, "you'll be done in a few days and can go home. Sarah's got at least seven months before she's due. She'll be fine. I made it through days like this when I was carrying her, and she'll make it too."

Matt nodded. She was right.

"Would you like something to eat?" Irene Taylor asked.

"I'd love to," Matt assured, "but I'm meetin' Fred DeCamp over to the Argonaut. Then I'm gonna get ready to ride. I've got to get enough supplies to last at least a week."

"I'll get some things together for you to take. You can stop back by later. Maybe John'll be awake by then, and you can see him before you leave."

Matt nodded. "Will do." He leaned over and kissed her on the cheek, then turned and left the house.

When he entered the Argonaut and Mary saw him, the color drained from her face. Matt saw it but didn't understand why.

"Mary? You okay?"

"Oh, Matt. I'm so glad you're back."

"What's up?"

"It's them prisoners."

"Something wrong?"

"Wrong?" Her nostrils flared as she moved toward him. "Wrong? I'll say there's something wrong. They could've killed Harvey, that's what's wrong!"

"What happened, Mary? Is Harvey okay?"

"He's shaken up. He's in the back. I won't let him go out alone."

Matt was bewildered. Why did women always take so long to get to the point?

"Mary, would you please tell me what happened? Is this about the prisoners?"

"They broke out."

"What?"

"That's right. They overpowered Harvey, took his gun, and locked him in the cell, then high-tailed out of town on a couple stolen horses."

"Did one of them have a funny gait?"

"Huh? One of the outlaws—?"

"The horses, Mary, the horses."

"I-I don't know Matt. What—"

"You say Harvey's okay?"

"Yes. I'm fine, Matt." It was Harvey, coming out of the back room wiping his hands with a dishtowel. "Mary's just upset. They didn't hurt me."

"They could've," Mary said contritely in her defense.

"Yes, dear," Harvey said gently. "But they didn't. Get us some supper, would you, honey? I'll tell Matt all about it."

Fred arrived at the restaurant just then, and the three of them enjoyed a hearty lunch while they exchanged stories.

"We got a wire after they broke out," Harvey told the deputy. "Nevada never heard of Patrick O'Shea. Must be an alias."

"I figured that much."

"They said the descriptions were too general to put a name to. They wanted more details. I didn't wire back, of course, since they'd gotten clean away. By the way, they still deny blowing the powder magazine."

Matt shrugged. "Don't much matter now even if that's true. They broke out of two jails and tried to murder Sheriff Taylor. I've got to bring them in, and every hour I lollygag here in town is another hour farther away they get," Matt explained.

Harvey nodded. "True enough."

Matt stood and set a couple coins on the table. "Here, that's for both of us."

"You don't have to—" DeCamp began to protest.

Matt quieted him with a raised hand. "I don't *have* to do anything," he said. "It's my pleasure."

"Well, thanks, Deputy. Thank you." DeCamp held out his hand, and Matt shook it.

"See you later, Fred. Harvey, you too. Glad you're okay. Sorry I got you into that. I'll never ask that of you again." He shook the other man's hand vigorously, then stuck on his hat. "Wish me lu— no, not luck. God speed. Somethin' tells me I'm gonna need it."

Matt stopped briefly at Harvey's store for supplies where he was waited on by Harvey's new assistant, a winsome, though plain, young girl in her early twenties.

"Good morning!" she said cheerily as Matt came in. She waved at him and in doing so knocked over a display of boxed items on the counter.

Matt smiled. "Good morning. You must be Jane Canary, Harvey's new clerk. He told me about you."

"He did?" She beamed and stacked the boxes. "Actually, my name's Martha Jane Canary, I just go by Jane. I hate Martha, it sounds so . . . feminine. Can I help you with something?"

"Well, I need to get a few things. I'm taking a little trip."

"Okay."

"A pound of jerky—no, make that two pounds. And a pound of sugar, two pounds of flour, a pound of coffee, a pound of beans. That oughta do it."

"Okay," Jane repeated from memory. "A pound of jerky, two pounds of sugar, a tin of coffee, and a sack of flour."

Matt shook his head. "I'll get it," he offered, and went about collecting his own supplies, adding to his list a box of shells for his revolver and a package of bacon.

He set everything on the counter for Jane to tally. She moved each item to the side as she added it to the tally sheet so she wouldn't count it twice, but the sack of flour she set too close to the edge and moving the sack of beans next to it pushed it over the side. It hit the floor with a slap and split open, flour spreading out for several feet in all directions.

"Oh dear," she said, her shoulders sagging.

"That's okay," Matt told her. "I'll get another one." While he moved off to replace the sack of flour, Jane busied herself with the broom. She swept the flour into a dustpan, holding the straw broom near the bottom, allowing the handle to waggle above her as she stooped. With her last stroke, the handle knocked a jar of jelly off a shelf behind the counter, and it exploded on the floor. Jane was surprised and turned abruptly, flinging the dustpan full of flour out over the store, including Deputy Page. He ducked but couldn't avoid being covered with the white powder.

Jane's sudden twirl also unleashed the broom handle, raking a whole row of metal pots and pans onto the wood floor with a deafening clamor. Matt jumped toward her before she totally destroyed the place, grabbing the broom out of her hands and pinning her arms to her sides to keep her still. She gazed at him in horror, then child-like admiration, then, upon seeing his flour-covered face and chest, broke out into laughter.

"Well, it's good you can laugh at all this calamity, Jane," Matt told her, dusting himself off. "I suppose it could have been worse."

"I'm sorry," she said, controlling her mirth. Just as easily as she laughed, she began to get upset. "I didn't mean to—"

"It's okay," Matt said. "I'm not mad. Here, let's clean this up before Harvey finds out."

"You—you're not going to tell him? Oh, I hope not. He's send-ing me to Lundy with a big order in a couple of days."

"By yourself?"

"Oh, no. One of the men is driving. I'm going along to keep the tally sheets."

"Oh. For a second there I was a little concerned. Lundy isn't the kind of place for a woman alone."

"I can take care of myself," Jane bragged. "I learned how to shoot when I was little. Here, let me show you." She reached for Matt's gun, but he turned his hip away from her and stayed her hand.

"Uh, that's okay, Jane. I believe you."

"So you won't tell then?"

"Course not. It was an accident . . . wasn't it?"

"Not really," she said.

"You did it on purpose?"

"No, not exactly. It's just that . . . I'm always doing this kind of thing. I'm clumsy. Except when I shoot."

Matt smiled. "Clumsy Jane. Naw, doesn't have much a ring to it. Come on, Jane. Give me a hand." Matt took the broom and bent to the task. He and Jane managed to finish the cleanup with-out any more breakage. Matt paid for his supplies, stuffed them into his saddlebags and rolled them into his bedroll, and gave Jane a smile and a wave.

"Be careful," he said. "And try not to shoot too many men in Lundy. Harvey won't like you killin' all his customers."

Jane blushed and giggled as Matt rode off.

Matt dismounted at the Taylors' place and knocked lightly at the door. Mrs. Taylor answered it with a smile.

"He must be doing better," Matt observed, the smile on her face giving it away.

She nodded as she let him in. "He woke up growly, but that's nothing new. I got some broth into him, and his fever's broke. He's still laying in there, though. Too soon to be up."

"Can I go see him?"

"Please. He's been waiting for you."

Matt removed his hat and crept cautiously into the bedroom. Sheriff Taylor had been looking at the door when his son-in-law pushed it open and followed him with his eyes as he walked to the side of the bed.

"Afternoon, Sheriff," Matt said. "You're lookin' fit as a fiddle. Considerin', that is."

"Considerin' I had a ham-handed whuppersnoot a diggin' in my back with a fishin' pole, you mean."

Matt couldn't stifle a grin. Sheriff Taylor was his old self again.

"You're lucky I was there to save you," Matt pointed out.

"I'm lucky you didn't ram that pole into my lung," Taylor countered. Then he let the corners of his mouth curl up under the shaggy overhang of his mustache. "Thanks, Matt. I appreciate it."

Matt shrugged. "No problem, Sheriff."

"What about them two hombres, the ones you brung down from Bodie?" Taylor was all business.

"Well, they broke out, and—"

"What?" The sheriff tried sitting up, but the pain contorted his face and forced him back down.

"Overcame Harvey at breakfast the day you were shot. I'm on my way out now to find them."

"By yourself?"

"You got another deputy up your sleeve you haven't told me about?"

Another flash of pain contorted Taylor's face, then it slowly relaxed, and he shook his head.

"No," he admitted quietly. "Got any ideas?"

"I know they passed through Coleville. Fred DeCamp saw them on his way out of town. Don't you remember?"

"I barely remember my name, son."

Matt nodded. "Listen, Sheriff, do you have any clue why they might have been following you and wanted to shoot you like that?"

"What makes you think they were shootin' at me?"

"Stands to reason, you being sheriff . . . and the one who got shot."

Taylor grunted. "Why not you? As I recall, at the moment I was shot we were right close together. Maybe he just missed."

That was a possibility that hadn't occurred to Matt, but it didn't shed any light on the situation.

"Either way, I got to go after them," he said.

Taylor was pensive, looking at the ceiling, then said quietly, "I know."

Matt stood up slowly. "Well, good-bye then. See you in a— when I get back."

Taylor turned his head and locked eyes with Matt.

"These ain't ordinary men, Matt. You be careful. I don't want my daughter widowed at her young age, you hear?"

"Yessir."

Taylor's face betrayed a flicker of a smile, then he closed his eyes and was still, except for the regular though shallow heaving of his chest. Matt backed quietly from the room.

CHAPTER

TWELVE

SMOKE CURLED LAZILY from the stone chimney of the house, a white-washed cabin with board siding and thick shingles brought in by wagon from Carson City, Nevada. The windows were shuttered against the cold, and snow stuck to the ground in patches and to the tops of the fence rails that surrounded a yard outside the barn. No trees adorned the property, just the rice grass and sagebrush native to the area, although the sagebrush had been cleared well back from the house by the insightful owner because of the fire danger.

The house was quiet and peaceful, and there was little breeze disturbing the smoke. No birds were about, and small animals had learned to stay clear of this place, for at any time one of the occupants of this residence might exit with a gun strapped to his hip, take aim and fire, and another member of the animal kingdom would meet its demise.

The only sounds this sunny, cold morning were those coming from the small stamp mill a quarter mile from the house, a private mill operated by William Bodine and his sons, Jefferson and Joshua. They spent most of their days in the mine, blasting and carting out the ore from their father's claim that they'd been working for the last five years, ever since they'd come out West.

William Bodine had preceded them, made his strike within the first year, and they soon followed, although the boys' mother hadn't been well enough to finish the trip, and now lay six feet beneath New Mexico soil. In her honor, the mine was named the *Rebecca*, and from her, the Bodines eked out a living. They did well enough to stop having to pay high fees for their ore to be crushed at a Mexican's arastra ten miles away in Nevada, purchasing a small, surplus stamp mill and carting it to their property.

They mined for a month, then milled for a month, and every now and then paid Wells Fargo to stop by and haul their bullion to the U.S. Mint in Carson City. In the meantime, what they gleaned from the rock was kept in a safe in the house, relatively secure because of the remoteness of their claim and the fact that no one could see it passing by on the road. If passersby listened when the mill was operating, they might have been able to hear it but would likely think it was just sound drifting over the hill from Bodie by some quirk of nature.

Jeff and Josh were like any siblings: fiercely loyal to each other, yet they fought no one else as hard as they fought one another. Jeff, being the oldest, resented Josh's recent foray into the world, where he'd taken a portion of his inheritance and squandered it, then returned home when he came to his senses and sought to be reunited with his father. Jeff's idea was to turn him away, but William Bodine would have none of that.

"He's my son," he had explained to Jeff.

"He left us," Jeff argued.

"But he returned," Bodine explained.

"Having that big party was a bit much, don't you think?" Jeff asked. "Roasting that pig you had brought up from town and inviting all those strangers? Shoot, Pa, I never deserted you. I stayed right here with you and kept working, and you never did that for me."

Bodine regarded his son with compassion, yet his eye had a glint to it. "And I appreciate it, son. As I recall, you ate your share of that porker. Besides, you never came back from the dead before, as I recall. Your brother did." And that was the end of the conversation.

For his part, Josh spent a full month absorbing his brother's abuse out of a sense of guilt and penance, but soon the old relationship returned, and one day Josh had had enough.

"Bring me that pick," Jeff had ordered, standing in the mouth of their mine and pointing to the tool he himself had thoughtlessly left there the day before.

"Get it yourself," Josh mumbled lazily. "I ain't your slave."

"I don't need your lip," Jeff said. "Now do as you're told."

"You don't order me around."

"Yes, I do. Pa put me in charge of this operation. That means you do what I say."

"Most everything," Josh corrected. "I don't do your work, and I don't fetch your pick."

"I suppose you'd like me to make you?"

"You're welcome to try it."

"I've been waitin' for this," Jeff said as he walked to where his brother was sitting, pushing up his sleeves. Without any further invitation, Josh jumped up and threw off his hat, and the two of them took to fisticuffs, the fight lasting nearly a full minute before they both rolled off each other holding injured body parts: Jeff his nose and Josh his eye.

Later that night, when they were patched up and fed by their father, who hadn't said a word to them about the incident, they sat around the table swollen, bruised, and discolored while their pa stared back and forth from one to the other, thinking.

"Go ahead and say it, Pa," Jeff said. Josh looked at his father with his one available eye but said nothing.

Bodine cleared his throat.

"You two beat all, you know that? We're family, and you two act like worst enemies. It pains my heart to see you such, and I know your mama wouldn't approve. Don't you ever think of her?"

"It was his fault—" Jeff started to say, but the elder Bodine held his hand up.

"I know the argument. I've heard it many times before. And I've told you, Jeff, it's history. Josh left, but he come back, and that's all there is to it. He is no less my son than you. The only difference is you being the eldest, which, I might point out, you had nothing to do with."

Josh never did say anything that evening. He still was feeling mighty guilty for his poor judgment and happy that his father had allowed him back into the home. He was grateful to be working in the mine, even though he didn't like it much, and grateful to have a bed to sleep in every night and food to eat regularly. About the only thing he wasn't happy about was the way his brother treated him, always throwing his excursion into the real world into his face.

Despite the bad feelings between them, they worked together without a problem because that's the way it had to be in a mine. You couldn't let petty differences get in the way of your responsibilities. That could be deadly—to everyone. It was during their breaks and after work that they took to spatting. Jeff still couldn't understand Josh's fascination for the pistol, and even though Josh had learned it wasn't as glamorous out there as he had once thought, he still enjoyed reading the dime novels he got in the mail and practicing with his revolver in the yard, shooting bottles off the fence rail and smoothing out his quick draw. And he was learning something new: twirling the gun.

It slapped plenty of dirt as he began, and Josh was smart enough to unload the piece before he tried spinning it around by the trigger guard. He'd jerk it out, toss the barrel up but keep his finger in place and watch the gun turn circles, then try to grab it by the grip and slip it fluidly back into the holster.

It didn't quite work that way at first, spinning right off his finger a couple of times before he realized gravity needed to be thwarted by keeping his finger pointing slightly upward. He kept working at it, however, and soon he could clear leather, spin the gun three or four times, and send it home, all in one motion and in just a few seconds. Once he became proficient with that, he'd try reversing direction.

He was anxious to get out of the mine and up to the yard, having learned a new trick from reading about it in a magazine. Jeff was even slightly talkative and peaceful this day, which made Josh all the more anxious, knowing he wouldn't be fighting him first.

They emerged from the dark stamp mill, the sun waning over the hills, so the light they came out into wasn't blinding and disorienting. Josh wiped his brow with his neckerchief. Jeff put on a more controlled air, as though the sweat on the back of his neck didn't mean anything.

The ribbon of smoke rising from the chimney was a welcome-home signal, a portent of warmth, comfort, security, and a hearty dinner. They did not speak during the walk back to the house, but as they neared, Josh said, "I'll be in shortly. I got some things I need to do."

"More gunplay?"

"Just never you mind."

"Do you have to do that all the time? Didn't you learn nuthin' while you were gone?"

"Yeah. A man needs a gun to get along in this world."

"Only if he plans on living by it. Or dying by it would probably be more to the point."

"Fine. One of these days, when you're in a bank and some desperadoes come in to rob it, you can jerk off your belt and whup 'em. That'll come in real handy. Or maybe you can scald them with a harsh word or two."

Jeff just shook his head and waved his brother off as he continued toward the house. Josh turned aside at the end of the fence and walked to a little shed on the far side. He unlocked the door and went in to his own private world, where his six-shooter hung in its holster from a peg on the wall, and pictures he'd cut out of his magazines adorned the walls. He'd built the shed and the workbench inside it himself where he could clean his gun after complaints from Jeff, supported by his pa, that the solvents he was using were smelling up the house. Like they all didn't smell bad themselves most of the time anyway.

As he always did, he pulled the gun from the holster respectfully, almost caressing it, and ran his fingers over the smooth, shiny metal, feeling the curve of the cylinder and the warmth of the walnut stocks screwed to the grip. He pulled the hammer back a notch and spun the cylinder, then eased the hammer back down.

Jeff was partly right, Josh knew. He'd learned that during his adventures. Those who live by the gun die by the gun, regardless of which side of the law they're on. But everyone . . . well, most everyone, carried a gun. It just made sense. The world was full of rattlesnakes, the slithering kind and the two-legged kind, and it never hurt to be prepared. With the skill Josh was developing, wouldn't be too many men dumb enough to challenge him. Besides, he wasn't a gunfighter or a robber. A gun in the hands of Josh Bodine was for protection, not an offensive weapon. And it had already gotten him out of one scrape.

"Josh!" The shout came from the house.

Josh mumbled to himself. "Must be time for dinner." He turned his head and shouted back. "Coming!"

"It's Pa!"

The meaning of that shout didn't register.

"What?"

"It's Pa!" Jeff's voice was drawing closer. He was headed toward the shed. There was an edge to his voice, and Josh could now hear his brother running. His gun still in his hand, Josh stuck his head out the door.

"It's Pa!" Jeff repeated, his breathing hard, much harder than necessary considering the short distance he'd run.

"What's the matter?"

"He's been . . . he's been shot!"

Josh needed no more encouragement. He charged past his brother across the yard and tore into the house, skidding to a stop inside the door as he realized he didn't know where his pa was. Jeff followed on his heels.

"The den!"

Josh moved again and entered the small room, seeing his father spread out face down on the floor, his arms tucked awkwardly beneath him. An ugly red stain had spread out across his back.

"You move him?" Josh asked.

"No."

Josh dropped down, setting his gun on the floor, and gently grabbed his pa's shoulder, turning him so he could see his face. William Bodine's eyes were open and glazed. A line of blood had run from the corner of his mouth and was now dried and cracked. Josh let him back to the floor gently.

"He's gone, Jeff," he said quietly.

"What do you mean? Do something. We need to get him to town."

"What do you think I mean, Jeff?" Josh looked up at the frantic face of his older brother. "He's dead. Been dead most of the day, the way I see it. Look here, he's stiff." Josh raised his father's arm, the rigor mortis apparent.

"What happened?" Jeff asked, staring at his father in disbelief. This couldn't be, his pa couldn't leave them like this. Jefferson Bodine, who seemed so capable and independent, and who was quite comfortable running a mine and a stamp mill, suddenly found himself the head of the family, such as it was. This was all his responsibility, something for which he had never prepared himself. He assumed his father would always be there or would at least go slowly so they'd have time preparing for the transition of leadership from William Bodine to his eldest son. Jeff sat down on a straight-backed chair, eyes locked on the corpse that had been his father.

Josh was not thinking as far ahead as his brother. He was concerned right now with the immediate crisis: figuring out what had happened. He looked around for a clue and was not long in finding one. The open door on the small safe in the corner told him everything he needed to know. Jeff heard Josh's oath as the younger Bodine spied the safe, and his concentration was broken. He looked over and spied it too, and they both knew their pa had been robbed, then murdered. Shot in the back after opening the safe for the crooks. No words passed between them for several minutes as they both made a silent appraisal of their predicament, both of them thinking what it meant only to them, not to the other.

After a time, Josh stood up. "Come on, we've got to take care of him."

"What do you mean, take care of him?"

"Jeff, you're not that dumb. We've got to bury him. Help me take him to the sofa."

Josh bent over and picked his pa up by the arms and waited for Jeff to get the legs. The older Bodine did so slowly, reluctantly, then they carried their father to the sofa and laid him out, folding his arms across his chest and closing his eyelids. The Bodine brothers retired to the kitchen to think.

Jeff sat with his face in his hands, his shoulders racked with silent, dry sobs. Josh brooded. He'd been on his own before; it wasn't so fearful of a thing now. Jeff was still older, but he'd never functioned without his pa. While Josh's experience couldn't be termed a rousing success, what with getting duped by robbers, arrested for a bank robbery he didn't commit and barely getting off during the trial, then watching his entire fortune in gold dust drift down a canyon wall in the breeze. But he'd learned. He faced adversity and come out okay. Jeff's biggest problem in life had been the loss of their mother on the trail, when both of them were little, Josh too little to remember much.

They sat for a full fifteen minutes before Jeff finally spoke.

"We've got to do something."

"Durn right, we do," Josh agreed. "You got any ideas who did this?"

Jeff shook his head. "No one knows about us."

"That can't be true. Pa buys supplies. There's a sign on the gate by the road."

Jeff looked up at his brother. "You been to Bodie, tossing gold around. Shoot, Josh, everybody knows about us. It was you, it was you brought these men down on us."

"What do you mean, these men? How do you know it wasn't one? And how do you know why he came here? Maybe he was just passin' through, came up for a drink of water or something, and heard the mill."

"There's a stream by the road, and a sign that says 'No Trespassing' on the gate."

"Okay, he didn't stop by for water. That don't mean it's somebody from Bodie that knows about us because of me. Besides, this is a little, three-man operation. Any intelligent person'll know three men ain't gonna be digging up enough gold to kill a man over."

Jeff regarded his brother with a hard eye. "Men kill other men for a look they don't like, or because they was snorin'. I know all about them kind of men."

"Been readin' my magazines?" Josh asked, a slight hint of glee in his voice.

"Yeah," Jeff admitted. "Once, just to find out what it is you see in them things."

"Well, it wasn't my doing brought them here. And I'm tired of hearin' you carp about that. It's over, Jeff. I came back. I'm sorry I left in the first place but grateful for the experience. Now swallow it and don't mention it to me again."

He pushed himself out of the chair and stormed outside, slamming the door behind him. For the first time in their lives, the argument wasn't stopped by their father. Not directly, at least.

Josh hiked up the hill behind the house to the crest and sat down on a rock to watch the sun set over the snow-capped peaks of the Sierra Nevadas. The red-streaked sky faded into purple and colored the snow, which stood out in contrast to the dark shadows of the rock below snow level. It was a beautiful sight, one he had never taken the time to enjoy before. It was dark when he decided on a course of action and had picked his way carefully down the slope.

He let himself back in, avoiding a glance at the sofa where his pa lay under a blanket. Jeff was by the fireplace, drinking a cup of hot coffee. When he heard Josh come in, he didn't look up but poured his brother a cup and handed it to him. Josh took it with a quiet "Thanks" and sat down in the other chair.

"We've got to bury him," Josh said.

"Yes," agreed Jeff. "I know. I thought about that. Where'd be good?"

"By the mill?"

Jeff considered it. "No, be in the way there. How about farther up the hill, behind the house, overlooking the whole property?"

"I just came from there," Josh said. "It's a good place."

"Tomorrow."

"Tomorrow." They drank their coffee, then Josh spoke again. "I gotta do something, though. You ain't gonna like it."

Jeff gave him a look, but it wasn't as hard as the others. "What?"

"I need to get the bullet."

"What for?"

"Caliber. I need to know what size gun killed him. That'll narrow down the search, help me know what I'm lookin' for."

"What search?"

"The one I'm startin' right after we're done puttin' him under."

CHAPTER

THIRTEEN

J EFF BODINE TOSSED THE LAST shovelful of dirt on the grave and
stuck the shovel in the ground. He joined his brother by the
marker Josh had painted and helped raise it, letting it drop into
the small hole they'd dug at the head of the plot. They back-
filled around it and tamped the dirt down with their boots, then
more dirt and more tamping.

When they were finished they stood back, both of them removing the hats they had worn to keep the sun out of their eyes. It was
cold, but the sun was bright, especially reflecting off the patches
of snow that still clung to the ground.

"Good thing the ground wasn't froze," Josh commented quietly.

Jeff nodded but remained silent.

"I suppose we ought to say something," Josh said.

"I reckon."

"You first. You're the oldest."

Jeff nodded again. He thought a second, then cleared his throat
and picked up his father's Bible he'd brought out from the house
in anticipation of this. He opened it reverently.

"It took a mite a lookin', but I found a good one," he explained,
and began to read. "'When the even was come, there came a rich
man of Arma . . . Arima . . . of Someplace, named Joseph, who also
himself was Jesus' disciple: He went to Pirate—'"

"Pilate," Josh corrected. "Even I know there's no pirates in the Bible."

Jeff scowled at him but continued. "'He went to Pilate and begged the body of Jesus. Then Pilate commanded the body to be delivered. And when Joseph had taken the body, he wrapped it in a clean linen cloth, and laid it in his own new tomb, which he had hewn out in the rock; and he rolled a great stone to the door of the seplacree, and departed.'"

"What was that about?" Josh asked, puzzled by the reading. "And what's a seplacree?"

"It was the burial of Jesus," Jeff said. "Don't you know? The seplacree is the tomb."

"Why don't they just say that? And by the way, what's that got to do with what we're doin' here today?"

"I don't know, I just thought that's what should be read. They buried Christ; we're buryin' Pa."

"Christ came out of the tomb. Pa ain't goin' nowhere but to heaven."

"You find something, then." He handed the Bible to Josh, who accepted it somewhat tentatively but had no choice. He'd criticized his brother, now he must accept the challenge.

"Where's it say something about ashes to ashes and dust to dust?" he asked rhetorically as he leafed through the pages. "That's what they always say at burials, isn't it? And something about your eternal soul?"

"I don't know. How about the twenty-third Psalm? Ma liked that, Pa used to say."

"Okay. What page is it on?"

"You don't go by pages, you look up the book, then find the chapter, simple as that."

Josh grumbled but thumbed through the big, black book, not willing to admit defeat to his brother under any circumstances.

"How do you spell it?" he asked quietly after a few futile moments.

"P-s-a-l-m."

"What's it got a 'P' in front of it for?"

"I don't know. Just read it."

Josh obliged him, reading the archaic language haltingly, stumbling over several words on the way, and in a few minutes, the service had ended.

"That was pure poetry," Jeff said sarcastically.

"Next time Pa dies I'll do better," Josh replied and, turning on his heel, strode back to the house.

He came out of the room a short while later finding Jeff sitting at the dining table.

Looking up, Jeff noticed the six-shooter strapped around his brother's waist. Josh also was wearing his hat and coat, and his saddlebags were draped over his arm.

"What are you doing?

"What do you think I'm doing? I'm going after Pa's killer."

"Sure you are. And where you gonna look?"

"There's tracks. I scouted 'em out this morning, early. They headed off toward Bodie. There was three of 'em. One came up here, the other two waited below on the main road."

"So now you're a tracker."

"I picked up a few things."

"You gonna do this by yourself?"

"You're welcome to come along."

"Josh, we've got a mine to work. Pa or no Pa."

"Jeff, I worked the mine because of Pa. I've got no reason to stay now. Besides, everything we ever brought out of it is gone. They cleaned out the safe, remember? It's over, the way I see it."

Jeff scowled. "What are you going to do if you find them?" he asked. "And that's a big 'if'! You got about two chances of findin' them: none and none."

"Maybe. But I got a whole lifetime to do it in, the way I see it."

"Okay, say you do come across them, and they confess to you they killed Pa. What then?"

Josh thought, then shrugged. "Kill 'em, I suppose. They'll probably not go down easy. Them kind rarely do."

"Like you know all about it. What about the law?"

"The only law out here is this." He drew the gun from its holster.

"Seems to me you tried that before."

"Last time I hadn't just buried my pa. Come with me Jeff. He's your pa, too."

"I know he's my pa. And he'd want us to stay here and work the Rebecca."

"Work the Rebecca!" Josh scoffed. "When's the last time you saw any gold of consequence come out of her? If Pa was paying us by the hour, he'd have to close down, couldn't meet his payroll. That's why he let Jim go when I came back. Did you ever think about that?"

Jeff was pensive. He had thought about it and knew full well Josh was right. But there was more to the Rebecca than gold, and he told his brother so.

"Tradition, Josh. Pa handed the mine down to us. He'd expect us to keep it going."

"Not when it was tapped out. Maybe one of the big companies could make it pay still. They have better equipment than we do. Shoot, our stuff is what the big companies throw out. Come on, Jeff. We've turned the page. It's over. You stay here now, you'll die here. I'll come back someday when this business is over to bury you, if you don't keel over in the mine or outside where the coyotes will get to you."

Jeff shook his head. "Sorry, Josh, I can't."

Josh sighed and dropped his head. When he lifted his face, there was uncharacteristic compassion in it. He stuck out his hand.

"Okay, brother. Like me, you're doin' what you gotta do. I gotta respect that. Good luck."

Jeff took his brother's hand and grasped firmly. Neither of them said good-bye but locked on each other's eyes for a few seconds, then Josh flipped his saddlebags over his shoulder and walked out, shutting the door behind him, knowing he'd never be back.

Not this time.

Josh saddled his horse and rode easily down the trail to the road that led to Bodie, eyeing the tracks left by the killers. The bullet he'd dug out of his father was burning in his pocket. He couldn't make anything of it, but there was undoubtedly a gunsmith in Bodie who could help him identify it. Maybe he'd even look in on that deputy there, the young one, Matt Page. And Billy O'Hara, the big, black man who gave him a room, and that attorney fellow, Pete Jensen, who gave him back his horse that he'd turned over to pay his legal fees. And that young gal, Sarah, Matt's wife. Boy, could she cook! He'd have to finagle a meal from her somehow. Could be the last food he'd get for a while. Josh had

enough money to situate himself with supplies for a week or so—
including more ammunition. He'd just about used his all up
practicing.

As he rode, he recalled that last time he'd taken this track alone,
how he'd met up with them robbers, the two Ezras. Never did find
out their real names, not that it mattered. They were both deader'n
hammers now. Ashes to ashes, dust to dust.

It wasn't a trip he remembered with pleasant thoughts, and he
forced himself to think on other things: on how he was going to
go about catching the men and what he'd do with them when he
found them.

The chill in the air was getting to him. He pulled his collar up
and kicked the horse to an easy lope, anxious to make Bodie before
nightfall.

Bodie wasn't visible when entering from the north until one was
almost within the town limits due to the hills that surrounded it
and the large bend in the road that approached the camp from
downhill. Although, from the west, a panorama of the whole valley was provided; from the east, the town could be ten buildings
or a thousand; it was impossible to tell.

Josh had passed the first scattered buildings on the northern
outskirts when Main Street came fully into view— not only Main
Street but the rest of the town that flanked Main on both sides.
Main Street was Bodie's only flat spot and during rainy weather
would have been the channel that collected all the runoff were it
not for a seasonal creek that paralleled the street on the east a couple of blocks away, running the length of town and continuing
down the canyon. The town rose gradually on both sides of Main,
and Josh could see how much it had grown since he had last been
there. What had been twenty, thirty buildings was now several
hundred, many of them houses.

Saloons lined both sides of the street, and as he passed the intersection with King Street, he could see the greatly enlarged Chinese
district. Green Street once had been the south edge of town; now
it marked the center. The mills on the hillside to his left continued
pounding the rock into gold, only now there were several, and
more mines were plainly visible, the pile of pastel rocks below the
dark shadow of the entrance to the shaft marking each one.

"Hold it!"

The cry startled Josh, and he reined up, instinctively reaching for his six-gun.

"Whoa, cowboy, wait!" the shouter said. "Friend. I'm a friend."

Josh finally noticed the man, who was standing by a large camera mounted on a tripod that he had placed in the street. It was pointing across Main at the buildings and the Empire Mill, visible above the rooftops on the hill beyond.

"Didn't mean to alarm you, friend. Just didn't want you to ruin the shot. It's on a time lapse to take in more light since I can't use a flash, and there isn't enough sun."

"What's that for?" the ever-curious Josh Bodine asked, relaxing his grip on the revolver.

"History, my good man, history," the photographer proclaimed. "Someday people will look at these photos and know what it was like to live here."

"Oh." Josh understood, but he couldn't figure out why people would care. Those that lived here would know for themselves; others would have no reason he could think of to wonder about it.

"Say," said the photographer thoughtfully, "would you mind posing for a shot? It'd be something to have a real cowboy pictured."

"Well, I—"

"Don't be bashful, friend. Look, if you're a little shy, maybe I could entice you with, say fifty cents? It's all I can afford."

"Fifty cents? Just to sit here?"

"Sure. I suppose I could arrange to get you a free copy of the photo instead, but you look like a man on the move, and I figured you'd rather have the fifty cents. Course, most people don't get either, so I guess you could say I'm doing you a favor in exchange for you doing me one. Most people pay me to take their picture."

"Then why are you willing to give me fifty cents?" Josh asked suspiciously.

"Let's just say it's that persuader on your hip. It's my way of apologizing to you for startling you and of thanking you for not ventilating me. So, what do you say?"

"What do you want me to do?"

"Move your horse out in front of me, about the middle of the street." He carefully pulled out the glass negative he had just exposed and prepared another while he spoke. "Yes, that's it. Good. Now gaze on down the road—no, look at me. That's better. No, don't smile. No one smiles. People's teeth are usually too bad to smile. Besides, you're a cowboy. Cowboys got nothing to smile about. They lead a hard life. Yes, that's it. Good."

He stuck his head under the black cloth at the back of the camera. "Okay, hold real still for about thirty seconds, starting . . . now."

Josh did as he was instructed, suddenly noticing every itch and tick on his body. A fly buzzed his face, and it was all he could not to brush at it. His eyes watered as he kept from blinking them, and he was about to have a fit when the photographer shouted, "Okay, you can relax!"

Josh sighed, then hurriedly rubbed his eyes and attacked the itches. He eased his horse over to the man, who handed him four bits.

"Thanks," he said. "Name's William H. Jackson. When I get done here, I'm on my way to Yosemite. Hear tell it's gorgeous there."

"Josh Bodine," Josh told him, taking the coins and sticking them in his pants pocket. "Never been there." He didn't have the heart to tell the man he was a miner, not a cowboy. Mr. Jackson must be new out here. There wasn't a cow within miles of this place—on the hoof, at least. Bodie cows were already cut up and hanging in a cool place. But it didn't matter, not to Josh. He'd just gotten to town and already made fifty cents and hadn't even gotten off his horse.

Maybe his luck was changing.

Josh dug his heels in gently and clicked his tongue, his tired horse plodding slowly down the street. He continued on through town, taking in the sights and sounds of the gold camp, remembering his previous encounter, mostly with disdain. Uncomfortable in the saddle from the months of not riding and aware that the horse was at least as bad off as him, Josh looked for a place to stop and sit so he could devise a scheme, a plan of action. He wisely ignored the saloons, then spied the Empire Boardinghouse and recalled the big Negro who ran the place, Billy O'Hara. "Uncle Billy," everyone called him.

He climbed off the animal and tied her to the rail out front. Mounting the wooden steps, he removed his hat as he pushed the door open and entered the parlor, drawing brief glances from some of the miners and other tenants sitting around the cozy room and playing cards for matchsticks or reading newspapers from Aurora or Bishop.

Josh paused and took in the room with a sweep of his head, but Billy was not in it. He cleared his throat and stared at a man nearby dealing a hand of five-card draw until his counterpart felt it and looked up.

"Excuse me," Josh said.

"It's okay. You can belch in here," the man said. "It's just us men."

His cronies gave him a laugh, then went back to their game.

"Uh, excuse me, no, I was going to ask a question."

"Go ahead, then. Maybe I got an answer."

"I, uh, was looking for Mr. O'Hara."

"He ain't lost is he?" The man looked under the table, then at one of his friends. "Did you lose Billy again? He's so big, how do you keep doing that?" Another round of crony chuckles.

Josh smiled to appease the man. "Do you know where he is?"

"Nope, can't say that I do. Best guess is over to the Quicksilver, getting us some supper."

Josh was puzzled. "I thought he cooked it here."

"He's too busy these days, stranger, now that he's acting deputy in the absence of the regular feller. He could be anywhere in town."

"You just said he was at the Quicksilver."

"No, I said that was my best guess. He probably stopped in—" The man looked at his pocket watch. "—about twenty minutes ago, told them how much to bring over. Rent here includes supper, and since Billy can't cook for a spell, he has to have Mrs. Page do the honors."

Mrs. Page. He must be talking about Sarah, Josh calculated.

"What happened to the deputy?"

"You're sure full of questions, young feller. Maybe you ought to find Uncle Billy. If you're needin' a room, you're out of luck. This place is plum full up of long-timers. We all work for the mining companies. The hotels take in folks just passin' through. So do the saloons, if you don't mind sleepin' in a chair or under a table."

Josh nodded. "Okay. Well, thanks." He turned to leave, then had a thought. "Excuse me, if I could."

"What?" the man said testily, his concentration on the game broken a second time. He eyed Josh up and down, noting the young stranger's clothing that was the same as his own, but the polished gun on his hip in a well-cared for holster was unlike anything any miner he ever knew to carry. Just who was this stranger asking all these questions? Maybe he was a miner who had been denied a job at the Empire and meant harm to Billy.

"Any of you men seen three men ride into town yesterday?" Josh addressed the whole room, since everyone was listening anyway.

"Strangers ride in every day," someone said.

"These three came in together, would've had some gold in their possession."

"Lots of men have gold in their possession," pointed out another man.

"Amalgam nuggets and coins, a whole sack full?" Josh clarified.

"Sack full!" barked the card dealer. "You say these men would've come in with a sack of nuggets and coins?"

"That's what I said."

"What's it to you?" asked a well-dressed man suspiciously from his chair by a lamp table. His newspaper he'd folded in his lap.

"My pa was robbed." There was silence, so Josh continued. "We have a private mine down the road some." Josh pointed toward Nevada. "They came in when my pa was alone, made him open the safe, then shot him in the back."

"Can you prove this?" the card dealer asked, suddenly more interested in this stranger than his penny-ante game.

"He's dead. The gold is gone. What more proof do you need?"

"I don't mean that. I mean can you prove the gold is yours and which three men took it?"

"Sure, but I don't need to prove it to you," Josh challenged, getting annoyed. "Now either you seen 'em or you didn't. Just tell me which, leave the rest to me. It ain't nobody else's business, the way I figure."

"Don't get your hackles up, son," the well-dressed man said. "We'd like to help, but we got to be sure you're not the robber going to steal from three honest men."

"Look at me?" Josh said. "Do I look like a robber?"

"Don't know," said the dealer. "What's one look like?" He got some more laughs, but the well-dressed man stood up, and the men quieted out of obvious respect for him. Josh figured him to be a leader of sorts who carried some weight, at least with the men in the boardinghouse.

"Well now, son, you dress like a miner, that much is true. But you're heeled like a gunman. Isn't a man in this room wears a rig like that. Most of us have never seen fancy leather like that. If we pack a pistol, it's stuck in our belt or pocket."

"Deputy Page can vouch for me. So can Mr. O'Hara. And Sarah Taylor—uh, Page, I guess it is now. She knows me too."

"Fair enough," said the well-dressed man. He looked around the room. "Any of you gents see the three men he's looking for?"

There was much murmuring and shaking of heads, but no one volunteered in the affirmative.

"Sorry," the man said.

"Much obliged anyway," Josh said. "I'll be in town, if you do see them. Just let Mr. O'Hara know. I'll be checking in with him."

Josh stuck his weathered, floppy hat on his matted hair and passed from the room, the cold of the evening air chilling him. Sizing up the street from the boardwalk, he located the Quicksilver and walked across the street in its direction, leaving his horse tied up in front of the boardinghouse. He'd unsaddle it and feed it later.

The Quicksilver was bustling inside as he peered through the window. Billy wasn't there and neither was Sarah Page, just a hefty woman rushing from table to table, bringing food and carrying off dirty dishes. Mrs. Page must be in the kitchen, he thought. She'd be busy. He decided to check back later. Anyway, his first mission was to find Billy.

With little else to do, he began to wander the streets of Bodie. People passed by on foot on the boardwalks or in the street, most of them giving him no mind except for the lone women eyeing him suspiciously until he smiled and tipped his hat and continued walking. A couple of fallen angels smiled back, and one of them asked if he was lonely. "No, ma'am," was all he said, and he kept going, speeding up a little.

The tinkling of pianos and sour plucks and strums of banjos floated out from saloons, carried on the smoke of pipes and cigars and propelled by the raucous laughter of the men smoking them while they drank and played faro. Josh looked inside each one, glad Uncle Billy would be easy to pick out in a crowd, but he was disappointed each time.

He decided after an hour that it was time to care for his horse, since he had no idea how long this was going to take. He was tired—not just sleepy but fatigued from the ride as well—but he couldn't bed down for the night until he'd at least located Billy O'Hara.

Josh untied the animal, whose face reflected her general languor and reluctance to bear her rider another step.

"It's okay, girl," Josh said gently. "No sense me climbing all the way up just to have to climb off again in a few minutes."

He took the reins and led the horse south on Main toward the livery that was sure to be at the south edge of town, near where most everyone came in. There hadn't been one at the north end. Josh sighed resignedly as he pulled the reluctant horse, anxious himself to be fed and bedded down, but knowing that wasn't an option for awhile.

An eruption of noise from a saloon he was passing caught his attention, as it was more boisterous than the sounds he had been hearing. He paused and gazed toward the place, curious but not so much that he wanted to tie the animal up and go inside.

As it happened, he didn't need to enter. The door opened and a man was heaved from the place by two burly toughs. He toppled down the steps and into the street, landing face first in a pile of snow at Josh's feet. He laid there motionless for so long that Josh began to wonder if he was alive, but even in the pale glow of the coal oil torches, he could see the man's back heaving with regular breaths.

"Drunk," Josh muttered with scorn. The man was encased in a long, buckskin coat, dirty and with evidence of grease in several places. His hat had become dislodged during his brief and awkward flight and lay on the ground beside him, a well-worn black hat with dented Montana peak and a flat brim, frayed at the edges and lacking in the stiffness it must have had when first bought. The odd hat band appeared to be made from a pelt of some kind, the kind of animal sacrificed to make it Josh couldn't begin to guess.

His hair was long and mostly straight, curling near his shoulders. He wore it parted down the middle, though now it was a touch disheveled, and hadn't been washed in a long time.

The man groaned and managed to push himself up from the ground onto his hands and knees. He vomited, rubbed his face with snow, then stood up shakily, muttering obscenities about the men who had done this to him.

Josh watched the whole scene. When the drunkard was finally erect, he noticed the young man inspecting him and eyed him back suspiciously.

"Ah, there you are." He reached back down, carefully, to avoid falling and retrieved his hat, which he plopped on his head backwards. "Brought my horse around, did you?"

The man continued eying Josh with squinting, piercing, bloodshot eyes under heavy brows. He sported a large, thick mustache and was in need of shave but didn't appear otherwise to wear a beard. There was something about his face that intrigued Josh, and he ignored the man's claim to the horse Josh held.

The vagrant wiped his hands down the front of his coat—as he quite obviously had done many times before—and walked past Josh, keeping his eyes on the young man's. He stepped directly to the side of Josh's horse and suddenly pulled himself into the saddle before Josh realized what was happening. Josh shook off the trance and quickly drew his six-shooter, pointing it at the man's belly.

"Get off my horse," Josh ordered coolly, cocking the gun with a deliberate and slow action.

"Nice move," the man said, "but are you as fast to kill as you are to present?"

Josh was a little taken aback, for this man did not appear armed, and both his hands were busy holding on to the pommel just to keep himself upright. Was it a challenge? Or just an observation?

He might never find out. A booming voice behind him told him to drop the gun.

"Do it now, stranger, or live to regret it!"

Josh slowly let down the hammer and, with his left hand still clutching the reins, bent over and set the pistol on the ground. There was no way he was dropping his prized revolver.

"Turn around," the voice ordered. "Nice and slow."

"I'm glad you're here, Sheriff," the vagrant slurred.

"Shut up."

"Yes sir." The vagrant mumbled something Josh couldn't understand.

Josh obeyed slowly and in a few seconds was staring into the face of Billy O'Hara and down the barrel of a Sharp's carbine.

"He's tryin' to steal my horse," Josh said as he raised his hands.

"On the contrary," the vagrant objected, "I was merely riding by, and he grabbed the reins and jerked his iron to take this horse out from under me."

"That's a lie!" Josh said, suddenly frantic. "I, uh . . . I know what's in the saddlebags."

"I saw him peekin' in there earlier," said the drunk, thinking quickly for one so inebriated.

"Ahh, well now," said Billy slowly. "That'd account for it, by golly." He eyed the man in the saddle. "But can *y'all* tell me what's in them bags?"

Josh ventured a peek back at the man, just in time to see him slowly lean to the side, then topple off the horse onto the street.

Billy sighed and lowered the Sharp's.

"What's yer name, son?" he asked Josh, while lumbering over to the unconscious tramp.

"It's me, Mr. O'Hara, Josh Bodine."

Billy stopped in his tracks and looked closely at the young man, his face dark under his hat brim with only the occasional coal lamp and the pale light that shined out from the various open establishments on Main Street illuminating it.

"Josh? Why, it sure enough is you!" Billy stepped over and wrapped a beefy arm around the young man's shoulder and shook him. "Ah'm mighty glad to see you. What're y'all doing back in Bodie?"

"Pa got killed," Josh said quietly.

"Oh, mah goodness," Billy said, drawing back. "Ah'm sorely sorry to hear that. What happened?"

"He was robbed while me and Jeff were in the mine. Cleaned us out and shot him in the back."

"That's terrible. So, what brings you to town? You know who they are?"

"No, not a clue. I was hoping Deputy Page would be here to give me a hand or at least tell me what to do."

"He's away. Don't know when he'll be back. Ah'm afraid Ah'll not be much help to you. Ah'm just fillin' in here till he gets back. But you're welcome to stay—"

"There's no place, and I . . . I don't have much money."

"Shoot, that ain't no problem, Ah'll—"

A groan from the prone drunk interrupted them.

"Guess we better do somethin' with him," Billy concluded. He moved slowly. "Where'd he come from?"

"They tossed him outa there," Josh said, jerking a thumb toward the nearby saloon. He bent over and retrieved his pistol, wiping it off on his pants before dropping it back into the holster and slipping the split leather thong over the hammer to keep it in place.

Together, they picked the drunk up.

"Sorry, girl," Josh told his horse softly. "I'll get you taken care of in a bit."

"Your horse ain't been took care of?" Billy asked.

"Haven't had the opportunity," Josh explained. "I was on the way there when this guy claimed her, then you came up."

"I'll take care of it," Billy said. He whistled sharply and called "Noah!" and soon an old geezer came out of the shadows.

"Uh, yessir, Unca Billy? What'cha need?"

"Take this man's horse to the livery. See that she gets some oats, too, not just hay. But not too many oats, we don't want to give her stomach problems. And be sure to give her a turn at the trough after, and a good brush down . . . not just with straw, neither. Use the brush. You hear?"

"Okay, Uncle Billy." The old guy nodded and took the reins as Josh set down the drunk's feet. Then he picked up them up again, and he and Billy hauled the man off to the Graybar Hotel—what the locals called Matt's jail—for a sleep-off. Not once during the short trip did he take his eyes off the vagrant's wet face.

CHAPTER

FOURTEEN

BILLY PUSHED THE UNLOCKED DOOR open with his foot, and they carried the man to the cell, dumping him unceremoniously on the mattress. The acting lawman searched his prisoner for weapons, found none, then shut the door and locked it. He and Josh filed out, Billy repeating the process with the outer door that led to the two cells.

Only then did he loosen his lawman face and give Josh a wide smile and two big arms to engulf the young traveler.

"It's real good to see ya," Uncle Billy said, slapping Josh's back and raising a cloud of trail dust. "Ah'm awful sorry it has to be like this. Awful sorry!"

Josh shrugged. "Me too, but there it is." He didn't quite know what else to say at this point, and his thoughts turned to the vagrant. "Do you know that man?"

Billy shook his head. "Nope, can't say as Ah do. Must be new in town. He's a sorry one, ain't he?"

Josh didn't respond but looked toward the door leading to the cells, as if doing so would provide an answer to the question forming in his mind.

"You want to swear out a complaint?" Billy asked.

"Huh? Oh, no . . . I don't think so. He was just drunk."

"Somethin' botherin' you, son?" Billy asked.

"He . . . just looks familiar, that's all." Josh chuckled. "Ain't that a riot. Like I seen enough people that somebody looks familiar. I tell you, Mr. O'Hara—"

"Call me Billy, Joshua. Mr. O'Hara is my pappy, you know what Ah mean?"

Josh smiled. "Sure, Billy. I know what you mean."

"Now you was sayin' . . ."

"I was just sayin' that it's good to get out of that mine. Not with Pa being dead. I don't mean that. And it ain't like before, when I left kinda with the wrong idea. It's just that after all them years workin' the mine, I'm happy to get out, once and for all."

"What do you mean, once and for all? Ain't you goin' back?"

Josh shook his head and slumped into a chair beside the desk. Billy took Matt's chair behind it.

"What for?" Josh asked. "It's tappin' out, at least for us. Especially now with all our reserves gone. Workin' a mine costs money, and unless you sell stock, you need some financial backing or have to have the money yourself to make a go of it. And Pa wouldn't sell stock or borrow money because he didn't want someone else telling us what to do. Besides, there's just two of us now, and that ain't enough. I think we should sell it, take what we can get, and get on with our lives somewhere else while we're still young enough to do it."

"What's your brother say?" Billy inquired quietly, leaning forward, his arms on the desk.

"When I left him, he was determined to keep it going, but I don't see how he can. And I'm not going back."

"Well, maybe that's a decision that would best be left until the time it has to be made. Never know, things may change. God has a way of switching everything for good, of makin' things happen you'd a never thought could happen, not in a million years."

Josh grunted but didn't contradict Uncle Billy. The young man figured the former assistant to a riverboat captain had seen more life than he had and maybe knew something he didn't, although he couldn't possibly figure out how God could make something good out of this. Or why He'd want to.

"You said you needed a place to stay," Billy said. "Why don't you stay here tonight? There's a cot over in the corner with a couple blankets and a feather pillow . . . it's warm and secure. When Ah come

over in the mornin' with breakfast for our prisoner, Ah'll bring some
for you. That'll be payment for guardin' that desperado." He winked.

"Okay," Josh said. He wasn't of a mind this late at night to be
overly polite or to turn down a gift. He was tired and hungry but
figured he could wait until morning for food, as long as he could
get a good night's sleep.

Billy stood. "Ah best be gettin' to the boardin' house. Them
miners are like kids, you got to watch them every minute or they
get themselves into trouble, fightin' and shootin' like it don't hurt.
Lock up after me, would you?"

Josh nodded and followed Billy to the door. O'Hara stepped
out and shut the door with another smile, and Josh threw the bolt.
He stretched, rubbed his eyes, and sat down in the chair to take
off his boots. Rubbing his sore feet and examining his dirty socks
with no toe or heel left in them, he thought again of the man in the
lockup, wondering what it was about him that bothered him so.
But his fatigue overruled any further effort in that regard, and he
curled up on the cot. It was only a minute before he was fast asleep.

*Pounding stamps slammed down on the quartz, pulverizing it into
fine sand that turned into silt when mixed with water and washed
down over the amalgam table, where quicksilver leached the precious
gold out from the dross, which was washed away. After days of this,
the bottoms of the stamps would be coated with a crust of soft gold
that had to be scraped off. But stopping the whole battery took too
long, so Josh waited for a stamp to be brought to its apex by the
revolving cam, then stuck a board under the collar, preventing it from
dropping down. With the stamp thus hindered, he could go down
and scrape off the gold that prevented the stamp from doing its work.*

*It was dangerous because the stamps next to it were still rising
and falling, all eight-hundred pounds that would pulverize his hand
quicker and easier than it would the gold-bearing rock. With the
scraper he adroitly pried the slab of almost pure gold off the bottom
of the stamp and was just about to pluck it from the trough when
something popped above him. In an eye-blink he knew the board
had come loose and slipped out, and the stamp was on its way down.
He began to pull his hand out, but there was no way he could do it
in time. Maybe just the fingers would be lost, maybe . . . The pounding of the other stamps continued as the fatal stamp hit home—*

Josh bolted upright on his cot, sweating with the fever of a dream, his breathing rough and deep, and he panicked at the unfamiliar surroundings. But in a few seconds his head began to clear, and he recognized the pounding as something other than the stamps or even his heart. It was the front door, and it was being soundly rapped.

"Josh, open up!" Billy O'Hara ordered.

Josh jumped up from the cot and did as he was ordered, and Billy—both his hands full with a tray of food—stepped into the jail.

"Ah been bangin' for five minutes," Billy exaggerated.

"Sorry," Josh apologized. "I guess I was asleep."

"Well, no harm. How's our prisoner?"

"Uh, I don't know."

"Well, let's go see," Billy suggested. He took a plate of food and unlocked the door to the cells, pushing it open with his shoulder. The vagrant was still asleep and snoring loudly.

Josh looked down at him and noticed for the first time a red sash around his waist. It struck a cord of remembrance in him, but he couldn't place it. Could it be he knew this man? And if so, from where?

"Wake him up," Billy ordered. He unlocked the door, and Josh went in.

"Come on," Josh urged, shaking the man by the shoulder. "Time for breakfast."

The man snorted and mumbled, then smacked his lips together and exhaled heavily. His dirty clothes, stale breath, and other assorted offensive odors drove Josh back, and he retreated from the cell. Billy laughed, set the tray down inside the cell, and shut the door so hard the noise startled their guest, and he jumped out of the bed, much the same as Josh had done. But he was used to waking up in strange places, and his first act was to head for the metal pot in the corner.

"When you're done, your breakfast is ready," Billy told him. The man mumbled an answer and waved them off as they retreated to the office.

Billy divided up the rest of the food, and he and Josh ate heartily, engaging in general discussions about the weather, the prospects for growth in Bodie, and the price of tea in Chinatown. Billy noted that it was cheaper than in the general store, but that was because the Chinese had an edge.

Josh commented, as he mopped up some maple syrup with the remains of a biscuit, that their prisoner looked familiar somehow.

"How can that be?" Billy inquired, washing down his meal with a long draft of dark, hot coffee.

"Don't know," Josh admitted. "Can we find out who he is?"

"Ah think we have an obligation before we let him go to do jus' that," Billy said. He wiped his mouth and put his napkin on the tray, then pushed away from the desk. Josh followed him into the cells.

"Ah," said the man looking up. "That was a fine meal, to be sure. My compliments to the chef. And I do appreciate the bed for the night. Uh, may I ask what I did?"

"You tried to steal my horse," Josh said.

"I did? Oh, that's most unfortunate. I'm sorry, I can assure you. The last thing I remember is sitting down at the faro table in . . . in one of your finer establishments. The name eludes me at the moment."

"So does yours," Josh said. "Who are you?"

"Oh, so we weren't introduced. My apologies. My name is William Severe. And despite my momentary lack of immediate recall of all the details of the previous evening, I'm quite sure I wasn't really trying to steal your horse."

Josh was disappointed. The name didn't mean anything to him. Severe continued his repartee.

"I believe it's safe to assume I was intoxicated. Is that a fair assessment?" He glanced down at his bespoiled shirt. "Either that or I suffered a short but rather harsh bout with the influenza."

"Drunk as a skunk," Billy said dryly.

"Are you the sheriff, then?" Severe asked. "We don't have too many Negro sheriffs where I come from."

"Just fillin' in. Deputy Page is out of town."

"Ah. Well, as they say, it must be time for me to go." He felt around his waist. "My pistols—I assume you will release them to me now that I'm myself again."

"You didn't have any," Billy said.

"They tossed you out," Josh told him, "and you climbed immediately onto my nag. You wasn't armed."

Severe sat on the edge of the bed with a dour expression, thinking. "I must've lost them in a game," he lamented finally. "Again. Well, I'll just have to find the man I lost them to and convince him to give them back."

"Ah think it best you catch the first ride out of town you can finagle," Billy told him. "Bodie don't need your kind."

"Not very hospitable," Severe said. "But I can't say as I blame you. However, I must inform you that, near as I can tell, this is a free country, and as I'm doing no one any harm, I shall leave as soon as I recover my pistols. They are quite special to me."

"So special you gambled them away?" Josh pointed out.

Severe laughed. "Ah, but I didn't expect to lose, you see. I seldom do."

"Seldom lose or seldom expect to?"

"Both, I assure you."

Josh and Billy let that one go, even though Severe'd already admitted having lost his pistols gambling at least once before. Billy opened the door.

"We ain't mean people here," Billy said. "But this is a hard town, and we don't cotton to troublemakers. Your inebriation last night notwithstandin', you tried stealin' this man's horse. Should y'all prove to be troublesome again, he just might reconsider wantin' to prosecute you."

"That would be sad, indeed," Severe said. "Very well. I'll locate my pistols, then leave town immediately, walking if I have to. Fair enough?"

Billy nodded. "Okay by me. Josh?"

"Yeah, sure," Josh said. Then he asked, "Mr. Severe, do I know you?"

"You do now. But I don't recall we've ever met. You ever been to Abilene, Kansas? Or Springfield, Missouri?"

"No."

"Then I doubt it." He stepped out and straightened his garments as best he could, slicking his greasy hair back and replacing his hat. Billy called him by name. When he looked at the temporary lawman, O'Hara flipped him a coin.

"For a bath and laundry," Billy said. "Not a bottle."

"Wise advice," Severe said. "I'll heed it." He winked at Josh and strode out of the jailhouse into the bright, cool morning.

Billy closed the door.

"Bet he drinks it," he said.

Josh just shrugged. "I don't know enough about people to figure it one way or the other."

Billy sat back down at the desk. "So what are you going to do? Ah have no idea when Matth—er, Deputy Page will be back. Do you know who you're lookin' for?"

"No, not really. Three men with our gold, that's about all. Oh, and this." He remembered the lump of lead in his pocket and pulled it out, holding it up so Billy could see it clearly. "One of 'em packin' a gun that'd shoot a bullet like this." He flipped it to Billy.

"This the one what did it?" he asked reverently.

"Yeah."

"Hmm. Looks like a .44 or .45 from the size of it. That don't help much."

"It rules out men with .32s."

"True enough," Billy admitted. "Now you narrowed it down to half the men in this part of the state. Course, if them three stick together, they'll stick out like sore thumbs. If they split up, y'all have to keep an eye out for men who are suddenly rich, who don't necessarily fit in. Stands to reason they're not from too far away. Think they might be in Bodie?"

"They headed this way according to the tracks they left on the road below our place. Should've got here the day before I did."

"Tell you what. Ah'll spread the word around. Maybe someone saw them. If they kept goin', they could be halfway to Bishop by now or past Bridgeport if'n they went that direction. But let's make sure they ain't here first. Ah'd hate to lose them if they're right under our noses. Ah'll start now, canvas the saloons. You do what you want, and Ah'll meet you at the Quicksilver at noon for lunch." Billy rose, the chair groaning as his bulk was eased off of it, and grabbed his Sharp's.

"Thanks, Billy," Josh said.

"Aw, you're welcome son. What're friends for?" Billy cuffed him on the back and left the building.

Josh wandered through town, looking at everyone he saw with a critical eye, trying to imagine them holding the gun that shot his father. A few regarded him back with puzzled looks, and Josh glanced away, embarrassed. He saw Billy once or twice as the man went from one saloon or business or mine office to the next, but Billy just shook his head and kept going.

Josh checked on his horse, then wandered into the stage office. The clerk greeted him.

"Need a ticket out? That seems to be the popular thing these days. Not too many jobs opening up, things are leveling off in the mines."

"No, I'm not ready to leave," Josh said. "I'm looking for three men. Did anyone buy tickets out yesterday or the day before?"

"Like I said, I've been busy. Can you be more specific?"

"Well, there were three of them. They might have left together or separate, I don't know. Maybe only one of them left, maybe none of them. They might have paid with gold."

"We did have one gent pay for his ticket with gold dust," the clerk said. "As I recall, he bought a ticket for Los Angeles. No, two tickets. He mentioned something about a lady going with him."

"His wife?"

"I assume so, but he didn't say, and I didn't ask. None of my business, you know?"

Josh nodded.

"Why the big interest?" the clerk asked.

"Three men killed my pa, stole our gold. We have a mine up the road a piece."

"I'm sorry to hear that. Oop, here comes the stage. I've got to greet it, help unload. Excuse me." The clerk walked around the counter. Josh followed him outside, watching with idle curiosity as the passengers disembarked. One woman got off, a fair, slender gal with a ready smile who had the look of a rough life about her, the kind Josh imagined would come to a woman of ill repute. The rest of the passengers were men of different sorts. Two obviously were miners, one a dandy-looking fellow wearing a brocaded vest with a gold watch chain hanging between the pockets and a black derby. His thin mustache and demeanor spoke loudly of gambler, even to the uninitiated Josh Bodine.

The next man out Josh recognized and, for a second, gaped at him in disbelief. Then his eyes caught Josh's, and they both adopted questioning looks.

"Jeff?" Josh said, his way of asking his brother what he was doing here.

Jeff shrugged and stepped down from the stage, picking up his bag that had been tossed down from the top. Jeff wore his best suit—

his only suit—a black three-piece that was just a trifle too small and a strange, black hat with narrow brim. The knot of his tie was cock-eyed under his chin. He looked ridiculous, and Josh stifled a laugh.

"What are you doing?" he asked his elder brother.

Jeff sighed and set down his bag. "I got to thinkin' about it and decided you might be right. We can't work it by ourselves. I certainly can't work it alone. I brought the deed. Maybe we can sell it."

"You thought I wasn't coming back, didn't you?"

"Were you?" Jeff caught the challenge and flung it back at Josh.

"Probably not. I hadn't thought that far ahead, actually. But I know I don't have a future there."

Jeff looked around at Bodie. "And here?"

"I'd like to get as far away from here as possible, but I don't have any money. Looks like I'm stuck for a while." It was an open invitation for Jeff to offer a solution, but he didn't respond. Instead, he ignored the comment and inquired as to Josh's progress.

"Nothing, so far. Uncle Billy—you remember him?—he's doing some checking for me. Somebody had to have seen them three."

"Not if they rode in and kept going right on through," Jeff offered.

"How'd you get on the stage?" Josh said suddenly. "Don't you have to have a ticket?"

"I was walking. Stage stopped when it passed me, and the driver said he'd take me in. Said this wasn't good country to be out in on foot. Listen, I'm pretty tired. Where're you staying?"

"Nowhere. I'm broke."

"Excuse me?"

"I've got a couple dollars is all, and I'm trying to hold on to it as long as I can."

"It's about time."

"Enough about that, brother. Unless you want your hat pulled down around your eyes."

"Oh yeah? By you and who else?"

"I don't need no help to take you, Jeff. You might be older, but you ain't bigger or stronger."

Jeff locked onto his brother's eyes and began peeling off his coat. "That's it, little brother. Time to have us a showdown."

Josh didn't wait for a second invitation. While Jeff's arms were both entangled in the coat, he lashed out with a right jab and caught the surprised man on the chin. The older brother went down like a sack of grain falling off the back of a wagon.

It was over before it started. Jeff lay prone on his back in the street as a crowd gathered. There were shouts of "Fight! Fight!," which drew even more people, but they were soon disappointed as Billy pushed through the crowd like a freight train through a herd of chickens. He looked at Josh, then down at his opponent, then back up at Josh.

"Is he one of them?"

Josh shook his head as he flexed his right hand. "Naw, that's Jeff, my brother."

"Your bro—what're you doing deckin' your brother?"

"We got to arguin', and he asked for it." Josh shrugged. "He's been askin' for it for years. Up till now Pa always stepped in."

Jeff groaned, and Billy stepped over to see to him.

"I'll take care of him," Josh said, moving in. "He's my brother." He bent over and helped Jeff up, picking up his hat and plopping it on his head. Josh pulled his brother's coat back up over his shoulders.

"That was the cheater's way," Jeff said angrily, his eyes narrow. He rubbed his jaw, and the crowd began thinning.

"Time you learned a thing or two about living in the real world," Josh told him. "It ain't always fair. Don't ever forget that. Now that's settled, what are we going to do? Where are we going to stay?"

"I don't have much money, either," Jeff admitted.

"Ain't you two somethin'," Billy said with a shake of his head. "You come to town full of vinegar, but you don't have two nickels to rub together."

"I've got the deed to the place," Jeff said. "Maybe we can find a buyer."

Billy was thoughtful. "Tell you what. You meet me over to the Quicksilver. Order some lunch. Tell Sarah it's on me. I'll be along in a few minutes. And try to keep from fighting until I get there."

He turned and hurried off.

"The Quicksilver?" Jeff queried.

"The deputy sheriff, Matt Page . . . his wife runs it," Josh explained. "Best restaurant in town."

Jeff nodded and bent over to pick up his bag. "If my jaw still works," he complained.

Josh began walking. "It ain't stopped you from talkin'," he mumbled.

CHAPTER

FIFTEEN

THE BODINES TRUDGED into the Quicksilver without having spoken to each other the entire way. Jeff, wearing his outgrown suit and carrying his bag, looked around with wonder at the town that had grown so much since he'd seen it last. He stared at the women who passed by and peered with curiosity into the saloons. He commented to Josh—although it drew no response—about the volume of the stamp batteries on the nearby hill being so much louder than their own had been.

Sarah came out from the kitchen as they were taking their seats and gave them the same genuine smile she gave all strangers. Jeff noticed her pale-yellow taffeta dress and the way her curls fell onto her forehead and found himself staring at her until Josh poked him in the ribs with an elbow.

"Afternoon, Miss Sarah," Josh said, removing his hat. He left it off, tossing it onto a chair at an empty table next to him. She raised her eyebrows in mild surprise.

"Excuse me, have we met?" She thought she knew just about everybody in town, except for each day's new arrivals, and these men, especially the man carrying his bag who had obviously just arrived, would have no reason to know her.

"It's me, Josh. Josh Bodine." He stood up, and Jeff followed suit, taking off his cap and holding it in two hands in front of him, then cleared his throat. "Oh," Josh continued, "and this is my brother Jeff."

The recognition came to her and she grinned. "Oh my goodness gracious. Please forgive me, Josh, but you look so different than you did at the wedding, so . . . grown up. I'm sorry, I didn't mean it like that. But it's true. And this is Jeff, your brother? Nice to meet you again." She wiped her hand on her apron and held it out. Jeff took it, embarrassed as he touched her soft hand. It brought back memories of his mother.

"Good day, ma'am."

Sarah giggled, not at all bothered about being called ma'am, even though these brothers were only a few years younger than she. Sarah had heard it plenty of times recently, even from men twice her age. It went with the territory of running a restaurant and being the wife of the town's lawman.

"Please, sit down. This is a restaurant, not my parlor. If you wait for me to sit, you'll be standing all day." The Bodines looked at each other and slowly took their seats just as the door opened and a gust of cold air drove in two more hungry diners.

"Hey, Sarah," Uncle Billy said with a grin, stepping quickly inside. "I see you met up with my guests." He advanced to the table, followed by Jacob Page, who had also entered.

"Afternoon, Billy. Jacob." Sarah nodded. "Coffee?"

"Course," Billy said. "How 'bout the Bodines?"

"Yes, sir!" Jeff said, and Josh echoed the request.

Soon they were all seated around the table, warming themselves with Sarah's steaming black brew, into which Jeff Bodine and Jacob Page stirred several spoons of sugar and Billy dissolved a schooner of cream. Only Josh drank it unadulterated.

In a few minutes plates of hot food were set before them by Sarah and Rosa, and they ate like they hadn't eaten in days. Josh ate quickest of all, to his brother's chagrin.

"You might consider slowing down to chew," Jeff told him quietly.

With a full mouth, Josh answered. "You might consider minding your own business." He returned his attention to his plate and continued his efforts unabated.

As they were diving into their apple pie, Jacob Page turned the conversation in a new direction.

"Yeah, I'm real sorry 'bout yer pa. It's quite a man kin run a private mine and mill like yers. Takes a heap a innards to stick it out that long."

"Both of you boys, too," Billy said. "And Ah don't mean it like you're boys, 'cause you're men. Real men."

Josh shrugged. "It's what we had to do. Ain't no big deal." He glanced at Jeff in his too-small suit and snickered to himself, thinking, *He don't look much like a man.* But Josh said nothing.

"Well," Jacob Page said, leaning back in his chair, "Billy tells me yer in need of a stake, since yer all tapped out now that they stole your savings."

"Jeff can't run the place by himself," Josh added, the obvious implication being that he wasn't planning on staying and helping.

Jeff made a comment to that effect, but it was colored by a twinge in his voice. Josh ignored it.

"Well, seein's how that's the case," Jacob continued, "you two needin' a stake and havin' that property, with its house and mill and ev'rything, seems like what you need is a buyer."

Josh perked up. "You know someone?"

"Well, I jes' might. There's someone I know who's lookin' fer a place just like that, some place he can call his own without havin' to put a lot of work in it right off, and where he can work the mine at his leisure. If'n it pays off, that's okay, but if it don't, well, he'd be happy jes' to live there."

Josh was excited. Jeff was not overly pleased but resigned to it.

"What do they propose?" the elder Bodine asked, wresting control of the negotiations by right of his earlier birth.

"What do you believe to be a fair price?" Billy asked.

Jeff shook his head. "I hadn't thought about it, actually." He furrowed his brow, then came up with a figure.

Jacob whistled. "That includin' everything?"

"Everything 'cept our personal things, which we can get later." He looked at Josh, who shrugged and nodded.

"Sounds fair," Josh said.

Jacob looked at Billy, who dipped his head one time. "Yep, sounds fair."

"Okay," Jacob said. He reached into his coat pocket and pulled out a piece of paper and some crumpled bills. "Here's my promissory note . . . We can settle it later at the bank once you've gotten the deed . . . and here's five hundred dollars earnest money." He handed Jeff the currency and wrote something on the paper, then signed it with a flourish, sliding it across to Jeff. Jeff took the bills and stared at them with mixed emotions. Josh was delighted and snatched the promissory note from the table when Page let it go.

"We're in business," he said to Jeff.

"What do you mean, 'We're in business'?"

"Now we don't have to worry about what we're gonna eat. We can concentrate on catchin' the men who killed Pa."

"There you go, goin' off half-cocked again."

"Not this time, brother. I been thinkin' about this real deep, and it's something we got to do."

"Revenge is a hard thing," Billy O'Hara cautioned. "It can take a man over, make him do things outside the law, possess him."

"It's not revenge," Josh said. "It's justice. Our pa was murdered, our gold stolen."

"Yeah, but what's your plan?" Jacob Page asked. "What're you gonna do with them men when you find them . . . if you find them?"

"That's up to them," Josh said. "It's now my intention to bring them in to stand trial. They'll decide if I do that or not."

"You're gonna need help," Billy said. "Ah really think it'd be good if y'all wait till Matt returns."

"And when will that be?" Josh asked. Billy shrugged, and Josh said, "The longer we wait, the harder it'll be to catch them. I need to start now."

Jeff sighed audibly. "I better go with him," he said, "if only to keep him out of trouble. Goodness knows I don't have anything else to do now."

Billy nodded. "Can't go lookin' like that," he said. "We need to get you some decent clothes and a horse."

"And a gun," Josh pointed out.

Jeff shook his head. "No gun, Josh. You know how I feel about that."

"I ain't askin' you to become a gunfighter," Josh said. "It's for protection."

"We'll see," was all Jeff would say.

After lunch, the four men told Sarah good-bye and ventured again out into Bodie's cold streets. Jeff complained about having to lug his bag all over town, so Billy took them to a hotel, where the Bodines rented a room. Jacob had to return to the Bodie Unified Mine, where he worked as supervisor, and Billy, due to his capacity as temporary deputy, was summoned to a minor problem on Bonanza Street regarding a woman who had knifed an unruly customer. Something about an unpaid bill.

Josh and Jeff stopped at the bank to exchange one of their larger bills for something smaller and more easily passed, then Josh took his brother to the general store for some new clothes.

Jeff picked a new pair of Levi's, a cotton shirt, and a decent hat and coat, while Josh added a long slicker and new Stetson to his wardrobe. Both of them dropped their old garb into a refuse basket outside the front door.

At the gunsmith, which Josh practically dragged Jeff into, the clerk displayed several weapons. Jeff disliked even the idea of considering a firearm but was ultimately convinced of its utility.

"Bottom line," Josh said, "is you can always leave it holstered if you don't want to pull it, but you'll be mighty sorry if you reach for it to protect yourself and you don't grab anything but air."

Reluctantly, Jeff agreed, and settled on a small Smith and Wesson self-cocking .38 that tucked nicely into his belt. He waved off a holster, saying that was just looking for trouble, wearing it openly like that.

"Suit yourself," Josh said with a shrug. They took their gear and left the shop, heading down for the livery to check on Josh's horse and get one for Jeff.

The big doors were open, and they wandered inside. Josh's horse wasn't visible. In fact, only one horse was in the building, waiting to get a new set of shoes. The blacksmith was in an office, smoking a hand-rolled cheroot and reading the town newspaper. He saw the Bodines and called out his window for the stable boy, who was apparently in the corral out back, to come in and see what they wanted. In a moment a lad of ten or eleven, wearing scruffy pants, dirty shirt and coat, weathered hat with a torn brim and a crushed crown, trotted in. His shoelaces were untied.

"My name's William," he said with a smile revealing a couple of missing teeth. "What can I do for you?"

"Why ain't you in school, Billy?" Jeff asked impulsively.

"Aren't," William corrected. "And I go by William. Billy's a kid's name. You the truant officer?

"I don't think Bodie has one, William," Josh said. "We're here about a couple horses. One of 'em's mine. The dappled—"

"Oh, yeah. The quiet one. Just stands there. She's out back." He jerked a thumb over his shoulder. "Wait, didn't Mr. Porter bring him in for Mr. O'Hara?"

"Yes, he did," Josh said. "As a favor to me. You got my saddle put away nice?"

"Yep, all polished up with saddle soap, too. I, uh . . . ." He suddenly realized something that disturbed him, and he looked down, pawing the ground with his feet.

"Something wrong?" Josh asked, worried. "Come on, you can tell me. Someone steal my gear?"

"Oh, no, nothing like that. I, uh . . . when I took your saddlebags down, I dropped them, and a magazine fell out. I kept it and have been reading it. I hope you don't mind. I was going to put it back, honest. I—"

"Whoa, partner, calm down. It's okay. So, you read my magazine?"

He nodded, still keeping his head down.

"Which one?"

He reached inside his coat and pulled the folded magazine out from the back of his pants, extending it toward Josh, who took it. Jeff immediately plucked it from his brother's hand and glanced at the cover. A gunfighter with long, black hair hanging out from under a dark hat was simultaneously firing two silver pistols at another gunfighter in the middle of the street as townspeople looked on from the boardwalks. The other man was clutching his chest as his gun dropped from his limp hand.

"Oh, brother," Jeff mumbled.

"Shoot, kid," said Josh, "you can have it. I've read it several times."

He looked up. "Thanks, mister. It's real exciting. I hope you're not mad." He reached up and took it from Jeff, sticking it back in his pants.

Josh pulled the boy's hat down to his eyes. "Shucks, William, I don't mind. That's kinda why I brought it."

Jeff had been looking at his brother with a smirk. "You actually brought your magazines?"

Josh shrugged. "Why not? Something to do when I get bored."

Jeff just shook his head. "Don't you pay them magazines no mind, William. Them are just stories. They ain't real."

"I want to be in one someday," William said proudly. "Like Wild Bill."

"You stay in school, get a good job. That's the only way to get by in this world," Jeff instructed the kid. "Now, down to business. I need to buy a horse," he told William. "Cheap one."

"Oh, we got a good, cheap one. You can ride him all day, just so long as you aren't in a hurry. If you hurry him up, he won't go all day. He's kinda old, horse-wise, but he comes with a saddle."

"I'll take him. How much?"

"Twelve dollars, plus two bits."

"What's the two bits for?"

"Me. It's what I get when I sell something."

Jeff smiled. "Okay. Bring him on up. Let me take a look. No need saddling him, we ain't leaving just yet."

"Okay!" William whooped and ran out to the back corral, returning in a few minutes pulling a mangy-looking beast that snorted and tried to shake off the lad, to no avail.

Josh moved forward casually and stroked the horse on its velvet nose. When it didn't draw back or try to snort his hand away, he lifted its top lip to check its gum line. "Kind of long in the tooth, don't you think?" he asked the boy.

"I already told you he was old. 'Sides, what do you want for twelve bucks?"

Josh grinned. "He's perfect. Any more horse and my brother here would spend more time gettin' back on than he would ridin'."

Jeff glared at him but couldn't contradict. He hadn't ridden that much, preferring to take the buckboard, especially since most of his trips involved bringing back supplies.

"Let's see the saddle," Josh said. "See if it'll fit Jeff's backside."

William led the horse into a stall and forked him a wad of hay. The horse stood without being tied, indifferently munching the alfalfa.

"By the way, his name is Polo," William said as he made his way to the nearby tack room. "Don't know why."

William soon emerged with the sorriest saddle any of them had ever seen, but since between them they hadn't seen that many, they figured it was okay, and Jeff handed over the twelve dollars. The boy thanked them. Josh told him they'd be by in the morning to ride out and would square up then with the storage and care fees, and the boy ran into the office of the blacksmith, who had watched the scene with apparent disinterest but a sharp, calculating eye. He laughed when the boy told the whole story, but the Bodines didn't hear it. They were already outside and walking to their hotel, both of them tired from their trips and slightly befuddled by the turn of events the past few days. Although neither of them spoke it, the future for them was very uncertain and not a little frightening.

As they were passing the Shortbranch Saloon, a disturbance inside attracted their attention. Josh immediately diverted and went for a look. Jeff was several steps past the place before he noticed that Josh was no longer with him.

"Wha—? Josh? Where are you?" He stopped and craned his neck, then retreated to the saloon and peeked in. A beer mug flew past his head and bounced once on the dirt before hitting a rock and bursting apart. Josh was standing inside the door and noticed his brother, then grabbed him by the sleeve and dragged him inside out of harm's way.

A fight was in progress. One of the combatants was a gambler, the kind of man who stayed in a gold camp only long enough to relieve a goodly number of folks of their money, then slip away during the night before they could get their hands on him, catch a ride to the next camp, and start over. In fact, it was the man in the vest who had been on the stage with Jeff.

His opponent was a familiar figure to Josh: a tall, long-haired vagrant whose clothes and person looked no cleaner than they had when Billy had released him from jail.

The purpose of the fight seemed obvious, so Josh didn't ask. Men stood in a circle around them, cheering them on and encouraging their favorite, although neither man seemed to have achieved a majority. A vagrant fighting a gambler: who could be the favorite? Many of the spectators, in fact, were probably hoping for a draw . . . a dead draw. The kind where both parties jerk pistols and fill each other full of lead at close range while holding the other by the lapels so innocent bystanders didn't get hurt.

But it was not to be. The vagrant was apparently unarmed. He reached inside his coat a couple times to great anticipation, but both times came out empty. Since he wasn't heeled, someone on the fringe managed to finger the gambler's revolver while he was occupied in a stranglehold so he couldn't murder the vagrant. This was destined to be a fistfight.

And it was soon over. The vagrant gave his opponent a few good licks, and the well-dressed gambler toppled like a man with no spine onto the sawdust-covered plank floor. In his victory salute to the adoring fans, William Severe turned a full circle in place and held his arms out, his smile wide. It was when he momentarily faced the Bodines that Jeff grabbed his brother's arm.

"Ouch," Josh complained. "What're you doin'?"

"That man," Jeff said, lowering his voice and leaning toward his brother. "Do you know who that is?"

"Yes, I do, as a matter of fact."

"You do?" Jeff was incredulous.

"Of course. That's William Severe."

"No, it ain't."

"What are you talkin' about?"

"He's on the cover of your *Beadle's* magazine, the one you gave the kid."

Josh looked at his brother suspiciously. "What? Are you sure?"

"Yeah. I didn't read the name, but he looks just like the picture. You know, the guy with two silver guns, wearing a black hat and long coat and a red sash?"

Josh was thunderstruck. He abruptly turned without a word and ran back to Bonney's livery and, as he came into view of it, began calling little William. Jeff ran along behind him, and when he entered the stable, Josh was already there, William running in from the back.

"If it's about the horse, my pa says it's too late, the deal's done."

"Naw, it ain't about that," Josh said. "Let me see the magazine I gave you."

"You takin' it back?"

"No, just need to see it." William handed it over slowly, suspiciously, and Josh snatched it out of his little hand. He unfolded it and there, on the cover, just as Jeff had said, was William Severe in a showdown.

"See?" Jeff told him, looking over his shoulder.

Josh scanned the caption, incredulous. No wonder the man looked familiar. He read out loud, reverently, "With dual pistols blazing, he ends the career of another desperado. Outlaws have given him the nickname William Severe because he is merciless in dealing with their treachery, but the rest of the nation knows him as Wild Bill Hickok."

Josh looked up from the magazine at his brother, his eyes wide, then narrowing as he began calculating.

"I thought I recognized him. Do you realize what this means?"

Jeff stared at his brother. "No, I don't. Why does it mean something?"

"Wild Bill. In the flesh!"

"Maybe. We don't know it's him. Could be someone pretending to be him. Besides, what if it is really him? He's a far sight different in real life than he is in those stories. I told you they were nothing but—"

"Don't start, Jeff. I'll bet you didn't think any of these people in here were real." He held the magazine aloft and shook it. "Here's your proof, right here."

"If that's him," Jeff cautioned his younger brother, "it might just be some guy trying to cash in on fame that ain't his."

"Yeah," said Josh. "Well, if that's true, then why ain't he goin' around town claiming to be Wild Bill? Seems to me he's not too anxious to have people know it."

"Okay, maybe you're right. But if that's so, then he's not going to be real excited to have you talkin' to him."

Josh grinned. "Oh, I think he'll listen."

"And how do you figure that, little brother?"

"He owes me."

"This I gotta hear."

Josh smiled. "I caught him tryin' to steal my horse. I can hold that over his head."

Jeff snorted. "So much for him being a hero. Furthermore, why would you want to ask him for help? What can he possibly do for us? Sounds like he's just a common drunk and horse thief."

"You may think he ain't much," Josh said, "and maybe he ain't. But he's better than nuthin', which is what we got now."

Josh tossed the magazine back to the wide-eyed William, who watched his brother as he strode out of the stable, a new spring in his step, born of hope and a vision. Jeff shook his head, then sighed and followed him out.

"Take care of our nags," he told the boy.

William nodded enthusiastically, staring after the Bodines, then down at Wild Bill's picture on the cover of *Beadle's*. He couldn't believe he was taking care of the horses of two friends of Wild Bill Hickok, and they'd given him twenty-five cents to boot. Wild Bill! What a day this had been!

CHAPTER

SIXTEEN

THE BODINE BROTHERS TRUDGED AGAIN up the street. Josh was disappointed, for upon returning to the Short Branch, Wild Bill was no longer there, and no one knew where he'd gone.

The sky was darkening, now that the sun had receded behind the Sierra-Nevadas, and the deep blue was streaked with purples and reds. A storm was coming in from the east, rolling clouds fronted by a thick fog that had already obliterated the road to Aurora. It could be raining or snowing within the hour.

"I'm hungry," Josh informed his brother.

"It ain't often I side with you, Josh, but I got to this time. Where shall we go?"

"How 'bout the Quicksilver? Deputy Page's wife is a mighty fine cook."

"Suits me. We gonna find this Hickok fella first?"

Josh shrugged and slowed down to look around. "Where? He might be difficult to locate right now, and I'm starving."

Even as he said this, a brawl erupted in a saloon across the street. Shouting and the crash of furniture and glasses spewed from the place, along with several patrons who wanted no part of it.

Jeff looked at Josh with disdain. Josh smiled sheepishly and shrugged, and they both walked toward the saloon without comment. They'd located their man.

Pushing their way through the doors, they spied Hickok right away, squaring off against his opponent, both fists raised in classic boxing style. But he wavered, and his eyelids drooped. His adversary wasn't so disabled, however, and he pushed up his sleeves to expose sinewy arms in preparation for pounding Hickok into a lump of dough. Josh knew that if they didn't do something—and do it quick—they'd never be able to hire Hickok to help them. You can't track desperadoes if you're lying on your back watching stars float around your head.

Josh lurched in between the men and held his hands up.

"Hold on, you two. Whatever's at the bottom of this, isn't there some way we can solve it peaceably?"

"No!" twenty men shouted at once. Hickok's opponent made his two eyebrows into one.

"Get outta the way, kid, or I'll make mincemeat outa you, too."

"What does he owe you?" Josh pleaded. "I'll pay it. He's drunk. He don't mean nuthin'."

"Yes, I did," Hickok slurred. "I meant every word. He's a liar and a cheat."

The man lunged at Hickok, but Josh stepped in the way and played like he was holding Hickok back, then warned Wild Bill's opponent.

"Listen, slick," the man growled, "get your carcass away from here, or you'll feel the sting of my anger as well."

"Is that all this is about, an insult?" Jeff asked from the fringe. He wandered out into the arena. "My brother told you, this man's drunk." He smiled a devilish smile. "And lucky for you, too. If he was himself, you'd be on your way to the doc's, being carried by your friends. Do you know who this is?" He pointed to Hickok.

"No!" Josh said. "Don't tell them." He didn't want anyone getting the idea that they could make a name for themselves by taking out the infamous Wild Bill Hickok.

Jeff turned to Josh and gave him a wink. "No, brother, I've got to. If I don't, I'll never be able to live with myself. Why, what would I tell this man's—" He cut himself off and leaned toward the fighter. "Your name?"

"Peevey."

"You married, Mr. Peevey?"

"Uh . . . yes, I am." He was so baffled by the question that he forgot about the fight and kept his eyes locked on Jeff.

"As I was saying, what would I tell this man's widow if I just stand here and let Pistol Pete have his way with him? It just wouldn't be right."

"Pistol Pete?" the man said. The crowd passed the name around reverently.

"That's right. Oh, you might knock him down once, Mr. Peevey. But you'd regret it. Pistol Pete is so quick on the draw and so deadly a shot that even when he's drunk as a skunk, there's no man alive a match for him, not even . . . not even Wild Bill Hickok."

Josh nearly swallowed his tongue.

"He's so good, he don't even need his own pistols. He'll use yours." Jeff pointed to a bystander. "Or yours."

"Or mine," Josh said with a smile. "Pistol Pete, Junior, at your service."

In a swift, fluid motion, Josh slipped the leather thong from the hammer of his pistol and drew it, spinning it on his finger, then cocking it and placing the muzzle against Peevey's forehead, square between the eyes. Peevey gulped audibly.

"And I ain't even begun to learn what my daddy can teach me," Josh said quietly with a menacing grin. "Ma sent me to bring him home for supper, so if you'll all kindly make way, we'll head on out." He smiled again and waved the gun casually around the room, clearing a path as he did so. The dumbfounded Hickok let himself be led out, posturing as he did by raising to his full height, as much as the booze would allow, and glaring from man to man.

Once outside they lost no time packing Hickok away, dragging him directly to the Quicksilver and sticking him in a chair with a pot of hot coffee in front of him. They ordered from the large, smiling woman, and soon three steaks with all the trimmings were set before them.

"Thanks, Jeff," Josh said as they dug in, watching Hickok struggle with the knife and fork. Jeff reached over and plucked the knife from his hand, then cut the man's meat.

"I did it for Pa," Jeff said. "That was a durn fool thing, butting in there like that."

"I couldn't let him get clobbered," Josh said, cramming a forkful of mashed potatoes and gravy into his mouth.

Hickok ate greedily, the fringe on his buckskin coat brushing his mashed potatoes as he reached across them for the bread. He largely disregarded his hosts, flicking a peek at them from time to time but snapping his eyes away when one of the Bodines looked at him. He gave Rosa a more serious eye on several occasions, and once Josh noticed the corners of his mouth flicker up as she refilled his mug with hot, black coffee.

Josh eyed him now and then, sometimes with admiration, sometimes disgust, but always with a wary glint that revealed his apprehension. After downing a fifth cup of coffee in a single gulp, Hickok leaned back and patted his stomach. His bloodshot eyes were keener than they had been earlier, and his speech seemed to be clearing.

"Well, gentlemen, that was a right tasty meal. It seems I owe you for the trouble, but for the life of me, I can't understand why you'd want to come to my aid. Nor, for that matter, why you thought you needed to in the first place. Not that I was willing to look a gift horse in the mouth, mind you."

"You remember me?" Josh asked.

Hickok leaned forward and squinted.

"Great, he's near blind," Jeff mumbled. Josh ignored him.

"You look familiar," Hickok answered. "Care to refresh my memory, or will I be sorry to have seen you?"

"That all depends," Josh said.

"On what? Oh, thank you darling," he said to Rosa as she filled his mug. She set a hunk of apple pie in front of him, which he attacked.

"On how you feel about what we aim to propose."

Hickok stopped eating and stared at them a moment as if sizing them up. Then his brow furrowed.

"So this was all just to propose something to me, is that it?"

"We need the help of someone like you," Josh explained. "Someone who can track and fight and shoot . . . if necessary, of course," he added, seeing the look his brother gave him.

"Hired gun. Is that what you aim to make me?"

"Not at all," Jeff quickly interjected. "We need someone who can help us find three men and bring them to justice."

Hickok chewed thoughtfully. "Too bad," he said. "I wouldn't mind being a hired gun. This bringing to justice stuff doesn't set well with me."

Josh lowered his eyebrows and gave Jeff a disgusted look.

"What'd these fellers do?" Hickok continued.

Josh smiled. He was interested.

"Killed our pa."

"In cold blood or in a fair fight?"

"Does it make a difference?"

"Yep."

"Cold blood. In our house. It was a murder."

"Where were you two galoots?"

"In the mine—" Jeff began, but Josh kicked him under the table. It was too late, though; the cat was out of the bag.

"You fellers own a mine?" Hickok asked.

"Owned," Josh corrected. "We sold it."

"So, these three men—did they just murder your pa, or did they murder your pa and steal your gold?"

The looks on their faces alone answered that question.

"You got any idea who did this deed? We need to start somewhere."

Josh shook his head. "No, we don't cl—"

"I got an idea," Jeff said.

"Huh?" said Josh, whipping his head toward his brother.

"I meant to tell you before but never had the chance. I got to thinkin' about it after you left. It must've been Jim Wheeler. That's why I came to Bodie, Josh, to tell you that."

"Who's Jim Wheeler?" Hickok asked.

"Hired hand we had for a spell while Josh was away. Pa let him go when Josh came back a little sooner than expected. He wasn't too happy about it."

"Did he threaten you?"

Jeff shook his head slowly. "No, he didn't. Just took his pay and left peaceful."

"Hmm," mused Hickok. "The quiet ones, they're usually the worst kind. The big mouths, like Peevey, they're all talk. So, let me get this straight. Three men kill your pa—Jim Wheeler, let's assume, and two friends—they took your gold and rode thisaway, I presume. How long ago this happen?"

"Two days."

"Where's this Mr. Wheeler live?"

"Bodie," Jeff said. "But he spent time in Lundy, too."

"And you want me to help you find him."

Josh nodded. "Him and his friends."

"Why should I?"

Josh cleared his throat. "Well, Mr. Hickok—"

"Name's Severe."

"Wild Bill Hickok, also known by his enemies as William Severe because of his harsh treatment of criminals," Josh quoted.

Hickok was quiet and stared at Josh, so long that Josh began to get uncomfortable, but soon a smile began to work at the corners of his mouth, visible even under the heavy mustache he'd grown many years before to disguise his long, dropping nose and protruding upper lip.

"All right then, have it your way. But what makes you think I'll do it, even if I say I am Hickok?"

"It's either that," Josh said confidently, "or you go to jail for trying to steal my horse."

The memory, foggy as it was, returned to Hickok, and he set down his fork and leaned back in the chair.

"Seems you got the drop on me," he said. "Okay, I'll do it."

"Thank you, Mr. Hickok," Josh said excitedly.

"But for a price. You can't expect me to go traipsin' all over the country, riskin' my life to recover your gold, without some kind of compensation. Plus I need a horse . . . obviously." He smiled. "And a couple sidearms of my own choice. You buy the horse and guns up front, we'll settle on the rest later, but it'll be in direct proportion to the danger involved. No less than . . . say, ten percent of the total we recover."

"Deal!" Josh said.

"Wait a minute!" Jeff said. "How do we know he can even live up to his part of the bargain?"

Hickok was amused. "Seems to me you don't have any alternatives, or you would've already exercised 'em."

"What's to worry about?" Josh said. "If he fails, we're out a horse and a couple guns. Ten percent of nuthin' is nuthin'."

"Besides which," Hickok said slowly, leaning back in his chair and picking his teeth. "I already earned half my fee."

"By showing up?" Jeff said dryly.

"No. By knowing who those men are . . . and where they're going."

"How do you know that?" Josh asked.

"Why, I played cards with them. They played with gold. They beat me outa my pistols, and I sure got a hankerin' to get them back. All I needed was some help, and it looks like you're it."

"Where are they?" Josh asked.

"When the time comes," Hickok said, stroking his mustache.

"If I tell you now, you could cut me out of the deal and then where am I? I'll let you know when we're on the trail." He glanced outside. "Boys, we're burning daylight. I suggest we get a move on."

An hour later the three men were at the livery, saddling up and preparing to depart. Josh had gone with Wild Bill to the gunsmith and general store for the pistols and some grub, while Jeff saw to it their horses were ready, and now they were together again, cinching their saddles and strapping bedrolls to their saddles.

Bill picked out his own horse, a mean-spirited animal that he got for half price after consenting to autograph little William's copy of *Beadle's*. They mounted and pointed the horses south toward Mono Lake by way of Cottonwood Canyon.

"It's a two-day ride, they tell me," Hickok said. "We best be getting part of it out of the way quick." He heeled his mount and the protesting animal, fire in its eyes, took off.

Jeff wondered where they were going and who told Hickok it was a two-day ride but didn't have a chance to question him. He followed on his nag, giving Josh a look that said, *this better work out right*. Josh could only shrug and let his horse fall in behind the others. He hoped they'd made the right decision. Even though Hickok wouldn't tell them where they were going, Josh trusted the legend, the stories he'd read. Their only hope, he knew, rested on the shoulders of the long-haired man wearing the buckskin shirt.

Old Noah Porter, Bodie's town character who'd been stirring things up with his own sense of reality since '69, stopped to watch three strange men ride out of town—two young ones and a long-haired fellow in a buckskin shirt, then, with a shrug, continued on his mission. He hurried to the jailhouse and burst in, seeing Billy O'Hara seated behind Matt's desk, dwarfing it with his bulk. The man looked up, his eyes tired, worry creasing his forehead.

"News from Matthew, Noah?"

"No, Unca Billy," Noah huffed, closing the door behind him and leaning against it, as though he had been chased there and was keeping his pursuers out. That he was several decades older than Billy didn't stop him from calling the man "Uncle."

"Well, Noah, what is it then? Why have you come in here in such a way, all out of breath and all?"

"I ran," Noah explained simply, missing the point of Billy's question.

"Yes," Billy said patiently. "The question is, *why* have you been runnin'? What's the matter, Noah? Speak up, man. Ah ain't got all day!"

"My, you're a mite touchy today," Noah observed.

Billy dropped his head and closed his eyes, taking a moment or two to compose himself.

"Noah," he began slowly, looking up, his voice controlled and quiet, "Ah am concerned 'bout the safety of Deputy Matthew and right now Ah'm respons'ble for the safety of this town, too. Ah got a ton a stuff to worry over, includin' the boardin'house, an' Ah ain't gettin' much help, neither. Then you come in all in a huff an' won't tell me what's up!" His voice had been rising, and now he was nearly shouting. "So could you pu-lease come out with it?"

"Okay, okay," Noah said, coming over to the desk. "You don't have to jump down my throat. Boy, ever since the magazine blew, you been—okay okay, I get your drift." He'd seen the look on Billy's face.

"I heard some things around town. Now, by themselves, they ain't much. But I kinda put them together and done some addin', you know what I mean? And when I done that they kinda summed up somethin'."

"What are you babblin' 'bout, Noah?" Billy asked, sitting back in his chair and folding his arms over his great expanse of a chest. "What things have you heard? And what do they have to do with anything?" Billy was all too familiar with Noah's vivid imagination and all the things he "heard" around town that didn't amount to a hill of beans, if he actually heard them in the first place. Usually, the voices were inside Noah's head, although Noah didn't know that. At least, he never acknowledged it.

Trouble was, because no one ever paid Noah any mind, he was often in a position to see and hear things, and occasionally his revelations contained a grain of truth. Billy's only beef was having to wade through all the tailings before finding the nugget.

"Well, Billy, you see, I was a talkin' to Doc Curtis, and he was tellin' me that James Nixon made a statement afore he passed on to that great powder magazine in the sky."

Billy was already suspicious. Why would Doc Curtis tell Noah anything? He leaned onto the desk.

"You was talkin' to the doc, and he tol' you what Nixon said before he died."

"Yep. Well, he weren't exactly talkin' direckly to me, face to face-like. He was—"

"Talkin' to someone else and you was eaves-droppin'."

"It weren't like that, Billy, honest. I was a standin' there in plain sight, not skulkin' around under his windows or stickin' my ear to the door. Nuthin' like that."

"Calm down, Noah. It's okay. Just tell me what you heard."

Noah took a deep breath. "He named his killer."

"What?" Billy jumped up, shoving the wheeled chair back against the wall hard. "Why wasn't Ah told?"

"I'm tellin' you now," Noah said, fading back from the desk.

"I mean, why didn't Doc Curtis tell me? Don't he know that's important information?" Billy's face was tight with anger, and the veins on his neck began bulging.

"Whoa, Unca Billy. Slow down. It ain't really that clear."

Billy shut his eyes. He should have known better than to take Noah completely at his word. He sat back down.

"Okay, Noah. Tell me exactly what Nixon said. Not your interpretation, not what you think he meant, his exact words as you heard Doc Curtis repeat them."

"Okay Billy, it was like this: he said, 'Make Wellman *puh*.'"

"Puh?"

"Yeah, you know. Like he was gonna say a whole word but just got out the first letter—a 'P' in this case—when God cut off his brain."

"Make Wellman . . . what?" pondered Billy out loud.

"Doc thinks he was going to say 'make Wellman pay,' like Thomas Wellman was the one who done the deed."

"Noah, go tell Doc I want to see him—no, on second thought, I'll go myself." He rose from the desk and reached for his coat. "In the meantime, Noah, not a word of this to anyone, you understand? Not a soul! Ah don't want this gettin' back to Wellman. If he's not guilty, which seems more likely to me, well, there's no sense gettin' him all worried or riled up. But if he's guilty and thinks we know it, he might do something stupid. Deputy Page would be none too pleased if Ah botched this thing up in any way."

As he said that, he stopped moving and regarded Noah with a worried expression distorting his face.

"If it's true, that means them men Matt took to Bridgeport are innocent."

Noah stared back at him blankly, unsure how to respond.

"Well, no matter," Billy went on. "First we need to check this out. See if there's any truth behind it."

"How you gonna do that, Billy?"

"Collect evidence, just like Deputy Page would." He opened the door. "Here, Noah," he said, flipping the rummy a coin. "Go git yourself a good lunch. No alcohol, you heah? Ah'm gonna check on you later."

"Yes sir, Billy. Thanks." Noah clutched the coin and scurried off like a kid headed for the candy store.

Billy left the doctor's office shaking his head. Noah had been right. Nixon's dying statement did seem to implicate Thomas Wellman. Fortunately, the conversation Noah overheard was between the doctor and Reverend Edwards, someone Billy figured wasn't likely to go blabbing it all over town. And neither of them had realized the significance of the statement, which is why they hadn't told Billy. Doc Curtis said they thought they'd just wait and tell Matt when he returned.

But now that he knew about it, what would he do with it? As he strode up the street, the Sharp's rifle dangling from his meaty fist, Billy ran the whole matter through his mind, seeing if there was any reason at all to take Nixon at his word. Assuming Nixon, with his dying breath, wanted to be sure Wellman was held accountable for having blown the magazine, he must have known Wellman was responsible. Billy didn't think any man wanted to meet his Maker with a lie on his lips. He also didn't know Nixon to be a liar or even especially unreliable. Nor had he ever noticed Nixon to be vindictive. Therefore, his statement had to be true . . . or at least Nixon himself believed it.

In what way could this be so? Well, according to Matthew, someone had warned Nixon to leave the magazine. Why? So he wouldn't get blown up. And whoever gave the warning had to know the magazine was about to blow. Therefore, that person must have been the one who lit the fuse. No, someone didn't light a fuse, at least not directly. They wrapped it around the end of a lit cigar, and it burned down slowly. Wasn't Wellman the one who found the cigar and alerted Matthew to it? Of course, that could have been a clever ploy to throw suspicion away from himself, Billy realized. And the cigar. Matthew had told him something about that cigar, but Billy hadn't really been listening and couldn't recall what he'd said.

But the big question that made Billy's forehead wrinkle was, *why*? Why would Wellman, who worked for the Empire, blow up the powder magazine belonging to . . . the Queen Anne? The question was almost self-answering as Billy remembered the feud between the two companies. Had the embers been fanned?

This was all very disturbing to him, and he decided not to wait for Matt but do some checking on his own, not wanting to confide in anyone else at this point and also knowing he couldn't confront Wellman with such a serious charge until he'd found some evidence to substantiate it.

Throwing caution to the wind that had just begun to sweep through the gold camp, Billy trudged up the street to pick up where Matt had left off . . . the tobacco shop.

Not thirty minutes later he reemerged from the shop, a fresh cigar dangling from his frowning lips, the smoke dispersed by the nor'easter whipping down Main Street. He stopped to button his collar and took a couple of pensive puffs, then skirted around the back of a passing teamster's four-in-hand rig and headed up the hill toward the office of Fred Smith, supervisor and a principal stockholder of the Empire Mine and Mill.

"To what do I owe this visit?" Smith said when he opened the door to Billy's healthy rap. He immediately stepped aside to let the large man in from the cold. "You usually don't come pleasure-calling with that cannon in your hands."

"Ain't a pleasure call, Ah'm sorry to say," Billy told the businessman, leaning the Sharp's against the wall.

"In that case, I'll not offer you a drink. And I see you brought your own cigar."

"Thanks," Billy said, reaching for the cigar box Smith hadn't proffered. "Don't mind if I do."

Smith watched, perplexed, as Billy reached in and plucked out a cigar, then pulled out the one in his mouth and held them next to each other.

"Seems we have the same taste," Smith said. "Care to tell me what's going on, Billy?"

Billy put the fresh cigar back and closed the lid of the humidor.

"Deputy Matthew's out of town."

He paused and drew long on his cigar.

"Yes, I know. The whole town knows."

Billy nodded. "Jus' layin' the ground work. Because he left me in charge of keepin' the peace, it fell to me to look into the matter of the powder magazine affair."

"Why does it need looking into? Deputy Page is gone because he's taking the perpetrators to Bridgeport so they can stand trial. Isn't that so?"

"As far as Matthew knows, that's true," Billy said. "But Ah've recently come into some information that may prove otherwise. Some of it involves cigars, jus' like these."

"Ah, yes, so Wellman told me. The powder was set off by a fuse lit by a cigar. You say it was like these?"

"Yep. Jus' like. And it was a fresh one. Accordin' to Mr. Gordon at the tobacco shop, only three people bought cigars like these in the days before the explosion. Bob Kitterman, who has an ironclad alibi during the morning of the incident—he was with me—a stranger, possibly one of the men Matt arrested, and yourself."

Smith recoiled. "You don't suspect me, surely."

Billy shook his head. "No suh, Ah don't. But Ah need to know everyone you gave a cigar to that day and the day before."

"Just those two days?"

"Yes, suh. You see, any longer'n that and they'd've been not so fresh. See the difference?" He again withdrew a new cigar and let Smith feel the two. Billy's was much softer. "Even in your humidor, they still don't have quite the same feel to them. It had to have been a cigar bought no more'n the day before. So, if it wasn't the stranger's, it had to have been one of yours."

Smith scratched his head. "Well, it makes sense what you say, but I don't see how it could have been one of mine. I only gave one cigar away out of the new box."

"Then if it wasn't you, the offending cigar was the one you gave."

Smith looked up, shocked. "That can't be! And I'll not implicate the man I gave it to."

"You were robbed then and a cigar stolen?"

"Well, I . . . no, Billy, I can't say that's a fact. I'll not lie. I wasn't robbed. But the man I let have a stogie—"

"Let have?" Billy queried. "In other words, you didn't offer, he asked?"

Smith just stared. That hadn't seemed an important distinction until now.

"Tell me, Fred. Did that man happen to be Thomas Wellman?"

The look on Smith's face told the tale. "I can't believe this, Billy. Not Thomas Wellman."

"Ah don't like it any more'n you, Fred."

"The cigar, is that all you're basing it on? If so, then the stranger is just as likely to be guilty, and he had a definite motive—"

"In the first place, we don't know that the stranger who bought the cigar is one of the men Deputy Matthew took to Bridgeport. That's jus' speculation."

"It's still more than you've got on Tom."

"Ah wish it were so," Billy said with a sigh, "but like Ah said when Ah started, Ah got new information."

Smith waited in silence, knowing Billy would get to it at his own pace.

"James Nixon named Wellman with his dyin' breath."

The silence in the room would have been haunting had it not been for the pounding of the stamps in the nearby mill. Smith stared first at Billy, then out the window as he digested this tidbit. After what seemed like an eternity, he finally spoke. "But why would Wellman do such a thing?"

"Oh, come now, Fred. Surely you haven't already cleared your mind of the doin's last year between the Empire and the Queen Anne. It ain't such a far stretch to imagine Wellman harboring a hate and waitin' for his opportunity to get back at your competitors."

"What opportunity?"

"Doin' it so them fellers Matthew hauled to Bridgeport could get blamed."

"No, I suppose that's not a big stretch," Smith admitted. "But I just can't believe it. Why, it was Wellman who found the cigar and showed the deputy."

"That's true," Billy admitted. "What better way to point away from yourself than to be the one who discovers the evidence?"

Smith sighed: a long, fear-laden sigh, a catharsis for his dread that he couldn't bring himself to express. "I hope you're wrong," was all he could utter.

"Ah hope so too," Billy said, rising. "And because Ah hope so, because Ah know Thomas and Ah don't like to think he done this thing, Ah'm gonna have to ask you not to say a word of this to no one. Ah think you can understand that, Fred."

He nodded. "Yes, Billy. I certainly do. Is there . . . is there anything I can do to help?"

"Pray, Mr. Smith. Jus' pray." Billy paused. "And if our hope is ill-founded and he did this thing, you can pray for Thomas, that God has mercy on his soul."

The outlaws rode hard all day, stopping only when necessary and then not for more than a few seconds. They had no food, and the wagon driver they passed as they approached Coleville didn't look like someone they wanted to tangle with after a hard day of riding on empty stomachs: a tightly-packed man with big arms and a thick neck, and a permanent scowl on his sun-reddened face.

So on they rode. Near dark they made the edge of Coleville, a sleepy little town in the shadow of some rather magnificent crags. The wind blew heartily through the pass in the middle of which the town was anchored, stirring dust and leaves and skirts and hats.

"Best we split up," Cole told his brother. "I'll check in at the hotel. Meet you for some supper at the restaurant over there," he pointed with a nod of his head, "and you can check in later."

"What are we gonna do for money?"

"Never you mind about that. I got a little in my boot I've been saving."

"Why don't we just take the bank. After all, we're the Y—"

"Shut up!" Cole demanded, his eyes narrowing to slits as he wheeled his horse around and glared at his brother. "Ain't you got any sense?"

"Ain't no one around to hear us," Bob protested.

"That ain't the point. You gotta get out of the habit of saying it. One of these days you'll slip when someone is within earshot.

Now you go on to the restaurant. I'll see you in a bit." He shook
the reins, and the horse flipped its mane as it moved forward.

Bob waited a few minutes then rode in himself, sticking to the
other side of the street and riding past the hotel without so much
as a glance that direction. He continued on to the livery at the
opposite end of town and left his horse there, giving the grizzled,
old cowboy who ran it his last two bits. Bob hated that horse but
figured he at least owed it a good feed for bringing him all the way
there. He planned, whether Cole liked it or not, to pick himself up
a new animal in the morning.

He walked to the restaurant, ignored by the few people he
passed on the boardwalk who were too busy shielding their eyes
from the swirling grit and trying, often in vain, to maintain custody of their smaller articles of clothing. It gave Bob a sense of
power, of invincibility—although he didn't recognize it as such—
to walk unhindered down a public street, and by the time he
reached the restaurant, he was more full of himself than usual.

But the glare from Cole, sitting at a table near the rear of the
small room, snapped him out of it.

"Where have you been?" Cole whispered through clenched
teeth as Bob took a chair on the opposite side of the table.

"Relax, Cole. I was puttin' up my horse. Don't worry. I ain't goin'
back for it. I just thought I'd give him a reward for carryin' me today."

"You always were sentimental about animals," Cole said.
"Let's eat and get on up to our rooms. I need some sleep. We've
got a lot of ground to cover tomorrow to make it to Markleeville."

"That where Jim's waitin'?"

"Should be."

"What about Jesse?"

"Gone back already. Says he's well. Says the stay in San
Francisco did the trick."

"I can't wait to get home. I hate it out here."

"Yeah, me too," Cole admitted. "Couple days, we'll be on our
way back."

Their food arrived and they dug in, the need for further conversation falling to a distant second place behind their hunger.

CHAPTER

SEVENTEEN

O N THE ROAD AGAIN, Matt allowed Blister to run a casual, easy pace, not so fast he'd tired quickly, not so slow the trip would take forever. Matt wanted to regain as much ground as he could before light gave out. If he could get near where the sheriff was shot, he'd be just two days behind the men.

A two day-old trail. Not the best for tracking. Matt hoped someone in Coleville saw them, or better yet, spoke to them and could tell him where they'd headed. Otherwise, it would be a hunt for a tick in a herd of cows. Not just any old tick but a particular tick.

As the day waned and the sun descended, the air took on a chill and the wind picked up. Blister made good time, never faltering and keeping a steady pace over the wagon road. There were few other travelers out, and Matt greeted them all the same way: a tip of the hat, a cheerful word or two, then riding on without slowing down.

With the last minutes of daylight upon him, he let Blister take a breather and walked off the road. They found a comfortable place for a camp on the far side of a large rock that would hide their fire from prying eyes. Matt let Blister drink his fill at a nearby stream, then picketed him to a bush and removed his tack. He rubbed the animal with dry grass and fed him some oats from his hat, then set about collecting dry sticks and grass for his evening fire.

When it blazed he made biscuits and beans and coffee and

leaned back against the rock as he ate, looking up at the stars and longed for Sarah, wishing she could enjoy this with him. Not that she would enjoy being out on the trail like this, but sitting with him and looking up at the stars.

But it wasn't to be, not tonight. Matt finished his meal and cleaned his pan in the stream, then settled in for the night, hoping to wake up in time to get an early start.

The morning broke, but the rising sun saw Matt's back as he was already back on the trail. He'd fried a hunk of bacon, washing it down with coffee, then saddled up his faithful Morgan and set out when it was barely light enough to see.

The place where Sheriff Taylor had been shot, he located early. Finding the tracks left by the shooter, he familiarized himself with them again, remembering the defective horse and the odd way the man rode. About the other man, the man the shooter met on down the road, Matt knew nothing. He'd only seen him through the spyglass, and the man was just a speck even then.

What did it matter? It was the shooter he wanted. Besides, if the two men were the escaped prisoners—though by the clothing description they might not be—Matt wouldn't have any trouble recognizing them. For that reason, Matt hoped it was them, and somehow they'd acquired some other duds. He shuddered to think how that might have happened.

The wary deputy headed toward Coleville, keeping an eye on the tracks just in case DeCamp had been wrong about seeing the same men Matt had. But the trail proved DeCamp's sighting true, as the wagon tracks left by the buckboard soon crossed the odd-gaited horse's marks at about the place DeCamp had remembered.

Coleville was just around the corner, and Matt could hear the sounds of the town. It was nothing like the continuous pounding of Bodie's stamp mills, but it was a good sound nonetheless.

It could be heralding the end of his journey, if the men he was after had stayed put.

Matt entered town around noon, passing tall trees that bordered the road, then gave way to buildings. Not unlike a thousand other Western towns, Coleville was filled with wood buildings, board-and-batten structures having false fronts adorned with colorful signs declaring what businesses lay within the walls. A two-story hotel, the Monarch, was the first brick structure he had seen in Coleville, and he didn't remember it from the time before.

A dog barked and chased Blister, but a glancing kick from the irritated horse sent it yelping away, unhurt but for its pride. Matt kept a wary eye on the horses and men that moved up and down the street, and upon the horses tied to hitching rails in front of the saloons. But there were more buckboards and wagons than saddled horses. This was primarily a farming town, with perhaps a few displaced prospectors and a very few rowdies or gamblers since there was no gold here attracting them. A solitary soiled dove watched Matt from her second-story window over a saloon, her elbows on the sill and her chin in her hands. Matt saw her but didn't let on.

He thought of Fred DeCamp and his family and wondered how they were faring. Over dinner DeCamp had mentioned that his little mine, the Golden Gate he had named it, had petered out, and he was back to dairy farming, as were most of the other Dutch settlers. But he wasn't specific as to the size or quality of his spread. Maybe someday Matt would pay them a visit.

Matt rode to the far end of town, disappointed at not seeing the distinctive horse he sought but not surprised. That would've made it too easy. He wanted to check in with Reverend Hinkle, see if maybe he'd seen anyone around town matching the description of the man. A shot in the dark, but one never knew.

This being around one o'clock on a Sunday, church was over and Matt figured Rev. Hinkle was probably at the parsonage enjoying a hearty Sunday meal. He eased up on the reins in front of the church and dismounted, tying Blister to the hitching rail. With a wary eye canted toward the people walking nearby on one mission or another, he stroked the horse's neck and said a few soft words. Blister leaned into his master's hand and switched his tail, then snorted contentedly.

Removing his hat and wiping his forehead, Matt strode toward the parsonage, opening the small white gate and passing between rows of dormant rose bushes. The wind blew lightly from the west but occasionally gusted, sending swirls of dirt spinning down the street. Women grabbed their dresses and skittered quickly to safety. Men held their hats on or clutched them in their hands to avoid losing them altogether. The sun was bright, but the air still spoke of winter just around the corner.

The front door of the parsonage opened before Matt mounted the four steps to the porch. The porch swing creaked as it swayed gently in the breeze.

"Is that Deputy Matthew Page?" Rev. Hinkle asked with a smile. He held out his hand. "Come in, Matt. Come in. Good to see you."

Matt took the offered hand firmly. "Thanks, Reverend. Good to see you too." He entered the modest house, and Hinkle closed the door behind him. Mrs. Hinkle came into the parlor wiping her hands on her apron. Matt nodded politely.

"Mrs. Hinkle."

"Matt, good afternoon. Please, sit down. Can I get you anything? Cup of coffee?"

"Water would be fine, thank you."

The three-room house was spartan yet comfortable, befitting a pastor and his wife. Their children were grown, and their only needs were for themselves and the frequent guests they entertained, most of them parishioners, but sometimes community leaders who would come calling for one purpose or another, usually to get the pastor's support for some project.

The walls were plastered and covered with colorful printed paper. They were also adorned with art work, most of it paintings by Mrs. Hinkle: still lifes, local scenes, and Biblical characters; some of whom Matt recognized because of the situation. David and Goliath. Christ on the cross. Christ rising on a cloud toward heaven. The humans in her paintings were slightly askew, but not having an artistic eye, Matt couldn't describe exactly what was wrong with them. They just didn't look quite right. The outdoor paintings were good, though, really good. Matt recognized the landscape in several of them as places he'd visited in Mono County.

Hinkle had removed his clerical collar and sat relaxing in trousers, white shirt, and slippers in a chair a few feet from where Matt had found a seat. The twinkle in his eye was as present as ever, and Matt figured a person in his position had to be ready at all times, not knowing when, without warning, he'd have to wrestle the devil.

"So, what brings you to Coleville?" Hinkle asked. "I'd like to think it was to see me, but I know better than that. You're dressed for business, and I'm sure Sarah would be with you if this were a social call."

"You're right about that, Reverend."

"How is she, anyway?"

"Oh, she's fine. Just fine."

"So, since it's business, and your business is the law . . . what can I do for you, Matt?"

"I'm trying to find two men, Reverend. They were last seen headed toward here two days ago. . . . Oh, thank you, Mrs. Hinkle."

She had brought his glass of water, plus a plate of brownies he hadn't requested but which she knew he wouldn't refuse. She didn't know a man on the planet who would refuse a plate of brownies.

"Those look mighty good," Matt said. "Almost makes me homesick."

"Sarah's cooking will do that to a man, so I'm told," she said. "We get a lot of men through here who've eaten at the Quicksilver. She's developing quite a reputation in the county."

"Thank you," Matt said, as humbly as if she'd been talking about him instead of his wife.

"How is she?" she asked.

"Sweetheart, I've already gone through that with the poor man," Hinkle said.

"That's okay," Matt told him. "There's somethin' I didn't tell you. I wanted to wait until Mrs. Hinkle was back."

"Ooh, this sounds exciting." Mrs. Hinkle sat down on the arm of her husband's chair. They gazed at Matt expectantly, used to being good listeners due to all the people they had counseled over their years in the ministry.

"She's going to have a baby." Matt beamed.

"I knew it!" Mrs. Hinkle clapped her hands.

"Good work," the Reverend congratulated. Matt blushed.

"When is she due?"

Matt looked at them blankly. "I don't know, actually. She didn't tell me. Her ma did. Sarah wrote her about it. I guess she was going to tell me, but duty called me to Bridgeport suddenly—" He cut himself off with a groan and a snap of his fingers.

"What's the matter?" Hinkle asked.

"That explains why she seemed so upset when I left. I think she was going to tell me but didn't want to distract me from my work."

Mrs. Hinkle smiled, stepped over to him, and patted him on the arm. "Don't fret none. She'll be fine. When you get back and she tells you, act as if you didn't know, you hear? That'll make it all right."

"Yes'm." Matt grinned sheepishly.

"Now I'll leave you two men to talk. I've got work to attend to in the kitchen."

She sauntered out of the room, and Hinkle urged Matt to continue. "What about these two men? What'd they do?"

"They shot Sheriff Taylor, that's what they did. One of them did, at least. But he met another man on the trail a mile or two away. I could see them through the spyglass but couldn't go after them because I had to take care of the sheriff."

"How is he? It's not too serious, I hope."

"Well, it was a mite frightenin' there for a while, but when I left, he was improving and able to talk."

"That's a relief. So now you're on the trail of his attackers."

"Well, it runs out here. That's why I came by, to find out if you'd seen any strangers in town."

"To be honest, Matt, I don't get outside much. People come by here all hours of the day, so I try to stay home as much as possible. And there weren't any new faces in church, I'm sorry to say. Sorry. I wish after all that buildup I could be of more assistance to you."

"That's okay, Reverend. I appreciate your time." Matt stood. "I best be gettin' on. I guess I'll be makin' my way through town, see if there's any witnesses."

"Try Toby at the livery. If they stopped there to take care of their horses, he'd know about them. He likes to gab."

"Thanks. I'll go there first." Matt donned his hat. "Thanks again. And tell Mrs. Hinkle thanks for the brownies."

"You got room for a few in your saddlebags?"

Matt grinned. "You bet."

Hinkle wrapped the brownies remaining on the plate in the napkin upon which they had been arranged and handed them to the young deputy. "Keep the napkin," he told him. "Maybe you can use it for something."

Matt thanked him and stepped outside, sticking his hat down hard to keep the wind from blowing it off and down the street. The last thing he wanted to do was spend his time looking foolish, chasing his hat as it rolled down Main Street.

Although the livery was close enough he could have walked, Matt took Blister with him in order to put him inside out of the elements since it looked like he might be in Coleville for some time locating someone who had seen the men. Two men. One who rode awkwardly. Not much to go on. But a horse with a gimpy leg, that was something a good stable boy would have noticed.

On the way to the livery, Matt passed the old jail, now kept locked and unused. Anyone who got arrested in Coleville was chained to a tree in the center of town until they could be taken to Bridgeport for trial. They didn't have too many prisoners in Coleville, and there wasn't much need for a full-time lawman. The town was on its last legs, or so everyone thought. Matt had once wanted to live here, to reopen the jail, but with the boom in Bodie during the past few months, Coleville had nearly cleared out.

He resisted the urge to peek through the dirty window. It would just remind him of his dream, make him feel bad. He wanted for himself what God wanted, whatever that was. At the moment, he didn't know, he just knew he was becoming unhappy with Bodie. Maybe he was too fussy, he told himself. Maybe Bodie was an okay place, or maybe it wasn't that much different from any other town. But was it a good place to raise a son or daughter?

That was something to give serious thought.

He pressed on.

The stable doors were closed against the wind, so he banged on them with a fist. He waited a minute, but there was no response, so he pounded again. In a moment, someone shouted for him to hold his horses, which Matt found simultaneously amusing and annoying. Then one door opened slowly.

"Yeah, whaddya want?" a scruffy old man growled. He was missing most of his teeth, was in need of a shave for about a week gone by, and his years in the sun had given him a serious case of squint-eye, which the wind did not improve. His cheek bulged from a wad of tobacco.

"Deputy Matt Page," Matt said, pulling back his coat to reveal his badge. "Can we have a word?"

The man eyed Matt up and down, then gave Blister the once over as well.

"Nice piece of horseflesh," he said and opened the door wider for them to enter. Matt wondered if he would have been let in if Blister had been a nag.

After the man had shut the door behind them, Matt strained to see in the dark stable. The bright light outside had made the transition into the murky blackness of the livery difficult.

"Well, whaddya want?" the man repeated.

"You Toby?"

"Yep, that's my handle. Now, you got something to parley with me about?"

"Yeah. I'm lookin' for two men, rode into town a couple of days ago. I figure maybe they stopped here with their horses."

"That was purdy good figgerin' considerin' this is a stable an' all and the only one in town," Toby said, punctuating it with a spit of tobacco juice onto a nail head sticking out of a nearby post.

"You seen two men?"

"I seen a lot of men," Toby said. "Not many folks live in Coleville, but a heap of 'em pass through. That's why this here liv'ry stays in business like it do, day after day, week after week, year after year. What'd they do?"

Matt figured this wasn't the old boy's business and told him so.

"You're a young whippersnapper of a lawman, now ain't you? You ain't likely to get too much information talkin' to people like that. That's like tryin' to tickle someone with a length of bobwire. You got to make 'em want to tell you. Sometimes that means tellin' 'em somethin' that ain't none of their beeswax." He spit again, hitting the same nail head.

Matt pressed his eyebrows together, thinking about the old man's wisdom.

"Okay, you made your point," Matt consented. "They shot Sheriff Taylor."

Toby raised an eyebrow. "Do tell. Now why'd they want to go plug a man like John Taylor fer? He ain't never done no one no harm."

"Don't know," Matt said. "Maybe someone's been carryin' a grudge for a time, someone he put in prison in the past, and they just got out."

"Mebbe. Where'd this happen?"

"Between here and Bridgeport. By the Walker River."

"Hmm," Toby scratched his whiskers. "I seen several diff'rent men in the past few days, some alone, some in pairs. Can you tell any more 'bout 'em?"

"Well, one of 'em rode a horse that had a lot of wear on the outside of one shoe. From a distance it didn't appear to have any trouble runnin', though."

"That narrows it down," Toby said. "Only one horse been in here like that. Man came in with it, wanted it fed and watered, kept overnight."

"So he left yesterday?"

"Don't know. If he did, he left without the horse. Here she stands."

Toby pointed to a reddish brown mare in the last stall. Matt dropped Blister's reins and walked over to it, slowly so as not to frighten the animal, his hand outstretched before him. She shied from it, but he spoke softly to her and stroked her nose, then moved up to her neck until she was comfortable with him.

"She's been rode pretty hard," Matt noted out loud.

"Yep. But that's what they're for, ain't it? Jus' so long as we take care of 'em, they're for ridin' until they can't go no fu'ther."

Matt didn't respond but gently lifted the animal's left front hoof. Sure enough, the shoe was well worn on the outside edge, a perfect match for the prints he saw at Walker River.

"Yeah, this is the horse," Matt confirmed. "This is the horse the shooter rode."

"Then you s'pect he's still in town?"

"Where else could he be?"

"Well, there ain't but one hotel. Course, he coulda got a ride on the stage. It left yesterday, headed north. Don't know the destination. Or he coulda borried a horse from someone who didn't know he was gonna do that, if you catch my drift. Or he coulda bought one, but he didn't, not from me, and offhand I can't think a no one else. Course, all that is assumin' he ain't still in town. He might be in his room sleepin' or in the restaurant stuffin' some vittles down his shirt. Lots of options for ya, Deputy."

Matt scratched his ear. "How much to take care of my horse until I get back?"

"Ten cents a day, up front." He held his palm up.

Matt fished the coin out of his pocket and handed it to Toby. "Tell me, Toby, what'd this man look like?"

"Ordinary-lookin' feller. Shorter'n you a touch. In fact, he was several inches your lesser but looked to be about the same age. Wore brown pants and a long coat over a dirty, white shirt. I noted he had a shootin' iron in a fancy rig up under here." He put his hands under his armpits.

"Shoulder holster?"

"Yep. Funny name, since they ain't on the shoulder. Course, armpit holster don't sound too appealin'." He chuckled at himself.

"Anything about his face stand out?"

"Just his nose." Toby lit into a loud guffaw this time but quieted when the deputy didn't follow suit. "No sense of humor, I take it. Typical lawman." He shrugged. "He also had beady, narrow eyes."

"Age?"

"Mebbe twenny. Hard to tell with hombres like that. They lead a hard life real fast. Burn it out quick and die before their time."

"Men like what?" Matt asked, puzzled.

"A hogleg in a shoulder harness?" Toby snorted and spit a third wad of juice onto the pole, missing his mark this time. He swore at his error as it ran down slow, leaving a brown trail behind it. "He's a bad man, sure as I'm standin' here jawin' with a tin star. Up to no good and destined to stay that way or die tryin'."

"Was he alone?"

"He was when I saw him."

"Okay, Toby. Thanks. I appreciate the information. Uh, listen, if he comes back, let me know somehow, would you? Let him ride off if he wants, then get word to me. I'll be around town."

Toby flipped the coin Matt gave him into the air and caught it, then slipped it into his pocket. "Stay as long as you like, Deputy."

The hotel lobby was deserted. No customers huddled by the stove or read newspapers in the overstuffed chairs. The desk was silent, the mailboxes empty. Even the clerk was absent.

Except for the pot-bellied stove burning hot against the far wall, Matt might have concluded the place was closed. Taking privilege from his solitude, he sauntered over to the desk and glanced at the guest register, which was upside down from his vantage point. Even so, he could tell that in the last two days three people had taken rooms. Turning his back to the desk, leaning on it with his elbow propped on the edge, and craning his neck to try and read the register, he casually reached over and pushed the corner of it slowly to turn it to a more useful position.

"May I help you?" said a voice from behind him.

Matt spun guiltily and saw the clerk standing in a dark alcove beyond the counter, his arms folded, a look of disdain on his face.

"Ah, there you are," Matt said. "I wonder if you could help me."

"You could have rung the bell," the man said with a straight face, making his way slowly to his position behind the desk.

He was a fairly small man, slender, pencil-necked with room all the way around his starched, buttoned collar. He wore an arm band around his right bicep, such as it was, and a black vest but no tie. His greased hair was parted in the middle and small round glasses pinched his nose.

"Ah, yes," Matt stammered. "Yes, of course." He reached over and tapped the desk bell, causing the clerk to roll his eyes at the country bumpkin as he reached out and stifled the ring. Then the clerk made a show of returning the book to its proper position and closing it.

"Would you care for a room, or are you just catching up on your reading?" he asked.

"Neither," Matt told him. "Deputy Matt Page, Mono County Sheriff's Office." He pulled his lapel back to show the man his badge. "And you are . . . ?"

"Lewis." The man stopped there, apparently unwilling to provide more without it being mandatory. Matt didn't care. Who this man was really didn't matter, only the information he possessed.

"Lewis, I'm looking for two men. They came into town two days ago, may have stayed here."

"What makes you think that?" Lewis asked dryly.

Matt continued to be surprised every time someone he was questioning—someone who by all appearances had nothing directly to do with whatever he was investigating except as a happenstance witness—was reluctant to tell him the answers to his questions without first being told why he wanted to know. Why couldn't they just answer him? Human nature, he guessed. Besides, he was finding out that a lot of people who came west did so to get away from a problemed past as much as to improve their future. On the lam, so to speak, making them wary of lawmen asking questions.

Whatever his reason, Lewis the clerk was being very wary right now, even cagey, which could mean but one of three things: a predisposition against lawmen, involvement with the men Matt was looking to find, or just a plain-old bad attitude. Actually it could have been all three of those things but at least one of them. Since involvement with the bad guys seemed unlikely—unless, of course, Lewis had been paid for his silence—and he didn't look the part of a criminal trying to pass himself off as an honest citizen, perhaps the clerk was just overzealous in his attention to duty, namely the confidentiality of his guests. Matt had no choice but to go ahead and answer his question.

"Well," Matt told him, "the horse one of them was riding when he shot Sheriff Taylor is standing in a stall in the livery this very moment."

The set to Lewis's face dissolved into wide-eyed horror. "The man who—" He caught himself, leaned across the desk, and lowered his voice. "The man who shot the sheriff . . . and he might be here?" Taking a furtive peek to both sides, he pushed the register toward Matt and opened it.

"This man is still here," Lewis whispered, pointing to a scrawling signature with a bony index finger, then sweeping his digit slowly upward toward to the ceiling.

"Jones is still here? What about the others?"

"Smith checked out early today. The third man isn't in the hotel right now, but he's still a guest. Listen, could I be in danger?"

"Their names are Smith and Jones and Hardin?" Matt read. "John Smith and Bob Jones?" He looked closer at the last name, then regarded Lewis with total disgust. "And Wes Hardin."

Lewis put his nose on his book in apparent surprise and read carefully, his finger leading the way, then looked up at Matt, his eyes wide. "You don't think . . . ?"

"Of course not. Those are aliases. Hardin rides in Kansas. Smith and Jones. Could it be more obvious?" But Matt was bothered. Three men using aliases, and he was only looking for two.

Lewis sighed in relief, then took a defensive attitude and shrugged. "Yeah, well, so what? That's what they wrote. Hey, we don't make folks prove who they are when they stay here."

"They all come in together?"

Lewis thought about it. "No. Smith came a half-day before the other two, who were about a half hour apart."

"The man upstairs, what does he look like?" Lewis described him and Matt shook his head. "Can you do better than that?"

"I really wasn't paying that much attention, Deputy. Nothing stood out, so he must've been ordinary. I think he had a neat mustache but needed a shave otherwise."

"Could be him," Matt mumbled, thinking of O'Shea. "What was he wearing?"

Lewis shrugged. "Beige duster, white shirt, black hat."

"Was he kind of young, skinny, about like yourself only more muscle?"

Lewis didn't appreciate the comparison, but he nodded. "Yeah, now that you mention it. Hard to tell for sure under that coat, though."

"What about the other one, the one who signed in as Wes Hardin?"

"Oh, you know what?" Lewis said abruptly. "I got confused. The salesman isn't Jones, it was Smith. And he had a trunk of samples with him."

"So Smith, the salesman, is the one who's gone."

"Yeah, that's right. Sorry about that but I—"

Just then the front door opened, and Lewis swallowed his sentence, a look of fear gripping his face. He quickly plastered a smile on himself and gazed at Matt.

"So, Mr. Peters . . . that'll be a room for one night?" he asked theatrically, his head facing Matt but his eyes following the new arrival as the man crossed the lobby and headed toward the staircase to the second floor.

Matt forced himself not to look and joined in the charade, and while hunching his shoulders to minimize his stature and hide his face let his hand slip casually onto the butt of his shooting iron. When he spoke, it was with a different voice. "Uh, yes, that's what I need. One night. How much?"

"Half-dollar."

"Here you go." Matt reached into his pocket, dropped a coin on the counter, and Lewis picked it up.

"Here's your key," he said but made no move to get it. By now the man was ascending the stairs, and Matt ventured a peek out of the corner of his eye. All he saw were boots and tan pants.

He quickly snatched his half-dollar from Lewis's hand. "What was that all about?" he demanded.

"Speak of the devil," Lewis said, his voice quavering. "That was Wes Hardin."

Matt glanced again at the now-empty staircase. Somehow he'd have to get a better look at that man, hoping he was right about John Wesley Hardin being in Kansas.

CHAPTER

EIGHTEEN

A S HIS QUARRY REACHED THE LANDING and disappeared down the hall, Matt moved toward the staircase, thankful once again for his choice in footwear. His soft, silent gum-soles, while perhaps not the best for riding, certainly paid dividends when he was afoot in stealth as well as comfort. He pulled himself up by the rail while keeping a sharp eye ahead of him, in case the man was tipped off somehow and waiting for him.

He wasn't. The hallway was clear. But all the doors were closed, and Matt couldn't tell into which room the man had gone. There wasn't time to go back down and ask Lewis. It struck him that the man had disappeared awfully quick, and yet he hadn't heard a door close, so it must've been done carefully to prevent the noise from giving him away. Matt drew his revolver, having no choice but to begin a room-by-room search.

The first was empty, the bed neatly made, awaiting the next customer. The second door was locked and Matt heard a muffled noise inside. Without a thought, he took a step back, then gave it a hard kick near the knob. The wood splintered and the door flew open. Lewis, having heard the telltale sound from downstairs, protested, but Matt was too busy to care. He crouched in the hall, ready to fire, but there was no response inside. The room was empty, the wind blowing through the open window, flapping the curtain like a Fourth of July flag.

Matt's instinct was to charge to the window and look out, to see which way the man had run, but he thought better of it since he did not have a view of the whole room from his position in the hall. Instead, he moved cautiously one step forward, then another, until he was at the door, then he ducked low and dove over the bed, coming up on the other side with his back to the window and his Colt trained on the dark corner where he hadn't been able to see.

But his precaution was unnecessary; there was no one there. Thinking himself safe, that his quarry had escaped out the window, he relaxed. What he had forgotten to do was make sure it was clear under the bed, and just as he realized his error, a hand shot out, grabbed his ankle, and jerked, throwing him down. He landed awkwardly, and the Colt was jarred from his hand, sliding across the wood and coming to rest against the far wall. At the same time, the man he had been following stuck his head inside the window from the balcony outside and shouted to his partner under the bed.

"Come on, Bob! Let's git before the whole town comes down on us!"

Even from his precarious spot on the floor, Matt got a good look at the man at the window. This was not just the man from the lobby, it was also the formerly-bearded man from the Nugget and the man from the stagecoach.

Therefore, the man under the bed had to be O'Shea, the bowler-hatted hot-head. And they had the drop on him.

This all took a fraction of a second to occur, and Matt had barely landed when he assembled all the information and realized he was in a dire predicament. His only hope was to act and to act fast.

That could be the key to getting out of this alive, Matt told himself. These men were basically cowards. Given the chance, they would run. Not once had they tried taking a stand against him; only to his back had they shown any gumption. Without waiting a second longer, Matt brought his heel down on the hand of the man under the bed, who was just now emerging, and rolled away from him, then dove for his pistol.

The man yelped, and Matt expected gunplay from his partner at the window, hoping he could keep moving to minimize the target he presented and regain his own gun. He was surprised when no shooting commenced, and, upon grabbing the butt of his Peacemaker, he looked to see O'Shea diving through the window out onto the balcony. He could hear them running on the boards and climbing the railing. He lunged toward the window in time to see them jump off onto the dirt streets of Coleville. They picked themselves up quickly and began running in the direction of the livery. The one in the Stetson, known as Patrick O'Shea a few days before but called Bob by the other man just now, looked back and saw Matt watching them. He jerked a pistol from a shoulder holster and fired two wild shots at the window, both missing comfortably but forcing Matt to duck back. He would have returned fire, but a woman chose that moment to panic and run across the street, putting herself close enough to Matt's line of fire to make the risk too great. He let the hammer down on the pistol as the fugitives disappeared from view.

Rather than risk injury jumping off the roof, Matt turned and retreated down the stairs. As he took them on a dead run, he heard a single, muffled shot, and fear coursed through him. He flew through the lobby and out the door, ignoring the protestations of the clerk. As he ran up the street, he saw Toby hobbling awkwardly toward him, calling and waving his arms wildly. Seeing the deputy, Toby stopped and cupped his hands around his mouth.

"They done took their horse!" he shouted. With a strange, distant look on his face, he added, "And yours," then fell face first into the street and was still.

Matt raced over to him and knelt by the old cowboy, turning him so he could see his face. His eyes were closed, the first sign he was alive: folks usually don't take the time to close their eyes when they're dead. And Toby's chest heaved in and out. Matt patted his cheek.

"Toby, you okay?"

He groaned.

"Toby, wake up," Matt implored. Other townsfolk converged on the scene in the middle of the street, attracted by the gunshot. First to arrive was Lewis, the hotel clerk.

"He's fine," Lewis said laconically. "He's a big actor. Oughta be on the stage."

"Get him some water," someone said.

"Was he shot?" asked another.

"I seen 'em ride off," said a small boy, and Matt thought he recognized the voice. He looked up onto the blue eyes of Samuel DeCamp.

"Which way?" Matt asked.

Samuel pointed north and said, "That was your horse, wasn't it, Deputy Page? The one you once said no one could ride but you."

Matt grinned. "Yeah, looks that way." Toby groaned and began coming around.

"Am I dead?" he asked in a moaning, pitiful voice.

"No such luck," said Lewis.

"Where's it hurt?" Matt asked.

"My side."

Matt checked the cowboy's flank and found the wound, a bullet crease about a half-inch long. It was almost bleeding.

"You'll be fine," he told him. "Look, Toby, I need to borrow a horse. I have to go after them varmints and they took mine. I'll pay you for the use of it when I can."

Toby winced as he tried sitting up. "There's a black in the corral. Name's Shadow. He'll come to you. Take any saddle you want from the tack room." He grimaced, and it was all Matt could do not to smile.

"Thanks." Matt looked up at the ring of onlookers. "Somebody want to take Toby and fix him up? I've got me some outlaws to catch."

"We'll take him," Rev. Hinkle offered, stepping forward with his wife.

Matt moved aside to let them in, then told them he'd be back as soon as he could and took off at a trot toward the livery. He just then realized that he was not only missing his horse but his saddlebags, supplies, bedroll, and coat as well. It was going to be a long trip, he feared.

The black was where Toby said it would be, and Matt had no trouble getting hold of it. He threw on a plain brown saddle and climbed on the animal, which was so docile that Matt was afraid it didn't know how to run. But once clear of the livery and on open road, the beast took on a new life. In no time Matt was flying down the track, the long, black mane of the animal flipping back into his face as he crouched over its neck.

It felt different than having Blister under him. Thinner, yet muscular, he could feel the tensing of the animal's sinewy flanks as it gave him a ride he could only have hoped for.

The tracks of his quarry were easy to follow, and it was a

strange sensation for Matt when he realized he was virtually tracking himself, what with one of them riding Blister. Matt felt personally affronted, not much different than he'd have felt watching
from the side as someone else danced with Sarah.

But he kept riding. He was bound to catch up to them sooner
or later. A mile from town they left the road and cut across a
meadow of dry grass, leaving a swath anyone could follow. They
didn't separate, and Matt presumed they had a specific destination
nearby they wanted. They could also be planning something, he
told himself, so he cleared his mind and kept on the alert.

Several hours had passed with no sighting of the outlaws when
their trail veered and took a slope up toward the foothills. There was
a pass through the mountains there, and on the other side of the
range was Markleeville. Several days ride would take them ultimately to Sacramento, then San Francisco, if they kept going. Matt
knew he couldn't follow them that far. They could too easily lose
themselves, had too many ways to get away such as by stage or train
before Matt could reach them. He had to catch up to them by
Markleeville or forget it, turn back, and bid Blister good-bye forever.

Losing his quarry was not something he looked forward to
doing. These men, whoever they were, had shot Sheriff Taylor,
blown up the powder magazine, and killed James Nixon. Plus they
had stolen several horses and assaulted Harvey Boone, and who
knew what else? These were bad men of the highest order, there
was no doubt about that.

Their trail continued to be clear and undisguised. They weren't
concerned about losing Matt, just staying ahead of him. After all,
they would probably kill him as easily as look at him, and they certainly had plenty of guns. Plus, they knew Matt was alone. So on
they rode, hard and fast.

Definitely, Matt thought, Markleeville was where they wanted
to be.

He crested the ridge of the mountain in the afternoon, having
run the black all day without letup. Only now, beside a clear, cold
creek, could he allow himself to stop and water himself and the
horse. Hunger was something he couldn't think about, so he drank
a little extra to take up space in his stomach. While Shadow slaked
his thirst, Matt climbed a rock that afforded a view of the valley
below. There, just specks in the distance, were the outlaws head-

ing in a straight line for the town as Matt had suspected, a town he could see only as a dark spot in the distance.

If he rode straight through, he figured he could be there by daybreak. It didn't look like the outlaws were going to stop before arriving in town, so he couldn't either. He knew Blister would make it. The Morgan was strong and strong-willed and would run all day just to prove he could.

Matt climbed back onto Shadow, talking to the animal in soothing tones and stroking his neck. Shadow responded to his new master's gentle, yet firm, touch and was ready to go. Matt squeezed his knees together, and they were off.

Markleeville was like any other town out West, only older and more established than most. The whitewash had faded from many of the buildings, and there were more brick structures than in Bodie (which had one) and Bridgeport (four). At least a third of the town was brick. Of course, the materials were more accessible in Markleeville due to its proximity to several large cities, so it stood to reason.

Otherwise, it was much the same as Bodie. Men on horseback and folks in wagons and carriages moved up and down its streets. People walked. Kids ran and chased each other. The tinkling of pianos emanated from the saloons mixed with conversation. Boots clumped on the boardwalk. Wagons creaked down the dusty street. The only noticeable difference was the absence of the pounding of the stamp mills, something Matt didn't miss at all. In fact, to be in town without it was like the feeling one gets when a headache goes away suddenly.

As Matt rode slowly, he scanned the main street for Blister, his only clue as to the whereabouts of the outlaws. After a pass through, he decided to hit the major side streets, then stop in at the sheriff's office and solicit some help. These were tough, desperate hombres, he'd come to realize, and alone, he was no match for them. He shivered when he thought about the stage ride into Bridgeport and how only the element of surprise had made it possible. He cringed even more when he thought of how Harvey Boone had been left in charge of these men. That was a mistake he'd never make again. Not that it was his decision, but he could have protested, could have postponed the fishing trip until the men had been tried and sent to prison.

But hindsight was always clearer than foresight. It had been a fiasco, that's for sure. Things were changing in Mono County, Matt concluded. The times weren't as peaceful as they had been in Taylor's day. One man in each town wasn't enough to keep the peace, especially in a place like Bodie. A whole police force was needed.

Bodie. Matt shuddered to think what might be going on there with him gone, chasing all over the state for two outlaws instead of keeping Bodie safe for its citizens. He hoped Billy O'Hara wasn't running into too much difficulty. Matt regretted his decision to leave, even though it had seemed necessary at the time. He should have locked the two men in the Bodie jail and posted a twenty-four-hour watch until the circuit judge came to town. Then he would have been there to do his job, Sheriff Taylor would never have been shot, he'd be with Sarah now that she was pregnant, and Blister would still be his.

Matt patted Shadow's neck. He was a good horse, and next to Blister, Matt would as soon have Shadow as any other horse he could think of.

A commotion up the street drew his attention. A circle of men had surrounded something or someone, and they were shouting, jostling, and catcalling. Curious, Matt allowed Shadow to amble closer.

From his perch high in the saddle, Matt could see a small figure in the middle of the men, dressed in black with a brown coat and a black skullcap, being pushed back and forth between the men, as though they were schoolchildren with a ball. Racial epithets sprang out now and again about the *yellow heathen* and the *Chinee*.

Whatever brought this on, Matt was pained to see such blatant bigotry. If the man had done something wrong, let them take it to the law or give him the chance to make it right. This was pure harassment, and Matt figured they had no good reason except the man was Chinese and they thought he'd gone where he didn't belong. This was not, after all, the Chinese district, and there were no other Chinese anywhere in sight.

Without a second thought, Matt shook Shadow's reins, and the horse sprang forward. Matt shouted and caught the attention of the circle of men. They looked up in time to see a galloping black horse bearing down on them. Confused, not knowing this man's intentions, they hesitated. Was he going to run the Chinaman down? Did they want that? Or was he coming for them? They looked around at each other. No one seemed to know who he was or what was his purpose. But they didn't have time to discuss the matter, the black was nearly upon them. With split-seconds to spare, the black broke the ring, sending men scattering and diving for safety.

One brave soul tried to grab Shadow's reins and got a boot in the face for his trouble. The Chinaman, dazed by the treatment he'd received, could do nothing but stare at the oncoming apparition in bleary-eyed wonder.

Without slowing, Matt reached down as he was upon the Chinaman and snatched him under the arms, the momentum of Shadow jerking the man off the ground and onto the horse's rump behind Matt. His passenger safely aboard, Matt pulled the reins and Shadow put on the brakes, skidding to a stop. He immediately turned the horse and the ring of men closed ranks behind him, some of the more alert gents beginning to shout in protest.

Matt raised himself up in the saddle and let the sun play off his badge, then drew his Peacemaker and held it casually across his lap as he walked Shadow back into their midst.

"You gents got a problem with this man?" Matt challenged.

They murmured, and one man suggested the lawman mind his own business, but Matt answered that with a look that urged the man to shut up or pay the consequences.

"In that case," Matt said slowly, "break this up, or I'll do it for you."

"Yeah?" the apparent leader of the group said in defiance. "And how you gonna do that all by yourself?"

"One at a time," Matt said, and cocked his pistol as he directed the end of the barrel toward the speaker.

"On what authority?"

"On mine," came a booming voice from behind them. They turned abruptly and stared down the double-barrels of a scatter-gun held by the sheriff of Markleeville, Bill Chance. Matt recognized him from the big fight in Slinkard Valley so long ago.

"Come on, men," the leader of the band of rowdies growled. "No sense any of us wasting away in jail for some ignorant chink." He turned and plodded off, followed by his men, the last of whom held a bloody neckerchief over his nose as he walked slowly by Deputy Page, his eyes squinting their hatred. Matt smiled and gave

Shadow a little kick, causing the horse to jump ahead a step, which sent the man scurrying into the backs of several of his friends.

Matt laughed and was the recipient of several glares, but the men moved on.

Sheriff Chance lowered the gun and walked up to Matt's side.

"Good afternoon, Deputy Page. So we meet again. What brings you to Markleeville? By the way you're decked out, I'd say it's business."

"'Fraid so," Matt lamented. He turned to the Chinaman. "You okay?"

The man nodded. "I believe my head has cleared."

"You're safe now. You can be on your way." Matt let him jump off the horse without help.

"Thank you. If I may be of service, please to let me know how I can assist you."

"Well, I might need some laundry done before I go home, if you do that."

The Chinaman smiled, for he detected no malice in his deliverer's comment.

"Alas, I do not." He bowed. "But I'm fairly handy fixing a pistol and manufacturing ammunition. The Chinese invented gunpowder, you are aware I'm sure. The technique has been handed down through my family for many generations. I am at your service."

"Ammo?" Matt said blankly.

"Dang good ammo," Sheriff Chance said. "Never had a misfire, and all loads are the same."

"No misfires?" Matt repeated. "If it don't misfire at least one out of six, it ain't proper ammo."

"Not Chang's ammo. Show him, Chang."

Chang bowed. "Please to follow." He turned and scurried off, his oversized boots plodding noisily on the boardwalk.

Matt shrugged. "You coming, Sheriff?"

"Can't. I was on my way to something. What did you say you were here for?"

"Tracked a couple of outlaws here. They blew a powder magazine in Bodie, then broke out of jail in Bridgeport and shot Sheriff Taylor."

"Whew! He dead?"

"No, I think he'll pull through. Should be right as rain in a few weeks."

"That's good news. Listen, I'll be back in a couple of hours. Can it wait until then? I'd like to be in on this."

"Sure. I'll just nose around town, see if I can get a line on where they are, then we'll get together and arrange a little surprise for them."

"You bet." Chance put an index finger to the brim of his hat. "Two hours. Meet you outside Chang's."

Matt nodded, then hurried to catch the Chinaman, now several blocks away. Matt caught sight of him just as the man disappeared into his shop.

After tying Shadow securely to the rail, Matt sauntered inside the small establishment. It smelled of gun powder and oil, and a case with a glass top held all sorts of weapons, from new Peacemakers to old, reconditioned Dragoons, double-action Smith and Wessons, and Colt's 1860 Army. A beautiful gun to look at as well as shoot, it used percussion caps and lead balls instead of metal jacketed cartridges, and Matt wouldn't have one. Not with the modern Peacemaker available. Still, the Army was a pretty piece of shootin' iron.

Chang brought out a box of shells, gleaming brass with shiny lead bullets stuck in the end.

"Look mighty nice," Matt said. "All exactly the same. But the end of them things, what's the matter with them?" He extracted one of the rounds and examined the tip of the molded lead bullet. Instead of being rounded, the tip had been cut off and a hole bored partway into the end.

"I call it the toadstool tip," the Chinaman explained slowly, his words carefully chosen. "On impact, instead of boring a hole through a man, it expands and flattens out into the shape of a toadstool. It makes a more grievous wound, yes, but more important, it prevents the bullet from continuing on to strike another person, perhaps a bystander."

"Won't that slow it down before it gets there, catching all that wind?" Matt asked.

"Does not do so. And it is just as accurate."

"Well, that seems like a good idea, Mr. Chang. I hope it works out for you. But you know how it is—you bein' Chinese and all. Ain't too many folk likely to give you a hearin'. They'll steal your idea, if it's any good, or try to cheat you out of it, figurin' what difference does it make, you're a yella man. I don't mean no disrespect, just tellin' you how people are." Matt noticed Chang grinning at him and the deputy was forced to blush.

"Like you don't already know all about that," he said sheepishly. "Sorry, Mr. Chang."

"That's okay, Deputy. I thank you for your concern. Perhaps someday you could help me. We could help each other."

"How's that?"

"Since I would not be well-received, as you say, perhaps you could represent my ideas to the small arms makers. They would not need to know where the ideas came from. You could present them as your own, and for that, I would pay you a handsome percentage."

"Well . . ." Matt responded slowly, "that's a right clever idea. But I don't have the talkin' ability to go to people thataway. And I don't even know if what you say is true, to be honest."

"Oh, it is true," Chang assured with a wise nod. "I have proven it on animal carcasses and will prove it to you so you can attest to it."

"Seems to me you're a bit too trusting, Chang, tellin' me this. I could rob you blind myself if I was of a mind to."

Chang shook his head. "I think not. You saved my life today, for no reason. You did not know me. I am Chinese—"

"Oh, that weren't nuthin'. I just can't stand seein' bullies act that way to people, that's all." He waved his hand once in a backhand motion as if to brush off the idea as he would a pesky fly, then changed the subject to avoid further embarrassment. "Listen, why don't you sell me a box of them cartridges?"

"Please," Chang protested. "I would be most honored if you would accept them as a token of my gratitude. Please not to dishonor by refusing." He pushed a box across the counter and gave Matt a humble bow that told the young man he ought to accept.

"Well, okay, if you say so. Thanks, Mr. Chang." He took the box, then glanced outside. "I best be gettin'. I got me some outlaws to find."

"Yes, I heard you tell Sheriff Chance. Is there a way I can assist you in your quest?"

Matt scratched his head, pushing his hat a little to the side to access the itch. "Well, another pair of eyes would be nice, Mr. Chang, I'll admit that. But what about your shop? You don't want to lose any customers."

Chang smiled a bittersweet smile. "The truth, Deputy, is that I would have more customers if I ran a laundry as my uncle did. I would be honored to ride with you. I assure you, I can shoot straight and true."

"I'm not asking you to get into any shootin' matches for me, just help me look around town for my horse they stole. Once I find them, I'll get Sheriff Chance and his men to help me capture them outlaws."

"Then a pair of eyes I will be," Chang said.

"In that case, let's go." Matt adjusted his hat, sweeping the hair back that had trickled onto his forehead, and went out into the sunshine.

They were an odd-looking pair to say the least. A tall, youthful lawman on an ink-black horse, followed by a diminutive Chinaman in white man's clothing and sagging felt hat, his black queue hanging down in back, bouncing from side to side as he rode on an old nag better suited for carrying little kids at the fair. The gun he wore in a holster hanging from his pants belt was hidden by a heavy, tan, rawhide coat with sheepskin collar.

Matt's plan, as he explained it to Chang, was to ride around town and look for his horse, Blister, which he described in great detail to the Chinaman. Once located, he'd find a comfortable place to stake it out while Chang went for the sheriff. It wasn't much of a plan, but it was all he had.

Unless the outlaws were in town to rob the bank, Matt figured, they were there to meet someone. They didn't figure to be from this area, based on their manner of speaking, which Matt recognized from his youth in Illinois as Missouri or Kansas or Iowa speech.

That they were outlaws on the lam was obvious. Phony names, jailbreaks, robbery, horse thieving, no regard for human life . . . these were desperadoes of the worst sort.

In a way, Matt hoped he wouldn't find them. After all, they were well out of his jurisdiction and not likely to come back. He hated thinking that way but somehow couldn't help himself. With Sarah back home waiting for him, pregnant, he was anxious to be in quiet, little Bodie.

The deputy sighed and pressed on. He described Blister to Chang, who nodded his head. Yes, he'd recognize the horse if he saw it. Agreeing to meet back at Chang's store in two hours, they parted company.

CHAPTER

NINETEEN

TAKING STOCK OF THE HORSES tethered up and down Markleeville's streets, Matt's thoughts wandered as he rode casually down the dirt track. They wandered to Sarah and her pretty face, and not for the first time since he'd left on this journey, he wished he was home. This job was fun, yes, but not as much as he'd thought at first. Now part of him regretted taking it. If he'd had any idea it would take him away from home so much . . .

Matt had considered the possibility that the outlaws would dump Blister but quickly dismissed it. However identifiable the Morgan might be to Matt, to anyone else he was just a handsome, fine horse, the pride of his rider. No one would realize just by looking at the stallion that he was stolen. The outlaws might not even know it was his horse they had hastily stolen.

No, they'd hang onto Blister . . . unless he balked under their hand, which Matt didn't think he'd do. As smart as he was, Blister was just a horse after all, one of the dumbest breeds of animals on earth. He hadn't balked at first under Matt, and he wouldn't under the hands of experienced riders such as these outlaws.

For the better part of an hour, Matt traversed the busy town, up one street and down the next, until the whole place had been searched at least twice, maybe even three times. He'd even passed the Chinaman a time or two headed the opposite direction. Chang hadn't seen anything either and sadly shook his head. No words were necessary.

Matt was finally ready to give up, call off the search and chalk it up to experience. He turned Shadow toward the Sheriff's office and planning on leaving Chance a note. It was not an easy decision; he wanted his horse back, if nothing else.

It was not the first time he'd lost a horse, and Matt resigned himself to it. Shadow was a nice animal; maybe Toby'd sell it to him. Matt slunk down in the saddle with a sigh, squeezed his eyes shut, and dropped his head for a reflective, conceding moment before turning the animal around in place and putting heels to its flanks. No sooner did the animal leap away than a hard-riding Chang headed toward him, forcing Matt to pull the black up sharply. Chang did the same when he came abreast of the deputy.

"I have seen him," Chang said breathlessly.

"Where? Close by?"

"A man on your horse rides north from town with two others."

"They met someone," Matt concluded. "So there's three of 'em. Three against one."

"Please to reconsider," Chang said. "Three against two."

"This isn't your problem, Mr. Chang."

Chang shrugged. "You saved my life, perhaps. Who knows what those men would have done to me. It is a small thing for me to go with you."

"Whatever you say, Mr. Chang. Glad to have you."

Still, these were not the kind of odds Matt had hoped for. Three outlaws, experienced with guns and not hesitant to use them ruthlessly, against a wet-behind-the-ears deputy and a Chinaman of unknown skills.

Oh . . . and God, the Creator of the universe.

Matt chuckled nervously to himself. Those outlaws were hopelessly outmanned.

"Let's go then," Matt said.

Chang spun his roan mare without a word and dug his heels in, the horse surprising Matt with the quickness of her response and her light, eager stride. Like himself, Chang's horse had more in her than her appearance revealed.

Shadow followed without prompting, sensing Matt leaning forward slightly in the saddle as he anticipated his command to "giddap."

Through town they ran and out of it, heedless of the looks directed toward them by some of the townsfolk.

They rode hard, Chang's mare able to keep ahead of Shadow for a good half-mile before the black overtook her. The tracks of the three outlaw's horses mingled with others on this well-traveled road, but the disturbance in the dust ahead as it floated over the trail before settling was as good as a big sign with an arrow on it pointing after them.

About two miles from town, over the crest of a rise, Matt reined up and Chang settled in next to him. They both scanned the road below. It didn't take long to pick out their quarry.

The outlaws were riding three abreast. They moved at an easy lope, Blister plainly evident even at this distance, running in the lead, centered between the other two horses. A swallow caught in Matt's throat to see his horse. He wanted to whistle for him, to call him back, but he held his peace.

If they were aware of their pursuers, the outlaws gave no sign of it. As they approached a narrow pass where the road had been cut between two rocks, one of them fell back to follow the others through. Not wanting to be spotted should one of them glance back, Matt sucked his cheek sharply. Shadow responded to the sound, and they rode quickly down off the crest.

Suddenly a feeling rose up inside the young deputy, an apprehensive emptiness in the pit of his stomach. With confrontation imminent, Matt almost regretted finding them. He tried to fight off the notion that he was afraid, but what else could it be? He wanted to go home again, see Sarah, hold her in his arms, smell her hair and kiss her mouth, and someday hold the baby she carried.

He was a fool to think he could have it both ways: ride the open range and make a home for his wife. It was one or the other. He could ride back to Bridgeport, resign, and be back in Bodie in three days if he pulled up now and quit while he was still ahead.

Yet on he rode, wanting to stop, bid farewell to the outlaws, and ride home as fast as he could, but he didn't. Something inside him made him continue going, continue riding toward whatever destiny awaited him. He was a deputy sheriff, a representative of the law, and protector of the citizens, the good people of Mono County who paid his meager salary and expected him to do his job.

And he had a responsibility to God. It was God, after all, who had arranged things, who had put Matt in the place he now found himself. And if that was the case, who was Matt to shirk from his duty? Wouldn't the God who put him there watch over him? Would God, a God who loved him enough to send His Son to die for him, take care of him?

"I hope so," Matt muttered out loud. *Dear God*, he prayed silently as he rode, *watch over us.* He paused to let God mull that over, then added, *And please make Mr. Chang a help rather than a hindrance.*

In a few minutes they reached the place in the road where one of the outlaws had fallen behind his partners, the place where it narrowed between the rocks. Since coming down from the rise, they hadn't been in a position to see the outlaws again, and Matt's uneasy feeling swelled. He leaned back and pulled hard on the reins, Shadow's nose coming up as his hind legs squatted in a fast stop. Chang pulled up beside him.

"What is the matter?" Chang asked. "Why do we stop?"

"I don't know," Matt admitted, not taking his eyes off the road ahead as Shadow danced and turned in excited irritation. "I don't like this. I got a bad feeling about it."

"You think they are waiting for us?"

Matt grunted. "Don't see how. They don't know we're here. Least, I don't think they do."

"Then what troubles you?"

"You got me. I—"

A shot exploded behind them, the bullet creasing his shoulder. Instantly he half-fell, half-jumped off the black as the horse bolted and he dove for cover by the side of the road, trying to catch a glimpse of his assailant as he did so. One of them had circled back, Matt realized.

He scrambled to the edge of the road and rolled into the brush as additional volleys were fired, some from the rear as the first had been, others from in front of them. Matt grabbed his Colt's as he tumbled, firing an unaimed shot in response. When he could, he ventured a peek for Chang. The Chinaman had dove for cover also and was lying low on the opposite side of the road. They were pinned down.

Best Matt could figure, the outlaws had been waiting on the far side of the rocks beyond the narrow passage, but when Matt and Chang stopped, one of them doubled back. Now the pursuers had become the pursued and were caught in a crossfire. There was no place to hide, no retreat . . . they were at the outlaws' mercy. Without a really smart plan or divine intervention, they were goners.

One thing Matt couldn't do was just lie there. He remembered the shootout at Monte Diablo and how Robert Morrison, the Wells Fargo agent, lie wounded in the clearing, his pistol empty, as one of the convicts walked casually up to him and put a bullet in his head.

Crazy or not, Matt had to do something. If he was going down, it would not be lying in the grass. He would die on his feet, his gun blazing. Not for glory, not because of pride, just because when he faced God, he wanted to be able to say he did all he could and didn't just give up. If there was anything Matthew Page wasn't, it was a quitter.

He brought his legs up underneath him, then lifted one knee so his foot was on the ground, cocked his Colt, then sprang up and darted across the road. His hat flew off as he ran low and fast, and he fired his pistol first to his right, then across his body to his left, feeling the heat of his own muzzle flash on his left sleeve as the fabric scorched. He slid into the gully beside Chang as the return fire from both sides whistled past and sent rocks and stinging dirt flying. Chang remained prone, face down, becoming one with the earth.

"You okay?" Matt asked breathlessly.

"Yes," came Chang's reply, muffled by the ground. "For the present."

"I hear that," Matt grumbled. He hurriedly thumbed open the loading door on the gun and dropped out the expended brass cartridges, replacing them with new ones. "That's pretty heavy ammo," he complimented the gunsmith. "No misfires and a recoil that nearly drove the gun up into my forehead the first time."

"Thank you," Chang said.

Matt shifted his position and tried catching a peek of their assailants but could see nothing. "If those empty-nose bullets of yours work as well as your powder loads, they'll tear a man in two."

"That's the whole idea," Chang said.

They fell silent and waited. The only sound Matt could hear was his own breathing, the only movement, the rise and fall of his chest. He could feel the blood pounding in his temples, the fear rising in his throat and lodging there, like layer upon layer of shingles on a roof. He couldn't swallow or spit to save his life.

"What do we do?" Chang asked.

"Well," Matt told him thoughtfully, "if we move, we get shot. If we sit tight, we live, at least for a while."

"Why they not come for us?"

"Don't know, Mr. Chang. Long as we can shoot, they're not going to be real anxious to walk up on us. Our best chance is to keep firing. Maybe we'll get lucky."

They paused and listened for approaching footsteps or the telltale noise of a man crawling through the dry brush. Surely murder was their intent. Why else would the outlaws bushwhack them since Matt and Chang had done nothing to draw their ire? Matt still couldn't believe the outlaws knew they had been following them.

"Deputy? You still alive?"

The voice had come from back up the trail. Patrick O'Shea, or whatever his name was. Matt didn't answer. Maybe if they thought he and the Chinaman were dead, they'd ride off or step out into the open.

"You're alive, Deputy. We know you are. You're the most tenacious lawman we ever met, I got to hand you that."

"Let my friend ride off!" Matt called back.

"Can't do that," O'Shea told him. "He might go back to town, bring a posse down on us."

"No, I won't!" Chang shouted.

"Nice try, Chinaman," a man shouted from the other direction. The voice wasn't familiar. It must be the man they met in Markleeville, Matt figured.

Matt whispered to Chang,"How do they know who you are?"

Chang looked up, a sheepish grin on his frightened face. "I sold one man ammunition this morning." He shrugged. "It must have been one of them. I know my work when I hear it. Sorry. I didn't know who he was."

"That kind of thing happens, I guess," Matt said. "No point frettin' about it now." To the outlaws he shouted, "What do you want?"

"Toss out your guns!"

"You know I can't do that."

"We won't hurt you."

"You expect me to believe that? You killed a man blowing up that powder magazine, then you shot Sheriff Taylor."

"Self-defense!"

"He was fishing!" Matt protested.

"Oh, *that* Sheriff Taylor. Maybe self-defense isn't the right word. That was our little brother did that. Besides, he wasn't trying to shoot the sheriff, he was trying to shoot you. You can thank your lucky stars he was anxious and squeezed off too soon. And by the way . . . we didn't mean to hurt no one. We told him to get out of that powder magazine, but the fool stayed in there too long."

"You killed him just the same." Matt rolled over so he could get a good peek, see if anyone was sneaking up on them while they were distracted with talk.

"So there it is. Now you know why we can't let you and the Chinaman go. We don't want to kill you, Deputy . . . well, Bob does, that's true enough. The way you showed him up in the saloon, well, that just didn't sit too well with him, you know?"

"Tell him to get over it," Matt ordered.

"Hear that, Bob? Deputy says to get over it!"

Bob responded with two shots in Matt's general direction, the second kicking up some rocks and sending them into Matt's face. Luckily, the first volley served as a warning and Matt had turned his head before the second shot struck closer to home, sending stinging pieces of gravel into the side of his face. Ignoring the blood now trickling down his cheek, Matt decided it was time to act. No longer could he lay there like a scared rabbit; it was time to take the offensive. He gauged Bob's location and distance by his last shots, then took Chang's gun from the ground beside the Chinaman.

"Sorry, Chang, but I'm gonna need this for a few seconds."

"Okay, Deputy, I have another." Chang patted his coat pocket.

"I shoulda known a gunsmith would have extras," Matt said, then mouthed a quick prayer for accuracy and sprang up and darted into the road, cranking off shots in both directions. He ran a ragged, twisting path to make hitting him harder and made it safely to better cover, a low rock that he crouched behind, where he could return fire and could also peek out with more safety.

They didn't fire on him while he ran, so Matt figured his aim was pretty close and they'd been doing some ducking of their own. He called to Chang.

"I'll cover you! Run over here!"

Chang didn't answer but abruptly bolted from his prone position, shooting wildly with his pocket pistol, a double-action Smith and Wesson. Several of Chang's shots clipped the rock Matt was squatting behind, making it impossible for Matt to provide the cover fire he'd promised, so busy was the deputy trying not to get shot by Chang.

Little did it matter, as Chang slid into place beside him unscathed, his eyes wide and the veins pulsating on his skinny neck as his heart pounded. Matt grabbed him by the coat and hauled him the rest of the way in out of harm's way. He finally managed to cap off two more rounds, both in Bob's direction. Then he quickly reloaded.

"Now what do we do?" Chang asked, following Matt's lead and chambering fresh rounds of his hollow-tipped ammunition.

"Try to talk sense into them. They got us pinned down, that's for plug sure. Barring a miracle, we got nuthin' else."

"I heard you pray earlier," Chang said. "Your God, He will deliver you?"

Matt shrugged. "That's up to Him, Mr. Chang. He has so far. I don't suppose He's obliged to, but I reckon it can't hurt to ask."

"But you have nothing to give Him out here. No offering, no candles."

"God don't have to be bribed, Mr. Chang." Matt chanced a peek out from the edge of the rock. All was eerily quiet. "He understands our predicament."

"Buddha is capricious," Chang admitted. "He likes to be appeased, or we can't expect him to do anything for us in return."

"I don't know much about your Buddha," Matt said. "But I know something about God. He created the universe. He made this clump of dirt," Matt scooped a handful of soil and let it drain from his hand, like through an hourglass. "And He made you and me. Your Buddha, can he claim that?"

Chang didn't answer.

"God made Buddha, too," Matt said. "The way I look at it, why go to the middle man when God says we can take our problems directly to him?"

"How is it we can talk directly to God?"

"His Son, Jesus Christ, came to earth as a man, lived a perfect life, and was killed by the religious leaders. He died for our sins, so we wouldn't have to be condemned."

"Buddha died," Chang said weakly.

"Christ rose to life again," Matt told him, "just as He said He would. It's all in the Bible. Did Buddha bring himself back to life?"

"No."

"That's because he wasn't God. Jesus is God, the Creator. He's the only way we can get to heaven. No one can be good enough to get in just on their own merits."

Chang was silent. What he was thinking, Matt would never know, for at that moment, a twig snapped behind them. They both jerked around to see the youngest of the three outlaws, vengeful Bob—formerly known as Patrick O'Shea—drawing a bead on the deputy. In a flicker of an eye, Bob thumbed back the hammer. Chang shouted and threw himself in front of the deputy as the outlaw's gun barrel flashed and roared. The bullet tore through the Chinaman's leather coat, plunking him square in the center of the chest. The impact and his own momentum drove Chang into Matt, knocking the deputy back against the rock. He struck the back of his head on the hard granite and stars exploded in front of his eyes as his Peacemaker fell from his grasp , landing worthlessly in the dirt.

His vision blurred, his head thick, and a searing pain in his side, Matt struggled under the weight of the motionless Chinaman as a vague, dark shadow approached him slowly. He vainly felt the ground for his pistol, but his assailant kicked it out of his reach, then reached down and grabbed the Chinaman, pulling him off the deputy and tossing him aside like so much scrap lumber. Matt was defenseless and prepared for the inevitable. He tried focusing on the outlaw's face, reading the intent in his eyes, but his vision had failed him.

"Sorry about the Chinaman," the outlaw said slowly. "I wasn't trying to kill him. And I wouldn't have been gunning for you if you hadn't been so persistent."

"I'll . . . remember that next time," Matt said with some effort.

His hand was unconsciously pressing on his side, and blood trickled out between his fingers, though he was as yet unaware of it.

The gunman raised his arm slowly to take careful aim at the center of Matt's forehead. He closed one eye as a wicked smile slowly curled his lips. His thumb slowly pulled the hammer back, and Matt heard each click as a thunderclap. He closed his eyes and prepared to meet his God, an image of Sarah reaching out to him, the last thing he expected to see in this life.

The shot came, and Matt was instantly puzzled. There had been no pain, no flash of bright light, no angels . . . just an easy transition from alive to eternal. Slowly, almost reluctantly, he opened his eyes to gaze into Christ's face but was sorely disappointed. The face he saw was ugly, mostly bald with long sideburns and a scraggly mustache. Squinty, laughing eyes gazed at him.

"I have to leave one of you alive," the face said. "I wanted it to be the Chinaman, but since he chose to take your bullet, so be it."

"Why?" Matt asked dumbly, not understanding. On the ground, Bob writhed and moaned, holding his wrist where Cole's bullet had nicked it.

"To take back the message that the Younger brothers did not mean any harm to anyone in Bodie. I told you we tried to warn that idiot in the powder magazine, and it was his own fault he didn't get out in time."

Bob suddenly grabbed his gun from the dirt with his good hand and swung it toward Matt.

"This is for tripping me in the saloon," Bob Younger said through clenched teeth as he cocked the gun.

But as he fired, his brother Cole flicked out a foot and deflected Bob's arm, causing him to miss.

"Don't you never learn? Next time it'll be your jaw," he spat at his little brother. "If you don't stop going off half-cocked, you're going to get us into bigger trouble for sure. Don't cross me when I've made a decision."

Bob glared at Cole but wisely said nothing and put his gun away into the well-worn holster hanging off his shoulder. The third man moved in, the one Matt hadn't yet seen close up. The family resemblance was unmistakable.

"Our brother," Cole said. A strange place for a sociable introduction if there'd ever been, Matt thought. He didn't respond.

"As I was saying, you go back to where you come from and pass the word, the Younger brothers is innocent of murder."

"What . . . what are you doing . . . ?" Matt was having trouble forming the words.

"In California?" Cole guessed. "Things is hot in Missoura and them parts. That's why I had to bust Bob out. I couldn't risk you figurin' out who he was and tryin' to take me and him back. You can understand that."

"Jesse . . . ?"

"Naw, Jesse James ain't out here. He went home. That's why we're in such a hurry. We're headed back now. Jesse, he was out here for a while, though. Took sick, spent some time recuperating in San Francisco. But he's better now and waiting for us. Time to move on. Don't try to find us. We're leaving your state. This time next week we'll be back with Jesse and Frank." He laughed, long and hard, then turned to leave.

Something stopped him, and he turned back to face Matt.

"That your horse?" He didn't say anything more, but Matt knew what he meant. He nodded once, the pain when he did so unbearable.

"Thought so. Good horse. Thanks for the use of him." Cole Younger spun on his heel, and the three outlaws trudged off. Matt couldn't see where they went. He could only hear them as they mounted their horses—Matt's Blister being one of them—and rode off.

It was some time before Matt could move. His head still throbbed, but the pain in his side had dulled. He removed his blood-caked hand from where he had clamped it over the wound in his side and ventured a look at the damage. It was only creased, although the channel was fairly deep, and had stopped bleeding. Judging by the obvious wound in Chang's back as he lie dead a few feet from him—evidenced by the six-inch circle of clotted blood on his coat—Bob Younger's bullet had gone clean through the Chinaman, then clipped Matt's side. He noted wryly that Bob must not have gotten any of the hollow-nose bullets. Cole had kept them for himself.

Matt crawled over and felt the Chinaman's neck for a pulse in his jugular, just in case, but at first feel it was obvious; he'd been dead since the moment he was struck. He was cold and stiff. Matt didn't know how long he'd laid there and even wondered if he'd passed out for a time. He didn't think to try reading the sky; it was all he could do to keep from dropping over in a heap. His head hadn't recovered from the blow he'd gotten in Chinatown.

He did have enough presence of mind to realize God had taken care of him, and he closed his eyes to pray. It didn't last long, however, as closing his eyes made his head swim, so he apologized to God and prayed with them open.

"And please take care of Mr. Chang," he finished. "He saved me, I'd be much obliged if you'd save him."

Matt didn't know if God could do that, what with each person having to trust Christ on their own. But with Christ dying for the whole world, as the Bible said, maybe God would see to it that Mr. Chang was taken care of. Maybe Mr. Chang's last thought was one of trusting Christ. Matt didn't know. But he was confident that God did know and left it up to Him to decide. Either way, he thanked Him and said, "Amen."

And now it was up to Matt to take care of Mr. Chang's earthly remains. The lawman picked himself up by pressing his hands against the rock. When he'd regained control of his balance, he looked around in vain for their horses. They were nowhere to be seen, which didn't surprise him. The Youngers would have been foolish to have left them. Matt had no choice but to bury Chang. He had no idea whether or not the man had any relatives and no way of finding out right then. The man had to be buried.

Matt also had no shovel. He took a deep breath and scouted around until he found a fairly large, flat rock and set to work in the softest soil he could find. He labored for a couple of hours until the hole was deep enough, then as gently as he could, he dragged Chang's body to it and rolled him in, after checking his pockets for anything he could hang onto just in case one day he could locate a relative.

But he found nothing, other than the man's gun belt, which he kept, and some scraps of paper with strange, oriental writing on them. He slipped these into his shirt pocket.

Matt said another prayer over the body, then pushed and scraped the dirt in place over it, making a mound that he covered with rocks to keep the animals from digging and spoiling the body. He stuck a stick at the head and placed Chang's hat on it.

Searching the road, he managed to locate his own and stuck it on his head, the pain a reminder of the gash on the back of his cranium. He tied his neckerchief around it, then replaced his hat gently. Looking around somemore, he concluded his gun was gone and both their horses had been stolen or run off by the Youngers. They'd cleaned him out pretty good.

With Chang's gunbelt—also minus its six-shooter—hanging over his shoulder, Matt took to the road and walked, not knowing where he was going or how long it would take to get there. But there was a small plume of smoke in the distance, or so he thought, and he headed for it. It had to mean there were people there, people who could look after him and maybe even loan him a horse.

He hoped that they were neighborly.

CHAPTER

TWENTY

WITH A GRUNT AND A TUG and a pull, Sarah buttoned the last button on the back of Rosa Bailey's costume.

"Let me know when I can breathe," Rosa quipped.

"Anytime you want. I don't see how you can, though," Sarah retorted.

Rosa turned and regarded her friend with a scrunched up face. "Kinda tight, huh?"

"Let's just say you best not eat too much tonight." Sarah smiled apologetically.

"Oh, shoot," Rosa said, her face relaxing. "I probably won't take off my coat, anyway."

"I have to admit, that's a right fair costume."

"Princess," Rosa informed. "Complete with pointed hat and lots of lace hanging down all over the place."

"You got your mask?"

"You bet. I'll tie it on. They won't know who I am."

"You sure are brave."

"You don't think I should go to the social?"

"Yes, I absolutely think you should go. You've got every right."

Rosa looked momentarily sad. "I don't know, on second thought . . . maybe I—"

"Nonsense. You've come this far. Your apple pie has got to be the best in town. You made your costume and put it on . . . what's left but to go?"

"I wish you could be there, Sarah."

"Well, Rosa, I do too. But with Matt gone and all, I just don't . . . truth is Rosa, I'm not feeling too well. Besides, if I go, they'll know for sure who you are, and I want your pie to win on its own merits. It's good enough. We need to show these women that you belong, that your past doesn't matter."

"But it does matter, Sarah. It matters to them a lot."

"They're wrong."

Rosa frowned and turned to look at herself in Sarah's dark, flawed mirror. "Maybe we shouldn't be tryin' to make a point this way."

"Rosa, you don't have to go if you don't want to. I'm sorry if you feel like I'm pushing you. I don't want to use you to prove anything to these women. But the fact is, you have just as much right to be there as anyone else, and your cooking is getting so good, you should be able to show it off. Look, you go if you want to. If you're uncomfortable, please, don't go just on my account."

Rosa set her face and spun around.

"You're right, Sarah. I belong. I'll not cower under the glare of those women, I'll not give in to their prejudice. I'm going!" She thrust her chin out and stuck her hands defiantly on her hips, then added, "Now where's my mask?"

Sarah giggled, and handed it to her. After Rosa had placed it over her face, Sarah handed the determined woman the apple pie, carefully protected in a box, then went to the door and peeked out.

"Okay, Rosa. All clear." She held the door open, and Rosa pattered out, stopping at the threshold and taking a deep breath.

"Wish me luck," she said.

"Even better, I'll pray for you."

"You think God cares if I win the pie-making contest?"

"God cares about *you*, Rosa, whether you win or lose. You take care. See you tomorrow."

"Tomorrow's Sunday."

"Oh, yes. That's right," Sarah demurred. She'd hoped Rosa would take the hint and join her in church. Maybe another Sunday. Sarah patted her arm. "Have fun."

Rosa smiled. "Wish you could go."

The younger woman smiled back, and Rosa stepped out the door and off the porch.

Sarah shut the door behind her and faded into the upholstered chair closest to the stove, drawing her shawl around her. She bent her head, folded her hands, and had a little chat with the Lord.

"Dear God," she began slowly, "please watch over Rosa tonight. I'm trying to get her to realize she needs to come to know You for herself, and it's a little difficult with people like Flora— Flora Bascomb, I mean—and Molly and the others treating her like they are. Maybe you can work things out so they realize what they're doing and so Rosa comes to know You." Sarah paused and took a breath. "Well, that's about all, Lord. Oh, and watch over my husband, wherever he is. I know he has an important job to do, but I have to admit, Lord, I miss him. If I'm being selfish, forgive me."

She paused again and thought. "And please help me to feel better. I've probably been working too hard, Lord, so now that Rosa's getting to be a good cook, maybe she'll consent to doing more of the cooking at the restaurant. But as Jesus said in the garden, 'Your will be done.' In the name of the Savior, Jesus Christ, I pray these things. Amen."

She relaxed back into the chair, keeping her eyes closed, and trained her thoughts on Matt, imagining him riding tall and handsome in the saddle, so proud to be a lawman. Sarah was proud too, proud to be his wife and the mother of his child.

Her heart ached for him. When was he coming home?

Her husband filling her thoughts, Sarah finally drifted off into an uneasy sleep.

Even before she arrived at the Miners' Union Hall—where all Bodie affairs were held, seeing as how it was the only room in town large enough—Rosa could hear the gay music playing a foxtrot and the stomping and scraping of the dancers' feet on the hardwood floor. Men loitered outside the place, most of them having come out to smoke so as not to offend the ladies inside. Not a few of them turned their heads at the shimmering princess floating by, carrying a box, her head thrown back with an air of confidence that, had they but known, she didn't actually feel.

One of the men, whom Rosa recognized despite his mask by

virtue of his solitary arm, stood closest to the door. He watched her intently and held the door open for her to pass.

"Smells good," he said quietly. "The pie, I mean."

She nodded once and continued on her way, keeping silent lest her voice and unschooled speech give her away.

Inside, Rosa spied the judging table and headed there directly with her entry. Receiving her number from one of the judges, a corresponding number on a folded card being placed on the table in front of her pie, Rosa removed her sumptuous confection and set it delicately on the table where directed, then quickly removed the box and melted into the background, finding a chair at the perimeter of the room where she could sit and wait nervously.

She wasn't alone for long. The one-armed gentleman soon strolled by, ignoring her, then "suddenly" realized she sat behind him, and he bowed and apologized for blocking her view of the festivities. Rosa tittered in a manner quite unlike her usual guffaw and bent her head down humbly.

"Care to dance?" Jacob Page asked, extending his hand toward her. When she hesitated, he said, "You ain't married or nuthin', are you?"

She shook her head.

"Is it my arm? I only got one, that's true. But I got two legs. I kin dance jes' fine."

Rosa stood quickly and took his hand as he led her out onto the floor. A waltz had just begun. Jacob put his good arm lightly on her waist and began shuffling about the floor. Rosa noticed that his hand quivered, and it made her smile.

"You're light on your feet, miss," Jacob Page noted, unaware he was making a veiled reference to the fact that she didn't *look* light on her feet, what with her being plump. Truth is, he didn't notice. He was just complimenting her on her dancing ability.

Rosa seemed to know this intuitively and wasn't offended. In fact, she wished she could speak and thank him. But she was afraid that would give her away, and that was something she couldn't do before the judging. Once the winner was announced all the folks would remove their masks revealing the identity of the champion pie-maker of Bodie, and there was nothing anyone could do about it.

If she won, of course, which Rosa was certainly not confident she would do. For her, it was enough that she had tried, for she hadn't been cooking very long, and most of these ladies were veterans of cooking contests. Pies, cakes, cookies, jams, everything the mind could imagine they had probably entered in socials like this one and county fairs all over the country. Rosa nearly laughed. While they had been slaving away in their kitchens, Rosa and her ilk had been keeping their husbands entertained.

But that was before, and Rosa had determined never to return to that life again. She knew it would kill her, just as it had killed her daughter. Maybe not the same way. Maybe by the opium or alcohol to which so many of the girls turned to numb their guilty consciences or ease the pain of their social diseases. Or a drunk patron, upset at the price, or the inability of the girl to please him, striking out in anger with fist or knife or gun. Or to suicide, the way out of the lifestyle chosen by far too many of the girls.

Seeing the broken body of her Nellie had done the trick for Rosa, but even these many months later, she still blamed God for the tragedy. It had not sunk in to Rosa's grieving mind that her choices in life had been her own, not God's. Oh, Sarah had told her many times the truth of the matter, but Rosa still wasn't ready to believe in a God who would let that happen to someone so . . . so innocent as Nellie.

There was no doubt everyone knew it was Jacob Page behind that nondescript mask. But he did not have a wife, or even a sweetheart, so who was this mystery woman he twirled around the floor in such a shameful manner? Women gathered in small circles and questioned each other: Who has he been seeing lately? Did you notice him giving anyone the eye in church? Was it Sarah, wearing padding to hide her figure as part of the costume?

But no one could decide, and as the evening wore on, Jacob's delight in the blue princess attracted the attention of other single men and probably a few of the married ones, and he had to contend with others cutting in and interrupting his turn. After about the fifth time he turned on the man and gave him a piece of his mind, quietly, face-to-face, so no one else could hear, not even the princess.

"Git lost!" he said through clenched teeth as he grabbed the man by his tie. "And pass it on, y'hear? If'n you don't, I'll make you wish I had two arms."

When he thought about it later, he had to laugh. He didn't

know what that had meant, just that it sounded mean. But it did the trick. No one bothered them again.

"Kin I git you some punch there, miss?" Jacob asked as they completed a fandango.

Rosa nodded.

"Okay. Be right back." He turned to leave, then turned back with a sly smile. "You be there when I git back, y'hear?"

His tone wasn't demanding, and she took it as it was intended: hopeful. Again she nodded.

Jacob nodded once to put a period at the end of her silent sentence, then hurried off to the punch bowl. Realizing after he got there that he couldn't easily carry two cups back without spilling (which normally wouldn't have bothered him), he quickly downed his glass in a single gulp and took his partner's cup to her with a large cookie balanced on the top.

"Here ya go." He handed her the cup, which she took graciously, then watched as she started to take a sip, hoping she'd remove her mask to drink from the cup properly. She saw him staring and turned away slightly, taking a small sip without maneuvering the mask more than an inch, then set the cup down.

"You know," Jacob said slowly, "I ain't never spent so much time with a woman without them chatterin' like a creek with a rocky bed. Cat got your tongue, or did you lose your voice somehow? Not that I care, mind you." He glanced down at his empty sleeve, folded in half, the cuff pinned to the shoulder.

She motioned him closer with a finger and whispered in his ear.

"I don't want no one knowing who I am yet. The contest."

Jacob leaned back. "Oh, I get it. Sure, that's a good idea. A lot of the women here feel the same way. That way the judgin' is fair. Course, they aren't all so judicial. Take Flora Bascomb over there. She couldn't hide that figger of hers under a tent. She ain't fat at all or nuthin' like that, but her head is always throwed back so far, if yer brave you kin look clear up her nostrils and see her little pea brain. And she walks so stiff, like she got a—er, excuse me, I wasn't thinking there fer a second. You catch my drift, though. She thinks she's got the right to win the contest jes' because of who she is. I ain't quite figgered out jes' who she is, but she apparently has."

Rosa stifled a laugh, and began really appreciating Jacob for his simple honesty. Men like him made good husbands: hard-working, truthful, unaffected by other folks' money or position.

No, she scolded herself, these were not thoughts she should be having. In fact, she probably shouldn't be spending so much time with one man here. People would think something was going on, and she didn't want that to happen to Jacob Page.

Or herself, she realized.

But, then again, people had been thinking bad things about her and talking amongst themselves for months now, so what difference did it make? She came to have fun, and by golly she was having it!

Then a man Rosa recognized, but whose name she couldn't recall, mounted the platform at the front of the hall and rang a small bell. The band became quiet, and those revelers who were outside were rustled up and herded in. The judging of the pies had been going on for the last hour and the winners were to be announced.

"Good evening, ladies and gentlemen of Bodie. Are you having as fine a time this evening so far as I am?"

There was a chorus of agreement from the folks, a few of the rowdier men whistling and stomping their feet.

"I'm sure we're all anxious to find out who the winner of the pie-baking contest is"—more cheers—"and we have another surprise for you."

"You're gonna sit down and shaddup!" shouted a man at the back of the room.

Jacob chuckled and leaned over to Rosa, speaking quietly.

"Thomas Wellman, the man up front, is known in Bodie for being one who enjoys hearing himself talk," he explained. "He's prob'ly talks to a mirror so's he kin watch them golden tones drip off'n his tongue."

Wellman ignored the heckler. "This year we're giving a prize to the best costume for men and women as well as a prize for the best pie. While you were all enjoying yourselves our judges, whose identities will forever remain secret—"

"Must be fixed!" the heckler shouted.

"—were circulating amongst you good folk, making their choices," Wellman continued without pause. He turned to a another man who handed him a slip of paper. "Here are the winners." He cleared his throat and looked around the room, trying to create tension. At his prompting, the band's drummer began a quiet roll on the snare.

"For the men, the winner is the man in the pirate costume!"

A swashbuckler, wearing a homemade black felt hat, the brim folded up in front and pinned with a cut-out paper skull and cross-bones, and having a real peg leg came forward to scattered applause. He wore a sword made from sticks painted silver—the envy of many of Bodie's ten-year-olds—and a patch over one eye. The patch had changed eyes several times throughout the evening, and now adorned his left.

"That ain't a costume!" the heckler yelled. "That's his real clothes!"

"Okay, Finch," Wellman said, "that's it. Throw him out, boys."

Finch wasn't far from the truth, for the costume winner, Tom Fleming, did indeed have a peg leg, acquired after a fall down a shaft shattered his real limb beyond repair. Tom now worked in the office of the Queen Anne, fortunate that he had made it through school as a lad and could cipher. Nonetheless, the heckler Finch was grabbed and tossed out into the street, kicking and screaming, by two of Wellman's biggest miners.

Fleming made it to the stage and accepted his prize, a certificate and a five dollar shopping spree donated by Albert Fosdick of Fosdick's General Store.

"Take off your patch and hat, let us all see who this fine costume belongs to," Wellman suggested as if they didn't already know. But Fleming readily complied and was rewarded with another smattering of applause.

"Now the ladies' division," Wellman said. He read the paper to himself and looked around the room while motioning with his hand for another drum roll. The banjo player kicked the percussionist lightly with his shoe. The kid woke up and began drumming.

"The winner is . . . the blue princess!"

Suddenly, all eyes were on Rosa, although it took a few seconds for her to realize she had won. Jacob was applauding—striking the bottom of his shoe with his only hand—and Rosa began to comprehend.

"Go on!" Jacob urged. "Go claim yer prize."

Rosa stood hesitantly, then slowly made her way to the stage, trying to walk as petitely as she could. When she arrived she was handed a certificate and a note for the shopping spree as had Fleming, and Wellman called for her also to take off her mask.

Rosa shook her head and pointed to the pie table.

"You want to wait until the pie contest is announced? Okay by me. We might as well get on with it then. I believe our judge has made his decision. Come on out, Judge, I mean Reverend, and make your pronouncement."

Reverend Edwards was pushed onto the stage and made his way to Wellman. Apparently not realizing his identity would be exposed, he had agreed to judge the pies. The last thing he wanted to do was alienate any member of his congregation. It was sparse enough as it was. But the cat had been let out, and he had no choice but to reveal his findings.

"Uh, ladies and gents . . . third place tonight goes to pie number twenty-three, a delicious cherry pie."

"That's me!" exclaimed a women at the foot of the stage. She was dressed as a scullery maid, only with a small mask tied over her eyes with holes cut out. She climbed onto the stage with the assistance of several men nearby and with a flourish removed her mask to reveal herself as Henrietta Butler, wife of superintendent Hiram Butler of the Queen Anne. She accepted her ribbon and was directed to the back of the stage to await the other two winners.

"In second place," said the Reverend, "is pie number ten. Rhubarb."

The crowd looked around expectantly, and Molly Carter, surprise evident on her uncovered face, made her way to the stage as the crowd parted for her pregnant girth. She had decided not to wear a costume, since nothing she had in that vein fit and hiding her identity would have been impossible anyway. Plus, she considered costume parties a little pretentious, so she concentrated her efforts on her pie, and it had paid off.

Flora Bascomb stood near the edge of the stage, beaming at Reverend Edwards. This could only mean one thing: She had won. Flora was not surprised. Her apple pies had always won first prize in every fair she'd entered them, and Bodie would be no different.

With Molly now standing next to Henrietta, whose worried

gaze kept flickering over to Molly's large stomach, Reverend
Edwards was ready to announce the blue ribbon winner.

"And now, the winner of our pie-baking contest. The blue ribbon goes to . . . pie number sixty-four. A scrumptious apple."

Before the winner had revealed herself, applause began. Flora
started to step toward the stage, then caught herself as the smile
quickly drained off her face. She double-checked her ticket, then
shot an evil look toward the Reverend and her husband, who stood
next to her. Mr. Bascomb immediately realized what had happened
and unconsciously took a couple steps away from his wife.

Rosa was nervous when the announcement was made but
totally shocked when she opened her claim ticket and realized
she'd won. She shut it quickly as if to keep the numbers from
escaping, then opened the folded piece of paper and read the numbers again. Sixty-four, just as the Reverend had said.

Methodically, almost imperceptibly, she headed toward the
stage. Jacob abruptly realized why and rushed forward to take her
arm to guide toward the platform. The crowd applauded, a few
men whistled, and Rosa's head began spinning. But she made it
without collapsing and accepted her ribbon.

"And now," Wellman said, "we must know who this fair
maiden is, who not only has won the costume contest but the pie-
baking as well. Please, remove the mask so we all may see."

The moment of truth had come. Rosa reached up and untied
the knot then pulled the ends around, letting the mask slip down
from her face. There was at first some sprinkled applause, but as
more and more folks recognized Rosa, a deathly still settled over
the room. Then Flora realized what had happened, that not only
had she not even placed in the contest, the blue ribbon was won
by . . . *a prostitute*. Flora gasped, and the murmuring began
spreading across the crowd.

Flora immediately reached up and grabbed the Reverend by the
elbow, dragging him off the stage. Wellman came also, wanting to
see what was up. There was some animated whispering among the
three of them, which did not escape the notice of Jacob Page. Then
Wellman returned to the stage and held up his hand for silence.

"Excuse me, but there's been a mistake. Our apologies,
madam," Wellman said to Rosa, his use of the term no coincidence, "but a protest was lodged, and it was decided that since this

is an amateur contest, it would be unfair to allow a professional cook to win. So while we acknowledge your delicious entry, we must award the blue ribbon to someone else. The judge, the Honorable Reverend Edwards, has given the prize to number forty-six. We're sorry, ma'am. Would forty-six like to come forward, please?"

"That's me!" Flora shrieked, waving a handkerchief as she leapt onto the stage. She all but grabbed the blue ribbon from Rosa and nearly shoved the stunned woman out of the way to gain her place in the forefront, though there was no applause from the audience except for a few of the more intimidated ladies from the sewing circle Flora headed. How Flora could go from an also-ran to blue ribbon was one for the books, and most everyone smelled a rat. Some, however, were willfully ignorant, others thinking the alternative was worse. No woman from Bonanza Street should even be allowed to attend a social such as this, much less win anything. It's even possible some of the attendees respected Flora's stand, but no one was happy about the way things had occurred this night.

Rosa staggered back, first numb and embarrassed, then confused; then anger began welling up inside her as she realized what had really happened. Jacob Page perceived it too as soon as he saw who Rosa was and then noticed Flora chewing on the Reverend's ear. He surprised himself by not being shocked that he'd spent the evening in the company of a former madam and fallen angel, probably because he'd had a good time and recognized, even through the costume, the real virtue of this woman in blue.

But before he could rise to her defense Rosa threw her mask on the floor as she stormed from the room into the cold night air, her face flushed but her tears held back, ignoring the pain of her eyes and throat.

CHAPTER

TWENTY·ONE

JACOB PAGE WAS LIVID. At first, though, he had been a little stunned upon learning the identity of the woman he'd been paying so much attention to all night, but he had gotten over it quickly and his surprise turned to anger toward Flora Bascomb. No, not Flora, he corrected himself as he thought about it, her husband, for letting his wife get away with being a domineering, conniving . . . Jacob checked his thoughts there lest he stray too far from what was proper. He shot first Flora, then her husband his best look of complete contempt, daring either of them to react in kind, then followed after Rosa.

Exiting the Miner's Union Hall, he stood on the porch and looked up and down the street as best he could in the dark, the coal oil lamps hanging here and there from posts doing little to illuminate the town, the night easily swallowing the light that strayed no more than ten feet from the lamps. Rosa wasn't visible. She'd gone too far, and he'd lost her. She could be anywhere.

Oh well, he thought, she's a grown woman. She'll go home and have a good cry and be okay in the morning. Right now he had something to take care of, something that couldn't wait until daybreak. First the Bascombs, then the Reverend. He set his jaw, narrowed his eyes, and stormed back into the hall.

Rosa couldn't quell the flood from her aching eyes as she hurried up the street nearly at a run. The sight of a princess with no coat on this cold night, rushing up the street blubbering, turned quite a few heads, but Rosa saw no one. She wasn't even sure where she was going until she got there. Left at the jailhouse, then past it and right on Bonanza, she found herself standing at the door of her old crib.

Whether someone else owned it now she wasn't sure. She reached up hesitantly to knock but lost her nerve and dropped her hand. She stood on the step, her shoulders shaking in time with her sobs.

The door to the adjacent crib opened, and a woman stuck her head out into the dim light. A blanket was wrapped around her, and she held it together at the throat.

"What's all the racket?" she asked, squinting toward Rosa's shadowy figure. "What in tarnation are you—Rosa? Is that you, sweetie? What in the world are you wearing? Rosa, are you crying?" She ran out in bare feet, taking Rosa by the arm and guiding her into her crib and out of the cold night.

Once inside, with the door shut behind them, Rosa's tears flowed freely, and Betsy wrapped her arms around her friend.

"There, there, Rosa. Somethin' must've hurt you bad," Betsy said soothingly. She kept her in an embrace until Rosa's sobs had quieted, then held her out at arm's length to look her in the face.

"Care to tell me what's goin' on?" Betsy asked. "Why you're bawlin' so and why you're all dressed up in that strange outfit and why you're knocking on Nellie's old door?"

Rosa spasmed and wiped her face with her sleeve.

"This is a costume," she explained, and told her the tale.

Molly Carter's heart began aching as soon as the "correction" was made by Wellman. She knew it wasn't true, and she knew Flora was at the bottom of it and why. Molly hadn't wanted Rosa associating freely amongst the rest of them. It didn't seem right. But after her talk with Sarah God had been dealing with her, and she was beginning to think perhaps she had been hasty. Maybe Rosa had really reformed, and if so . . . well, then what right did they have keeping her away?

Now she knew in her heart—could feel it in her heart—Flora had crossed the line. This wasn't right. Rosa had won fair and square. She'd been the best pie-maker and wore the best costume and deserved to win. If she was a twelve-foot tall ogre with green, scaly skin, she still made the best pie. The prize was hers, whether Flora or anyone else wanted her socializing with them or not.

Molly set her jaw and marched toward Flora, throwing her second-place ribbon at the woman, then grabbed her coat and told her husband she'd be back shortly. He nodded, finding the proceedings inside just beginning to get interesting, and settled in to watch as the old one-armed miner moved in on the Bascombs.

Molly turned north on Main Street, her intuition telling her that Rosa was likely to go where she was the most comfortable at an emotional time like this. Especially since the reason for the injustice was because she had come out of the red light district, Molly figured that's where Rosa was most likely to head.

She turned on King Street and walked, with not a little trepidation, toward the Chinese District, hoping she'd been right about Rosa's destination. It was only when she saw the sign post declaring Bonanza Street that she realized she didn't know where to go next. Taking a deep breath, Molly turned up the narrow street and walked past the row of identical cribs, really just a flat wall the entire length of the street with no breaks in between the shacks, just a window, a door, a window, a door, repeated many times. The rooms couldn't be much larger than the beds they contained, Molly surmised, and she suddenly became afraid as she realized how she might be mistaken for one of the soiled doves, even in her condition, by a drunken man seeking companionship.

She almost wished she hadn't come, but knew deep inside, she had done the right thing.

If only she knew for sure where Rosa had gone.

Inside the Miner's Union Hall, the social had all but broken up. No one had left, but they'd stopped dancing and eating and had divided into small groups to discuss what was happening. Some of the more astute partygoers were keeping an eye on Jacob Page, sensing that something was brewing in his mind and heart. They also made sure they weren't in his way if he blew up.

With his fist clenched, then stuffed into his pocket to control it, Jacob made his way across the room to Clyde Bascomb, who stood mute as his wife, Wellman, and Reverend Edwards cloistered at the edge of the stage, a heated but quiet discussion rebounding between them. The crowd saw Jacob coming and parted for him like the Red Sea, then closed in behind him.

Clyde happened to glance over briefly, nothing registering on his face as he stuffed his hands in his pockets, then resumed gazing at the three coconspirators. Immediately something clicked in his brain, because he did a double take and realized that the one-armed miner was headed directly for him, a man on a mission if he ever saw one. Just what that could be, Clyde Bascomb couldn't tell, willfully ignorant as he was of all that was going on. Over the years, he'd discovered living with Flora was a much easier proposition if he made it a point to stay uninformed.

Clyde was the first to speak.

"Good evening, Jacob." He smiled dimly.

"Don't good ev'nin' me, you lily-livered, apron-wearin', spineless—"

"I beg your pardon," Clyde said, recoiling. Onlookers would later claim Clyde's hair was blowing back from Jacob's tirade, like Bascomb had been standing on the bow of a fast ship.

"You beg my pardon all right," Jacob predicted. "Come outside with me."

"I'll not fight you, Page. I don't even know why you're upset."

"That's the problem. Yer woman is stirrin' it up, and you stand there like a person what had his brain removed 'cause it itched. I ain't takin' you outside to fight—that's what'll happen if'n you don't come willingly. I'm takin' you out to fill you in."

"I don't see—"

"'Zactly. Now come on out."

Clyde looked around, noticing there were plenty of witnesses, and figured no harm would come to him. Besides, the man only had one arm. How much damage could he do?

"Okay, Jacob. Don't get so worked up. I'm coming." He handed another man his cup with a roll of his eyes and followed the miner outside.

"What's all the fuss?" Clyde asked when they were alone in the dark outside the hall, standing facing each other in the middle of the road.

"Seems plain as a carbuncle to me," Jacob declared. "But I'll humor you, Clyde. It's that wife of yer'n. She's made a career out of meddlin' and lookin' down her nose at folk, and she done the same to Rosa Bailey since she moved offa Bonanza Street and tried to reform herseff."

"So what is that to me?"

"That's my point, Clyde. What is that to you? And what is it to Flora? Flora's made life tough on Rosa, and she's also turned the church women agin Sarah, Matt's wife, for hirin' Rosa to help her in the Quicksilver."

Clyde was momentarily silent, looking away from Jacob while he thought.

"I can't deny what you've said," he admitted. "But so what? We don't welcome her kind in with us, you know that."

"She ain't a prostitute no more, Clyde. And Sarah ain't never been one. It's time for the meddlin' to stop. It's high time you took control of yer wife, put her in her place. If you ain't man enough to do that, I'll be happy to do that fer ya after I give you a once-over."

"You'd strike me to prove your point?"

"I don't need to hit you to prove my point. If I slug you it'll be to let you know I'm serious, so you can't say you didn't understand me. You straighten that woman out or—" Jacob straightened to his full height and looked Clyde directly in the eye. "I aim to protect my family, and if that's how I have to do it, so be it."

Clyde suddenly wasn't so sure no harm would come to him, and when he chanced a frantic look around, he realized the people who were watching probably wouldn't intercede. It struck him that they might even be on Page's side! He was at the miner's mercy, and the veins on the man's neck were extended and throbbing. He was obviously working himself up to a fever pitch.

"W-well, there's some things you need to know then, Page, before you commence to assaulting me. Things that'll maybe change your view of your son. He ain't the perfect man you think him to be."

"What's that wisecrack supposed to mean, Clyde? You best back that up and quick."

"I saw Matt come out of a Bonanza Street crib a few nights ago, just before he left town, some little blonde-headed thing standing at the door, watching him leave."

"Oh, is that so?"

"Yes, it is."

"Why don't you just tell me about it and don't leave nuthin' out."

"Okay, if that's what you want. It's like I said. It was late, maybe eleven o'clock. He come out and staggered off, and she stood there, gawking after him."

"Yeah. So?"

"Well, don't you—"

"Is that it? That's your whole terrible story. You didn't leave out a single detail?"

"No, I—"

"You left out a lotta details, Clyde. How long was he in there?"

"Well, I don't—"

"You don't know because you didn't see him go in and don't know why he was there. You made an assumption and couldn't wait to get home and tell Flora about it."

"That's not—"

"Shut yer trap, Clyde! You left out something else, too. Like jes' why was you on Bonanza Street at that hour of the night? Care to reveal that to me?"

"It's not what you're thinking," Clyde said, quickly finding himself on the defensive.

"Then just what was it?"

"I, uh . . . Flora wasn't feeling well. I had to get her something."

"Ain't nuthin' 'vailable on Bonanza Street," Jacob observed, "so you musta been headed to Chinatown. An' about the only thing you kin git there at that hour is likker or opium. Just what does Flora have that makes her feel bad, Clyde? An addiction, maybe? This would make fer some juicy gossip, don't you think?"

"Y-you can't do that, Jacob. You can't go around spreading lies and turning people against Flora just because of appearances!"

"Why not? She does it all the time. Yer doin' it right now 'bout Matt."

Clyde was dead silent, the truth beginning to sink in.

"Matt got clubbed on the head in Chinatown," Jacob explained. "He collapsed as he was leavin', and a woman happened by who helped him out, patched him up, then turned him back out into the street. What her profession is had nuthin' to do with what happened. And Matt's the law in this town. He had a right to be there. That's more than you can say."

Clyde's face burned as the blood rose into it. He knew Jacob was right but couldn't bring himself to say it. He couldn't say anything against his wife.

"So, what was it, Clyde? Likker? Opium?"

Quietly, Clyde responded, his head dropping. "You're right, Jacob, Flora sticks her nose where it doesn't belong. And I suppose she has been trying to raise some support for her stand against that woman, but she's just trying to keep the church pure, free from the evil influence of women like her."

"She's afeared too many of the husbands in the church know that woman better'n they ought, that what she's afeared of," Jacob concluded. "But I think she'd be better off worryin' 'bout her own purity. I don't want to know why you was in Chinatown that night, Clyde. But *you* know. And if I understand things rightly, *God* knows too. You can fool me and the rest of the town, maybe, but you ain't foolin' God."

Jacob stared at Clyde for a moment to fix the thought, then turned and went back to the hall. He was done with Clyde. If Bascomb had any manhood left in him, he'd do something about Flora. If not, well, Jacob always had his ace in the hole: Flora's little "problem," whatever it was.

Now it was Reverend Edwards's turn.

Molly took several sharp breaths, wrapped her arms around herself against the cold, and stepped onto the boardwalk that ran down the length of cribs. She walked slowly, as softly as she could, listening, hoping to hear something that would reveal Rosa to her. Something like crying, which she was sure Rosa would be doing.

Rosa was a woman, wasn't she? And she fled the social because she was upset. Wasn't she already in tears before she cleared the building? Molly had to admit she wasn't sure about that. Rosa might have been angry, not weepy. She wondered about those kind of women. Were they different than she? Did they get emotional? They always seemed so hard when Molly saw them on the street, so bitter. She imagined a life like they led could do that to them so very easily. Didn't many of them commit suicide?

Maybe this trip was senseless. Maybe Rosa Bailey was sitting in a dark room somewhere, drinking and laughing and cursing the silly women at the social. Maybe she didn't care at all but came to the social and entered the contest just to needle them.

Molly decided to go back. It was cold; she really didn't know where Rosa had gone; her husband would be concerned about her—

A door creaked open and a woman came out in a tattered coat, her hands in fingerless gloves clutching her coat to keep it closed as it had no buttons. Her head down, she almost bumped into Molly, looking up at her with suspicious, bloodshot eyes, deep set into a face that had once been pretty, now leathery and lined.

"Excuse me," the woman muttered softly.

Molly stared, and the woman began to walk away.

"No, wait, please," Molly begged.

The woman stopped and looked back puzzled but said nothing.

"Please, maybe you can help me."

"Yeah?" She did not come any closer and her voice had an edge, a wary tone.

"I'm looking for someone."

"Husband?" the woman queried with a smirk.

"No. No, certainly not! I-I'm trying to find Rosa Bailey."

"Humph. Rosa Bailey don't live her anymore, honey. She done moved uptown. Now she associates with all them society types, like yourself. No, you'll find her somewheres else."

"Please, no. I tried to follow her this way but lost her. I'm sure she came here."

"Well, if she's here, she'd be at Betsy's."

"Betsy?"

"Yeah. Third door up from mine." The woman turned and disappeared into the darkness.

Molly hurried ahead to the door indicated and reached up to knock, but something stayed her hand. She listened and, through the thin wood, could hear the sobbing. Quietly she tapped on the door.

"Go 'way!" came the blind reply. "I'm closed tonight."

But Molly tapped again. "Please, Betsy. Open the door."

It opened shortly, just a crack, and a blonde-haired female head stuck itself out.

"Yeah, whaddya want?"

"I'm looking for Rosa Bailey. Is she here?"

Betsy looked back into the room, then again at Molly.

"Who wants to know?"

"My name's Molly Carter. I was at the social tonight. I feel bad about what happened. Is Rosa okay?"

"Yeah, she's fine. Go away."

A shiver ran up Molly's spine. "Please, I'm cold. May I come in for a minute?" She let her hands fall away from in front of her so Betsy could see she was pregnant. Immediately Betsy opened the door wider and stood back. Molly stepped in hesitantly but sped up when she saw Rosa curled up on the bed. Rosa looked up at Molly and, when she recognized her through the tears, bared her teeth.

"Get out!"

"She's pregnant, Rosa," Betsy told her friend. "She came lookin' for ya. Says she sorry about what happened."

"Sure, she is."

"It's cold out there, Rosa," Betsy said. "Maybe she really means it. Would she have come at all in her condition, if she didn't mean it?"

"Does it matter?" Rosa spat, sitting up. "Does it matter what she thinks? Can she change anybody's mind? Sarah couldn't. Why should this one?" She pointed an accusing finger at Molly, who shrank back from it, fear growing inside her. She didn't belong here; she needed to go back. Rosa wasn't finished. She got up and grabbed at the costume she still wore, ripping it in two as she pulled it away at the collar. "Here's what I think of you and your kind. Take this silly costume with you. Tell everyone you took it from me, to put me in my place. Maybe then you'll all be happy and will leave me and my kind alone."

Molly was afraid and sorry at the same time and began to cry. "Rosa, I don't want this."

"Sure, you do. Sure, you do. Here take it!"

"Rosa, this ain't like you," Betsy said. "Please stop."

Molly didn't take the pieces of torn cloth Rosa threw at her. Her hands shook, and she backed toward the door, ready to flee. Maybe Rosa was right. There was nothing she could do to help—

A sudden pain racked Molly's belly, and she cried out, doubling over and nearly falling. Betsy moved over next to her to steady her.

"Are you okay? You look kinda pale." She helped her into the room's only chair. "Here, take a seat . . . uh oh."

She looked down at the floor boards where Molly had been

standing. They were freshly wet, as were Molly's shoes. Betsy looked Molly in the face, shocked by the expression of fear that had seized it, the woman's eyes wide and staring.

"You ain't goin' anywhere, lady." She turned and barked at Rosa. "Rosa, get off the bed. This lady's having a baby . . . right now!"

"What?" Rosa abruptly snapped out of her tirade.

"You heard me. She's about to give birth. Her water just broke."

"Uh oh," Rosa said, jumping up, her problem momentarily forgotten. "You done this before?"

"Who you askin'?"

"You, Betsy. I know Miss Carter ain't give birth before. Sarah Page told me that. That's right, ain't it?" she asked Molly.

Molly could only shake her head and groan as she was led to the bed and the clothes under her dress were removed by Betsy. She did not protest, but began crying softly out of fear and bewilderment. This wasn't how it was supposed to be.

"No, I ain't never done this," Betsy said.

"In that case, better let me in there," Rosa said. "I know what to do."

"Be my guest," Betsy said, stepping aside. "What do you want me to do?"

"Get all the clean linens and towels and clothing you can find. We're gonna need some hot water, too. Your stove up to that?"

"Yeah, it'll boil broth."

"Good, get some started. Not broth, just water. Okay honey, it'll be all right. Just relax, I'll talk you through this, okay?"

Molly nodded dumbly, still frightened but sensing in Rosa's voice a calm confidence that what she said was true: She had done this before.

"Let me take a look in there," Rosa said. "Oh, my. I'll say you're ready. Didn't you have any warning?"

Molly shook her head.

"You must be one of them quick types. Get up, make breakfast, have a baby, clean the rugs . . . you know, the kind that don't waste a lot of time when it comes to labor. That's good, really, but it can create a lot of problems, as you can well see. Some women take all day, and no one else can get anything done for a while."

"Okay, here's the towels and things," Betsy said, coming back to the bed. "Ain't too many of them."

"It'll do," Rosa said.

"Now what?" Betsy asked.

"We wait. And we won't be waiting long. There's its head."

Molly shrieked in surprise and pain as another contraction pulsated across her body.

"Breathe even-like, honey," Rosa encouraged. "Nice, even, deep breaths. That's it. You're going to feel more of those. Don't worry. That's normal. That's your muscles contracting, getting ready to push the baby out. Pretty soon now it's gonna slide right on out, and it'll be over. Just keep breathing. Betsy, wipe her forehead, please."

Betsy responded as asked, gently dabbing the beads of perspiration from Molly's face. With her other hand she held Molly's, and the birthing woman's fingers locked tightly around those of the prostitute.

Rosa kneeled on the foot of the bed, watching, ready to reach in and help.

"Good girl," she told Molly. "You're doin' fine."

When Jacob Page had finished giving the Reverend—and, as a bonus, Thomas Wellman—a piece of his mind, he stormed out of the hall, intending to go home. But outside stood a nervous Joseph Carter, looking up and down the street.

"What'cha lookin' fer, Joe? Stage ain't due till mornin'."

"Molly took out after that woman," he said. "I figured she'd be back by now. Something must have happened to her."

"What's that s'posed to mean? Rosa wouldn't hurt her."

"No, I didn't mean that. It's just that . . . Molly's expecting, you know. Any day now."

"Well, I s'pect we ought to go hunt her down, then. Why don't you leave word with someone here that you'll be back in case we miss her and she returns. That way she won't have to come lookin' fer you."

Carter nodded and spoke to a man on the boardwalk, then he and Jacob headed off up the street.

They hadn't gone far when a woman wrapped in blankets could be seen running down the street toward them.

"Ain't that a sight?" Jacob said. "Prob'ly got chased out of someplace right in the middle of things."

As she drew closer, though, she called out to them.

"Either of you Mr. Carter?" she shouted.

"I am!" Joseph yelled back with a wave.

"Come on then, I'll take you to your family." Betsy stopped running and gave a wave, then turned and headed back where she had come from.

Joseph Carter didn't move. "Family? Did she say family?"

"That's what it sounded like," Page said. "Come on, before she gits too fer away." He took off at a trot. "I hope nobody's watching this little scene," he mumbled to himself. "Be mighty hard to explain later." But he kept going and soon Joseph Carter passed him at a dead run.

They followed Betsy to her crib, where she opened the door and let Carter inside. When Jacob got there he could only stick his head in because the room was full. There was Molly lying in the bed, a baby in her arms wrapped in some soft linens. The exhausted woman was a mess but a beautiful mess. Her disheveled hair, just a short time ago done up about her head, now fell about her shoulders. Joseph sat on the edge of the bed, grinning like a simpleton at his bride and their delicate baby girl.

Jacob smiled at the scene.

"Now I got an idea what it looked like in the stable when the baby Jesus was born," he said reverently.

CHAPTER

TWENTY·TWO

FLORA BASCOMB PEEKED OUT THE DOOR cautiously, then her face relaxed as she saw the friendly face of Reverend Edwards peering in at her.

"Oh, Reverend, it's you. I'm surprised to see you out on a Sunday afternoon. Please, come in."

"Thank you, dear Mrs. Bascomb," he said, removing his low-crowned, black hat with the flat, small brim as he stepped over the threshold.

"Let me take your coat."

"Certainly. It's nice and warm in here," he commented as he peeled it off, "contrary to the mean streets of Bodie." He laughed uneasily at himself.

"That was a fine sermon this morning," Flora told him. "Would you like some coffee? I also have some fresh pie."

"You're too kind, Flora, but . . . perhaps not this time. Thank you just the same."

"Very well. Please, Reverend, sit down. Now, what brings you to our humble abode this afternoon?"

Edwards regarded the woman with no expression on his face: her pinched nose, most often held up more highly than she ought; that thinning hair with streaks of gray that she tried to hide with shoe black; her stale breath that Edwards suspected was due to late night imbibing on the sly. Yet her husband was a major contributor, if not *the* major contributor to the church. Still, as a minister of the Gospel, Edwards recognized his duty to address problems within his congregation, even if they were social in nature. Jacob Page had made that abundantly clear after the pie-baking contest.

"My good woman, so as not to interrupt you any longer than necessary, I'll get right to the point. It has come to my attention . . . how shall I say this ? . . . that some of the ladies in the fellowship have been indulging in a little, uh, class distinction regarding other people in the congregation. As you I'm sure are aware, God is no respecter of persons, and we are not to be either."

Flora regarded Edwards with surprise and innocence painted on her face.

"Reverend, of course I agree. All good people should be treated equally, regardless of their station in life. I know I am a leader among the women—I didn't ask to be, naturally—but they all just seem to gravitate toward me. I don't understand the phenomenon, I can assure you. But there it is, nonetheless."

"Yes, Mrs. Bascomb, and that is precisely why I have come to you. I would ask that you use your influence with the ladies and try to stop this terrible thing."

"I'd be happy to oblige, Reverend. May I ask one thing . . . who is this poor person so that I might make an extra effort toward kindness in their direction and perhaps see that a few coins find their way to—"

"It's not a poor person, Mrs. Bascomb."

"No?"

"I referred to their station, not their bank account. I speak of the treatment that's been directed toward Sarah Page, and her friend, Rosa Bailey."

Flora nearly shrieked, and her face turned crimson.

"Reverend, how can you suggest that that . . . *woman*! be accepted into our flock with open arms?"

"I never said—"

"Do you realize she's a . . . I can't even say the word, it's so horrible."

"Waitress?"

"Yes, it's so—no, not that!"

"That's what she is. She works in the Quicksilver, waiting tables."

"I'm talking about her other habits."

"Her former profession?"

Flora didn't answer. To do so would be to acknowledge the concept of "former."

"Mrs. Bascomb, the Bible is quite clear, God can save anyone from anything. And we are to accept all people who want to come into our midst, even sinners." His irony was lost on Flora, however, so he continued. "Mrs. Bascomb, were you born a Christian?"

"Certainly. I was born into a very well-behaved Christian family."

"That's not what I asked. Were you personally saved when you were born, or did that happen to you later in life?"

She could only stare at him blankly.

"Mrs. Bascomb, have you not been listening to me these past few months? Salvation is not something we can claim based on our heritage. It is a personal relationship with God through Jesus Christ, based on His death for us on the cross."

"You don't need to teach me, Reverend," she said snidely, folding her arms. "I'm well aware of the cross. I'm also aware that Christ drove sinners from the temple with a whip because they were desecrating it."

"Very good, Flora. Except their sin was greed and using a house of worship for personal gain. They were sinning in the temple. The discussion here is something entirely different, and it is a past sin, not a present one. I'm sure you know all about the conversion of the woman at the well, the Samaritan woman who had seven husbands. And what about the woman caught in adultery? Christ did not turn them away. Nor did he reject Mary Magdalene but praised her for anointing him with costly perfume. I believe we should keep these things in mind."

He put his hat on and picked up his coat. "And that's not all. Surely you've read in Hebrews about that great heroine of faith, Rahab the harlot. And let's not forget Hosea and his wife. These are things you should think on, Mrs. Bascomb. Well, I've taken enough of your time. Good day, Mrs. Bascomb. See you Wednesday evening?"

"Of course."

To Edwards her icy words sounded more like a threat, but still he managed a smile before turning and letting himself out.

Flora seethed as he shut the door and determined to solve this problem once and for all. She'd go directly to the source . . . that troublemaker, Sarah Page. Especially now that the woman's husband wasn't in town to throw his weight around. Then she'd speak to her husband, and he'd see about a replacement for Reverend Edwards.

She closed her eyes and patted her chin as her plan began to take shape.

Betsy watched in wet-eyed silence as Rosa Bailey stuffed clothing into a small canvas bag. She took no particular care with her things, and when the bag was full, she had several items left over. She thought about it for a second, then dropped them onto the bed.

"They're too big for you," she told Betsy. "But maybe you can find someone who'll fit. Goodness knows there's plenty of fat women like me on Bonanza Street."

"Please don't talk that way," Betsy begged, wiping her fingers across her cheek.

"What, saying there's fat women on Bonanza Street?"

"No, Rosa. You know what I mean. Why do you have to go?"

"What's the point of goin' over it again, Betsy? I've done all the talkin' and cryin' I'm gonna do. I ain't wanted here in Bodie, so I'm go someplace where I'll be welcome."

Betsy had no answer to that so she kept silent, watching Rosa's face for a sign of a tear as Rosa stared at her own hands. But Rosa wouldn't crack and finally Betsy called up her courage and said what was on her heart.

"That was a really good thing you did, Rosa, deliverin' that baby like that."

Rosa didn't respond or react.

"If you hadn't done that, she coulda died or even lost the baby."

"Yeah," Rosa mumbled. "An act of real Christian charity."

"Please Rosa, don't talk that way. You can't deny what you did . . . or why. Rosa, you got a heart as big as all outdoors, you can't deny it. If that had been your worst enemy, you'd a done the same thing."

Rosa shook her head, tears now forming in her eyes.

"*Pah!*" Betsy chided. "You're a lousy liar, Rosa Bailey."

Rosa smiled, but it faded quickly. "Don't matter one way or th'other. Next stage out, I'm on it."

"Have you spoken to Sarah, the deputy's wife? I think she has a right to know."

"You know she'll take your side. Try to talk me out of it."

"Rightly so, Rosa. She gave you a job, invested a lot of time in you, not to mention putting her faith in you, too."

At this Rosa looked up at Betsy, her brows knit. "What're you talkin' about?"

"Oh come on, Rosa. Don't play stupid. It took a lot of faith for her to take you in like she did, let you work in her restaurant. And the way you been talkin' about how Sarah's friends been treatin' the two of you, she's stuck her pretty neck out a country mile. The way I see it, Rosa, you at least owe her a good-bye."

"I can't." Rosa's voice was small.

"You got to."

She shook her head emphatically.

Footsteps outside the door, then a light rapping ended the debate. Rosa gazed at Betsy who just shrugged and opened the door.

Outside in the cold morning air stood a pale Sarah Page, her eyes red. She wore a heavy, gray woolen coat, the hood up over her head so only her dainty oval face showed. In another time or place, she'd be the perfect homeless street urchin, a waif, an orphan, come to beg pennies for bread.

But this was not another time or place, and Betsy immediately reached out and pulled her inside by the arm.

"It ain't much warmer in here," Betsy told the deputy's wife, "but a few degrees are better than none."

Sarah didn't respond. She was unconcerned with the cold, having obviously ventured out into it despite not feeling well. Rosa was on her mind, and her moist eyes locked onto Rosa's and wouldn't let go until Rosa forced her head to turn toward Betsy. She gave her friend an accusatory look. This was too much of a coincidence, Sarah coming by just when they were talking about her. Betsy had set this up. But Betsy wouldn't commit. She just stared back at Rosa defiantly.

Sarah didn't come so they could all gaze at each other, though, and reached out to take Rosa by the hand. Rosa turned toward her, and they embraced. When she broke free, Rosa turned her face away.

"Don't try to stop me," she asserted quietly.

"I haven't said a word," came Sarah's soft reply.

"Didn't need to. It's that look in your eye."

Sarah dropped her head so the hood blocked her eyes from Rosa's.

"Sorry. I didn't mean to. I didn't come here to pressure you into staying, just to say good-bye."

"Who's minding the restaurant?" Guilt was evident in Rosa's voice, knowing she should be at Sarah's side, taking orders and pouring coffee.

"It's closed for now. Not much point opening with so few customers."

"Come to think of it," Rosa said slowly, "you're probably relieved to see me go. I've been driving all your customers away."

"Nonsense, Rosa. That's not true and you know it. Flora Bascomb's running them off. She and all the women she—" Sarah suddenly doubled over, sucking in her breath. Betsy had been watching her face and grabbed the woman, helping her sit on the edge of the bed.

"What's the matter, honey?"

"She don't look too good," Rosa said.

The strain and pain gripped Sarah's face, and she was unable to speak, her breathing shallow and forced.

"Oh dear," Rosa lamented. "Look what I've done. I'm sorry to have caused all this, Sarah."

Sarah managed to shake her head while Rosa patted her hand, and Betsy wiped her moist forehead with a delicate handkerchief. Finally her breathing slowed allowing her to speak.

"No, Rosa, this had nothing to do with you or the restaurant or Flora. I'm in a family way."

"You're pregnant!" Betsy declared.

"Honey, that's wonderful!" Rosa said, a smile brightening her heretofore lined faced. Then the creases returned and she said, "You're having a tough time with morning sickness, ain't you."

Sarah shrugged. "I don't know. Never been pregnant before. Aren't they all like this?"

"Some," Rosa said. "Mine wasn't too bad . . ." She trailed off as the memory of Nellie surfaced again.

Betsy sensed Rosa's unease and changed the subject. "Speaking of pregnant, did you know Miss Molly had her child last night?"

Sarah nodded her head. "I heard about it in passing. Jacob

came by early this morning, but he didn't have time to say much, had to go see about a few things at work. Other than that, I haven't spoken to anyone since a couple of nights ago."

Betsy beamed. "We delivered it for her, right here."

"*Pah.*" Rosa waved her off. "Molly and the baby delivered themselves. We just watched."

A strange look crossed Sarah's face. "What was—how did—she birthed it here?"

"Yep," Betsy stated. "She come by after the social to apologize."

"Betsy!" Rosa scolded. "Keep ahold of your tongue!"

"Why? It's important. Besides, this is my crib, I'll say what I please." She turned back to Sarah. "She came by to apologize about the way Rosa was treated at the social and got all upset like, and suddenly she gushed her water and just like that—" snapping her fingers— "Bodie's population grew by one."

Sarah wondered what had happened at the social, but the look on Rosa's face told her not to ask. The woman was obviously uncomfortable about the whole affair. She concentrated on Molly and the baby.

"Boy or girl?"

"Beautiful little girl," Betsy said.

"They okay?"

"Oh sure, they're fine. But it's a good thing Rosa was here. It happened so fast. If I'da been alone or if Mrs. Carter had been walkin' outside, well, who knows what might have happened. I shiver just to think about it."

Rosa turned away, whether embarrassed or ashamed Sarah couldn't tell. She stood on shaky legs and put her arm around the woman.

"Rosa, I know you've got to do what's on your conscience. It's true, I need you here. But if you have to leave, then it'll be with my blessing. I'm proud to have known you." Sarah stood on her tiptoes, leaned over, and kissed the former madam on the cheek, then smiled at Betsy and nodded her thanks as she bundled her coat around her and stepped out to brave Bodie's severe morning.

A weary lawman trudged up the muddy track, head bent from trying to keep the rain out of his eyes, shivering from the cold, his pace slow and unsteady. He rarely looked up, beyond caring where he was headed, wanting only to make it someplace where he could get out of the rain, drink something hot, and sleep for a few days. He'd long since left the road. When it wound down into a canyon for what he figured to be mile upon mile, he remembered the smoke he'd seen and stayed on high ground. Then the rain came and in a few hours so did his fever.

Whatever smoke there had been, he had lost sight of hours before. Whether the rain had masked it, put the fire out, or it had all been his imagination in the first place, Matt Page didn't know and didn't care. He only knew he had to get out of the rain.

His mind wasn't working well, though, for he'd passed several places wherein he could have taken refuge had he but put some thought to it. Caves, even an overhanging rock not fifty yards off to his right, would have sufficed. But he plodded ahead, heedless, thinking only of the smoke he'd seen until he realized he'd been walking too far. He should have been there by now. He'd passed it somehow, missed the cabin. He was no longer even sure which direction he was headed.

He stopped and leaned against a rock, wiping his wet face with wet hands and rubbing his tired, stinging eyes. He'd be sick to death if something didn't happen soon. He shielded his eyes and gazed into the distance as the rain slacked suddenly. He thought he spied two shadowy figures walking toward him. Try as he might, he couldn't make them out, couldn't tell if they were friend or foe or even human. No, they had to be human; they walked on two legs. Could be bears, he supposed. Real thin bears. No, they weren't animals. Maybe they were angels, and he was finally dead after all. Was there rain in heaven?

Suddenly his head grew light and the ground rose up swiftly and slammed the side of his face. The lights went out, the rain stopped, and the shadowy figures faded to black along with everything else.

He was on his back when he awoke, but he wasn't staring up into the sky. There was no rain on his face. He reached up and pressed his eyes, rubbing them with his fingertips, then wiped them slowly down his face. His face was overgrown, his beard gone unshaven for so long that the whiskers were long enough to be soft. His body was dry. That realization came to him before his vision returned. He was also warm. He could feel blankets and, on his right side, a fire. He could hear it, too, the crackling of the wood and the whooshing and flapping of flames.

He was indoors. Above him was a ceiling of sorts, but he couldn't make out exactly what it was made from. His mouth was dry too, his throat sore, and a bitter taste permeated it. Bitter, yet familiar. The fever was gone, he knew that. And he was powerful hungry.

Struggling to sit, Matt rolled toward the heat and propped himself on one elbow, stretching the kinks out of his neck. Slowly his vision cleared, and he could make out the fire. He stared into it, watching the flames dance, until a face beyond came slowly into focus.

Matt suddenly recoiled in fear and gasped but in his weakness could not retreat, and in a minute, his senses returned. The face was friendly, very smiling and friendly. And very Indian.

The old woman wore a faded, calico dress and a moth-eaten, yellow sweater, with a blue bandanna tied over her gray hair. Her face was a road map of wrinkles. She smoked a long, thin pipe carved from bone while grinning toothlessly at Matt. He smiled weakly in return and looked around for someone else. He was not to be disappointed, seeing another woman, a young maiden, a few feet away deftly weaving a basket with quick, sure hands while she watched the white man wake up.

The animal skin over the entrance to the wikiup flipped back, and a man ducked in. He wore wool pants, a cotton shirt, and old, black lace-up shoes. His long, black hair was tied with a piece of bright-red cloth. His age was indecipherable, but he appeared to be closer to the age of the older woman than the basket weaver.

"Ah, you wake," he said. "That good. Give us many worry. You breathe but rest of you dead we think. Hungry?"

"Yes," Matt said weakly, his parched throat burning with the effort. "Water."

"Ah, yes, water." The Indian gave Matt a drink from a skin, then offered some small pieces of pine nut bread. Matt took it with his fingers and stuffed it into his mouth, forcing himself to chew and swallow, then washing it down with more water. He wanted more but was too tired and let himself back down onto his side, resting his head on a small pile of skins.

Presently the Indian left, then returned with a tin mug full of pungent tea, emanating a strange yet familiar odor. It was the squaw tea Charlie Jack had made for him once after he'd been shot at the shootout with the convicts and was the source of the bitter taste in his mouth—the same tea he'd tried to make for Sheriff Taylor at the hot springs. But his hadn't smelled like this. The Paiutes obviously had a secret about their tea that they didn't share, something that made it stronger and better. Matt held his breath and took it all at once, then gasped. His tea hadn't tasted like this, either. He laid himself back down.

"*Su-du-pe,*" the Paiute said. "Very good, make well. You sleep now, eat more when wake," the Indian said. Matt nodded, closed his eyes, and did as the Indian instructed.

The next time Matt woke, nothing much had changed. The old Paiute woman still busied herself at the edge of the fire, only now instead of weaving she was making small cakes of acorn mush to cook on a flat stone. The younger woman, maybe a teenager, was now at her side, helping pat the meal into the small cakes and placing them on the hot rock. She smiled coyly at Matt.

He watched them, not attempting to get up, until the first batch of cakes was finished. Then the elder woman whistled through the space where her two front teeth should have been, and the man of the wikiup came with a leather bag. He smiled at his guest and motioned for him to sit up.

Matt did so with some effort and was surprised at how good he felt. The old woman handed the man a cake and he in turn gave it to Matt, than accepted one for himself. On his own, however, he sprinkled some yellow grains before taking a large bite.

Matt looked at his own cake, figuring it to be rather pungent but otherwise tasteless and viewed the bag with a pout. The Indian gave him a questioning look.

"You no like?"

"*Koochabee*, very sweet," Matt said.

The Indian smiled broadly and sprinkled a handful of the stuff onto Matt's cake. "You very smart white man."

Matt smiled and bit into the stuff. He knew what *koochabee* was, and knew also it was very nutritious and quite good, once you got used to the idea of eating fly larvae. To the Paiute, it was a delicacy and the main reason for their annual festivities at the shores of Mono Lake where it was harvested from the salt water.

Matt finished his meal and nodded. "Thank you," he said to the man, then repeated it to both of the women in turn, the elder woman first.

"Tomorrow, you walk," said the Indian. "Today sleep, rest, grow strong."

"I'm okay," Matt said. "I want to get up."

"No, better you not. You tired, have bad wound. Tomorrow."

"I don't want to be in the way," he protested.

"If you in way, Sally John move you." The Indian nodded to the elder woman, who just smiled at the white man. "I, John. Some call John Horse. I catch horse, very good."

"You like to catch horses?" Matt understood the Paiute practice of naming themselves after the first name of white men they respected, sometimes adding a descriptive term. There was Matchie Fred, who was always begging matches, and of course Cornbread Tom. Their wives were called by their husband's first name after their own adopted name.

"Yes. Catch one two moons past. Sell in town three moons."

"Maybe you won't have to," Matt said. "I'm gonna need a horse to get back to Bodie."

"Bodie? You go to Bodie?"

"Yes. I'm the deputy sheriff there. Matt Page."

"Ah, Matt Page. Hear of you. Charlie Jack tell many stories, Deputy Matt Page. We laugh." As if to prove it, he chattered something to the women in his native tongue and they all laughed. Matt flushed, though he had no clue what had been said.

"You good friend, Charlie Jack say. He say you smart." The Paiute looked at his bag of *koochabee*. "He right."

The Indian got up. "You sleep. Tomorrow you walk. Two days you ride home Bodie." He and the women all left the tent, leaving Matt nothing to do but to obey, and he settled once again under the skins, suddenly very tired, his stomach full and satisfied.

Three sharp raps on the door prompted a verbal response from the occupant.

"Hold your horses. I'm coming!"

Billy O'Hara, substitute lawman, stood patiently on the porch, his silent eyes staring off at the town below this hillside house. The natural wood and whitewashed homes and businesses, most with gray smoke puffing from chimneys and flues from fires lit against the hint of winter in the air, stood in tranquility that contrasted with the turmoil churning inside the man holding the Sharp's rifle.

His companion for this visit to the home of mine superintendent Thomas Wellman was Jacob Page. Both men were friends of Wellman, and neither of them wanted to be there, at least not for this reason: Billy was about to place Wellman under arrest for the destruction of a private building and for the murder of James Nixon.

Wellman came to the door as promised and opened it enough to peek out, then, seeing his friends, opened it wide and beckoned them in. Solemnly, Billy accepted.

"Sit down, gents," Wellman said. "Libation?"

"No, thank you," Billy deferred. "On both offers."

Wellman was puzzled. "You look so serious. Do I take it this is not a pleasure call?"

"It is not."

Ever mindful of his manners, Wellman included the one-armed miner in the conversation. "Jacob? What's wrong? Is there bad news? Was there a cave-in? This isn't about the pie contest at the social, surely."

"No, nuthin' like that, Tom. Go 'head, Billy. Tell 'em. Yer the official man here." Wellman looked back at O'Hara.

Even in this weather, a sweat had broken out above the big man's upper lip, and he wiped it with the sleeve of his free hand.

"Thomas Wellman, by virtue of the power given me by Deputy Matthew Page in his absence, Ah'm afraid Ah must place you under arrest for the Queen Anne explosion and the death of James Nixon."

Wellman leaned back, as though the words had driven him like a stiff wind.

"What are you talking about?"

"There's evidence," Jacob said, almost apologetically.

"Evidence?" Wellman adjusted his wide-eyed gaze to Page. "What evidence? What are you talking about?"

"We don't like this, Tom. Don't think we do," Jacob said. "But we cain't disregard what we know to be true. Maybe it's all a mistake. I pray to God it is a mistake. But until we can check it out completely, we're gonna have to take you in."

"Billy?" Wellman was pleading, not just for his freedom but for the wise, friendly man to make some sense out of this for him.

"It's true, Tom. There's circumstantial ev'dence 'gainst you."

"Circumstantial . . . you can't arrest me on just circumstantial evidence."

"That ain't all. Nixon named you before he died."

The color drained from Wellman's face, and he collapsed into the chair behind where he stood, staring blankly ahead of him, seeing nothing.

"Come on, Tom. This is hard enough as it is."

He shook his head slowly, eyes still focused at some point in the room straight ahead. "What'll this mean? You're taking me to jail?"

"Got to."

"Why, Billy? I'm a danger to no one."

"For your protection, Tom. Someone gets wind of this—and they will, there's no doubt 'bout that—some people might want to take it upon themselves to try you and convict you with a few balls of hot lead in some dark alley."

"But, I'm innocent . . ."

"Ah'd like to believe you, Tom, but Ah've got a duty to do. We'll hold you until Matthew gets back, then—"

"Matt! He already arrested the men who blew up the Queen Anne magazine!"

"Yeah, that's what he thinks. That's why we're gonna wait until he gets back. You'll be comfortable and well-fed, and if you're not guilty, Mr. Smith has agreed not to dock you any pay."

Wellman leaned forward and put his face in his hands. "This is all too much."

"Come on, Tom, please," Billy appealed.

"You going to handcuff me, Billy?"

"Do Ah need to?"

"No, of course not. I'll go peacefully. I'm not only civilized, I'm innocent. Jacob can follow with a gun in my back if that would make you more comfortable."

"Nope, I think not," Jacob said, but he had a revolver in his pocket just the same and had every intention of keeping it at the ready. Friend or no, Thomas Wellman was being arrested for a capital crime, and desperate men have been known to do desperate things.

"Get your coat and a change of clothes, Thomas, and whatever else you want to make you . . . well, Ah was gonna say 'comfort-able' but that don't sound right, so Ah'll just leave it unsaid."

"I know what you mean," Wellman said as he got up slowly. He walked with uneasy steps into his bedroom, followed closely by Jacob Page, and collected the items he would need. Jacob tried to act nonchalant, but both of them knew he was keeping the prisoner from making a break for it or arming himself. It was a tense moment that neither of them would remember fondly, yet both of them knew was mandatory.

When Wellman came out carrying a carpet bag, Billy nodded. "Ready?"

"As I'll ever be," came the reply, and together the three men walked to the jail.

CHAPTER

TWENTY·THREE

THREE RIDERS CRESTED A ROCKY BUTTE and hundreds of square miles of California's high plains stretched out below them. In the distance to the south rose the White Mountains, beyond which rested the lowest spot in California, Death Valley. To the east were the deserts of Nevada; to the west stood the rugged, magnificent Sierra Nevadas, including Mount Whitney, the highest spot in California. Snow-capped virtually year round, but certainly now, they rose almost immediately from the plains, not bothering with foothills. At their feet, and directly below the riders, Mono Lake sat as still as death, the black island in the center rising like the hub on a discarded wagon wheel in the sand. On the opposite side of Mono Lake were over twenty lifeless volcanoes, their gray-ash flanks dotted with belligerent vegetation.

"Magnificent," Jeff Bodine breathed quietly.

"Breathtaking," remarked his brother, Josh.

"Let's eat," said Wild Bill Hickok, dismounting his horse and reaching into his saddlebags.

Jeff looked at him askance, then rolled his eyes for his brother's benefit. Josh accepted the challenge.

"Good idea. I'm famished." He threw a leg over his steed's neck and slid down. Bill tossed him a biscuit and a hunk of smoked ham. Jeff watched them for a moment from the saddle, then reluc-

tantly climbed down and took some food. After all, beautiful
scenery doesn't feed the bulldog.

"You can gaze in wide wonder while you chow down,"
Hickok told him, his own back to the view. "I seen things you
wouldn't believe. Trees so big twenty men with their arms out
couldn't wrap all the way around 'em. And mountains as purple
as a blood blister. And flat plains so vast you could see the curve
of the earth."

Jeff snorted. "All in one place?"

"You got me there," Hickok chortled.

"I believe the mountains and plains parts," Josh said with his
mouth full of buttermilk biscuit, "but trees that big? Come on, Mr.
Hickok."

"It's true, son. They're called redwoods, and you've got some
not too far from here, just over them mountains, in fact. Two day
ride. Ain't you ever been nowhere?"

"Not much," Josh said sadly.

"Well, when we get done recoverin' your gold and my pistols,
maybe you two can take a ride over there, see if Wild Bill ain't
tellin' the truth."

"Speaking of which," said the ever-practical Jeff. "Just where
are you takin' us?"

"To find Mr. Wheeler, your gold, and my pistols. We're going
to Lundy, boys. In the mountains. It's a little place built pretty
much on the side of a hill, overlookin' a lake."

"How far away?" Josh asked.

"We'll be there tomorrow, maybe the next day, dependin'."

"On what?" Jeff asked, his voice dripping of suspicion.

"On these horses, mostly. They ain't much. I hope you get your
gold so we can buy some decent creatures to ride home on."

After they had finished eating Hickok put the remains away
and mounted his horse, turning it in a circle as he waited for the
Bodines to follow, then headed down the hill toward the lake.

The descent took a half hour and once they bottomed out
Hickok paused giving the horses a rest. Though it hadn't been
long, the slope was somewhat steep and covered with loose rocks,
and the horses were worn out. They weren't fresh, young horses
to begin with, and Hickok didn't think any of the animals could

carry two riders, nor did he think any of the men, he nor the Bodines, wanted to walk. At least, he didn't.

They all took slugs from their canteens and watered the horses, then after a rest they rode on again at a slow, even pace. They were not in pursuit. Their quarry had lit out a couple days before for his hometown, and that's where they'd find him, Hickok believed. There was plenty of time.

Josh, however, was anxious.

"Can't we ride a little faster?" he asked.

"Sure, you can. But it ain't a good idea. We want the horses to make it all the way there, don't we? Sure, we do. And it ain't that far. There's not enough daylight left to get there before dark even if we galloped. We'll ride for a few more hours, get within striking distance, then bed down for the night and discuss our strategy. Then in the morning we'll ride into Lundy, find that hombre and his friends, and see what they have to say."

Josh relented. Jeff didn't say anything but just brought up the rear in silence. They did as Hickok said, and at the base of a mountain in some trees by a creek, they made camp. Jeff stood off a ways from them while Josh and Hickok made a fire and put on some coffee and bacon and beans, gazing up at the line of trees winding up a canyon from where they had settled, back and forth, cutting through and around the rising hills until it disappeared.

"This crick flows from the lake," Hickok called out to Jeff. The town is back 'bout a mile or two from where you can see up there. Grab some firewood before you come back."

Jeff didn't acknowledge the gunfighter but did as he was told and returned with an armload of dry sticks. He dropped them by the fire and was handed a plate of grub by his brother, taking his turn as cook.

"You get to make breakfast," Josh told him.

"That so?"

"Pretty much. We're takin' turns. It's the only fair way to do it."

Jeff gave him a disgusted look but ate his food, his hunger overcoming his desire to argue which of them was the oldest and which gave the orders. Hickok ate like he'd fasted a week, noisily sucking black coffee and talking with his mouth full.

"So, you fellers know how to use them things?" He nodded in the general direction of Josh's six-gun.

"I do. He don't," Josh stated to the point.

"Never had no need or no desire," Jeff said in his defense.

"No?" Hickok raised his eyebrows. "Well, that's good, I suppose. Keeps a man out of trouble if he knows he ain't up to meetin' it eye to eye. Time consumin' too, learnin' how to shoot fast and accurate, and how to keep 'em clean so's they won't let you down. I wonder what woulda happened, though, had you been there when them outlaws braced your pa."

He went back to his food, showing no interest in what Jeff's answer would be if he'd been inclined to give one. Which he wasn't.

Josh knew the answer. Jeff would've got himself shot too. He changed the subject, not to save his brother from embarrassment but because the subject was boring and predictable. Who cared what Jeff would've done anyway?

Josh began to speak to the gunfighter: "Hey, Mr. Hickok—"

"We're trail partners, son, you call me Bill."

"Excuse me," Jeff said, "But your name is James, isn't it? Where's the 'Bill' come from?"

"Don't remember exactly. It was attached to the 'Wild' part somehow."

"Who gave you that name?"

"Well, it coulda been my schoolmarm or a couple ladies in Texas or John Wesley Hardin—"

"That's right. I read about him," Josh said, his eyes growing wide. Jeff just shook his head.

"Is it true about him shootin' a man just for snorin'?" Josh continued, ignoring his brother. "Weren't you sheriff in Abilene when he done that?"

"Abilene, Kansas, to be exact. Yes, I was. But it didn't quite happen like that. If it had, I'da had no choice but to arrest him. Truth is, he wasn't shooting at the man directly. You see, the man had an adjoining room in a cheap hotel, the kind with thin walls. He commences to snoring and after a while John Wesley couldn't take no more, so he fires a round through the wall just to wake the man up. One shot ain't never enough for John Wesley, so he fired another, only the second shot kills the man deader'n a beaver hat. John Wesley never met him in life, and in death he couldn't say he had anything agin him, so it was officially recorded as an accident."

"What was he doin' with a gun in town?" Jeff asked.

Josh gave him a surprised look. "I thought you never read my magazines," he said. "How'd you know about the ban on guns in Abilene when Mr. Hickok was the law?"

Jeff's face reddened. "I . . . uh . . . accidentally skimmed through one of 'em once, when I had nuthin' better to do."

Hickok laughed. "He's right, Josh. I did have a ban. But John Wesley Hardin was a hard'n all right, and me and him came to an understanding. I promised not to take his guns and he promised not to shoot me." Hickok guffawed at himself, then said, "Seemed to have worked pretty good. Here I am."

"Yeah, here you are," observed Jeff. "A drunk in exile in California, only out of jail because my brother thinks you can recover our gold for us."

Not seeming to take offense Hickok said, "I can help lead you to it, but you're gonna have to take it for yourselves. I'm here for my pistols, that's all. If I help you too, well, that's okay by me. I don't mind being your friend, Jeff, but you're sure makin' it awful hard. You either don't think I can deliver, or you don't trust me. Think I'm after your gold."

"Jeff," Josh said testily, "why don't you stick a cork in it?"

Jeff flashed his brother a menacing stare. "You know, I've had about enough of you tellin' me what to do. In case you forgot, I'm still the oldest. You're to do as I say."

"Says who?"

"Says Pa, that's who."

"Look around you, Jeff. He ain't here."

"That's your fault, Josh. Your little escapade of ridin' off to Bodie with your fortune, then losing it to them two cowboys foolishly and almost goin' to prison for robbin' that bank. That put Pa in an early grave."

"That's your opinion."

"Excuse me," Hickok said.

"It's the only possible answer," Jeff asserted. "If you hadn't gone off like that, Jim Wheeler woulda never been hired and never been let go, and he never woulda come back to kill Pa!"

"May I—" Hickok tried again but was ignored.

"You're guessin'."

"Boys, I—"

"It was you, and that's all there is to it!" Jeff concluded, pointing a finger. That was all it took, and Josh flew off the rock he had been straddling and tackled his brother, knocking him off his log onto the dirt. As they rolled around, delivering weak, ineffective blows to each other's midsections, Hickok crossed his leg at the knee and leaned back on one elbow to watch.

"That's pretty lame," he encouraged. "Oh, good one. Too bad you hit like a woman. That's it, right in the eye—oh, you missed. Tough break."

Finally Jeff and Josh grew tired, not so much of fighting each other as listening to Hickok's derision, and rolled away from each other, panting in the dirt.

"All done?" Hickok asked. "Now let me tell you boys something. I know you're brothers, and you got a wild hair for each other—for whatever reason I'm sure I don't know—but we got a serious job ahead of us. We're gonna need to be able to trust each other. When this is all over I'll personally referee the match, but for right now I hope you got it all out of your systems. Understand?"

Josh nodded. Jeff just glared but eventually mumbled his consent, picked himself up, and walked off to be by himself while dusting off his pants.

There was silence around the campfire for a time, and Hickok took out the makings for a cigarette and rolled it skillfully. Josh watched him, interested, but Jeff continued ignoring the both of them. Then, while Jeff watched the small flames dance in the fire ring, a thought formed in his brain without him putting any effort to it, and he suddenly shouted, "Wait a minute! Lundy! How'd you know the man was Wheeler and that he was going to Lundy?"

Hickok grinned slyly. "I wondered how long it would take you to ask. He said so when he was beating me at cards."

"Yeah?" Jeff said. "Maybe we should make sure the man you lost your pistols to is Jim Wheeler. What'd he look like? Or were you too drunk to remember?"

"Oh, I remember all right, drunk or not. Yes siree Bob, I remember. He was a regular-lookin' cuss, I'll grant you that. 'bout five-eight or nine, heavy mustache like mine, weak chin, squinty eyes, wore a tan Montana hat with a concho band around it, real fancy-lookin'. Sported a single revolver, a Smith & Wesson like yours, Jeff. Wore it butt first in a holster hung from his pants belt. His boots were miner's, with his jeans tucked in 'em. Kind of an odd duck, now that I think about it. Half-cowboy, half-miner, and half-trail dog."

"That's three halves," Jeff pointed out in derision.

"Did good in math when you was in school, did you?" Hickok asked, rightly figuring Jeff probably hadn't been to formal school. Hickok tore off another chunk of ham and worked it over, wiping the small flakes from his mustache with the back of his hand.

Jeff would not be intimidated. "I do okay in math. But the man you described ain't Wheeler. Wheeler's no more'n five-five, clean-shaved, wears a bowler and carries a Colt's self-cocker in his coat pocket."

"Course it ain't him," Hickok said. "I described one of his partners, just to test you. Wheeler's just like you described him."

Jeff wasn't satisfied, but there was nothing left to say. Had Hickok actually met Wheeler as he said, or did he trick Jeff into revealing his description? Hickok testing *him*. Jeff kicked at the dirt, frustrated. He had started out disliking Hickok, and that attitude was growing, but there was something about the gunfighter's ways, his ease of manner, his sharp eye, that stayed Jeff from speaking his thoughts. Besides, he acted like he had a good idea where their gold had gone, and if he could help them recover it, well, Jeff supposed he could put up with the man's bad points.

Assuming, of course, that in the end Hickok wasn't going to just help himself to their gold once they found it. Jeff determined he'd follow the man's leading, but he'd keep an eye on him as well.

They all bedded down shortly thereafter, Hickok immediately falling into a deep, snoring sleep. Jeff drifted off after he was sure it wasn't a ruse on the gunman's part, but Josh stayed awake, looking up at the sky for what seemed like hours, counting the falling stars. He had gotten up to eight when sleep overcame him.

Jeff woke at dawn, though it wasn't the first time. He'd done so at least five or six times during the night. Whether it was Hickok's snoring, the noises of the night prairie, or his own uneasiness, he couldn't tell. Bottom line, though, he hadn't gotten much sleep.

He also ached all over. This wasn't the first time he'd slept on hard ground under the open sky, but it had been a long time. Once when they were little, Pa had let both of them camp out behind the house. It lasted all of three hours before they decided their beds were more comfortable and safe.

Without getting up, he stretched his whole body in sections trying to work out the kinks, especially his back. He longed for a clean change of clothing, for a place to wash up, for a home-cooked meal.

Suddenly he had to chuckle at himself. He'd been on the trail a whole day now and was already homesick. What a sissy. Of course he'd never let on to Josh. Jeff knew he'd never hear the end of that. So he gritted his teeth and determined that everything was just fine.

He lay still for some time, gazing up at the lightening sky and the colorful tricks the sun played on the scattered clouds: the pastel yellows, oranges, and purples against the deep but brightening blue sky. Then he became aware of movement and glanced over to see his brother getting up and stirring the coals, bringing up the fire that had ebbed nearly to extinction during the night. Josh tossed some kindling on them and leaned over to blow. In a few seconds, they ignited. He blew some, more then carefully placed a handful of twigs in the young flames, followed by sticks, then a couple of hefty logs. In almost no time, the fire crackled and roared, and Jeff could feel its warmth creep over him.

"You can get up now. The fire's ready," Josh muttered quietly.

Jeff didn't answer but sat up and pretended he had just awakened.

"Huh?" he said with a yawn.

"I said you can get your lazy bones out of the sack. I've got the fire roaring so you don't catch cold."

"Oh, thanks," Jeff said. "Can I do anything?"

"Yeah. Would you mind making breakfast, your highness, like we already said?"

"Sure, no problem."

Jeff threw off the blanket and pulled on his boots, then got up and did as Josh asked. Hickok continued snoring.

"What about him?" Jeff asked.

"Toss some bacon on the griddle and make some pan biscuits. He'll be up soon enough, I reckon."

Josh was right. About the time breakfast was ready, Hickok stirred, swallowed his final snort, then got up smacking his lips together. He rubbed his eyes and glanced around to get his bearings, his eyes finally alighting on the Bodines. The puzzled look fell from Hickok's face as he remembered, and he sniffed the aroma of Jeff's cooking.

"Ah, breakfast. Good thing. I didn't sleep a wink all night."

He trudged over to the boys in his stocking feet, stockings with very little toe left in them. Josh handed him a plate, and he sat on a rock by the fire and ate, loudly and greedily. Jeff took his own plate and moved as far away from him as he could. Josh stayed by the fire.

With breakfast out of the way, the dishes done, and the horses saddled and ready to move out, Hickok suddenly became once again the captain of the ship. He instructed the boys to mount up, heedless that they had already done so, then took off at an easy canter across the sagebrush plateau. A couple of hours later, as Hickok slowed the pace, Josh ventured ahead and rode abreast of the gunfighter. Just to keep himself informed, Jeff did the same, keeping himself within earshot.

"So what's the plan?" Josh asked.

"The plan?" Hickok stroked his mustache, picking out a small piece of food he'd left there during breakfast and flicking it away, then took a plug of tobacco from his pocket and bit off a chaw. "The plan. Well, son, that depends on what we find when we get to Lundy. If they're together, the three of 'em, we'll brace them together. If they're separated, we'll go after the man who used to work for your pa. Based on the way you describe him, that's the same man who took my pistols—"

"Won your pistols," Jeff corrected from behind them.

"Yes, of course," Hickok said sourly without turning around. He spit a black torpedo into the dirt and jerked a thumb over his shoulder. "The voice of truth," he said quietly to Josh but loud enough for Jeff to hear. "Anyway, we'll gang up on that man. He'd be foolish to try to shoot his way out of it against three guns, especially since one of 'em is me. He don't know you two are a couple of green miner's boys."

"Josh can shoot the tail off a lizard," Jeff said. Josh couldn't tell for sure if there was a slight sense of sarcasm in his brother's voice, but he assumed it.

"Don't listen to him," Josh told Hickok.

"He's the voice of truth," Hickok said, pulling his mount to a gentle stop. "If you're good with a gun, I need to know now. I've got to plan this around you two, and if either or both of you can shoot, that'll certainly make this a lot easier."

Josh sighed, gave his brother a look askance, then suddenly drew and fired at a nearby rock where a lizard had been basking in the sun. His bullet was close enough to the small target to send it scurrying, but the unexpected noise of the weapon startled the horses, and all three of them snorted in fright. Josh and Wild Bill slacked the reins slightly while their animals reeled, then pulled them to one side getting them to turn rather than run off, and soon they were again under control.

But Jeff jerked his reins back in a panic and the horse reared, tossing him into a clump of sagebrush. He landed with a grunt, and the riderless horse took off. Wild Bill leapt immediately into action, charging after the frightened beast. At a dead run he removed his rope from the leather straps on the saddle that held it and began waving it over his head. Soon he gained on Jeff's horse and with a mighty fling his lasso flew out in a gentle arc and found its way around the neck of the fleeing horse. He quickly looped the end of the lariat around the pommel and tightened his knees to stop his own horse, cinching the lasso and bringing both animals to an abrupt, dusty halt.

Josh jumped down to help his brother out of the prickly bush, not knowing whether he should laugh or apologize. He grabbed his brother's wrist and pulled, and the elder Bodine struggled and finally stood. He dusted himself off with a grumble as Hickok returned, leading the errant horse.

"You okay?" he asked Jeff.

"I'm fine," he said.

"The voice of truth," Hickok said. "You're a tough hombre. I used to get banged up pretty good falling off a horse. Good thing he didn't step on you."

"Yeah, good thing," Jeff agreed, giving Josh a glare. Josh just turned away and grinned.

"Well, I guess we all learned something this morning," Hickok said, slipping his lasso off the neck of Jeff's mount. "I learned Josh can shoot pretty good for a miner—and quick, too. At a lizard, at least. A man's a different thing. Josh learned not to shoot around skittish horses until he knows how they'll react . . . Some horses don't like sudden noises, son. Takes training to get 'em used to it. And Jeff learned how not to steady a scared horse." He tied his rope back on his saddle. "Been a good morning, so far." He turned and once again headed for Lundy.

"Oh yeah," he added over his shoulder, "we also learned why Jeff's horse is named Polo."

"Why is that?" Jeff asked.

"It's not actually Polo, you see. It's got two L's. His name is *Poy-Oh*. That's a Spanish word. In Spanish, you see, two L's are said like they was a 'Y.' Get it? Poy-Oh. It's scratched into his saddle on the pommel. See?"

Jeff did indeed See as he remounted the horse while Josh held it still. P-O-L-L-O scratched into the leather with an awl or the tip of a knife blade.

"So what?" Jeff asked defensively.

"Pollo. That's Spanish for *chicken*." Hickok roared and kicked his horse into a trot.

CHAPTER

TWENTY · FOUR

LUNDY WAS INDEED built on the side of a hill. What would have been the valley floor was submerged under a lake, and the buildings rose to the south of it, each street a story higher than the one below it. Not that there were many streets. About four, as best Jeff could tell. A small mine works was the highest building, the mill just below the opening of the drift. But the biggest business in town wasn't mining. It was a lumber mill at the south end of the lake. In marked contrast to the barren valley in which Bodie had been built, Lundy was surrounded by trees. It was apparent that the lumber company folks had begun by taking the closest trees first and clearcutting, then spreading out from there.

Most of the buildings, mostly one-room log shacks thrown together by their occupants, were scattered across the hillside without concern for design or order. The main street was short, only a block or so long, and contained a general store, a saloon, a chop house, a laundry, and an assay office. No jail that Jeff could see.

It had apparently rained recently in Lundy. There were spots of dirty snow in the shadows; everywhere else was mud or slush. It would be impossible walking across the street and ending up on the other side with clean boots. Jeff sneered his disgust.

The three of them rode into the town attracting the stares of everyone outside. In front of the store, a young girl wearing pants and a gun belt strapped around her coat lounged on the seat of a buckboard as two men unloaded boxes and crates off the back. She checked things off on a sheet of paper she held until she noticed Hickok, and her mouth dropped open, her pencil poised in mid-air. She watched them ride by as Hickok, noticing her as well, tipped his hat and smiled.

The men of Lundy—there were few other women about besides the girl on the wagon—were uneasy with the new arrivals. They weren't used to seeing strangers ride in unless they were leading burros laden with the gear of their trade, be it mining or logging. These men were wearing guns. This did not bode well.

A small boy threw a rock at Josh, then ran, the stone falling woefully short of its mark. A dog nipped at the heels of Hickok's horse, but the man let loose with a large glob of well-aimed tobacco juice and the animal yelped and ran off whimpering.

Hickok pulled up outside the chop stand and climbed down, tying the horse loosely to the rail. Jeff and Josh followed obediently, neither of them saying anything, both of them feeling very uneasy in this obviously hostile environment. Jeff unconsciously felt for the unwanted revolver he carried, and sighed in spite of himself as he touched the smooth, wood grip. They went inside.

"Three plates of pork chops," Wild Bill announced as he chose a table by the window where he could keep an eye on their horses. The cook nodded as the Bodines sat on either side of the gambler, finally catching each other's eye. Josh only shrugged.

They ate in silence, then Hickok leaned back in his chair with his cup of coffee and a toothpick and scanned the small group that had assembled outside, trying to act casual but watching them just the same. The cook—also the owner, waiter, and bottle-washer—came over to secure payment.

"Three dollars," he said.

Josh paid him in coins and the man bit one, then grunted his acceptance.

"What's your business in town?" he asked.

"Looking for someone," Josh stated.

Hickok cleared his throat. "What he means is, these boys lost their pa, and they're lookin' for their uncle. Heard he was last in Lundy. Maybe you know him?"

"Maybe. I know most everybody in town. Looking for their uncle, you say? What's your take in this?"

"This is a tough world we live in," Hickok said. "I wanted to make sure these lads don't have any trouble."

"That's mighty neighborly."

"Ah, it's nothing, really."

"Well, I wish you luck."

"Thank you. Thank you. Now, maybe you can help us find him."

"What's his name?"

"His name?" Hickok looked at Jeff and Josh. "What's his name, boys?"

Josh's face was a blank, so Jeff said, "Wheeler. Jim Wheeler."

"Hmm. Jim Wheeler, you say." The man chewed on it for a moment, sizing the three of them up, then shook his head. "Nope, ain't likely."

"You don't know him?" Josh asked.

"No, he ain't your uncle. He was an only child. Well, thanks for your patronage. Don't let the door hit your backside on the way out." He turned to leave.

"Ain't you gonna tell us where we can find the man?" Josh asked.

The restaurateur stopped and turned. "The likes of you three ain't likely to make me. Now you two, you look okay. But Jim Wheeler ain't your uncle. That lie, plus the squinty glare of your long-haired friend, tells me you're up to no good. You'd best get on out of town before something happens to you." He abruptly turned and walked back to the kitchen.

Jeff glared at Hickok. "Good job. Now we won't be able to find him. Why not just tell him the truth?"

"The truth? That he killed your pa and stole his gold? We'll have every man in town either taking up arms to defend him or to get to him first and take off with your gold before you can find him. Don't matter that they know we're lookin' for him. But we dare not tell them why. Besides, he's just one man," Hickok pointed out. "Others'll know him. Course, they may want their palms greased. Let's go."

He got up, replaced his hat, and strolled out into the dreary afternoon, the clouds dark and menacing as they blocked the sun. The Bodines followed, Jeff now more uneasy than ever.

"What now?" Josh asked as they stood by their horses. Hickok took a deep breath.

"Well, why don't we let your brother call the shots for a while? He don't seem to like my approach."

"Fine with me," Josh said.

Jeff only shrugged. "Why not? Couldn't do any worse than you so far. Your attitude puts people off."

Hickok only grinned. "There's as good a place as any," he said, pointing across the street to a ragged-looking saloon. "If he ain't home counting his money or sleeping, he's likely to be in there."

Jeff took a breath, suddenly sorry he'd said anything. Leaving Hickok and his brother loitering by the animals, he left his horse tied to the rail, trudged across the street to the saloon Hickok had indicated, and pushed his way through the batwings.

During midday in Lundy there was precious little action to be found in the town's only saloon. A few men stood at the bar sipping warm beers, several others huddled around a table playing penny-ante poker, and the rest played checkers by the stove. The bartender, tired of wiping and rewiping the same glasses, stood with his chin in his hands and his elbows propped up on the makeshift bar: a long, varnished plank set atop two fifty-gallon nail barrels. He occasionally yawned.

Inside, Jeff was greeted by the stares of more of the locals, but seeing he had come in by himself, they quickly went back to their drinks, games, and conversation, paying him no further heed. Jeff scanned them, one at a time, searching for the man he'd worked with those months but recognized no one. He went to the bar.

"What'll it be, stranger?" the barkeep asked.

"Water," Jeff said.

"Water?"

"Yeah, water. You got water, don't you?"

"Sure. Same price as whiskey, though. It's harder to come by."

"You got a lake full of water right there," Jeff said, pointing.

"Go ahead. Stick your head in it and drink up if you want. But if you want water that's been filtered of fish doo, it'll be two bits."

Jeff grumbled but paid what the man required and received a glass of pure, clean water. He drank it down, rinsing the trail dust off the back of his throat, then motioned the barkeep over.

"'Nother?"

"No, information. I'm looking for Jim Wheeler. He worked for my pa for a time, came back here a few days ago."

"What'cha need him for?"

Jeff hesitated, then said slowly, "Well, it's a mite personal."

"Want to kill him, eh?" the bartender asked with a smile.

Jeff recoiled. "No, good heavens. Why would you think that?"

"I don't know. Just the way that friend of yours looks, sitting outside twirling them guns around."

Jeff looked quickly out the window and saw Hickok mystifying his brother—and the girl on the wagon—with a display of gun-handling prowess the likes of which he'd never seen before. His mouth fell open and he stammered, "Uh . . . oh, he's just showing off. We met him a few miles back. He's not really with us."

"Yeah?" the bartender said. "Well, I'm gonna have a tough time buying that. Still, what do I care?" The bartender stroked his magnificent mustache. "You don't look mean or like you got a chip on your shoulder, so I guess I can trust you. I don't know where Wheeler is right now, but I know where he'll be later."

"Where?"

"Right here. We got a game going tonight."

"You're sure he'll be here?"

"Trust me, son. He'll be here."

"Thanks," Jeff said. "And thanks for the water."

Jeff plunked down a coin and left the saloon, then rejoined Hickok and his brother out in the street and told them of his success. As they stood by their horses, momentarily at a loss for what to do next, a small, bearded man stumbled out of the bar and staggered up the muddy street, glancing over his shoulder at them several times before disappearing into an alley.

"Did you see that man?" Hickok asked.

Josh nodded. "Yeah. What about him?"

"He's on his way to Wheeler."

"How can you tell?" Josh asked incredulously. "He's just a drunk."

"He ain't so drunk yet. Did you notice how he kept looking at us? He was thinking of us and hoping we weren't thinking of him. That tells me he's getting ready to warn someone we're here."

"That's nuts," Josh said.

"No, Josh, it ain't," Jeff said. "It makes sense. If I tell you not to think of pink elephants, you're gonna think about pink elephants. He's concerned about us, so he figures we're thinking about him. And he was moving kinda fast for just a drunk on his way home."

"Very good, Jeff," Hickok said. "See there, Josh, your brother ain't so slickered that he can't figure some things out. There's hope for him yet. I'd say he did something right in there to produce action so quickly."

"Well then, what do we do now?" Josh said. "Do we follow him?"

"No, there's no need. Wheeler'll come to us now, I think."

"How so?" Jeff asked.

"It's like this: Wheeler's gonna know there's three men looking for him, one of 'em a handsome fellow with long hair and a buckskin coat. He'll remember me, no doubt, but the last time he saw me, I wasn't myself."

"You were a common drunk," Jeff noted.

"I'm never a common anything," Hickok pointed out. "Nevertheless, he'll think I'm here to get my pistols back, one way or another, and brought reinforcements with me to make sure it happens. He'll be pretty confident hearing all I brought is two green kids and probably come on down to throw us out of town. Or he might even consent to another card game, but I doubt it. No, I think he'll want to be rid of us so he can get back to living a life of luxury and recluse. So he'll round up his cohorts, and they'll come looking for us."

"But then he'll recognize us," Jeff said.

"That's what I'm hoping for. When that happens it'll be too late for him. He'll know why you're here, of course, then he'll panic, and we'll have him."

"Huh?" Josh said. "I don't follow."

"Of course you don't. When a man panics he don't shoot so good. But I, being the Prince of Pistoleers, never panic. I'll simply tell him who I am and demand he turn himself in for the murder of your pa, and he'll give up or face the consequences."

"We didn't come here to kill him," Jeff protested.

"We didn't?" Josh asked his brother.

"Of course not," Hickok said. "But you best be prepared to do so. Wheeler just might decide the only way to avoid the noose is by killing you."

The Bodines were silent, each for their own reason, as they considered this possibility. Finally Jeff spoke.

"I'm not game for retribution. I want our gold, not blood."

"I'm pretty keen for blood," Josh said. "If he'd just stolen our money, that'd be one thing. But he killed our pa."

"Good point," Hickok said.

Jeff shook his head. "I'll not have it if it can be helped. He'll be given a chance."

"Of course." Hickok plucked off his hat and swooped his greasy hair back, settling the hat back down easily. "Of course. Then we'll kill him. Shall we go?"

"Where?" both brothers asked simultaneously.

"To wait for him. I think it might be a tactical mistake to stand in such a tight group out in the open like this. We might have more of a chance to accomplish our mission if we spread out. You two can pick you own spots. I'm going inside the saloon to wait for him there." He started to walk off.

"So you can get drunk," Jeff muttered. "I knew it."

Hickok stutter-stepped, and Josh thought he was going to turn on Jeff in anger, but the gunman picked up his pace again and kept going, paying Jeff no further heed.

"That was a fool thing to say," Josh scolded after Wild Bill was out of earshot. "He's come all this way to help us, and you insult him."

"He came all this way to help himself," Jeff corrected. "You threatened to have him arrested, remember? Besides, he wants his precious pistols and probably will try to help himself to our gold if he gets a chance."

"You're wrong about him, Jeff. That's Wild Bill Hickok. Why, he's a lawman!"

"He's a used-up gunfighter who sometimes got paid for being a gunfighter by virtue of a tin star."

"He brought us here, didn't he?"

"Yeah, but will we get back?"

"You can leave now if that's how you feel," Josh said. "Hop on that horse and go. I won't say nuthin'. But our pa's dead. If you can forget that, ride on out of here. But do me a favor and keep going, 'cause if you do, I don't ever want to see you again."

Jeff didn't move but looked down the street toward the lake and the hazy mountains in the distance that held their mine and their memories.

"No, I'll stay," he said quietly. "But only to keep you from gettin' yourself killed."

They separated and found places on either side of the street to sit and wait, Josh in front of the general store, Jeff under the town's solitary remaining tree within the city limits, left as sort of a monument to the lumber industry. He leaned against the tall pine and folded his arms.

Josh sat on a wooden bench a few feet from the buckboard that had been unloaded and now sat empty. The girl was gone. He pushed his hat back and stared vacantly across the street, thinking about what might happen when Wheeler came to town and how he was going to handle the murderer. He never considered the possibility that he might die this day.

"I said, 'Excuse me,'" a thin voice said beside him.

"Huh?" Josh looked up at the plain face of the girl wearing a large revolver.

"I guess you were daydreaming," she said.

"Yeah, I guess so," Josh said. "Sorry."

"That's okay. What were you thinking about?"

"Oh, nothing much, I guess."

"My name's Jane."

"Josh Bodine."

"That's a nice name. You live here?"

"No, just visiting."

"Me too. I came with the wagon of supplies for the store here. I'm from Bridgeport."

"Oh."

"Where's the man with the long hair?"

"You're sure full of questions."

Jane blushed. "I'm sorry. I was just wondering . . . . Say, can I sit down?"

"Huh? Oh yeah, sure." Josh slid over and made room for her.

"Thanks. Can you use that gun?"

"I do okay."

"I'm pretty good."

"Yeah? What do you need a gun for?"

"I don't know. Protection, I guess. I just like 'em. So where's your friend?"

"He's across the—why do you want to know?"

She smiled coyly. "Oh, I just think he's handsome."

Josh just shook his head. "Listen, Jane, I'm waiting for someone, and I don't think you should be here when he shows up."

"Why? Is he dangerous?"

"Could be. He killed my pa."

"And you're waiting here to kill him back?"

"Well, I—"

"Can I watch? I've never seen anyone get killed before."

"Well, I—"

"Say, where's that other feller? Wasn't there three of you?"

"I, uh, he—"

"Oh, there he is, under the tree. Hi!" Jane began waving. Josh grabbed her arm and pulled it down.

"Jane! Would you stop, please? We're tryin' not to be obvious, okay?"

"Oh, sorry. So, who are we gonna kill?" She put her hand on the butt of her gun.

"We aren't gonna kill anyone. We're here to arrest him and take him back to Bodie."

"Bodie? You're from Bodie? I know someone from Bodie."

"Yeah? Who."

"The deputy, Matt Page. He's a customer of mine."

"Yeah? I know him, too."

"Oh yeah? Wow, what a small world this is—"

A shrill whistle from Jeff interrupted Jane's discourse and brought Josh back to reality. He looked up the street as Jeff pointed with a thumb and saw the man who'd slipped out a short time before returning to the saloon, then duck quickly through the batwings after glancing at both Josh and Jeff in a manner Josh was sure made the man think no one noticed.

So, he's delivered his message, Josh thought. *Now it's just a matter of time.*

"Look, Jane, I enjoy talkin' to you and everything, but we got serious business to take care of and, well, you're kind of distractin' me. Maybe when it's all over we can talk some, okay? Right now I've got to pay attention. Mr. Wheeler could be coming any second now."

"Mr. Wheeler—is that who you're gonna kill?"

"I told you, Jane, I ain't gonna kill no one . . . if I can help it, that is. Now please, run along. And stay out of the way. I don't want you gettin' hurt."

Jane stuck her lower lip out and hung her head, but Josh ignored it. She then got up and shuffled back into the store. Josh happened a glance at his brother, who stood with his arms folded, a scolding look on his face. Josh shrugged and held his hands up in a helpless gesture. Jeff just shook his head and looked back up the street.

An hour passed with no change. No one came down the street. Jane stayed inside the store. Hickok never emerged from the saloon. In fact, there was no foot traffic at all. It was like someone had sent a warning out to stay indoors or risk getting hit by a stray bullet. Even the breeze had died down, and Josh noticed that breathing was a mite difficult with his heart in his throat.

Jeff, under his tree, was getting fed up and seriously considering riding out of there as Josh had suggested. He swatted a pesky fly as he weighed the idea, missing it by a wide margin, but he stayed.

Josh was antsy and kept a sharp eye up the street, anxious for action, for something to happen. Anything.

And just as quickly as he thought that, something did.

NOAH PORTER SHUFFLED HURRIEDLY up the street, glancing to his left and right and over his shoulder every few seconds making sure he wasn't being followed. He ducked down an alley, retraced his steps, avoided Main Street completely, and finally made his way to the back door of the office of the Queen Anne Mine and Mill. He rapped three times slowly, then waited, and after a few seconds, the door creaked open the width of an eyeball. Once recognized, Noah was let in, the door quickly shut behind him, and the bolt thrown.

A crowd of twenty men stood in the near dark, the only sounds the shuffling of their feet on the wood floor and the rustling of their clothing. Hiram Butler, superintendent of the Queen Anne, and his foreman, Aaron Goodhew, stood at the head of the group as all the men turned and faced them. He held up his hand for silence out of habit as it was hardly necessary in this clandestine rendezvous.

"Men of the 6-0-1," he began solemnly, "you all know why we're here today. One of our men, the beloved James Nixon, was cruelly and savagely cut down in the prime of his life, blown to Kingdom Come by that man languishing now on the county dole over in Page's jail, while the good deputy continues to stay out of Bodie in this most desperate time."

"He left Uncle Billy in charge," reminded Noah.

"Mr. Porter, you're here because of the important information you supplied that led to the discovery of the true perpetrator of the crime. I'll thank you to remain silent for the duration, otherwise be considered an enemy of the 6-0-1."

Noah nodded excitedly, a worried look creasing his face. To be an enemy of the vigilance committee was not a good thing. He could find himself looking down on the crowd, dangling from a hemp necklace himself.

Butler continued. "We have seen in the past the results of justice—and I use the term loosely—here in Bodie. When was the last time a criminal was convicted of a capital crime? Footpads and thieves, drunks and those who talk themselves into fistfights, are quick to be jailed and receive the appropriate castigation. But who can recall the last killer to be properly tried and executed in Bodie?"

"That rebel feller got hisself killed," someone in the back pointed out, recalling the incident during the mine war between the Queen Anne and the Empire.

"That's my point exactly. That's the only way justice is ever served around here: Someone kills the killer and saves the county the trouble of letting him go free and unpunished. Such will not be the case with Thomas Wellman, I can assure you. He will not get as far as a trial by the county, because we, the 6-0-1, the good citizens of Bodie who are tired of the injustice, will see to it that he is properly tried and executed."

"There's but twenty men here," Carl Gordon, the tobacconist, pointed out. "Do you think that's enough to carry the day?"

"Are you worried, Carl?" the Queen Anne superintendent asked. "Is our cause not just and right?"

Gordon didn't answer, not really sure whether it was just and right but unwilling to take on the other nineteen men at that moment. Assuming his silence to be an agreement, Butler went on.

"We have taken out an ad in the *Chronicle*, thanks to Mr. Farquhar, the owner and editor of that fine periodical." He gave a smiling nod to a man in the back of the room who smiled sheepishly, uncomfortable that his name had been spoken aloud. "At the next meeting, where we will discuss our strategy, I anticipate a strong turnout. And I want each and every one of you to talk it up to your friends. There's plenty of honest, hardworking men in

Bodie who are like you and me, who are tired of the worst criminals always slipping through the cracks.

"You know it as well as I do, you've seen it time and again: Two men have a disagreement, maybe a little tiff, then one of them leaves and arms himself and returns to shoot the man in cold blood, but the courts let him off for one flimsy reason or another. Well, I'm tired of that."

"S'cuse me," said a voice in the middle of the pack. "Jes' for the sake of argument—I know yer concerned with the truth, Hiram, jes' like me—it ain't always the court that cuts 'em loose. Sometimes the witnesses, good Bodie men like us, refuse to testify or they say they didn't see nuthin' when everyone knows they did. And sometimes it's the jury who lets 'em go. And the jury is also us, men from Bodie jes' like you, an' jes' like me. Is there any of you men what ain't never served on a jury?" He glanced around the room, receiving some nods and some shakes, but, in general, no definitive response.

"As you well know, Jacob," Hiram Butler said, "only people too stupid to read a newspaper or too uncreative to get themselves excluded ever have to serve on a jury. Twelve of the dumbest citizens in town are the jury."

"I never!" Noah protested, drawing some chuckles from the men.

"That's sometimes true," Jacob admitted, ignoring Noah. "But mebbe we shouldn't try to escape our duty so dang much. If'n you want murderers convicted, then you should be doin' all you kin to stay on the jury."

"For my part, I've tried," Butler argued. "But I usually know the defendant and so the lawyers get me booted off the jury. It's really the lawyers' fault, you know. But enough of this talk. We'll meet again tomorrow night, you all know where. Jacob, I know the deputy's your son, and I don't have nothing against him, but you know better than to stand against us in this."

"And you know better than to do this thing. I know it looks like Thomas is guilty, but he's entitled to a trial and to hear all the evidence agin him."

"We'll do just that. Then we'll hang him."

"Many a you are his friends," Jacob Page told the crowd.

"We was," a man pointed out, "until he killed James Nixon and almost killed Mrs. Calhoun and her baby."

"You don't know he done that."

"You were there when Billy hauled him off to jail," Butler accused. "You know the evidence as well as any of us."

"Better, most likely. Yeah, I helped. I didn't like it, but I done my duty."

"Now we're doing ours," Butler concluded. "Tomorrow night, men. Jacob, you needn't bother coming . . . if you know what's good for you."

Jacob didn't answer but gave Butler a glare that would come close to killing a weaker man. The men filed out slowly and quietly until only Jacob and Hiram were left.

"We been friends ever since I came to town, Hiram," Jacob reminded his counterpart.

"Not that close."

"Mebbe. But I'm as good a friend of Thomas as I am of you, and I don't want to see him deprived of his rights none. I'll fight you on this."

"You dast not. Your son neither. I'm warning you."

"Thanks for giving me that warning, Hiram," Jacob said. "Good evening."

He strode out into the cold, dark evening, wishing Matt would hurry home before it was too late, not just for Thomas Wellman but for Sarah and Rosa and the whole town. Things were ready to bust wide open at the seams.

Where was that boy?

Matt was alone in the wikiup when he woke. The sky outside was light. He could see that by how bright it was inside. He must've slept through the night. Taking a quick inventory of himself, he threw back the skins that covered him and sat up, stretching.

He felt pretty good. That squaw tea had done its work. A little stiff, perhaps, but to be expected considering how far he'd hiked. It was time to get up and stretch his legs. Then, once he was whole—or nearly so—he could figure out a way to get home. Maybe the Indian—what was his name? . . . John Horse, that was it—maybe John would let him use one of the horses he'd captured.

No, that wouldn't work. They weren't broken. Perhaps he had one for himself that had already been saddle broke.

Matt stooped over and passed through the small opening of the wikiup into the bright, morning sun. The old woman was there and smiled at him, then returned to her chores, some sort of food preparation as usual. It was pretty much a full-time job for her, Matt figured. Not unlike his own Sarah, though his wife certainly benefitted from the inventions of the white man with all their modern things, like skillets and wood stoves and such. The young girl was several yards away working in a small vegetable patch.

The old woman pointed to a basket, and Matt sauntered over to take a look. It was filled with several kinds of berries. Matt grabbed a handful and popped some in his mouth. The elderberries he recognized; another type he didn't recall ever having seen before and held one up for scrutiny as he chewed.

"Buffalo berry," the old woman said. She got up and offered Matt something from another basket, holding her fingers to her lips while making *ummm* noises and smiling.

Matt hesitated, not too sure about this stuff. It looked awfully like insects to him.

"*Pe-agge,*" she told him, as if the stuff having a name made it all right. She took a few of the short, plump worms—that's what they appeared to be—and stuffed them into her mouth. Matt wanted to pass on this one, not sure that the larvae of the Pandora moth was suited to his tastes, but the Paiutes had been so hospitable that he didn't want to offend. Besides, he had eaten *koochabee*. This couldn't be much worse.

He took one and ate it, swallowing quickly and following it with a handful of berries, then thanked her and turned away quickly. The young girl had ben watching and giggled at the face he made, having forgotten about her as he hid it from Sally John. Matt blushed and shrugged his shoulders sheepishly.

Matt walked slowly through the brush surrounding the encampment, heading for suitable cover to conduct his constitutional, and took in the view of the countryside. The Paiutes had picked a beautiful place to call home. Grand mountains behind them, a sloping sagebrush plain below, just enough Piñon pines to provide a source for food and fuel but not too many that they blocked the sun or the view. It wouldn't be such a bad life, he thought. No worries except the basics, food and shelter, which Matt had to concern himself about as well, plus all the other worries of life: catching bad men, dodging bullets, breaking up fights. And men in other professions had more than their share of concerns, too. Falling down a mine shaft, cave-ins, getting a hand crushed by an 800-pound stamp, scoliosis . . . .

No, being an Indian wouldn't be so bad. Except maybe for the food. But they didn't seem to mind. In fact, the *koochabee* harvest was the major event of the year in Mono County for the Paiute, where they would all gather at the shores of Mono Lake for a week of celebration, games, singing—

Matt stopped abruptly, not just his thoughts but his walking as well. He stared at the corral John Horse had made and the three horses that stood within its confines. An appaloosa, a sorrel, and a shiny black.

Shadow!

Matt looked around for the Paiute. Not seeing him, he walked quickly over to the corral, a small pen encircled by two strands of white man's barbed wire John had evidently acquired, probably in exchange for a horse sometime in the past. Shadow ignored him until he spoke, then the horse turned its head and flared its nostrils as it took in his scent. Slowly the horse dropped its head and sauntered over to the lawman, its tail switching back and forth in recognition. Matt let the horse smell his hand, then stroked its velvet nose.

"I'm sure glad to see you, boy," Matt said quietly. "So John caught you, did he? I wonder where your saddle is, huh? If he caught you, he's got to have that too. Where is it, boy?"

But Shadow couldn't tell him. Matt gave him a pat on the neck, then the horse moved away and began grazing on the rice grass at the fence line.

"He very good horse," said a man's voice behind Matt.

Matt nodded without turning.

"Yes, John. His name is Shadow."

"Why you name my horse?" The Indian moved up alongside the white man.

"He was my horse a couple days ago."

"I find in canyon." John pointed east, in a different direction than Matt had come.

"I can't explain what happened. I was knocked out, when I came to, Shadow had run off, so I started walking. That's all I know, except that's my horse."

"I need much wood," John said. "You make, I give horse."

Matt was about to protest, thinking the idea that he had to work to get back his own horse was a bit unreasonable, until he remembered all the Paiutes had done for him without any expectation of repayment. They had probably saved his life, at the very least had hastened his recovery. Gathering some wood was the least he could do.

"You have the saddle?" Matt asked.

John glanced away, then a smile formed. He looked Matt in the eye and nodded.

"Trade for belt."

"What belt?"

"You have two belt, very nice. John Horse have none."

"Okay, John, I'll trade you a belt for the saddle. But you have to throw in a blanket. I need a blanket."

"John have only basket to wear in rain."

So, Matt thought, *he wanted to barter.* "I'm a white man, and I have a long ride ahead of me. But all Paiute men have hats. You have at least three in the wikiup."

John Horse smiled. "Okay, you keep hat. But you help Sally John grind pine nut. She very tired."

Woman's work. John Horse was going to extract his pound of flesh for that blanket. Matt smiled and shrugged.

"Deal."

"Deal." John Horse extended his hand white-man style, and the arrangement was sealed. He told Matt where to find the best wood and where to put it.

"I need my hat first," Matt said, pointing up at the sun. Though the air had a cool edge to it, the sun was unobstructed by clouds and was as bright as a new bride's face. "I'll go back for that before I get started." John Horse nodded and walked off toward the wikiup.

Matt gazed at Shadow. "I hope you appreciate this," he said, then followed the Paiute.

It was nearly dark when Matt dropped the last of the wood on the pile and took off his weather-beaten hat to wipe his forehead.

He'd only stopped long enough for a quick lunch of greens from the maiden's patch and some pine nuts, washed down with water from the stream that flowed about a hundred yards from John's encampment, then was back to it, hiking the long trail to the stand of trees that provided the fuel for John's fires.

John himself was gone all day, returning at dusk empty-handed. No horses this day. But the skin sack he carried was weighted down, and he handed it to Sally. She cooed when she looked inside and set about preparing whatever it was for dinner.

Fresh meat, thought Matt. *Finally.*

John sauntered over and sat on his haunches next to Matt.

"Much wood," he commented, sizing up the pile. "Good for small pony, not big black horse."

Matt turned his head slowly to stare at the Indian.

"We had a deal," he reminded him.

John Horse nodded. "You work too slow, not gather enough."

"I've been sick," Matt explained. "Look, John, I appreciate all you've done for me, but I need to get back to my people, to my wife. She's waiting for me. So is the whole town."

The Indian remained stoic.

"Is there anything I can do?"

The Indian slowly looked down at Matt's shoes.

"My boots? What'll I wear if I give you my boots?"

"We trade," the Indian said.

Matt considered the idea. John wore the clothing of the white man, his winter garb. Summer usually saw only a breech cloth or pants. John had moccasins, but now he wore an old pair of scuffed, black shoes, the soles paper-thin from the abuse they'd been given, the heels worn to the last on the outside edges. For laces, John had used some twine.

Matt sighed. He could get a new pair of gumsoled boots when he got back. "Okay, but this is it," he declared, and pulled off the boots. He was fortunate, he felt, that the Indian's shoes came close to fitting but glad he wasn't going to have to walk in them.

Both men returned to the wikiup, John stuffing his pipe with store-bought tobacco and lighting it with an ember from the eternal fire burning inside his home. He offered it to Matt, who took it and puffed, careful not to inhale the acrid smoke, instead just sucking it into his mouth and blowing out again. That his guest was so anxious to do things the Indian way pleased John, and he took a leather necklace off and handed it to the white man.

Matt accepted the gift, admired the hand-carved obsidian stone dangling from it, then slipped it over his head. He had nothing to offer the Indian, but nothing was required. John set the stone mortar and pestle in front of Matt, along with a sack of pine nuts, then retired from the tent to let Matt work in peace.

An hour or so later, dinner was served. Matt enjoyed the savory meat, seasoned with salt and garlic and accompanied by acorn mush. It was strong, a mite gamey, but Matt had been expecting that. Still, it was a welcome relief from the insects and other disgusting things he'd been required to consume in recent days, and he ate until he was full.

As he sat back, satisfied, he glanced over at John, who was having his last morsel. The Paiute picked it up slowly with two fingers and a smile, evidently having left the best piece for last. As Matt looked on, John held the long, thin piece by one end and dangled it above his open mouth, then slowly let it down until it was all inside and he chewed happily. Slowly it dawned on Matt what John had just eaten: the tail of the animal. Rabbits don't have long, thin tails, he realized, but rodents do.

Fighting a revulsion that would've expelled his dinner, Matt grabbed the skin and drank some water, then held his breath and forced himself not to think of it. With all the things he had eaten recently, this had to be the worst. Maybe being a white man, even with all the problems and worries, wasn't so bad after all. He'd rather be in a shootout than eat a rat.

Suddenly Matt remembered Bodie's Chinese butcher shop, with its naked ducks hanging in the window and foul odors from the fish, and he had a new respect for them. At least they didn't eat rats and worms.

The nausea having passed, Matt got up and told John Horse that he needed some sleep because he had a long ride ahead of him in the morning. The Indian nodded and Matt retired to the wikiup, thankful to be warm and cozy wrapped in the skins, lying by the fire. He thanked the good Lord for his provision and prayed that He would provide him safe passage on the morrow, asking God also to be with Sarah and to do something about their situa-

THE PROVING GROUND   303

tion. Matt was tired of being away from home so much and told God so.

"So anyway, God," Matt concluded, "do what You will. Thank You for listening. Amen." He rolled onto his side, closed his eyes, and was asleep in minutes.

Billy O'Hara spread the newspaper open on the desk with a distressed sigh and leaned back heavily in the chair, which creaked and groaned its objections. With a chubby hand, he wiped his face, then scowled across the desk at the one-armed miner who had brought the paper and their breakfast in.

Uncle Billy took a slug of black coffee and another bite of cornbread, chewing thoughtfully.

"What should we do?" he asked, though not really expecting a definitive answer. And he was amply rewarded.

"I dunno," Jacob said. "We can't let this happen, but how kin we stop it? If'n they git the support they're rustlin' up, we'd be foolish to try and stop 'em."

Billy nodded, staring vacantly at the wall behind Jacob Page, then turned his head slowly to look Page in the eye, a strange look on his face.

"Since we can't stem the tide," the former ship pilot said slowly, "we'll have to take the boat out of the water."

Jacob gazed at him vacantly. "Huh?"

"We can't stand against 'em, so we take Wellman out of here, hide him."

"How? Where?"

"There's lots of places to hide a man. The problem's gonna be gettin' him out of here unseen."

They thought for a moment, then Jacob's gaze fell where his other arm had once been.

"We'll hide him right here," he said, holding up the empty sleeve with his other hand.

The door to the jailhouse creaked open, and Uncle Billy stepped out, his Sharp's carbine cradled in his right arm. Glancing up and down King Street, he took a step away from the stoop, then turned toward nearby Chinatown, away from Main Street.

He was followed out the door and into the street by Jacob Page, his empty sleeve hanging loose, flopping in the wind. Keeping his hat low on his head and his face down against the chill, Jacob rubbed his whiskers gently with his only hand as he walked with Billy up King Street. They drew little attention from the Orientals as they hit the outskirts of the Chinese sector and turned up the narrow confines of Bonanza Street. The cribs of the soiled doves were silent at this early hour, most of them sleeping in from the previous night's activities.

Billy and Jacob didn't speak, keeping to the middle of the deserted street, which was more akin to an alley due to its width. Wagons would be hard-pressed to travel down it without running aground. Billy and Jacob only left the dirt to tread on the echoing boards when they crossed the boardwalk to access a door. Knocking once, Billy was let in. Jacob followed, and the door was shut behind them.

The single window of the one-room crib let in little light, but it was enough. Billy sighed audibly as he looked down on the small, blonde woman who had let them in.

"We appreciate this," he told her.

"Shoot, this crib ain't bein' used anyhow. Man, you sure look strange, Mr. Page."

She regarded Jacob as he sat on the bed, only now removing his hat. Betsy gasped as a second arm snaked its way out the front of his button-up shirt and pulled at the whiskers on his face. They peeled off in his fingers, pulling the skin away from his jaw, then snapping it back as the glue released.

Billy clamped a meaty hand over Betsy's mouth as she sucked in air in preparation for a scream.

"It's okay, little lady," he comforted. "It's not Jacob."

"What's this about? Who are you?"

"This is Thomas Wellman," Billy introduced.

"Pleased to meet you, Miss . . . ?" Wellman said, standing and extending his naked arm through his shirt front.

"Betsy," Billy said, for the woman was too flabbergasted to speak.

Staring at Wellman with her mouth slightly open, she took his hand without a conscious effort and shook it.

"I appreciate the use of your abode."

"It ain't really mine," she said. "I just have first rights to it, is all."

"Just the same," Wellman concluded. He unbuttoned his shirt, put his arm in its proper place, and turned to Billy. "Thank Jacob for the use of his clothes and his beard. I trust he won't miss it too much."

"He says he'll stay in the jail till it grows back," Billy said with a grin. "And since your clothes are better'n his, he ain't complainin' much 'bout that. Ah'll bring him a change of his own clothes later. In an hour we'll all be safe and sound."

Billy escorted the woman to the door. "Now, you remember my instructions?"

"Yes, sir. Two meals a day, don't tell no one about this, and no hanky-panky." She smiled.

"Very good. And make sure no one sees you bringin' in the food, you hear? This man's life is at stake." He handed her a fistful of dollars. "That ought to take care of it ample. There's plenty in there for you, too. You need more, let me know, understand?"

"Yes sir, Billy. Thanks. I can use it."

"Run along now, honey."

He opened the door, checked to make sure the way was clear, and let her out. Turning back to Wellman he said, "And you make sure you don't leave this room. Ah don't want to have to handcuff you to the bed, but Ah'll do it if you make me."

"I'm no fool, Billy. I like my neck the length it is. I doubt you could get me away from here without force before this is over."

"That's what Ah'm tryin' to avoid," Billy said solemnly. "That's what Ah'm tryin' to avoid. Nonetheless, Ah'll be padlockin' the door after Ah go. Betsy has the key. It's more to keep them out than you in, but . . . well, you understand. Good day to ya." He stepped out onto the stoop and shut the door, slipping a padlock into the ring of the new hasp he'd installed the night before, then dropping off the key with Betsy next door before making his way back to Jacob's place. He took the long way through Chinatown to cover his tracks.

Billy hoped this ruse worked. If not, and if Matt didn't come back soon, Thomas Wellman might be living on borrowed time.

CHAPTER

TWENTY·SIX

DEPUTY MATT PAGE WAS AWAKENED before dawn by Shadow's snorting and his excessive pawing of the ground. Matt gazed through puffy, lazy eyelids, trying to see, but there was no light, the moon obliterated by clouds. Something was bothering the animal.

"What is it, boy?" Matt asked quietly. "You hear something?"

Matt threw off the blanket, pulled the knife John Horse had given him from the leather sheath that he'd kept beside him and pushed himself up, his body still sore from the treatment it had been given in recent days. Though not eager, he was primed for action. He'd slept with his boots on, ready as always to break away if need be. And lately, that was more likely than not to be needed.

Matt listened, his ears unhindered by the darkness that blinded his eyes. There was nothing, nothing but the wind in the trees. Still, Shadow was upset, and now that he was close enough, Matt could see fear in the animal's eyes. He stroked the horse's neck and spoke softly to him, soothing words the animal didn't understood but uttered in a tone he did.

Shadow was still jittery, though, yet he obeyed his master and remained placid, only his wild eyes and flared nostrils betraying him. Matt stood for a while listening, wondering what the sensitive horse had heard or felt. Or perhaps he had smelled something. Matt detected nothing from any of his own senses, however, and soon gave in to his fatigue and stretched back out on the ground under the colorful blanket given him by the Paiutes.

Matt had left the Paiutes' home early in the morning and ridden hard all day, eating his pine nuts and rabbit jerky provided by Sally John on the move, stopping only to let Shadow drink. He'd bedded down at dusk, tired and sore from his wood-gathering, and wasn't pleased with this midnight interruption. But there was nothing out there, and he consoled Shadow before bedding down once again.

He slept restlessly, though he wasn't disturbed again until dawn when a light rain tickled his face. He got up quickly and saddled the black, deciding not to bother with breakfast. Seeing to it that his coals from the night before were spread, his eased himself into a crude coat made by Sally John from blankets, then onto Shadow's back, and the anxious horse took off at the first hint of an urging from his rider.

Matt was unaware how much his appearance had changed in the past few days. He hadn't shaved, hadn't even given it a thought, and of course the Paiutes weren't equipped for such a task, not having the need themselves. His time in the sun had darkened his already tan face, and the exposure had leathered the texture of his skin. The clothes that were his were dirty and tattered, those given him by the Paiutes having a strange, almost comical hang to them on the body of a white man.

Matt rode steadily all morning, so eager to get home that he didn't care how soaked he got. He planned on obtaining some proper rain gear in Bridgeport, stop in and report to the sheriff, then excuse himself—perhaps after one of Mrs. Taylor's meals—and hightail it to Bodie . . . no, to Sarah. Hang Bodie, it was his wife he wanted to see.

This was beautiful country he traversed this inclement morning. Even through the rain he could see it: the green fir trees, the brown leafless alders, amber and yellow grass, a silver-blue lake. There was no trail, but the mountain peaks in the distance he recognized so he headed toward those, per the Paiutes' instructions, and figured he'd make it to Bridgeport eventually.

Several hours into his journey he crested a ridge to a spectacular scene. The rain had stopped a half hour before, and now the clouds were breaking. Miles to the southeast the clouds were still heavy and raining, but above him, the sun was shooting yellow rays like javelins and sticking them into the ground. Mono Lake at the base of the lavender mountains was visible as a gray mirror, and the end of a full rainbow dissolved into its saline waters. Matt sucked his breath in at the sight and pulled Shadow to a halt. The deputy drank in the view, offering a prayer of praise to the Creator not just for the spectacle but for allowing him to be alive to see it. He wished Sarah could be by his side at this moment, this once-in-a-lifetime moment.

The thought of her tore him away from the view, and he turned Shadow north, knowing his first destination was not far.

Thankfully, gratefully, Bridgeport came into view just after noon. Matt had never seen it from this direction before, and it took him a few seconds to be sure he was there and not at some other town in some other valley in this part of California—or Nevada if he'd gone too far.

Then he picked out a landmark or two and smiled for the first time in . . . he didn't know how long. Always thinking of his horse, he maintained his pace, knowing he'd be back on the road to Bodie in just a short while.

Matt cantered into town and pulled up at Sheriff Taylor's house, knowing that's where he'd be. Or, at least, where he should be. Matt wouldn't have been surprised to find the tough lawman propped in the chair in his office, even if he had to be tied to it to sit up straight.

But his first impression was correct, as he knew when a tired-looking Mrs. Taylor met him on the porch. At first she hesitated, unsure that it was really him, and gave him a once-over, frowning at his strange, dirty, and tattered attire. But when he spoke she relaxed and gave him a hug.

"What happened to you, Matt?" she asked, letting him inside.

"It's a long story," he deferred. "I'll tell you someday. Right now I'm kind of anxious to get goin'. Where's the sheriff?"

She directed him to the bedroom. Matt thanked her and walked down the hall.

Matt was a little stunned at the sight he laid eyes on. In the bed lay a thinning, pale remnant of the sheriff he remembered, his scraggly gray whiskers having gone uncut, his mustache shaggier than before, his hair wild and sticking in all directions. He didn't look as if he'd gotten out of bed during the whole time Matt was gone.

Taylor turned his head slowly toward the sound of shoes scuffing the floor boards. Matt rolled the brim of his hat loosely in his hands while he stepped to the side of the bed. The bedridden man stared at him a few moments, the look in his eye distant, unrecognizing or uncaring, then his eyebrows raised slightly.

"You look like something somebody dug up," he observed. "Did you get 'em?" His voice was scratchy, and Matt winced in sympathy just to hear it.

"Yes and no, Sheriff."

Taylor waited for Matt to explain.

"I caught up with them outside Markleeville, but they got away. They coulda killed me, but they didn't. Shootin' you was an accident. They meant to kill me, just like you said. But that was just one of 'em, Bob Younger, and his brother, Cole, kept him from tryin' again."

"Cole and Bob Younger? Them was the Younger brothers?"

"And Jim. They met up with him in Markleeville."

Taylor nodded, a little awestruck that Matt, having met the Younger brothers, was able to stand here before him.

"Did Sheriff Chance give you a hand?"

"No, he was on his way out of town when I came in, and I never saw him again."

Taylor closed his eyes, held them there for a few seconds, then opened them again slowly. "You don't look none too good," he noticed.

"I had me a time, that's for sure. But I'm okay. Cole told me he didn't mean to hurt anyone in the explosion. He tried to warn Nixon to get out, but the man was too slow."

Taylor nodded slowly, almost imperceptibly, then rolled his head away and was silent. Matt waited a few minutes, then realized the conversation was over for the time being. He backed out quietly and returned to the living room where Mrs. Taylor sat knitting, her face creased with worry. Her hands functioned on their own with no conscious direction from her mind.

"You hungry?" she asked her son-in-law.

"Yes, I am. But you look tired. I'll go to the Argonaut."

"Nonsense." She put down her knitting and got up from the rocker. "I need to keep busy."

"Is the sheriff going to be all right?" Matt asked as he followed her to the kitchen.

As she took out the makings for a beef sandwich, she shook her head. "I hope so. He seems to have lost his spirit. I don't know what it can be. I've never seen him this depressed before. He's been hurt and bedridden before but never became like this."

Matt stared out the window. "Yeah, I half-expected him to be pushin' his recovery, to be up and around and barkin' out orders."

"That's what I thought would happen. Doc says he's going to be okay, but he's not improving much."

"All we can do is pray, I guess," Matt said, accepting the sandwich from her.

"Yes," she agreed, and without prompting, they bowed in unison and did just that.

Filled with two sandwiches and an apple, Matt took his leave, heading to the sheriff's office to finish his paperwork before preparing to head home. He dropped Shadow off at the livery for food, water, and a rubdown, then stopped by Harvey's store to replenish his equipment. Harvey was behind the counter, his face dour.

"How's it been going, Harvey?"

"Oh, I'm fine, but you look like something the dog buried. What happened? You find them outlaws?"

"It's a long tale, Harvey. They got away, and it's probably a good thing, too. They were the Younger brothers."

Harvey's mouth dropped open, and his voice left him.

"So, where's your new girl, Jane?" Matt asked.

"Went to Lundy," Harvey croaked, still dumbfounded.

"Lundy? What for?"

"I sent her to Lundy to keep tally on a shipment. I hope she makes it home okay. I'm here all alone again."

"That's a blessing in disguise," Matt said. "You got some jerky?"

"A whole can."

"Pick me out a dozen good hunks, would you, and package them up?" Matt continued through the store, picking up a slicker and a few other things he'd need. He also bought a new hat, stuffing his old damaged one in a trash bin at the rear of the store. He then chose a new pair of saddlebags and took his purchases to the counter. He decided to wait on the boots. No time now to break them in.

"What did you mean, a blessing in disguise?" Harvey asked.

"Huh?"

"You said Jane being gone was a blessing in disguise. What did you mean by that? I need the help."

"Not her kind. She was well-meaning and mighty good-natured, but she kept breaking things."

"Oh? I never noticed."

Matt grinned. "You will when you take inventory." He collected his purchases and nodded good-bye to Harvey. "I've got to go, Sarah's waiting. Say hello to Mary for me, would you? And say hello to Calamity Jane, too, when you see her," he said over his shoulder as he walked out.

"What did you call her?" Harvey called after him, but Matt was already out the door and gone.

Matt retrieved his horse, saddled up for the ride home, and was about to mount when he was hailed from across the street. He turned to see who was calling but didn't recognize the well-dressed little man who trotted toward him, out of breath and sweating.

"I'm glad I caught you," the man huffed. "Mrs. Taylor said you'd probably be here."

Matt could do nothing but look at him and wait for him to state his business.

"I'm Frank Ferguson, I run the bank." He paused to take a breath. "The bank you saved a while back from those two men who were breaking in."

"Oh," Matt said, remembering. He'd only seen the man once and that seemed a long time ago.

"I'm also a member of the county council."

That's nice, Matt thought, *but what do you want?* He said nothing, however.

"It seems we're going to be in need of a sheriff."

"Sheriff Taylor's the sheriff."

"Well, technically speaking, I suppose that's true for the moment. But as you know, he's in no condition to fulfill his duties. So I've been empowered by the council to ask you if you'd fill in for him, at least until the next election. Perhaps by then he'll be well enough to be back on the job or to run for reelection, or perhaps not to run and someone else will win the post. Whatever, we're going to need a county sheriff, and the county doesn't want to spend the money on a special election for just six months of duty, so we voted to appoint you."

He paused for another breath as Matt took the opportunity to think about what he'd been offered. He looked down at his hands, then up and down the street. This was an interesting turn of events. But did he want to accept it?

"What's this mean to me?" he asked.

"Well, a raise in pay for the duration you hold the post. And of course you'd move to Bridgeport."

That was the best news he'd heard in a long time.

"But surely there are other deputies more qualified."

"Longer service, perhaps, but hardly more qualified. Please consider the offer."

"I'll need to talk to my wife. When do you need to know for sure?"

"Soon, Deputy Page. We need someone right away. If you'll come, then be here next week. If you haven't shown by next Sunday, we'll assume you don't want it, and we'll just have to find someone else, a task to which I don't look forward. You came very highly recommended."

"Oh? By who?"

"Sheriff Taylor, of course. And Harvey Boone. Several others said so too, and the vote was unanimous."

Matt wondered why Harvey hadn't said anything, but perhaps he'd been told not to. "Well, that's mighty humblin'," he said. "But what about Bodie? It's gettin' out of hand with just me there. It's growin' so fast. What's gonna happen when I leave? I was gonna ask for a police officer to help me."

The man thought for a second. "We discussed that, too. You'll just have to hire two men. Do you know anyone?"

"Not offhand, but I'll think about it. Can I have the authority to swear them in?"

"As your first official act as sheriff," Ferguson declared. "There should be badges in the sheriff's—rather—in your desk. And forms for them to sign." He reached out and took Matt's hand with his own sweaty palm. "I'll take this as a 'yes'. Congratulations, Sheriff. See you next week."

He turned and hustled off in the direction of his bank, leaving Matt staring after him, his head swimming as it had done so many times before.

The first time he came into Bridgeport he was a penniless drifter, afoot and without two nickels to rub together. Now, in what seemed like such a short time, he was the county sheriff with an expectant wife.

Expectant wife! Matt pulled himself onto Shadow and raced up the street to his new office. He took the sheriff's old revolver from the drawer, checked it for bullets, and dropped it into his empty holster, strapping the belt on for the first time in days. He grabbed the badges and forms from the desk drawer and stuck them into his new saddlebags, then climbed into the saddle and turned the horse toward Bodie with a kick.

CHAPTER

TWENTY·SEVEN

Y OU BOYS LOOKING FOR ME?"
The challenge came from the dark shape of a man who had
appeared at the top of the street. The sun was at his back,
just over the ridge of the mountain in the distance behind him. Josh
squinted to get a better look.

"Is that him?" he called to his brother.

Jeff leaned forward, trying also to get a clear view.

"Can't tell. Sun's in my eyes. Who else would it be?"

Josh hitched up his pants and moved away from the storefront,
heading slowly to the center of the street.

"You Jim Wheeler?" he called to the man.

"You know who I am," came the reply. "I worked for your pa.
Why have you come looking for me? State your business."

The batwings of the saloon moved and a man stepped out, a
man with long hair and a buckskin coat. But when he looked up
and down the street and saw what was taking shape, he quickly
ducked back into the saloon.

"Where's Hickok goin'?" Josh asked his brother worriedly.

"Where do you think?" Jeff said, shaking his head. "He's
chickenin' out, goin' back in to have another drink. Well, now
we've gotten ourselves into it for sure. It's not too late, Josh. Let's
back out now and go home."

"No!" Josh told him. "We can't do that now. Why, we're facing our pa's killer! How can we just tuck tail and run? I won't do it."

"Then he'll be your killer too, Josh."

"I can take him. Besides, there are two of us."

"Yeah? Look yonder."

Two more men appeared, one on either side of Wheeler and on opposite sides of the street. All three men were clearly armed. They began advancing down the street.

"Hickok!" Josh shouted in a panic, but there was no response from the saloon.

"I'm asking you again, boy," Wheeler shouted. "Why'd you call me out?"

"You killed my pa!" Josh spurted. "You killed him and stole our gold. All three of you!"

"Is that so? So what do you aim to do about it?"

"Give yourself up," Jeff demanded from his position under the tree. Josh glanced quickly at him in surprise, and Jeff said quietly, "You're a durn fool, Josh, but you're my brother. If you won't back down, we've got to see it through." He came out from under the tree, his hand nervously twitching as he wondered just how quickly he could pull the pistol he carried. His eyes darted back and forth for cover to throw himself behind.

"You've come this far. Come and get us."

"So you admit it," Josh concluded.

"We admit nothing," Wheeler said. "Where's your proof?"

"In your cabin," Josh said.

"Shut up, Josh," Jeff snapped. "Think about it. Do you think he'd leave the gold just laying around? And do you think he'll take us back there to look for it?"

"Ain't nothing in my cabin," Wheeler said. "You can look for yourself."

"See?" Josh told his brother.

"Yeah, he'll let you look. Ain't nothing there, that's why. He's hid it."

"It was you who killed him and stole the gold," Josh called to Wheeler. "No one else knew about it."

"Like I said, I didn't do it. Quit yer yapping and jerk your pistol, or turn around and ride out of here and don't never bother me again. I don't want to hurt you, boy, either one of you." While he spoke Wheeler remained in constant motion, with small forward steps and side-to-side swaying to keep from being an easy target. The other men kept to the boardwalk just a step or two from cover.

Jeff broke out into a sweat.

"Josh, we've got to do something. Either turn and walk away like he said, or let's take our chances. We can't stand out here and talk to him all day—"

He was cut short by a sudden shot from their left, the direction of the store. They both jerked, startled, and at the same time a cloud of dirt kicked up at Wheeler's feet. Someone was helping them.

Josh crouched and drew his gun, bringing it up to fire, but Wheeler was faster. Surprised by the shot from an unexpected source, the man immediately drew both pistols he carried and began firing. The first shot removed Josh's hat; the second, blasting a fraction of a second after the first, whistled past Jeff's ear and slammed into the tree trunk behind him. Startled by it, the eldest Bodine bolted for the side of the street but tripped and sprawled in the dirt, tearing his shirtsleeve and skinning his elbow. His hat went flying. As Jeff scrambled on hands and knees, Wheeler's bullets plinked the ground behind him, spurring him on.

Wheeler didn't stop there. While his two partners also dove for cover, he continued rapid-firing his two pistols at the Bodines, sending several shots into the wood transom over the door of the general store as well.

He walked as he fired, keeping the Bodines and their secret assistant so busy ducking and trying to make cover that they couldn't shoot back. None of Wheeler's shots connected, but they were all close, too close for comfort.

Finally the brothers both found themselves behind Jane's wagon as the shooting stopped.

"He's out of ammo," Josh said breathlessly.

"Oh, were you countin'?" Jeff mocked. "I was too busy gettin' to safety to worry about keeping tally of how many shots he was firing."

"Well, at least we know he's a bad shot. He didn't hit nuthin'."

"I hate to tell you this, Josh, but he hit everything he was aimin' at. And he did it without actually aimin'. I tell you, he was shootin' both guns as fast as he could and gettin' just close enough to keep us busy without hurtin' us."

"Why would he do that?"

"He don't want to hurt us, that's why. He's giving us a chance to leave here under our own power."

"That don't make sense. Why would he kill our pa, then let us live after we tried to take him in?"

"Maybe he didn't kill our pa," Jeff guessed.

"Then why didn't he just come out and say so?"

"He did."

"He just denied it like all guilty people do. If he didn't do it, why'd he come to town like this, ready to engage in a shootin' match? He coulda just walked up to us and said, 'Sorry about your pa, boys, but I had nothing to do with it.'"

"Would you have listened?"

"Yeah."

"Well, I don't know about that. And he obviously didn't think so either."

There was an unearthly silence as the boys stopped talking to each other. Josh could hear the blowing of the wind through the tree in the center of the street, the pawing of the uncomfortable horses hitched to the wagon, and the scuffling of feet inside the store. He ventured a look, but the reflection of the waning sun on the glass kept him from seeing inside.

Josh peeked around the wagon. Wheeler stood behind a post in front of the saloon, calmly reloading his second gun, having apparently already finished the first. When he was finished he spun the cylinder and twirled the pistol by the trigger guard, slipping it into his waistband with the butt forward in a fluid, easy motion.

"Why doesn't Hickok do something?" Josh asked frantically. "My gosh, Jeff. Wheeler has his back to him!"

"Your hero," Jeff said sadly, "has apparently retired to the bottle for good. I knew it was a mistake following him here."

Then Wheeler did something that caught Josh's eye. He turned his head toward the saloon door and said something. Josh couldn't hear him, but the way his head bobbed, Josh could tell he was speaking.

"Wait a minute," he muttered.

"What is it?" Jeff asked.

"Wheeler. Take a look at him."

"Yeah, so?"

"Did he have a mustache?"

"No, I don't recall one. What difference does it make?"

"Well, he's got one now."

"This is a fine time to be concerned with the sartorial habits of the man, Josh. He's got us pinned down and will kill us if we don't throw down our guns."

"No, he won't," Josh said, and took careful aim with his pistol over the edge of the wagon side. He cocked the gun and squeezed the trigger. The bullet whistled across the street and slammed into the post Wheeler leaned against, sending the man scrambling.

Josh fired once more, then again, each time sending the same message Wheeler had sent him: Hunker down or face the consequences.

"What are you doing?" Jeff asked.

"Don't it strike you odd that Wheeler's partners didn't join in but just took cover when it was Wheeler doin' all the shootin'?"

Jeff shrugged. "I suppose a little, now that I think about it."

"And aren't you surprised Wheeler is so good with a gun—no, with two guns at the same time? As I recall, he didn't even have anything but that little self-cocker in his pocket when he worked for us."

Jeff thought back on it, and as the riddle assembled itself, the concern melted from his face, replaced first by bewilderment, then insight.

"That ain't Wheeler," he concluded to Josh.

"No, I don't think it is."

"Then who is it?"

"One guess," Josh said. "You know anybody else around here who can shoot like that?"

"Hickok?" Jeff was incredulous.

"The Prince of Pistoleers."

"Why would he shoot at us?" Jeff looked at the man as he ducked behind cover on the boardwalk, then jerked his head toward his brother. "He's in on it!"

Josh shook his head. "No, he ain't in on it. He would have killed us already if that was the case. He wouldn't have come this far."

"This could be a setup to get rid of us and make Wheeler look guilty."

"Sometimes you think too deep," Josh criticized. "Here, I'll prove he ain't in on it."

"What are you doing? Stop, Josh."

But it was too late, Josh had already jumped up from his cover and was striding out into the street.

"Come on out, you coward!" he called. "Wheeler, come on out and face me, man to man."

"You wouldn't have a chance, boy," Wheeler called.

"That's my problem, isn't it? Come on out."

Wheeler responded with several quick shots to Josh's feet, but the young man stood rock steady. Wheeler hesitated, then peeked out. As quickly as he could, Josh drew and fired, missing intentionally but close enough so Wheeler could hear the bullets whiz past.

"Okay, Hickok," Josh said. "What's this all about?"

Wheeler stared at him for a second from around the post, then began to laugh and pulled off his hat. Long curly hair fell out of it, spilling onto his shoulders. He turned his head toward the saloon. "Come on out boys. It's over." Turning back to Josh he said, "Put away your irons, boy, you done real good."

"What's the meaning of this?" Josh demanded, as a man in Hickok's hat and buckskin coat stepped cautiously out of the saloon. He removed the jacket and handed it to its rightful owner, who pulled it on and was suddenly himself again. The two men who had pretended to be Wheeler's accomplices emerged from their hiding places and made their way to the saloon in silence, with a friendly wave from Hickok as thanks. He flipped them a coin for their trouble.

Jeff also came out of hiding, and the door to the store opened behind him. Jane emerged, her gun still in her hand, giving Jeff another surprise.

The five of them met in the middle of the street.

"Boys, you know Jim Wheeler." Hickok pointed to the man who had been wearing his buckskin coat. Jim nodded to the Bodines.

"Sorry to hear about your pa," he said. "I had nothing to do with it, I swear. He was a good man, treated me right. So did you, Jeff. Ever since I left your pa I've been here in Lundy, got a job at the new mine up the hill. I got plenty of witnesses and pay stubs to prove it."

Jeff just stared at him, then transferred his gaze to Hickok.

"Just what is the meaning of this charade?" he asked Wild Bill.

"Yeah," echoed Jane. "I coulda shot you."

"I weren't expecting you to get involved," Hickok admitted to the girl, giving her a little smile and a wink.

"Get on with the tellin'," Josh urged, starting to get a little testy.

"Why don't we do this over a libation?" Hickok suggested as he began to move toward the saloon.

"Hang your libation," Jeff said forcefully. "We want to know why you made fools of us."

Hickok stopped. "Okay, son," he said, turning toward the brothers. "I'll tell you. But what I did today didn't make fools of you. It was an education. First off, you two made up your minds pretty quick Mr. Wheeler here was guilty. I fueled that idea, I suppose, but that's because I knew more about your pa than I let on."

"Like what?" Jeff challenged.

"Keep your powder dry, son. I'll get to it. Now, Mr. Wheeler here wasn't in Bodie when I said he was, and he didn't win my pistols in a poker game. Someone else did, but when I heard your tale about your pa, I realized something I hadn't before and knew you two were so headstrong you'd get yourselves in a peck of trouble if I didn't help you out. So I let on that Mr. Wheeler had been in Bodie and was headed back to Lundy, to get you to come here."

"How'd you know he was in Lundy if he was never actually in Bodie?" Josh asked.

"You told me he was from Lundy, remember? I didn't know he'd really be here, but it really didn't matter. I brought you here to keep you from going after the real killers."

Josh's face flushed, and Jeff's hands clenched into fists.

"You better have a good reason for doing that, Hickok," Jeff threatened.

"Relax, you two. I ain't done. The first question is, how'd I know who killed your pa? Well, I don't know for certain, but I got a good idea. Day after I came into town I was standing on the corner, just taking in the sights, when I saw three hombres ride into town on a couple of sorry horses. Well, I recognized them as a set of brothers I'd heard of and seen pictures of before when I was sheriff in Abilene, and I was a mite stumped when one of 'em rides right on through town without stopping while the other two lay over. Now, this puzzled me, to be sure, but it weren't none of my business at the time, so I let it go. Then I meet Josh here, and he tells me his pa's been killed out yonder of town and robbed of his gold, and I just put two and two together."

He paused and looked from Jeff to Josh, staring them both in the eye. "I couldn't let you two go after the varmints."

"Why not?" Josh asked, sounding insulted.

"They're the Younger brothers, boy. Meaner'n a teased rattlesnake. They'd a killed you where you stood once they knew you were onto them about your pa. I brought you here to save your lives."

"But you let them get away."

"That's life sometimes. I ain't a lawman here. That wasn't my concern. I just didn't want to see two healthy lads like you get hurt and killed, that's all."

"I can't say I like all this deception, Hickok," Jeff said. "But I can't say I blame you, either. You're right about Josh wanting to go after them, and I'da probably gone along."

"Okay, that's the first question," Josh said. "What's the second?"

"Well, my main purpose was to keep you alive, but as I thought about it, I decided to teach you a little something about making hasty decisions."

"What do you mean?" Josh asked.

"Ain't it obvious?" Jane told him. "He wanted you to bite off more'n you could chew, thinkin' maybe you'd learn to be more cautious, more conniving next time."

"Young lady, you are wise beyond your years," Hickok told her with a winning smile.

"You think so?" she cooed.

"And you're not a bad shot, either."

"Yeah? Well maybe you could teach me some more."

"I'd love to," Hickok told her, "but it's time for me to be moving on. I've learned a few things myself, and I feel my destiny lies somewhere else. Like the Dakota country, maybe."

"I'm not entangled," Jane told him. "I wouldn't mind seeing the Dakota country."

Hickok glanced over at Josh, as if to seek his permission. Josh only shrugged.

"I've got no claim to her. We just met."

"Young lady, what about your mother? What would she say to you traipsin' all over the country with the likes of me?"

"I ain't got no ma or pa," she told him. "Just a cousin name of Dora."

"Well, I—tell you what, Jane. I'll meet you in Bodie in two days, lobby of the American Hotel. We'll see what happens then, okay?"

"You bet." She smiled ingratiatingly. Jeff rolled his eyes and turned away.

"One thing still bothers me," Josh told Wild Bill. "How'd you pull this off this morning?"

"Well, I was hoping Mr. Wheeler wasn't here, but when Jeff went into the saloon and that old geezer snuck out and hightailed it up the street, I knew he was around. So when I went over there, I snuck out the back and found him, and we set up this little charade." He grinned. "Pretty good, huh?"

Jeff growled as Josh said, "Yeah, so good I almost shot you."

Hickok's smile faded. "Yeah, you shoot pretty good. But I knew you weren't a dead aim. Remember that lizard out on the trail?" He grinned again, directing it toward Jeff.

"Let's get outa here," Jeff said with contempt.

"What's your hurry?" Hickok asked. "You got someplace to go?"

They didn't, and the Bodine brothers looked at each other. Josh spoke first.

"Can we stay the night at least? It's kinda late to be startin' out, and I ain't slept in a real bed for a week. A hot supper, maybe a bath . . ."

"Oh, all right," Jeff relented, then couldn't suppress the tiny smile that tickled the corners of his mouth as he thought about what his brother had said. Those things sounded mighty good to him, too. Without another word, he turned and headed for the small hotel at the top of the street.

CHAPTER

TWENTY·EIGHT

WITH THE RAYS OF THE NEW SUN dusting the tops of the trees and the lake still in shadow, the three horsemen loped their steeds out of town, skirting the placid lake along the north shore. Rings of water appeared and multiplied where fish broke the surface in their quest for food, but otherwise, there was nothing but the beating of the horses' hooves and the creak of the leather saddles to disturb the solitude.

They rode in silence the first few hours, anxious to put Lundy far behind them. Jeff and Josh were sullen now that the adventure was over, Josh because his father's death hadn't been avenged and the gold hadn't been recovered, Jeff because there was no reason to ride home. There was no home. Without the gold, what hope did they have?

For years he'd had a purpose: to blast the tunnel and process the ore. Yes, it was tedious, repetitive work. But what wasn't? Farming was nothing more than digging furrows and planting the same ground year after year, harvesting the same crops, taking them to market. Ranching was just raising cows or sheep year after year, day in and day out. So what did it matter that mining was tedious? At least then he had a home, a place he could stand on and survey, a place he could call his own . . . even if it was really his father's.

It would be his now, if they hadn't sold it to Mr. Page. What did he want it for? He only had one arm. He couldn't work the mine or run the mill. One man was hardly enough, much less a one-armed man. Jeff wished it was still his. Maybe he could buy it back . . . but he didn't have enough money. He'd have to go to work in Bodie for one of the mining companies. He knew the business, probably better than just about anyone in town. Surely he could get a job.

Four dollars a day, that's what they paid. He made more than that before but never spent much of it. He'd been saving it for later in life. Now it was gone.

Two hours of thinking these things and no progress was made, so Jeff sighed and tried enjoying the ride.

A few feet away Josh was working through his own thoughts, having no better luck than his brother. He was disappointed and angry that Hickok had intentionally led them on a wild goose chase and kept them from at least trying to recover their gold, but he knew the gunman was right; the Younger brothers would not be easily reckoned with. Professional lawmen hadn't been able to stop them, so what chance did a couple of greenhorns and a drunk have?

Wild Bill was thinking about lunch.

They camped that night by Mono Lake, not so close to it that the insects were a problem and not so far that they couldn't wash their dishes in the salty, alkaline water. The meal, beans and bacon and hot coffee, followed by some pie Hickok had brought from Lundy, pacified them all, and they settled down under their blankets.

"Tell me something, Bill," Jeff said quietly, staring up at the stars with his hands up under his head.

"Shoot, son."

"Them stories in the magazines, like *Beadle's* and *Deadeye Dick's* . . . are they true?"

Josh answered from the other side of Hickok. "Sure, they are."

"Whoa, partner," Hickok cautioned. "They're somewhat true, I suppose. But they exaggerate to make them interesting."

"You really had shoot-outs at high noon," Jeff asked, "where you faced men and both of you went for your guns?"

"Naw, it never happens that way. It's mostly like today, everyone hiding and running. Only once did I have it out with a man face-to-face in the street. It was against a Mr. Dave Tutt, as I recall, although the name is of no importance. His only claim to fame is to have been unlucky enough to draw on me."

"What happened?" Josh asked.

"I believe I won," Hickok said, and rolled over. In seconds he was snoring peacefully.

In the morning, when they had finished with breakfast and were saddling the horses for the ride home, Hickok asked if they'd heard anything during the night.

"No," Josh said. "Slept like a baby."

"A baby elephant," Jeff told him. "You need to do something about that snoring."

"Like what?"

"Like sleep on your side—or in the next county. Something. Anything."

"That's not what I'm talking about," Hickok said. "The horses were restless for a time. Pawing and snorting. You didn't hear it?"

"Sorry," Jeff said.

Hickok made a pensive guttural sound in the back of his throat but said no more, cinching up his saddle and climbing into it.

"Does it trouble you?" Josh asked.

"Horse are sensitive to things we can't hear or feel or see. There was something going on."

"Like what?" Jeff asked.

"Don't know," Hickok admitted. "Might never know. Could be we're being followed by Indians or bandits. Could be a coyote was nearby. Could be the wind blew in a smell or sound they weren't familiar with. No way to tell. I wouldn't worry about it, though. We'll be back in Bodie sometime after lunch."

They heeled the horses and rode off again, up the narrow, winding, rocky trail through the pass from Mono Lake to Bodie Valley. Several hours later they were nearly halfway through the pass when Jeff's horse faltered, stopping his forward progress and turning in circles, his head shaking.

"Stupid animal," Jeff muttered, trying to bring it under control while remembering vividly the incident a few days earlier after Josh fired his six-gun. But the animal would not be controlled, and Hickok rode back to help. But just about the time he leaned down to grab the reins near the bit, his own mount began acting strangely, and immediately Josh's horse followed suit.

"Whatever it is," Hickok observed, "it's contagious."

Then all three of the men heard a deep rumbling coming toward them up the pass from the rear, and the ground vibrated. Before they could even think about doing anything, the ground shook violently and kept on shaking.

"Earthquake!" Hickok shouted. "Stay away from the cliffs."

But they had little say in the matter, their horses going where they wanted. Large boulders broke from the cliffs that rose on either side of them, rolling and bouncing down the steep sides, crashing into the valley floor and bounding over the rough surface. Jeff fought hard to stay on his horse as it bolted from the path of a rock. Josh leaned over and tried comforting his horse by patting it on the neck, nearly getting himself thrown for his trouble, clutching his saddle only just in time. Hickok alone maintained control of his animal, doing his best to avoid rocks and shout warnings to his young charges.

After what seemed to be minutes, though was probably just fifteen seconds or so, the shaking ceased and the rocks stopped rolling. The horses calmed themselves, though their eyes remained wide, and in a while they were once again on the way to Bodie.

"Hope Bodie's still standing," Hickok remarked. "Town like that, it could be a pile of broken lumber and bodies by the time we get there." He kicked his horse's flanks and hurried up the road.

Shadow's black hide glistened in the sun as the sweat formed from his efforts, his lean flanks taut and powerful as his strides took Deputy Matt Page closer to Bodie and to his wife. The ink-black mane of the animal, whipped by the wind of his speed, lashed at Matt's face as he leaned forward in the saddle, riding for all he was worth. He wouldn't slow down until they began their ascent up the grade several miles out of Bridgeport, and he wouldn't stop except halfway, to water the horse. Food for himself was of no consequence now. He could always eat later.

But plans come with no guarantee, as Matt realized when Shadow hedged. He'd already made the grade, taken the Bodie cut-off, and was within sight of town when Shadow suddenly slowed, ignoring Matt's heels digging into his flanks. He whinnied and rose up on his hind legs, refusing to respond to Matt's tug on the reins.

"What's the problem, Shadow?" Matt asked testily. Shadow turned in place, and Matt quickly scanned the ground for a rattlesnake. There was none, and he tried settling the horse, but

Shadow wouldn't be still. His ears were perked, his nostrils flared, and he shook his head as though he was trying to dislodge something from it.

Matt barked commands to the horse while he held onto the pommel to stay in the saddle, finally leaning down and grabbing Shadow around the neck. Then he heard what Shadow had already sensed: a low-pitched roar rising from deep within the earth as the ground shook and rolled, like waves of the ocean. There was little Matt could do with Shadow until it passed but hang on and try keeping the horse from running into the ditch where he might injure himself . . . not to mention his rider.

And hang on he did, riding out the earthquake until the growling and the shaking diminished and finally went away. Shadow calmed himself as it dissipated, finally stopping, his right-front hoof pawing and scratching at the dirt. Matt's heart raced and his breathing was fast and shallow, but in a few minutes he returned to normal and was ready to go on.

"That was quite a shaker," he told Shadow quietly. "Is that you're first one? They're something, eh boy?" He patted the horse's strong neck. "We really need to get back to Bodie now, boy. Come on." He snap the reins lightly and jerked in the saddle, and his mount responded finally by moving out at his own pace, following the leading of the reins. When he'd recovered his stride, Matt hurried him and Shadow ran, ran as he had when they left Bridgeport, the earthquake already forgotten.

Flora Bascomb took a breath as she paused before the front door of the Page residence, then hiked her skirt and mounted the steps. She rapped solidly on the door four times and tapped with her foot waiting for it to be answered. Just as she reached up to strike it again, it opened. Sarah peeked out warily, then recognized Flora and stepped aside, opening the door fully.

"Please come in, Flora," she said, her voice betraying no particular emotion.

"Thank you," Flora said tersely. She stepped inside, avoiding Sarah's gaze. Sarah bid her to sit on the upholstered chair, taking a seat herself on a wooden stool.

"May I fix us some tea?" Sarah offered.

"No thank you, Mrs. Page," Flora declined.

"Please, Flora, call me Sarah. We've known each other long enough to use first names."

Flora cleared her throat, obviously uncomfortable with the familiarity, but complied.

"Sarah, I shan't be long. I've come to you directly today to let you know just how things stand in Bodie."

Sarah tilted her head slightly. "How things stand? What things, Flora?" Though she had a good idea what was coming, she wasn't going to make it easy for the woman.

"I think you know perfectly well what things, Sarah. Here in Bodie we have two classes of people. The respectable citizens and the riffraff. The people who obey the law and fear God, and those who . . . well, those who don't. They mock the law, and they mock God with the way they live."

"Yes, I know this to be true," Sarah admitted. "But there is a third class."

"Third class? I hardly think so. If you're not a law-abiding, God-fearing person, you're a scoffer and a mocker."

"Yes, that's true," Sarah agreed. "But the third class are those who mock God while they think they are doing His will. I'm sure you remember the Crusades from your history lessons. And the Inquisition. And the witch hunts in Salem in our own country. All things done in the name of God."

"Of course, but those were done by evil people. We don't have folk like that here, except those whose profession is blatantly anti-God. The mockers and scoffers I already mentioned."

"You don't think we have hypocrites in Bodie?" Sarah challenged.

"Just one that I'm aware of," Flora said, craning her neck forward and squinting one eye. The implication was not lost on Sarah, and her face became taut.

"I suggest you speak what's on your mind, Flora. But may I ask, first off, whom you represent? Is it the whole church, the ladies' group, or is it just Flora Bascomb? If the latter, save your breath. I'm not interested in what Flora Bascomb thinks."

"Those are harsh words, young lady," Flora snapped, "and they just might be your undoing. I represent all the people in the church who want what's good and right without the tainting influence of certain people, nor the woman who has made the church a haven for them."

"You certainly are one for beating around the bush," Sarah noted, keeping her voice pleasant. "Perhaps you lack the courage of your convictions to speak it outright."

"If that's your desire, then so be it," Flora concluded. "I'll say it plainly. Your prostitute friend has no business commingling with us good folk, and you have no right thrusting her into our midst."

Sarah was not unprepared for such a statement. "That's an interesting opinion, Flora, but I doubt the whole church holds it. You don't speak for the body; you speak for yourself."

"You're young, Sarah, and I don't want to see anything happen to you, but we can't allow you to continue this charade. Rosa Bailey has got to go, and if you continue to support her, then you'll have to go with her."

"You're throwing me out of the church?"

"If it comes to that."

"In the first place, Flora, you have no authority to do so. Your husband's position in the community does not translate to any particular standing in the church. God is no respecter of persons. If you ever read your Bible or listened to Reverend Edwards, you'd know that. We are all equals in the body of Christ."

"We are not to associate with sinners."

"We are all sinners, Flora. Christ ate with sinners and associated with them so much that he was criticized for it."

"She is a bad influence."

"You're afraid your husband has been with her, isn't that it, Flora?"

Flora's eyes and mouth widened, and her face turned crimson. "Why, you little . . . how dare you make such an insinuation!"

"Why else would you want to keep her away from the congregation? In your mind she's a temptation to the men, and you're so unsure of yourself and your husband's love for you that you think Rosa might challenge you for his affections."

"How dare you—"

"I dare, Flora, because you dare to accuse my husband!" Sarah stood up. "You spread the lie that he was with one of the prostitutes on Bonanza Street. Your husband saw him there, you said. Don't act so shocked. I've got plenty of friends who'll tell me what lies you're spreading. Well, let me tell you this, Flora. My husband was in that part of town on business. He's the deputy. What's your husband's excuse? Why was he on King Street in the middle of the night? Don't try explaining. We all know why he was there, don't we? And another thing, Rosa is not a prostitute. She is a *former* prostitute, just as Mary Magdalene was a former prostitute. There's a big difference. We all have former lives, Flora, even you. Yes, I know that's hard to admit, that the lily-white Flora Bascomb could once have been a sinner. Well I'll tell you, Flora, I wouldn't be at all surprised if Jesus came to earth now and you stood before Him, if He didn't say 'Depart from me, you worker of iniquity, I never knew you!'"

Flora jumped up. "Sarah, I'll not tolerate this insolence." She pointed a bony finger at Sarah, her voice quavering. "This is the last time you'll speak to me that way. I'll call a meeting of the elders and you'll be asked to leave, so the church might remain pure."

"You have no authority," Sarah reiterated, her voice suddenly calm. "And I believe God's truth will win out."

"We'll just see about th—" Flora never finished her sentence. There was a sudden movement of the floor beneath them and a small hurricane lamp on the table rocked, then tipped over with a crash. Fortunately it hadn't been lit, so there was no fire, but the pungent kerosene spilled out and soaked into the throw rug in the small room. The shaking continued growing rapidly in intensity until the whole house shuddered. Flora lost her balance and fell, and Sarah, struggling with her own footing, rushed to her aid.

"Come on, Flora. We've got to get to safety."

"What is it?" Flora cried.

God's judgment, Sarah wanted to say, but she held her peace. "It's an earthquake, Flora. We've got to get outside."

But Flora wouldn't stand, wouldn't even crawl for cover. Sarah was unable to drag her as the woman cowered on the floor, her head covered with her arms. Sarah had no choice but to get down with her and to pray.

"Dear God, protect us—"

It was all she had time for. A hollow, heart-sinking crack above them cut her prayer short, and she looked up in time to see a roof support beam split. She threw herself over Flora just as the rafter broke in two, and the unsupported half swung down, along with the boards and shingles it had been holding up.

Debris fell over and around them, but the heavy beam Sarah was expecting never landed. It had fallen to the sofa, which stopped its descent, hovering just inches above her back. Slowly the shaking subsided and finally stopped altogether, though small bits of wood and plaster from the walls continued drifting down on them. Flora's whole body shook and she whimpered.

"Flora, get up," Sarah begged. "We need to get outside. Please!" She couldn't stand, so she backed her way off the woman and pulled at her arm to pry her loose, but Flora wouldn't budge. Sarah yanked again and an abrupt, sharp pain surged through her abdomen. It went away as quickly as it appeared, then returned, harder this time, and stayed. Her belly, her insides, trembled, shaking nearly as much as the house had during the earthquake. The pain was intense, and Sarah cried out for help. But there was none. Flora didn't move, just curled up on the floor and moaned.

Sarah knew she couldn't stay there. Whatever was happening to her was making her nauseous, and she felt her bowels threatening to release. She crawled out of the debris and around Flora, then staggered to the bedroom and dragged out the chamber pot.

The pain in her belly was intense, but as she released, it suddenly subsided. She felt weak, drained, and sat there a moment gaining her strength back before grabbing a towel. It was then she noticed blood on her dress and the floor. Her face pale, sweat standing in drops on her forehead and running down the small of her back, Sarah became woozy and the room wavered. Thinking at first it might be another earthquake, she soon realized it was her head and not the room that was spinning.

Sarah clawed her way to the bed and dragged herself onto it as the pain returned. This time it increased in duration and intensity, and she felt another flow, only this time not due to nausea. When it had finished, the pain subsided and didn't return. Hesitantly, Sarah looked at what had been expelled, seeing a torrent of blood along with a small mass of irregular tissue, not half the size of her fist.

She gazed at it, stunned. Then the realization of what it was came to her, and she screamed.

CHAPTER

TWENTY·NINE

MATT RODE UP MAIN STREET at full speed, ignoring the confusion, shouting for the men and women running helter-skelter in the street to get out of the way. Several buildings had collapsed, he could see. In general the town didn't look too bad, at least at a cursory glance, which was all he was going to give right now.

He headed directly for his house, pulling hard on Shadow's reins and sitting the animal on its haunches as it slid to a stop. Matt leaped off and threw the reins over the hitching rail hard, causing them to twirl around twice, enough to hold most any horse. He noted with dread the damaged roof.

"Sarah!" he called as he hit the porch running. "Sarah!" He ran into the door, unconcerned with the abuse he might render the wood planks or the hinges, and it flew open. His first sighting was the debris under the hole in the roof, then he saw the crumpled figure of a woman in the midst of it, and fear gripped his heart.

"Sarah! Oh God, let her be okay." He dove into the rubble to rescue his bride, hearing her crying softly in an irregular fashion born of fright, but as he put a hand on her shoulder he realized the hair was not that of his wife. He turned the woman's head and recoiled at the distorted face of Flora Bascomb.

"Where's Sarah?" he asked, but Flora, though uninjured, was unable to answer, her fear having paralyzed her. Matt could see that she seemed to be okay, or at least didn't require any emergency treatment, so he picked her up out of harm's way and dropped her into a chair in an undamaged part of the room before tearing into the rear of the house.

The bedroom was the only other room of consequence, and he opened the door to see a pale Sarah on the bed, staring his direction with vacant, unseeing eyes.

"Sarah?" he asked softly. "Are you all right?"

She didn't answer, only gazed at him hopelessly, then down at the mess on the bed. It was then Matt saw it and came to her side.

"You're bleeding!" he said. "Where are you hurt?"

He checked her quickly but saw no obvious injuries, and she wasn't favoring anything. She stared at his face, then down at the bed, then back at his face, her eyes questioning but her lips motionless. Then the bottom lip quivered and a flood of tears and sobs broke free, spilling out in a horrendous rush that Matt couldn't even begin to understand.

She threw her arms around him and bawled unchecked. Matt held her, so grateful to be home and find her apparently unhurt that he was, for the moment, unconcerned with the reason for her sorrow. He figured she was just scared and relieved to see him. Women cried like this when they were scared, didn't they? But where had the blood come from?

"Oh, Matt," she said finally. "I lost it. I lost it."

"It's okay, honey, I'm home. What did you lose?"

"Matt, I lost the baby."

For a moment he didn't comprehend the import of that simple statement. Then he looked again at the blood on the quilt and the lump in the midst of it, and he knew. His heart rose up in his throat and tears sprang to his eyes as her pain became his. He closed his eyes and held her tightly as they rocked on the bed, crying together as they clung to each other for support, for comfort, for solace neither of them felt adequate to provide.

Matt didn't know how long they had sat there when a small voice called to them from the parlor.

"In here," Matt called, though he didn't recognize the voice.

In a moment a disheveled Rosa Bailey came in.

"You're back," she said. "Oh, Lord, you don't know how

relieved I am. I came over to check on her because I know she's been having—"

She stopped cold when she saw the blood.

"Oh, Sarah." Rosa came over and sat behind her, putting her arms around both of them. Sarah finally released Matt, who stood up uncomfortably, trying not to look at the remains of his first child. Sarah melted into Rosa's arms and the woman looked up at Matt with wet eyes and cheeks.

"I'll take care of it," she said. "You might want to see to Mrs. Bascomb. I checked her on the way in. I don't think she's hurt. A splash of cold water in the face will probably bring her out of it."

Matt nodded, peeling himself reluctantly from the room. He did as Rosa suggested, and Flora gasped at the shock of the water, then shook her head and regarded Matt with frightened eyes.

"It's okay, Mrs. Bascomb," Matt told her. "It's me, Matt Page. It's all over." He wiped the tears off his face and repeated his comment sorrowfully. "It's all over." He paused and turned his face from her, pressing his eyes tightly shut to stem the flow, then took a deep breath, wiped his face with a sleeve, and returned his attention to Flora, bending over with his hands on his knees.

"Come on, Mrs. Bascomb, you've got to go home."

"Home?" she asked weakly, staring past Matt to some unknown spot in the air.

She staggered to her feet and, with his help, made it to the door. Without so much as a "good-bye," Flora stumbled off.

"Matt!"

The voice hailed him from down the street, and he looked to see a one-armed, clean-shaven man running toward him, waving. Matt peered at him, making sure it was his father, then waved back.

Jacob Page leaped onto the porch, bypassing the steps.

"Boy, I'm glad yer back. Sarah okay?"

"She lost the baby, Pa."

"What do you mean she lost the baby?"

"She miscarried durin' the earthquake." Matt broke down, and Jacob put his arm around his son.

"Wish there was somethin' I could say. She in there alone?"

"Naw, Rosa's in there with her."

"That's good son, real good. I'm glad she didn't leave yet."

"Leave?"

"Yeah, Rosa's leavin' town. She's tired of the way the women is treatin' her. Thinks it'll diff'rent someplace else."

"Might be, but it's too bad. Sarah needs her, now more than ever." Matt broke away and sat on the step as he thought about it. "On the other hand, maybe it won't matter."

"What do you mean, son?" Jacob took a place beside him.

Matt looked at his father. "I'm the new sheriff of Mono County. At least until the next election. Sheriff Taylor can't come back for a while, so they appointed me sheriff."

"That's great!"

"Well, I'm not so sure now. I don't know how Sarah's going to take it. She might not like the idea of moving to Bridgeport right now."

"I think she'll jump at it like a chicken on a cricket."

"Who knows what she'll do now. She probably needs a doctor since the miscarriage—doctor! I need to get the doctor!" He started getting up, but Jacob grabbed his arm and pulled him back down.

"He's a mite busy with some injured folk, Matt. Rosa's in there. She'll know what to do."

"She's a good woman, Pa. If it wasn't for her . . . background."

"That don't bother me none," Jacob said. "Sometimes people do what they think they got to do. It ain't always right, but God can forgive them. Don't I know all about that."

Matt stared at his father, thinking, then asked, "Pa, why'd you shave off your whiskers?"

Jacob reached up to stroke his chin.

"Oh, that. That's what I need to tell you about. We got us a 6-0-1 workin' in town."

"6-0-1? What's that?"

"Vigilance committee. Lynch mob."

"What for?"

"They're planning to take out Thomas Wellman, string him up."

"Wellman? What'd he do to get them so riled?"

"Do? Why, Matt, he blew up the Queen Anne powder magazine."

"No, no, he didn't."

"Looks like he did, Matt. We got some new evidence after you left, makes him look mighty guilty."

Matt didn't know what to think. There were too many things going on right now for him take care of all of them at once. His only real concern was Sarah at the moment. He wanted to go in and console her, hold her, and stay by her side as long as she needed him. And as soon as Rosa came out and gave the okay, that's just what he was going to do. Wellman could wait until morning, couldn't he? After all, the whole town would be busy with the earthquake, treating the injured and fixing homes and businesses.

"I take it he's in jail?" Matt assumed.

"Not exactly. We arrested him, but when we got wind of the 6-0-1 we snuck him out and hid him."

Matt stared at his father. "Does that have something to do with . . . ." He rubbed his chin.

"Yeah, 'fraid so. Billy arranged it. Wellman's safe for now. But the fact is, I think he done it."

Matt shook his head, then put his face in his hands. This was all too much. How could he take on even more responsibility by becoming sheriff when he couldn't even control one little old gold camp. A vigilance committee. He'd seen what they could do and how helpless the law was when the committee was determined to do a lynching. The last time, with the convicts down in Bishop, there were plenty of lawmen around, almost as many as there were vigilantes. He wanted to stop it but his pa—though he hadn't known it was his pa at the time—kept him from it. Now the same man was asking him to stop it, even though he thought Wellman was guilty.

Only problem was, Matt knew different. But could he prove it? What was the evidence against Wellman? Could it be he was in on it with the Youngers?

But his thoughts kept returning to his wife inside, his wife who had just lost their baby.

It was too much. Matt put his head down on his arms and, though he fought it, his shoulders shook as he sobbed quietly.

Sarah stared wide-eyed at nothing, not unlike the gaze of a dead person. She saw only what was in her mind, and Rosa couldn't tell what that was, though she had an idea. She wanted to console the young woman but knew there nothing she could say that would help. Rosa had been there herself not too long ago. Only time could bring her back.

Still, she couldn't just stand there. Rosa sat on the edge of the bed and took Sarah's hands in her own, rubbing and patting them softly. Sarah didn't react, her only movement being the shallow expanding of her chest and the blinking of her eyes.

It seemed like a long time had passed before Sarah broke the silence.

"Why, Rosa? Why did this happen? Did I do something wrong?"

"What do you mean, did you do something wrong, child?

"Did I sin? Do you think God is punishing me?"

"I don't know too much about God, Sarah. But I can't imagine He'd want to punish a person by doing something like this, even an evil person. That punishes the unborn baby more than it does the mother, I would think. I don't think God works that way. Besides, how would He punish men? They don't carry the children."

"Maybe I work too hard. That could be it," Sarah went on, not really listening and her gaze still fixed.

"You do work hard, that's for sure. But no harder than anyone else."

"There's got to be something, Rosa. I feel so . . . so guilty, like I did something I shouldn't. There's no other reason for this to have happened."

"Why does there have to be a reason?"

"So I can make sure it doesn't happen again," Sarah said, and finally turned to look at her friend.

"It's not fair, Rosa. Molly was doing something wrong, and she had a baby girl." Sarah cried again, large tears sliding down her cheeks, her already bloodshot eyes getting redder. She slid down into the bed, the tears suddenly stopping as quickly as they started. Her face soured, a despondent look distorting her petite features.

"Why, God?" she muttered, then again, only her voice more defiant, then a third time she repeated the question. Rosa could almost see Sarah shaking her fist, her voice was so demanding.

"Matt!" Sarah said suddenly, sitting up. "He'll be mad. He wanted this baby so bad. He's going to kill me, Rosa. He'll put me out, divorce me. I'm not good enough to be his wife. He deserves better, someone who can carry his baby to full term.

"You're talking crazy," Rosa scolded. "I know you're upset,

but you know better than the things you're saying. Matt loves you. He wouldn't do no such thing."

"Then why does he leave me all the time? Leave me alone to fend for myself? Tell me that, Rosa. Why?"

"It's his job, Sarah. He only leaves because he has to for his job. And he works because he wants to provide for you, and so he can afford to have a family."

"And then I go and kill his baby," lamented Sarah. "Fine wife I turned out to be. I ought to go home to my parents, make Matt a free man."

"Something tells me he doesn't want to be free," Rosa said. "Besides, your parents wouldn't take you back. They know your place is with your husband."

"Oh, Rosa," Sarah cried, turning toward the woman and holding her hands tightly. "I feel so empty. Will it ever go away? Will I feel normal again?"

Rosa began shedding a few tears as well, and soon both of them were crying freely. "Someday," she said, "only don't ask when that someday is. I'm still waiting to find out. What's important is for you to know that it will get better. It will."

"I hope so," Sarah sniffed.

Me too. Rosa thought. *Me too.*

Matt came in hesitantly, peeking around the door as if to avoid a flying plate, not knowing what Sarah's mood would be. She rolled her head to gaze upon him as she heard his footsteps, and when he saw it was safe, went to her side, unbuckling his gun belt and dropping it on the floor in the corner. He sat on the edge of the bed and began stroking her forehead and telling her he loved her. Jacob followed him in and came to stand on the opposite side of the bed.

"How're you feelin'?" Matt asked.

"I'm tired," she said, her voice hoarse from crying. An occasional spasm still convulsed her chest. "It hurts, Matt, but Rosa says I should be all right."

"That's good to hear. We'll get the doctor here as soon as we can. Pa says the earthquake caused some injuries in town."

"Our little house," Sarah lamented. "It's ruined."

"It kin be rebuilt," Jacob assured her. "We'll git to it tomorrow, be done in no time."

Sarah's eyes teared again. "Oh, Matt, I'm so sorry."

"What for, honey?" Matt moved his face closer to hers.

"For losing your baby." Her bottom lip quivered.

"Sarah, it's not your fault. These things happen sometimes. God knows best. He hasn't left us."

"I know, Matt. I know. I just feel there must be something I did to cause this. Maybe I worked too hard, or maybe I let the ladies in the church get to me—oh my . . . Flora. She's under all the—"

Sarah tried sitting up, but Matt pushed her gently back down.

"She's fine, Sarah. She wasn't hurt, just scared out of her wits."

"Didn't take much," Jacob mumbled. "She was halfway there anyway."

"I sent her home," Matt continued. "I don't think she'll be givin' you any more trouble."

For the first time since his return, Sarah got a good look at her husband. "Matt, what's happened to you. You look . . ."

"Terrible? I've been told. It's a long tale. I don't want to worry you with it tonight. You need to rest, get well. We can talk about it tomorrow."

"You're not leaving, are you?"

"Well, I . . . I think there's a couple of things I have to attend to, isn't that right, Pa?"

Jacob shrugged.

"Can't they wait?" Sarah complained. "I hardly ever get to see you."

Matt looked at his father pleadingly, and Jacob cleared his throat.

"I suppose I can watch over things for a while."

"Thanks, Pa."

"Yeah . . . sure. Look, I'm gonna leave now, let you two be. I'll take Rosa with me, she can—" He looked around, but Rosa wasn't there, nor was she outside the room. Jacob leaned over and gave Sarah a fatherly peck on the cheek, then patted her shoulder and plodded out.

Rosa wasn't in the living room either, nor was she outside the house. She'd gone. Jacob stood on the porch, torn between the desire to go after her—a desire he didn't understand—and the need to keep his word to Matt and fill in for a few more hours.

At least, he hoped it would just be a few more hours.

He decided to have a quick look for her. A few minutes one way
or the other wouldn't make any difference. Besides, Thomas
Wellman was hidden, and everyone was too busy with the after-
math of the earthquake to be worried about lynching him.

Jacob stepped off the porch and trotted down the dusty street,
noticing how dark the sky had become and wondering how the
time could have flown so quickly. Then he realized it wasn't that
late. The clouds had rolled in during the day unnoticed and built
up until they were approaching storm caliber.

Ignoring the chill he felt now that he was aware of the snap in
the air, Jacob headed directly for the stage office. That's how Rosa
had intended leaving, and maybe the earthquake wouldn't affect
the stage line's schedule. Even if it did, the delay might be short and
she'd be there, waiting.

But the office was closed and dark, a hastily scrawled sign in
the window announcing that no stage would be leaving until the
next day. Jacob was crestfallen; then hope sprang again when he
realized Rosa would have to wait until then. She'd be back at
Betsy's, no doubt. He'd find her there.

But then what? What did he want with her? What did he have
to say to her? Everyone had already said all they could to try and
convince her to stay, but she would have none of it. She was determined to go and no one, not even Betsy, her best friend, could talk
her out of it.

What could a grizzled old miner say?

Jacob turned and walked to the Empire Boardinghouse, where
Billy surely had gone to check for earthquake damage, when he
was waylaid by Noah Porter.

"Mr. Page! Whooee! Boy, that was a whopper, weren't it? That
was bigger'n the big one we had up north in fifty-three. That one
shook pretty good, dislodged a few hats and dishes and knocked
Mrs. Carstairs out of bed—accordin' to Mr. Carstairs, you understand—anyway, this one was a mite stronger, I'd say, maybe longer,
too. Did you notice how it rolled, like waves on the ocean? Why I
remember when I was on board the *Monitor*—that's the Union's
ironclad, don't you know, fought to a draw with the *Virginia* off
Chesapeake Bay, as I recall. That was quite a battle between them
two ships. The *Virginia*—used to be called the *Merrimac* or some-
thing-like when it was a Union ship, but the Rebs, they yanked it

up after they sank her and rebuilt her and give a new name, a Southern name. Well sir, they fought all day, exchanging cannon balls, neither ship getting the upper hand—"

"Noah!" Jacob shouted, his face red.

"Huh?" Noah leaned back, driven by the force of Jacob's voice.

"I'm busy. What do you want?"

"Oh. Nothing, really. I was just wondering if you were looking for that woman."

"Woman?" Jacob asked suspiciously.

"Yeah, you know. Rosa . . . what's'ername, that wh—that soiled dove."

"*Former* soiled dove."

"Yeah, whatever. Ya lookin' fer her?"

"What if I am?"

"I was just gonna tell ya, she ain't here."

"I can see that, Noah."

"No, I mean here." He swept his arm in a wide arc. "In Bodie. She left town."

"When? How?"

"Just a few minutes ago. Caught a ride on a wagon leaving town, headed south. A man and his wife who'd had enough of this place, I guess. The earthquake put the period at the end of their sentence."

"Thanks, Noah," Jacob said. "Thanks." Jacob shook the startled old-timer's hand and ran down Main Street, bound for the livery stable.

CHAPTER

THIRTY

AS DUSK SETTLED ABOUT THE SHAKEN TOWN, a phalanx of men in dark clothing moved with all stealth and diligence up an alley. Some wore black hoods over their heads, others kept their hats pulled down low, many were unconcerned about their identities being known and walked almost proudly amongst the rest. Some bore clubs, others hunks of wood, but no guns were visible. There was no doubt, however, that to a man they were all armed. Every sunrise found them heeled with the weapon of choice. Certainly they would not put down their arms on such an occasion as this. But they were discreet.

The leader raised an arm as he arrived at King Street and the column halted obediently, no one speaking above a whisper.

"There's the jail," the leader said in a stage whisper through the hole cut in his black hood. "Surround it as we planned, and those already chosen by lot come inside with me. Now hurry and be quiet!"

He threw down his arm and the vigilantes went into action, running out from the alley to make a ring around the jailhouse. Once in place, the leader strode boldly to the front door and beat on it, then stepped back.

After a time the door opened, and Billy O'Hara, his Sharp's at the ready, moved over to fill the opening.

"Ah thought you might come by," he drawled slowly. "Don't

think you wasn't seen all sneakin' off to the rendezvous. Despicable behavior! Ah'm ashamed of all of you. Bodie's time of greatest need, people injured, three dead, and all you can think about is takin' justice into your own hands. Well, it'll not happen tonight boys. Why don't you take yourselves home, forget about this while it's not too late, while you can still sleep at night, while you can hold your heads up, while you can look yourselves in the—"

"Quit yer yappin'" came a voice from the rear, "and stand aside."

A chorus of agreement rose up until the leader held his hands up for silence. The tumult died slowly, but eventually he regained the floor.

"Billy, you best listen. This is not a mob, nor is this a spur of the moment decision. It is a well thought-out and reasoned responsibility we undertake."

"We aim to see Wellman undertook," yelled a hooded man near the leader.

The leader had to quiet the men once again, then continued as Billy remained silent but stalwart in the doorway.

"This is your last chance, Billy. Stand aside."

"Ah'll not budge," Billy said forcefully. "Which of you will move me?" He brought the barrel down until it was nearly level with the men's heads and looked all the men nearest him directly in their eyes.

"How many shots can you fire before we take you down?" the leader asked. "Besides, we know you too well. You'll not kill any of us. You're not the kind of man to shed blood. Anyway, I don't think that old carbine really works."

Before Billy could answer a stone was launched from his blind side and struck home, knocking him on the side of the head. As he recoiled from the blow, the men rushed him. Without aiming, he pulled the trigger on the Sharp's just before the first onslaught reached him, but his recoil from the rock had spoiled his intention, and the deafening blast went awry, over the heads of his assailants. Immediately they were on him and drove him to the floor of the jailhouse while taking the Sharp's from his hands.

While several men sat on him and others held his arms and legs, the leader and a few others raced to the cell, one of them grabbing the keys on the way. But a cry rose up from them as they discov-

ered it quite empty, and they returned to the office to confront
O'Hara.

"Where is he?" the leader demanded.

Billy sputtered, "He ain't here!"

"We noticed that right off," someone said.

"Billy," said the leader, "this is your last opportunity. At your
own peril you'll remain mute."

Billy struggled with the men, but they would not release him.

"Sorry, Billy." He nodded at the men, then turned away as the
beating began.

Betsy heard the shot and peeked out her door, shocked by the
sight of hooded men surrounding the jail down the street. Curious
and fearful, she wrapped her shawl around herself and ventured
out, trying her best to act disinterested. The attention of the men
was directed toward the jail, and none of them noticed her, but she
made it to King Street opposite the jail before she dared turn her
head to look. The door stood open and she could see men holding
someone down, many of them shouting angrily, almost cheering.
Betsy knew what this was, knew that what Billy had feared had
happened: The committee had come for Wellman. Then, to her
horror, a fight started inside . . . no, not a fight. A beating.

And Betsy knew Billy was the recipient. She turned and ran
back to her crib but passed it and went to Wellman's. She unlocked
the door, having trouble in her haste, while calling to the man
inside.

Opening the door finally, he pulled her in and shut it behind her.

"Are you mad, shouting my name like that?" he said angrily.
"I gave my word to Billy that I'd not run away, I expect you to keep
your word to him as well."

"But they're coming for you!"

"Yes, that's the whole idea of my being here."

"No, no, listen. They're at the jail, and they're beating Mr.
O'Hara mercilessly because he refuses to tell where you are.
They'll kill him, Mr. Wellman!"

Wellman hung his head. This was a decision he'd hoped he
wouldn't have to make. He pressed a hand to his eyes, then
slammed his fist into the door.

"I survived the earthquake intact to come to this," he muttered.

He looked into Betsy's eyes while grabbing her firmly by the arms, surprising her so much she yelped.

"I don't know where, Betsy, but you've got to get some help. I'm going out there. They'll take me, so hurry. Do you understand? Hurry!" He let go and turned to the door, then stopped and spun back to her.

"But in case you don't succeed . . ." He grabbed her, drew her to him, and planted a long kiss on her mouth, then let her go and stormed outside at a dead run.

Betsy took a moment to recover, then followed him out in time to see him get as far as the corner before the cry went up, and he was surrounded. Without hesitation, she was off, taking a different route to avoid the angry horde.

On his roan, the same horse he'd stolen from Matt twice a year ago, before they discovered each other's identity, Jacob Page raced out of Bodie and down the road to the south. Rosa couldn't have gotten too far, he thought, not in a wagon loaded with someone's earthly possessions and three people. They'd be taking it slow and easy. Even a one-armed man on an old horse could catch up to that pretty quick.

But what would he say to her? He'd asked himself that already and had come to a decision. There was no talking her into staying, so there was only one thing a man could say to a woman to keep her from walking out of his life. And say it he would, though he was stumped as to what had gotten into him.

The miles passed beneath the pounding hooves of his mount, and he struggled to hold on with one arm. But it was the first time he'd taken a ride such as this in a long time, and it felt good. Perhaps, he thought, it was because he had a purpose, something at the end of his ride that spoke to him of hope for the future and joy for the present.

Was that possible? Could he really be planning this? What would Matt say? Would he approve? Hang Matt. He had enough problems without taking this burden on. Matt could like it or lump it . . . but something inside Jacob told him Matt would give the nod.

He crested a hill, affording him a view of the winding road for several miles ahead, parts of it, at least. He pulled hard on the reins and the roan stopped, grateful for the rest. He wasn't used to this kind of activity. Though he was taken out at least once a week, it was never for more than a leisurely stroll around the perimeter of the town.

Jacob scanned the countryside as best he could in the waning light. He figured there wasn't much more than fifteen, twenty minutes of dusk that would allow him to see more than a few feet ahead of him. Either he caught up to them quick, or at least spied them, or he could count on riding blind or turning back, brokenhearted. The clouds were thick, dark, and heavy, and he feared a storm before morning, but right now they blocked the stars and the moon, not letting any light through whatsoever.

There, up ahead . . . movement. He leaned forward and opened his eyes as wide as he could, taking in as much light as possible. Yes, it was a wagon, fully loaded. He couldn't make out the people, but it had to be her. It just had to.

Kicking the roan hard, he shouted and bounced on the saddle. The animal responded. A mile was all he had to make up, but since the wagon was still moving, that meant a mile and a half before he caught up to them. And with his vision—and the roan's—so severely limited, he could only hope and pray the horse didn't step in a hole.

Pray. That was something he still wasn't used to, despite the teaching of the preacher and Uncle Billy and Sarah and Matt. He knew he'd been more than a mite cantankerous and had intentionally avoided supplication. But now was as good a time as any to repent, and with his eyes open, he appealed to the Lord.

"God, I know'd Yer list'nin', even though Yer purdy busy back in town with so many folk cryin' out to Ya. But if'n You got time, could You kinda help me some, and slow that wagon down? That's all I'll ask, the rest leave up to me. Wouldn't be fair to make You arrange ev'rything." He gave the horse a good *giddap*, then added, "Oh, and amen."

"Well, how was that, horse?" he asked. "I wish ol' Bonehead could be here to see this. He'd appreciate it, no doubt. You know, I miss that stubborn ol'—"

Rounding a blind bend as he spoke, he pulled the roan up sharply. Sitting by the side of the road, enjoying a few morsels from a picnic basket, were three people, their wagon stopped at the side of the road while the horses refreshed themselves at the seasonal creek at the road's edge.

They all looked up at the rider, the man and his wife with casual disinterest, Rosa with surprise at the recognition of the one-armed miner.

"Jacob? That you?"

"It is, Rosa," he answered as he swung himself awkwardly from the animal.

"What are you doin' out here? If you've come to try and talk me into goin' back, you've wasted the effort. I've made my mind up and nuthin' is likely to change it."

Jacob led the horse as he approached her, the man and wife watching with curiosity now as they chewed bread and jam sandwiches.

"Then you won't mind list'nin' to me one more time, since yer jes' sittin' there gnawin'."

She smiled at him, her first smile in she didn't know how long.

"No, I suppose that won't hurt. But make it quick. These good folk need to get back on the road before the storm breaks."

Jacob looked up, then back at Rosa. "I know you got to move on. That's okay. We all gotta do it sometime or other. But it wouldn't be fair if'n I didn't give you somethin' to think about. I, uh . . . Rosa, I'd mighty pleased if'n you'd consider . . . workin' with me."

The expectant look on Rosa's face dissolved. This was not what she had expected to hear. She wasn't sure what she had expected to hear, just that this wasn't it.

"Work with you? I've told you, Jacob, I'm not staying in Bodie. I ain't wanted there."

"Did I say work?" Jacob slapped the side of his head. "Sorry, Rosa, I'm a mite nervous. Makes me thick-headed like my ol' mule. What I meant to say was, if'n you'd consider stayin' with me . . . permanent. I want you to be my wife. I got me a place outside town. Bought it from them boys you heerd about. It's got a house and a mine and a stamp mill . . . we could make it a real nice place, jes' for us. And when we come to town, we'd come together, and no one would give us no lip. There'd be nuthin' for them hens to cackle about. Whaddya think, Rosa?"

"That all sounds very nice, Jacob. There's just one problem."

"You don't want to come."

"Well, it's not that . . ."

"Then what in tarnation is it?"

"Why, Jacob? Why do you ask me this?"

"Huh?"

"If it's pity, well, I appreciate the gesture. I really do. But I can't build a life on pity."

Jacob stared at her, the answer eluding him for a moment. It seemed so obvious, yet he couldn't find the words right off, and his eyes darted around, his feet shifted restlessly. Slowly it came to him, and he focused on her face again.

"It ain't pity, Rosa. Shucks no. It's because I love you, that's why! I want you to be wedded to me. Why else would I ask?"

Rosa grinned. "That's what I wanted to hear, Jacob."

"Huh?"

"Yes, Jacob, I'll come back and marry you."

"You will?"

Jacob was so surprised he could hardly believe it. He looked at his horse, then back again at Rosa, thinking maybe by breaking the spell she'd be gone and it would all have been his imagination. But she was still there and moving toward him. He dropped the reins and took her in his arm, and the couple by the wagon reached out and touched each other's hands, smiling at the miner and his newly betrothed woman.

"Looks like we lost us a passenger, Maggie," he said quietly.

"Yes, Ed. It looks that way. Isn't it grand?"

Night had fully enveloped the small gold camp, the clouds so low they could almost be touched, their undersides brushed with the yellow glow of the coal oil and kerosene lamps. And it had begun snowing, lightly dusting the shoulders and heads of the people who still ventured out, driven by the necessity of damage control after the earthquake, patching roofs or obtaining replacement supplies, some even transferring themselves and their belongings to other homes until repairs could be made.

When a level-headed assessment was finally attained, Bodie had gotten off easy. Only two structures had collapsed entirely, both of which had been unoccupied. Many roofs were damaged, several had fallen in, and a relatively small number of people had sustained serious injuries. Three were dead, another in danger, and most everyone had bruises and scratches, but that wasn't unusual in a wild town such as this.

Three tired riders penetrated the haze of light at the edge of town, their faces red from the cold. The eldest removed his hat and shook off the snow, his large nose and long, wavy hair making him a striking figure in the dull radiance. They turned their heads from side to side as they walked their horses up Main Street, solemnly taking in the damage to the town. When abreast of the American Hotel, they stopped and consulted each other.

"What now?" Jeff Bodine asked his brother.

"Room for the night, I guess," came the answer. "We'll think about tomorrow tomorrow."

"As for me," Wild Bill Hickok said, "I'll be moving on in a day or two, but I think I'll hole up in one of these establishments." He swept his arm, taking in many of the prevalent saloons that lined the street. "If I get tired, I can always crawl under a table."

"You don't have to do that," Jeff said, surprising both Hickok and Josh. "We'll see to it you have a bed to sleep in."

"Thanks just the same," Hickok told him. "But that's my element in there. I'm perfectly comfortable."

"Yes, I'm sure you would be," Jeff agreed, moving his mount next to Hickok. "But you and alcohol don't mix. You've got more worth than can be found at the bottom of a bottle. You dream of the Dakotas, but if you go in there tonight, you'll never see them. I'm not offerin' charity. It's just my way of sayin' thanks."

Hickok thought about it. "You know, Jeff, you got a level head on your shoulders. With your sense and your brother's skill, you two would make a good team."

"Team of what?" Josh asked.

But his question was never answered. A commotion up the street several blocks—a swarm of men, nearly a hundred by Hickok's estimation, shouting and scurrying all in the same direction—drew their attention.

"What's this?" Hickok said. "Mighty unusual."

"Aren't some of them wearing hoods?" Josh asked.

Jeff confirmed it. "And carrying clubs or rifles or something."

"Look, they're dragging a man along with them," Josh added. "What are they doing?"

"Unless I'm completely loco," Hickok contended, "that's a vigilance committee, and they've got their man."

"Vigilance committee?" Jeff asked.

"Lynch mob," clarified Josh.

A woman wrapped in a shawl turned the corner at a dead run and tore breathlessly down Main Street toward them, her face wide-eyed and terrified. She saw the horsemen watching her and hesitated but couldn't read their intentions, so she continued on her way, taking a side street.

"Where's she going, do you suppose?" Jeff asked.

"To the sheriff, I'd guess," Hickok speculated.

"Jail is the direction she came from," Josh said. "She must be goin' to Deputy Page's house."

Hickok scowled. "This is strange. If she's going for the deputy, then he don't know his prisoner's being lynched. We best go along." He kicked his horse and rode after the girl.

Josh started to go with him, but Jeff stopped him.

"Someone needs to keep an eye on them men. I'll go with Wild Bill."

That was all the encouragement Josh needed. He snapped the reins, and his horse responded, tired from the long journey but submissive to his rider. Jeff watched him ride off, then hurried up Green Street after Hickok and the girl.

When he saw them again, they had already made the deputy's house where he was on the porch, listening to the girl tell him what had happened. Jeff caught the tail end of it, hearing only that the mob had beaten up Billy O'Hara and was now taking the man, who had given himself up to them to stop the beating.

"We've got to stop this," Deputy Page asserted.

"He needs to be hung legally," Hickok agreed.

"Who are you?" Matt asked.

"James Butler Hickok, at your service." He doffed his hat while his horse pawed the ground impatiently.

Matt then noticed the other rider. "Jeff Bodine? Is that you?" He peered at him through the falling snow.

"Yes, sir. Josh rode on ahead to watch the men."

"Let's get going," Matt said, then remembered Sarah. He couldn't leave her alone. He turned to look inside, as though doing so would solve his dilemma, and she appeared in the doorway, clutching the frame tightly to keep from collapsing.

"Matt, please don't go," she begged.

"I've got to. I'm the law here."

"Please, I couldn't stand to lose you. I need you, Matt." She began to slip, and Matt hurried to her, steadying her.

"We'll take care of it on your authority," Hickok said. "You come when you can." He wasted no more time, spinning his horse and charging down the street. Jeff gave Matt a questioning look. He nodded, and Jeff took a breath and kicked Pollo in the flank.

Matt helped Sarah back into the bedroom as Betsy watched. As his wife tried to recover her breath, they were hailed from yet another rider. This one, however, had a passenger. As Matt paused to see who else had come for help that would be denied, he recognized his father.

"Rosa!" Betsy yelped as Jacob threw a leg over and jumped off, then helped Rosa down.

"Pa!" Matt shouted. "Rosa, get on in here. Take care of Sarah! I've got an emergency!"

Jacob sensed the urgency in Matt's voice, and they both ran inside. Sarah protested, but Matt took her face in his hands.

"Sarah, I love you more than anything. But I can't sit here and let them kill an innocent man. It's the last time, I swear. Please!"

Tears welled up, but she looked deep into Matt's eyes, then nodded. "Come back to me," she demanded.

Matt kissed her tenderly. "The gates of hell couldn't keep me from it."

Rosa moved in to steady Sarah as Matt broke away and ran out, followed by his father.

"They get to Wellman?" he asked as they mounted their horses.

"Through Billy," Matt said. "Beat him up. Wellman came forward to stop it." He *yeehawed*, and Shadow took flight, leaving Jacob to do the best he could.

Matt rode hard, forgetting he wasn't armed, thinking only of the innocent man who this very second could be dangling from the end of a rope, the victim of mob violence that Matt could have prevented if he hadn't been gallivanting around the countryside on a wild goose chase. He berated himself and pressed Shadow harder, listening for the telltale sounds of scuffling feet and shouting to guide him. There was enough snow on the ground now that they wouldn't be too hard find even if they were quiet as church mice.

He only prayed he wasn't too late.

CHAPTER

THIRTY·ONE

JOSH FOLLOWED THE GROUP from a safe distance, keeping them in sight but not so close that he could recognize anyone even if they hadn't been wearing hoods. He remained on his horse as they took their victim down Park Street to Green, to the wagon shop. A shiver—not from the snow but from the sight of the hooded men—snaked up his spine.

Outside the wagon shop was a hoist to help the wright with the repairs. It was a simple device: two strong supports with a thick cross bar, from which there was hanging a block and tackle for manipulating heavy wagon and stagecoach parts. Ready-made and perfect for hanging. Josh grew nervous when he saw the thing. It wouldn't be much longer before they tied the rope around the man's neck and pulled him up where he could dangle from it, try-ing in vain to breathe until, red in the face, his eyes bugging out and his tongue hanging like a dog's, he died. Might take two min-utes or so as he fought the rope, kicking his feet. Or maybe he'd resigned himself to it and would just hang there with his eyes closed. No, they'd probably put a hood over his head so no one could see how horrible it was. Yeah, they'd do that, so they wouldn't have to see their handiwork. Goodness knows, Josh thought, they got plenty of hoods among them. But who'd be will-ing to give his up?

"A horse!" someone shouted. "We need a horse."

"What for? Just tie him on and hoist him up," another man answered.

"Put him on it and let it run out from under him."

"There's one over there!" a man said, and suddenly Josh realized all heads had turned toward him. A few men advanced in his direction.

"Don't even think it," Josh warned.

"If you're not with us, what are you doing here, friend?"

The man speaking wore a hood, and Josh couldn't read his face.

"Just curious," Josh said. "I'm not with you, and I'm not against you. But you ain't using my horse." To punctuate his determination, Josh suddenly drew his gun and cocked it in a swift blur of a motion, surprising everyone. The man backed off, holding up a hand.

"Okay, friend, we won't press you for it. Just don't you try anything. We've got you highly outnumbered, and there's room up there for two." He pointed to the wagon hoist.

"Yes, I see that. But which six of you are willing to go to hell this evening just to use my nag?" His point was made, and the vigilantes turned back to their task, wisely deciding they could get by without the animal.

Josh uncocked the gun but kept it in his hand just in case someone got stupid. He watched as they stood the man on a box under the hoist and someone threw a rope over the cross bar, having apparently decided not to spoil the wagonwright's block and tackle. A noose was quickly formed and readied, and a man approached the prisoner with a hood, this one not having the eyes cut out as theirs had.

"No hood," the prisoner said. "I'm not guilty of this offense, and I want you to see what you are doing to an innocent man."

"Then why'd you give yourself up to us?" asked a man, obviously the leader of the mob.

"Hiram, you were going to kill another innocent man, Billy O'Hara, just to get to me, and I couldn't let that happen."

Josh recoiled at the idea. They were going to kill Billy O'Hara? He thought everyone in town loved Billy O'Hara. Of course, that was some time ago, and Bodie had grown. Maybe there were a lot of people in town who didn't know him, or just didn't like Negroes.

What had they done to him? Was it just threats, or had the prisoner interrupted a beating?

Didn't matter. The important thing was this man, who had been protected by Uncle Billy, was protesting his innocence. That was enough for Josh, having been in the same circumstance once—except for the lynching part. This man deserved a fair trial, even if he was guilty. But what was one man against this mob? A hundred men against six bullets. They'd have to be very well-placed shots. He hoped his brother and Wild Bill got there soon. Real soon.

Wellman was pushed up onto the box, his hands bound behind him, the noose slipped over his head, and the knot tightened behind his left ear.

"Any last words?" The man Wellman called Hiram asked.

"Certainly," Wellman said. "Most of you men, you are my friends, have been my friends for many years. Some of you worked for me. Many still do, I assume. You know my character. I wouldn't do such a thing."

"There's evidence."

"Yes, I've heard it. Circumstantial, all of it. You have nothing to prove me guilty because, the fact is, I am not. I never had anything against Nixon. I'm not feuding with the Queen Anne or anyone who works for her. That's about it, boys. If you still think you will be able to live with your consciences when you find out you've murdered an innocent man, then go ahead, pull away."

"I'll not have any trouble," Hiram Butler said, removing his hood, apparently no longer seeing the need to conceal his identity since Wellman had recognized his voice. He pointed to a small group of men huddled around the other end of the rope a few feet behind the hoist. "Are you ready?"

They all nodded, a couple of them weakly as though second thoughts had broken through, but none of them begged their leave.

"All right, then," Hiram said. "Thomas Wellman, you have been found guilty by the Bodie 6-0-1 Citizens' Vigilance Committee and are sentenced to death for the murder of James Nixon and the attempted murder of three other people and a baby. Pull him, boys."

They strained at the rope, and the slack went out of it. Thomas Wellman's facial expression changed from resolute courage to abject fear as the rope tightened around his throat, cutting off his air, and hauled him off the box. He closed his eyes, his lips quivering as he struggled to breathe.

Josh stared, transfixed, and hoped again for the others to come quickly. His hope was rewarded, for no sooner did he think that than two horseman riding hard swung around the corner, shouting. They split up, driving their animals directly into the midst of the crowd. Jeff drew his revolver and fired, causing men to duck as they ran.

Hickok shouted for them to let Wellman down, but no one answered or moved to accommodate. The men who pulled him had their attention diverted by the shot and still held onto the rope. They moved now to tie it off.

"What were you aiming for, Jeff?" Hickok asked as he drew both his pistols with a flourish and cocked them.

"Nothing in particular."

"Congratulations. You hit it." Hickok sighted down the barrel and squeezed the trigger, a flash spurting from the muzzle as the bullet slammed into the hand of the front man pulling on the rope. He yelped as his hand flew off it, carried by the force of the bullet, then hopped away, holding his injured extremity. The courage of the other men failed and quickly they too slackened their grip, despite encouragement from the leader to hold on. In a second or two Wellman's weight became too much for the rest to hold, and he came crashing to the ground.

Hickok didn't stop there, though. As guns began to be leveled in his direction by the members of the 6-0-1, he spun his horse in place, and with both revolvers blazing, the gunman scattered bullets wildly in all directions, seemingly indiscriminate in his aim.

Josh, now on foot and keeping low, made his presence known with a few well-placed shots into the thighs of men wielding guns toward himself or Hickok. He kept moving, keeping his head down so Wild Bill could shoot over him, managing as he ran to punch or drive a shoulder into a few men.

While the other two were raining terror and confusion throughout the crowd, Jeff rode his horse right into the mass of men and headed straight for Wellman. He jumped down while the animal was still moving and quickly yanked the rope down from the makeshift scaffold with one hand while slipping the noose off Wellman's neck with the other. One hooded man ventured too close, intent on intervening, and got a broken nose for his trouble, collapsing into the muddy snow to think about the error of his ways.

Jeff helped Wellman to his feet and steadied him as he ran back out through the crowd, his horse having been taken by someone anxious to make their getaway. Josh saw this and shot the man off the horse, a grazing blow to the shoulder that was sufficient to take the flight out of him. The now unencumbered horse kept going.

Out of ammunition, Hickok rode through the men passing out well-placed messages with the heel of his boot. Injured men were strewn about the ground, though, when later tallied, only three were actually shot. The rest were kicked, punched, or trampled by their escaping friends.

But there were still plenty of men left who were determined to see this through, and noticing that the gunman was conveniently short of firepower, they regrouped and converged, ready to string Hickok and his foolish partners up alongside the man who killed James Nixon in the Queen Anne powder magazine.

A rifle shot from the north split the air, cracking loudly. Then another, and Hiram Butler fell. And from the south two more riders, one hatless and wearing the shining star of the Mono County Sheriff's Department, raced their horses up the street, not bothering to slow until they reached the hoist. Matt rode his black horse right onto the platform, turning in a full circle and finally spying a large crippled man carrying a gigantic rifle hobbling down the street from the north.

Fighting the urge to go help Billy, Matt turned his attention back to the crowd and addressed it, his more urgent duty.

"Listen up, you men! This man is not guilty." He pointed at Wellman, still attended to and protected by a gun-wielding Jeff Bodine.

"A lot you know. You've been gone!" shouted a man in the crowd.

"Take your hood off, you coward," Matt challenged. "If you're so sure you're right, why are you afraid to show your face?" The man didn't do as ordered, but neither did he say any more.

"That's right, I've been gone," Matt said. "But I ain't gone no more, and I'm not alone. I've got the infamous Bodine brothers here to help me keep the peace, and I'm also aided by James Butler Hickok. Wild Bill, to you. Not to mention Billy and my pa. Now listen to me and no one else will get hurt. I've spent the past few days chasing the real guilty parties. The Younger brothers, Cole and Bob, that's who did this. Whatever evidence you got against Thomas Wellman, it won't stand up to scrutiny."

"What about Nixon's dying statement?" Hiram Butler said with some difficulty from the ground as he struggled to sit up, blood oozing between his fingers as he held a hand to a bad shoulder wound.

"What dying statement?"

"He named Wellman."

"Is that so?"

"Not 'zactly," said a contrite Noah Porter, slowly pulling his hood off. "He said, 'make Wellman,' then a 'p' sound."

"To who, Noah?" Matt queried. "You?"

"No, sir. To Doc Curtis."

"Was it clear and easy, or was he sputterin'?"

"Well, truth to tell, he was kind of sputterin'. We thought he was saying, 'Make wellman pay.'"

Matt shook his head. "Sounds to me like he was asking the doc to make him well . . . please." Matt let that sink in. "Anything else?"

There was murmuring from the men, but no one stepped forward with evidence.

"Well, just so you don't go home tonight regrettin' that you let this opportunity slip by, Cole Younger confessed to the deed. He told me he did it to create a diversion so he could spring his brother, who was languishin' in my jail. Which is what I was actin' on the whole time. Now, I been through hell this last week because of them, and I'm sorely disappointed to come home and find you men actin' like heathens. You all get on home now. Hiram, you're the exception. After Doc gets done with you, you're gonna be charged with inciting to riot and attempted murder. Anyone else wishin' to confess their role in this is welcome to present themselves at my jail in the mornin'. Now let's have this street cleared in five minutes. Help the wounded get home, gents."

Matt stayed on his perch and watched as the men meandered away, some helping those with bullet holes or bloodied faces vacate the area. Within the time allotted, the street was clear.

Without any more hesitation, Matt jumped down from

Shadow and ran to Billy, who had collapsed in the street. Thomas Wellman, shaken but otherwise none the worse for the wear, rushed over to help. They stood him and walked him to the nearest chair on the porch of the adjacent funeral parlor as Josh rode off to fetch the doctor.

With his handkerchief dabbing at Billy's face, Matt said, "Who did this to you Billy? Can you identify them?"

Billy shook his head. "Besides Hiram, Ah can't say for sure. Tomorrow you can walk around town, though, and see who has a guilty look on the face."

"Hmm," was all Matt could say.

Jeff sauntered over to Hickok, still seated atop his horse.

"That was right noble of you not to kill all them people," Jeff said, obviously impressed, "especially that fella holdin' the rope you shot in the hand. That was some pretty good shootin', I must admit."

"I was aiming for his chest," Hickok muttered to himself, examining the barrel of his gun as if he expected to see a curve in it.

CHAPTER

THIRTY·TWO

THE NEXT MORNING Matt assembled the Bodines in his office. "Sleep okay, you two?"

"Fine," Jeff said. "Thanks for putting us up. It took a while to get to sleep. We were both still keyed up."

"I suppose so. I hear from Billy you two lost your pa. I'm powerful sorry about that. Did you catch the man who did it and recover your gold?"

"No. That turned out to be the Youngers too, best we can figure."

Matt nodded. "Doesn't surprise me. Well, I suppose you two will be headin' back home?"

Jeff and Josh regarded each other.

"Uh, not exactly, Deputy," Josh said slowly. "We sold everything: mine, house, mill, and all."

"Oh. To who?"

"Your pa," Jeff said.

Matt stared at them wide-eyed, then slowly returned to normal, a smile flickering across his face.

"Then you're out of work."

"Looks that way, but it's only temporary, I'm sure," Jeff said.

"That's true enough," Matt said. "I've got a proposition for you. I've been named county sheriff, to fill out the rest of John Taylor's term. You remember him, Josh."

The younger Bodine nodded.

"I'm leaving this morning. That means Bodie won't have any lawmen, and as you saw last night, we need not one but at least two. It just so happens I've got two men in mind for them positions." He dropped the badges on the desk. "What do you say, boys?"

Two women, one slighter, younger, and blonder than the other, walked briskly up the boardwalk, chatting happily. They were bundled against the cold in heavy greatcoats, Betsy with her hood up, and Rosa with her head exposed but not caring about the cold. They were on their way to bid "so long" to Matt and Sarah Page as they moved to Bridgeport. Then the two friends would part company because just a few days before, Rosa had been married— by Reverend Edwards in a private ceremony with just Matt and Sarah as witnesses—to Matt's father, Jacob, and they were off to honeymoon for a few days at Walker Lake in Nevada, where there was no snow to bother them.

Rosa was excited and afraid all at once and had turned to Betsy for moral support. Finally settled down, they hurried to the Page residence for the farewell.

As they passed the general store, the door creaked. A woman stepped out onto the sidewalk in front of them, blocking their path. They halted, preparing to walk around her, when their eyes locked.

"Good morning, Mrs. Bascomb," Rosa said politely.

"Oh. Morning . . . Mrs. Page," came Flora's icy greeting. "I suppose you're on the way to see off the deputy and his wife."

"Yes, we are," Rosa told her. "You're welcome to come as well."

Betsy elbowed Rosa, but she ignored it.

"Thank you, no," Flora said. "Uh . . . unfortunately I have a prior commitment. Please extend my apologies and also for her bad luck with the baby."

"Tell her yourself, why don'tcha?" Betsy challenged.

"I doubt she'd appreciate that, to be frank," Flora said. "I'm quite sure she blames me for it all."

"You're wrong," Rosa said. "She feels sorry for you. That's what she feels. And so do I. You've done a lot of evil in the name of God, Flora Bascomb."

Several other citizens, seeing Rosa and Flora talking and knowing what had gone on, now gathered at a safe distance to watch things unfold, many of them secretly hoping for a brawl. The smart money would be on Rosa.

Unaware or unconcerned with the audience, Flora raised her eyebrows. "Is that so? Well, Sarah's miscarriage was not an evil I did. It was from God."

"God?"

"Surely. As punishment for her secret sins."

Betsy's mouth dropped open as her anger flared, but Rosa only shook her head. "No, Flora, even I know you're wrong about that. Dead wrong. God doesn't punish good people that way."

"No matter," Flora said snidely. "It's all for the better anyway. The baby was probably imperfect, having been fathered by that boy, that son of such an uncouth man."

"That tears it!" Betsy said loudly. "Sock her, Rosa! She asked for it, talking that way about your husband."

"No, Betsy, I'll not stoop to her level," Rosa declined, keeping her eyes fixed on Flora's. "She claims to be a Christian, yet she gossips and lies. I'll not let her incite me to violence so she can use it to fuel her slander. I really *am* a Christian woman, even if I ain't as close to God as Flora thinks she is."

Flora glared her.

"Yeah?" Betsy sneered. "Well, I ain't so inclined." And with that she abruptly turned toward Flora and shoved her as hard as she could, propelling the woman off the boardwalk and into a dirty snow bank, then brushed her hands together in triumph, locked arms with a shocked but not necessarily displeased Rosa Page, and together they marched off to the cheers of the onlookers who had gathered.

One of the curious was a young woman on a horse, wearing buckskin pants and coat and a man's black hat with a curved brim, sitting cocked off to the right on her head, her hair cut short. She watched the scene with a wry grin, then turned and rode to the American Hotel, tying her horse to the rail before stomping inside.

When she returned a few minutes later, wiping the back of her sleeve across her mouth, Wild Bill Hickok was not far behind. In silence they mounted their horses and rode down the street, stopping at the general store and hitching their animals out front.

There were many things that would be needed on the trip that lay ahead of them. South Dakota was a goodly distance away.

Matt lifted the last crate onto the back of the wagon and lashed it down with a heavy rope. They were fully loaded now and ready to leave. He stood back with his hands on his hips and took a deep breath. He was anxious to be gone, but something inside him made him sorry he was leaving. He was having trouble understanding how both feelings could be present at the same time. He listened wistfully to the incessant pounding of the stamp batteries on the hill, knowing he would both miss it and be relieved to be rid of it.

Sarah came out of the house carrying a pillow and her knitting, bundled in her greatcoat. She walked gingerly.

"You sure you're up to this?" Matt asked.

"No," Sarah admitted. "Matt, I'll be fine. It's time to go, and we can't wait for another storm." She put the pillow on the seat of the buckboard and the knitting next to it.

"You don't want to go, do you?"

Sarah walked over to him and slipped her arms around his waist, pressing hard against him. "I want to be where you are. It's my duty and my desire."

"You sure?"

"Yes, I'm sure. I love you."

"I love you too, honey." He hugged her and kissed her deeply on the lips.

"Is everyone coming to see us off?" Sarah asked.

"Yeah. Pa said so. They'll be here shortly. It's nearly eleven. Look, there they come."

Several people had rounded the corner and were walking toward them. Matt recognized a few by their distinctive silhouettes: his pa, Rosa and Betsy, . . . the others he couldn't tell at this distance. Jacob waved his arm in greeting.

Sarah waved back demurely and smiled in anticipation, then the smile turned to wonder as she recognized Joseph and Molly Carter. Molly was carrying a thickly wrapped bundle.

"Hello, Sarah," Molly said when she arrived, her tone apologetic.

Sarah took a breath and smiled in return. "Morning, Molly. How's the baby?"

"Fine, Sarah. Just fine." Her eyes became moist. "Oh, Sarah, I'm so sorry about your baby. About everything. How can you ever forgive me?"

Sarah shook her head. "It's Rosa you need to say that to, not me."

"I have," Molly said. "Rosa's a dear, dear woman. I don't know how I ever let Flora deceive me like she did."

"Satan's good at that," Sarah said, unable to take her eyes off the baby. Molly saw this, and her heart was heavy.

"Would you like to hold her?"

Sarah wasn't sure and said so.

"Please," Molly urged. "It'd be a privilege for me."

Sarah reached out tentatively as Molly placed the child in her arms. She held her close to her breast, looking at the cherubic face peeking out from all those blankets, A pain formed behind her eyes and a lump filled her throat, but she maintained her composure.

"She's so beautiful."

"Thank you. I feel bad for you, Sarah. You deserve one of your own. It's not fair. I feel . . . partly responsible."

"It's not your fault, Molly. It's not anybody's fault. It God's will. I don't understand it, and I'm not happy about it, but somehow I've got to accept it." No longer could she fight off the tears, and they flowed unabated and unwiped, her hands full of Molly's baby.

"What's her name?" Sarah asked through her tears, handing the infant back so she could get her hankie out.

Molly smiled. "We named her Rose."

Sarah glanced over at Rosa and the woman smiled broadly, as did Betsy. They already knew. Molly had told them. Rosa moved over and put her arm around Sarah's shoulder, giving her a gentle squeeze that said more than any amount of words could have.

Sarah hooked Rosa by the arm and took her aside.

"I'm going to miss you, dear," Sarah told her. "More than you'll ever know."

"Aw, that's nice of you to say. You've been a real sweetheart to me. Besides, we're related now. It's not like I'll never see you again."

"Yes, but I have the feeling you're going to be busy."

"Doing what?"

"Running the Quicksilver."

"What are you talking about, child?"

"The restaurant. It's yours. I'm giving it to you."

"Sarah, you needn't do that. Sell it. Make a little money."

"I was renting the building, and we didn't pay that much for the stove and tables and things. The man before us basically gave it away. Please, Rosa, if you want it, take it. We don't need the money."

"What if no one comes?"

"Oh, they'll come." The voice was Molly's, come over to join the conversation. "I'll see to it they come."

"But I can't do it alone, and Jacob has his own work to attend to."

"What about me?" Molly asked. "Rose can come with me, sleep in the warm kitchen."

"You sure?"

"Absolutely. It'd be an honor. I can cook, too, can't I, Joe?"

"With the best," agreed her husband.

"I think it's a grand idea," Jacob said, coming over.

"What about your new house?" Rosa asked. "And your mine and mill?"

"Aw, I don't want to do all that work. I'm happy here at the Unified. I think I can sell the property for what I paid for it. We'll fix this place up," he pointed with a thumb at Matt and Sarah's house behind him, "and live here. It'll work, Rosa."

Rosa looked at Jacob, then back at Sarah, then broke into an embarrassed grin. "Okay, Sarah, okay. I'll take it. Thank you."

They hugged, then Rosa hugged Molly as well.

"Injun!" Joseph Carter shouted from several feet away. Sarah and the others turned to find out what had alarmed him so and saw a lone Indian wrapped in a blanket riding slowly up the street.

"Don't worry," Jacob told him. "That's just Charlie Jack. He's a friend of ours with a knack for showing up at just the right time. Hey, Charlie!" Jacob waved.

Charlie Jack nodded, threw his left leg over his horse's neck and slid down, landing lightly on his moccasins.

"What are you doing here?" Matt asked the Paiute, stepping forward to greet him.

"Got to be someplace," Charlie Jack said. "Why not here?"

Matt grinned. "Yeah, but I thought you'd be someplace warm."

"Warm in blanket," he said. "I hear from father you stay with him."

"Father? Those were your parents I was living with?"

"And little sister. Good thing you no touch." He grimaced menacingly at the deputy, then looked down at Matt's new boots. "He like your boots."

"I'm glad. He drives a hard bargain."

Charlie Jack regarded the wagon. "Where go?"

"Moving to Bridgeport," Jacob said. "Matt's the new sheriff."

Charlie Jack raised his eyebrows. "Good. I see you there sometime. I go now."

"Wait a few minutes, can't you?" Jacob Page asked.

"Charlie Jack hungry. Go to Billy for pine nuts."

"I'll buy you a real lunch," Jacob said. "Besides, Billy ain't feelin' so well. He got into a little scrape."

"Okay, I stay. Later I see Billy. You drive hard bargain, Jacob Page like Charlie Jack father." Charlie grinned, ever so slightly and ever so quickly, then resumed his expressionless countenance as conversation resumed amongst the people.

A well-dressed man in a new bowler and smoking a cigar helped another man walking with a crutch down the street. The injured man, a large, black man with a bandage around his head, grimaced in pain as he lumbered slowly down the street but did not stop to rest.

"You're doing fine, Billy," Thomas Wellman encouraged. "You're almost there."

"Ah can . . . see that," Billy said with some difficulty through swollen lips, his jaw visibly distorted. "They beat me right good, but Ah ain't blind."

"That trouncing didn't alleviate your temper none. In fact, I'd say it made it worse." They were a few feet from their destination now, and everyone could hear their exchange.

"Wouldn't it make yours worse, gettin' beat black and blue like that?" Jacob Page asked.

"He already black," Charlie Jack observed. "He just beaten blue."

Billy looked up, his face suddenly brighter. "Charlie Jack, you old dog. Heard Ah was down and out so you come by to steal mah winter supply of pine nuts?"

"No, I not think of that. But now you say, I do."

Everyone laughed and Billy went up to his Paiute friend and gave him a delicate hug.

"Not too hard, Billy," Wellman reminded him. "Your ribs are broken, remember."

"Thanks," Billy said, breaking off from the Indian. "Ah done forgot what that pain was."

He patted the Paiute on the shoulder and moved over to Matt. "Matthew, Ah'm gone miss you sorely. You made mah life a lot brighter while you was here." He shook his hand. "And, Sarah, darling, you take good care of this man. Make sure he don't get into any more trouble than he can handle."

"I'll try Billy. I haven't done a very good job so far." She put her arms gently around him and laid her head on his chest. "Does it hurt there?" she asked.

"Not any more," he said quietly, stroking her hair. He winked at Matt, then peeled her off and gave her a kiss on the forehead.

"Good-bye, sweetheart," he said. "You'll be fine."

"Thanks, Billy." She turned and Matt helped her into the wagon.

A few feet away, watching the scene with casual disinterest, stood the Bodine brothers, sporting their new silver stars. Jeff nudged his brother, then nodded toward the street. Josh turned to see what was up and watched as Wild Bill Hickok rode slowly by, Martha Jane Canary dressed in similar buckskins riding next to him, chattering and gesturing happily. Hickok glanced over and winked at Josh, gave Jeff a little wave, then turned his attention back to Jane.

"Yes, that's very interesting," he said.

"And then, after that, I joined the army as an Indian scout," Jane told him. "Oh yes indeed, I did. They picked me because I could ride and shoot so well, of course, and because I could speak several Indian tongues as good any . . ."

Jeff smiled. "Perfect match, I'd say," he told his brother.

Josh didn't argue. "I wonder if she'll make it into *Beadle's* dime novels." He sounded almost hopeful.

"We'll ask Billy to keep us informed."

"Uncle Billy?" Josh screwed his face up, mystified that O'Hara would read those things.

"No, not Uncle Billy. William. You know, little Billy, the kid from the stable."

"Oh, yeah. Just the same, I think I'll get my own copies. Might be something in there I can learn to help me do this job."

Jeff just shook his head. Would his brother ever change?

"Who's that with Wild Bill?" Matt asked, noticing the pair.

"Jane, his new friend," Josh disclosed.

"Jane? Jane Canary?"

"The same. Only she says you nicknamed her Calamity Jane. She likes going by that now."

Matt could only grin as he watched her ride off with Hickok. She'd gotten her wish, apparently. He hoped she fared well as he watched them ride out of sight.

He walked to the back of the wagon and checked the knot on Shadow's lead rope one last time, then climbed into the seat of the buckboard and sat next to his wife.

"Sarah, you ready?"

She nodded sadly, sniffing back more tears. "As I'll ever be."

"We ain't goin' that far," he told her. "We'll see everyone again soon."

"As long as they come to see us and it isn't you going to see them. I want you staying with me for a while." She threaded her hand into the crook of his arm and held on tight. Matt leaned down and kissed her on the top of the head.

"I promise. Good-bye, folks," he shouted, and with a whistle and a snap of the reins, the wagon jerked forward and Matt and Sarah Page rolled out onto the muddy road, leaving behind them the *pound pound pound* of Bodie's heart.

AUTHOR'S NOTE

Though this book and the others in this series are works of fiction, all the towns and other locations are real. Some of the characters are actual people of the period (Hickok and the Youngers, obviously; others not as well-known, such as Harvey Boone, a descendant of Daniel Boone whose store in Bodie still stands).

As always, with historical fiction, much research must be undertaken if any degree of accuracy is to be achieved. Though most of the information used as a basis for these tales is a mattter of public record, the primary souce being the newspapers from Bodie, Bridgeport, and Carson City, Nevada, I owe a debt of gratitude to historians who have gone before me to do most of the tedious work of pouring through these archives.

I would like to thank these persons in particular (some of them, sadly, posthumously): Ella Cain, Warren Loose, George Williams III, Frank McGrath, Frank Wedertz, Margaret Calhoun, Thomas C. Fletcher, Emil Billeb, and Joseph G. Rosa. Their work was invaluable. Any deviations from historical accuracy one might note in this series of novels are the responsibility of this author and no one else. I would also like to thank the employees of the Nevada State Library in Carson City for their asssistance in researching microfiche copies of the Carson City *Daily State Register*, which carried day-by-day accounts of the prison breakout of 1871 and the chase of the convicts, as depicted in volume1 of this series, *The Gathering Storm*.